I0825072

THE DAUGHTERS

JOANNA MARGARET

THE MYSTERIOUS PRESS
NEW YORK

THE DAUGHTERS

Mysterious Press
An Imprint of Penzler Publishers
58 Warren Street
New York, N.Y. 10007

First edition

Interior design by Maria Fernandez

Library of Congress Control Number: 2025943819

ISBN: 978-1-61316-677-2
eBook ISBN: 978-1-61316-678-9

10 9 8 7 6 5 4 3 2 1

Printed in the United States of America
Distributed by Simon & Schuster

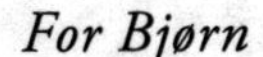

For Bjørn

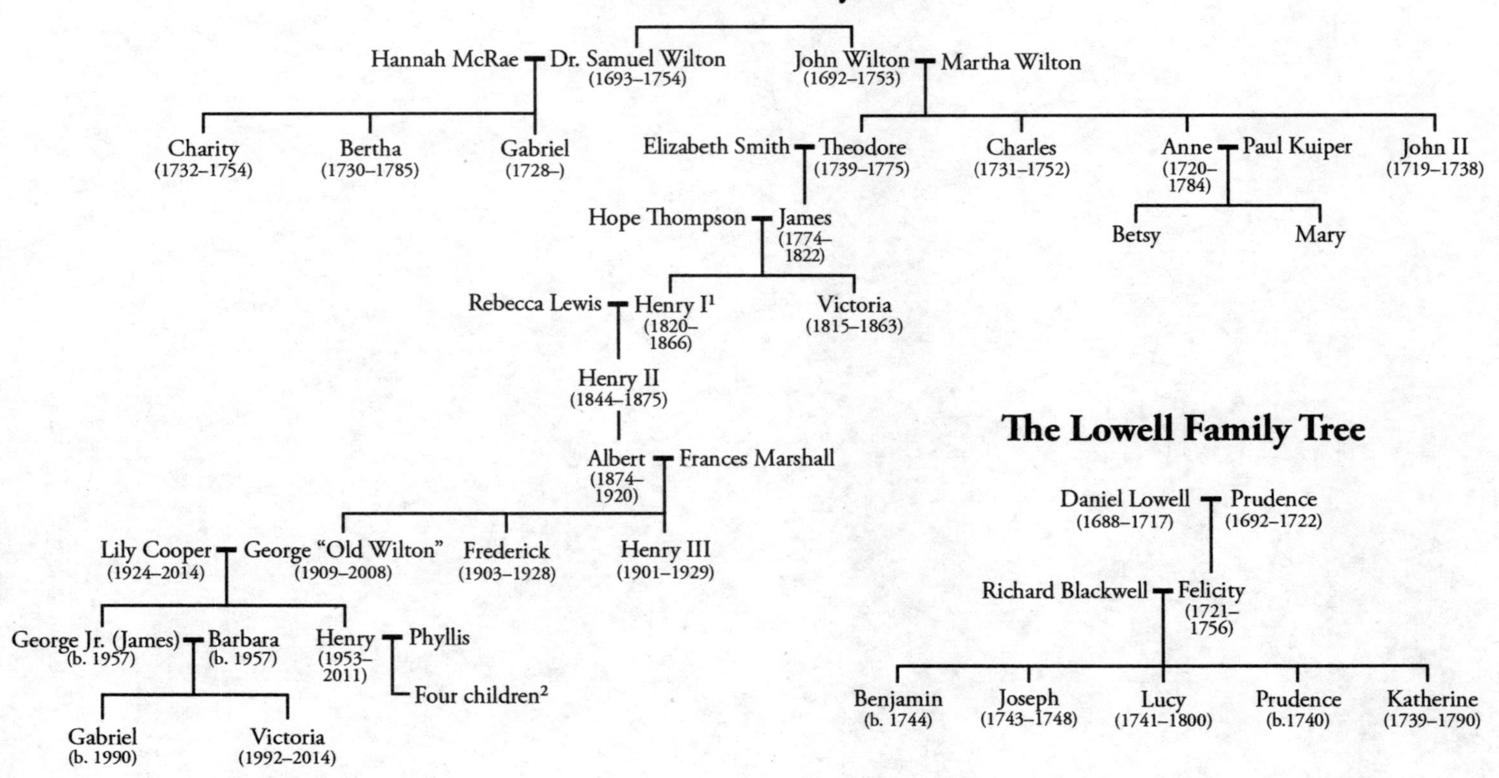
The Wilton Family Tree
Hannah McRae
Dr. Samuel Wilton (1693–1754)
John Wilton (1692–1753)
Martha Wilton
Charity (1732–1754)
Bertha (1730–1785)
Gabriel (1728–)
Elizabeth Smith
Theodore (1739–1775)
Charles (1731–1752)
Anne (1720–1784)
Paul Kuiper
John II (1719–1738)
Hope Thompson
James (1774–1822)
Betsy
Mary
Rebecca Lewis
Henry I[1] (1820–1866)
Victoria (1815–1863)
Henry II (1844–1875)
Albert (1874–1920)
Frances Marshall
Lily Cooper (1924–2014)
George "Old Wilton" (1909–2008)
Frederick (1903–1928)
Henry III (1901–1929)
George Jr. (James) (b. 1957)
Barbara (b. 1957)
Henry (1953–2011)
Phyllis
Four children[2]
Gabriel (b. 1990)
Victoria (1992–2014)
The Lowell Family Tree
Daniel Lowell (1688–1717)
Prudence (1692–1722)
Richard Blackwell
Felicity (1721–1756)
Benjamin (b. 1744)
Joseph (1743–1748)
Lucy (1741–1800)
Prudence (b.1740)
Katherine (1739–1790)
[1]Founder of Wilton Springs Township
[2]Henry, Phyllis, and four children perished in a car accident, 2011

Appendix A

The examination and confession of Mrs. Prudence Lowell

After hours of questiones which provoked negative answers, Mrs. Lowell, aged 30 yeares, at last confessed that she was a witch. And that earlier in the summer she left a red mark in the devil's book with the middle finger of her left hand that the devil would afflict Martha Wilton, wife of John Wilton, whom she named on the Sabath day for she wished so to seduce and have John Wilton for her husband, although he was married by law to Martha Wilton. She states to have borne a girl child that she claims to be the child of John Wilton. Says a witness wax poppits were found that she used to afflict Martha Wilton and the daughter of John Wilton, Anne, aged 2 years. Prudence Lowell confesses she attended the witch meeting and promised her body and soul to the devil and to worship him and that she hath lied when she said that she bore the child of John Wilton. She confesses that the child she carried and bore was not the child of John Wilton but the child of the devil. Reverend Dr. Samuel Wilton examined the widow and found the witch's teat, to suckle the devil's children. She promises to confesse what she will further remember.

Prudence Lowell Signed and owned the X Mark
The above said confession of Prudence Lowell
Signed 31st August 1722
Signed before John Wilton, Jus{tice} of the Peace

PROLOGUE

"Excuse me, miss, are you feeling okay? Your voice is . . ."

Rowena glanced at the reflection of the middle-aged man in her rearview mirror, then pumped the brakes, jolting both of them. "Fourteen Northview Court, right? We're"—she wheezed in a breath—"here."

"Thank you. Five stars. But. Are you sure you're alright?"

"Maybe you should mind your own business."

"Okay then. Goodnight."

She didn't wait for him to walk up the steps, didn't even peek through the window at what must have been a fancy house. After drop-offs she often looked up addresses on Zillow to see how much her riders' homes cost, giving lower ratings to those who lived in expensive residences but didn't tip well. The clock glowed green in the dark: 3:30. Tonight's last trip. Rowena's heart thump-thumped. She zipped up her hoodie and shivered as she clicked on the overhead light, and looked in the mirror again. Her face looked greyer than it should have, and a halo of dewy sweat glistened along her hairline. She was exhausted. She'd sleep it off.

She thought about the rich guy. He had promised a lot of things, then disappeared when things stopped going exactly his way. Now Rowena was staying at her cousin's place while they fixed the leak that had flooded her apartment. But everything would get better when the rest of the money arrived in her account.

She was thinking about her son, who had spent yet another birthday with his father—how she'd get custody soon, that the next court date was only weeks away—when she realized her hands were shaking. Looking down at her trembling fingers she didn't notice the stop sign and collided with the only other car on the road.

The ambulance took her and the other driver to the hospital. She drifted off as they wheeled her along a corridor. Then she heard talking above her, her eyelids heavy under bright lights. "Pulse . . . Overnight . . . Observation . . . Dehydration . . . 104 degrees . . . Septic shock."

When she woke up, machines beeped softly. There was an oxygen clip in her nose. It felt good to breathe so deeply. She looked down. Clear plastic tubes were snaking out of her bandaged arms. She was attached to an IV. She sat up. She couldn't be there. It wasn't safe.

"I have to go! Now! Someone, please! Help me!" Rowena shouted down the corridor.

By 4:58 A.M. her bed was empty.

PART I

CHAPTER ONE

I arrived in Wilton Springs on May 19, 2019 in the mid-afternoon. Wilton Springs was known for the three H's—health, hot springs, and something else beginning with the letter *h*. Horses? The place was knee-deep in horse country. Yes, that must have been it. I'd also read about a witch trial in the eighteenth century when a local woman had been subjected to a water test. There was a marker near the spot where she died what must have been a horrific death.

But in that moment, I wasn't focusing on the three H's, or witch trials, or death by drowning. It had been a seven-hour bus ride from Midtown Manhattan, and I needed to stretch my legs.

I'd been hired as a private archivist for a prominent family in a college town in upstate New York, hence the protracted bus ride. In photographs Wilton Springs looked postcard-pretty and bucolic, the perfect place to reflect on and figure out what I wanted to do with the rest of my life. Once upon a time I'd thought I wanted to study and teach history, but now I wasn't so sure.

I stepped off the bus carrying a backpack and a medium-sized duffle. The only thing of value I'd brought was my late grandmother's star sapphire ring, which looked silly on the finger of a woman in her twenties, but I wasn't ready to put it up for auction. Not yet.

The picturesque town appeared to have been pickled in 1889. On Main Street a series of elaborate, Victorian houses had been converted into specialty boutiques. Set back off the sidewalk near what appeared to be the center of town, a bronze statue of a stern-looking man stood eight feet tall. His cheeks were caved in and he was wearing an eye patch over his left eye. He looked war weary. The plaque on the base of the work identified him as *Henry Wilton (1820–1866), Founder of Wilton Springs Township, incorporated 1845. Civil War hero.* Henry Wilton. Wilton Springs' namesake.

Beyond the quaint commercial core was a broad, tree-lined avenue with huge mansions set back on sprawling green lawns. Heading in the direction of my rental, I saw a rectangular black sign on a dull brass pole in the middle of an unmowed patch of grass. I stopped to read the text, assuming it described the historic house behind it. The brass letters were obscured by a layer of grime and barely legible.

WITCH TRIAL

> On September 4, 1722, Prudence Lowell, suspected of witchcraft, was stripped of her clothes, bound by rope, and thrown into a nearby lake. Because Lowell floated, she was judged guilty, and was summarily convicted and hung by the neck on this spot.

The famous Wilton witch trial. So, the accused had been hung, and not drowned. I shuddered. Reading the marker, and the name of the woman, Widow Lowell, made the events of the past seem more real, more immediate.

The rental I'd arranged belonged to a friend of a friend of my employers, and I'd been instructed to pick up the keys at 12 Warwick Street. I stopped at 10, a hulking, beige Victorian that looked like a haunted house in a children's book. The sun still bright and high in the sky, I shaded my eyes to read the sign next to the blood-red awning. *Peyton's Funeral Home.*

I double-checked the address, then continued twenty feet to the neighboring mansion, constructed in a tacky, anachronistic half-timber Bavarian style. There didn't appear to be a doorbell, so I knocked. Despite the mild temperature, sweat was dripping down my face. I tucked a few strands of hair behind my ears, and knocked again. A middle-aged man with sloping shoulders, watery eyes, and a head of colorless hair emerged from a side door.

"Russell Bailey," he said. "You must be Miss Tompkins. Hello!"

He shoved his hand out, and I hesitated before shaking it. "Please, call me Genevieve."

"Follow me, Genevieve!" Russell said. "Glad it worked out and we're here this weekend, though my wife is out of town with the kids. So I should say *I'm* here. We just bought the carriage house where you'll be living." After walking to the back of the property and making a sharp left onto a side street, we approached a small turn-of-the-century structure, with various tones of pastel paint chipping off wooden curlicues. It looked like a derelict, Hansel-and-Gretel dwelling.

"Ta-da!" he said. "As a historian, you can appreciate all the nineteenth-century details." Without waiting for my reply, he continued, "So much history in Wilton. You'll love it."

As we walked inside, I coughed on sour-smelling dust. The wallpaper was faded and yellowing, curling over around the edges. I could see huge water stains, and coughed again.

"Sorry it's a bit stuffy," he said. "Miss Fletcher was still living here when we bought it. I thought we'd use it as a playhouse for the children, but my wife decided we'd rent it out to a student or someone else who was . . ."

"Unsuspecting?" I offered.

"Funny," he said, but frowned. A spiderweb that looked like cotton candy was draped across the largest window. Noticing me notice it, he said, "Hope you like spiders."

I smiled politely.

"Anyway, here are the keys. Give us a shout if you need anything." Russell stopped. "I mean figuratively. Old walls are built thick. We wouldn't be able to hear you through them." He took a step back. "Any questions?"

"Where's the alarm?"

This elicited laughter. "Alarm? People in Wilton Springs don't even lock their doors, it's that safe! No alarm. Just a key."

"Got it. Do you know the Wilton family?"

"Of course, of course I do. Junior's my age so we're in the same circles. Watch yourself though, there's a saying around here: Junior's out on the town, best lock up your daughters!"

He paused for laughter, but I filled the silence with a question. "Junior, did you say?"

"Yes, George Wilton. Junior. Come to think of it, he changed his name. Goes by Jim now. James was his middle name, but he and his father had a sort of falling out." He cleared his throat then looked down at his watch. "I'd better go—need to run an errand for my wife. Ring if you need me!" He turned and left, the still-bright sunlight casting a tall shadow of Russell walking across the green grass toward his house.

I opened all the windows to dilute the mustiness before closing them again. Then I looked up directions to the college campus, locked the door, and made my way there. As I walked, a fresh spring breeze tickling my face, I passed several white, many-gabled houses with manicured grounds and winding driveways. It took forever to walk by one lawn so large it could have been a football field. Who would need so much land and space in the twenty-first century? A thick forest flowed between that house and the next one. High in the tall trees, birds chirped. Following a long wall, I came to a stone block carved with the words *Bainsville College*.

I went through the gate and meandered through the vast grounds built into thick woods. At the end of one path was a pantheon, which housed the theater, funded by the same family who'd hired me. The Wiltons.

On the bus ride, I'd read about the history of Bainsville. Founded as a women's college in the 1940s, the school had expanded in the '70s after they'd started admitting men, and the campus stretched over nearly five hundred acres in a woodland preserve. The newest buildings were modern and grey, lacking the charm of the Victorian town. I hadn't seen anyone since walking through the main gate. It was outside of term, and although the trees were flush with leaves there was a stillness, a lack of vibrancy. No Frisbee throwing or laughing students. My phone had no reception. Someone could haul me away to somewhere deserted and no one would know.

I walked faster, noticing a sign on a tree that pointed in the direction of the library, which turned out to be a mass of concrete that could have been the abode of a James Bond villain.

I climbed the steps, followed the sign to special collections, and introduced myself to a woman in her early sixties wearing vintage-looking round-framed glasses, and a fluffy red sweater, which she needed as the air-conditioning was on full blast. She reached out and shook my hand.

"I'm Susan," she said, pulling her hand back to block her yawning mouth. "Really nice to meet you, Jennifer."

"Genevieve," I said.

"Oh, sorry," she said, already walking away from me and down a hallway. I followed her into a large workroom. Over the next few minutes, my new colleagues came in to meet me. Daniela Rodriguez, the head of Special Collections, said she was from Puerto Rico but had lived in Wilton for the past fifteen years. Mitch Lowell, somewhere in his sixties, wearing an Italian light-wool suit that looked expensive, worked as Daniela's assistant. Andrea Barker was a PhD student who was leaving the following week, and Luna Collins had started a few months earlier. Luna was the closest to me in age. She had straight, shiny black hair down to her waist, which she twisted into a bun and placed on top of her head, securing it with an elastic band. A thorny circle was tattooed around her left arm, and words in a language I didn't recognize were inked between her elbow and wrist.

After I'd met everyone, Susan walked with me through a hallway, opened a door, and led me down a flight of stairs to the basement room where I would be working. Large, grey boxes covered an enormous table, and others were spread out across the floor. There were no windows.

"These are the first twenty boxes," she said. "I hope you like organizational work."

"That's why I'm here," I said. It wasn't a lie.

"Old Wilton—that's what everyone called him—collected the materials in a garage for years, at which point his wife had them transferred to new boxes and donated one at a time. Every time we received a box there was more money. After he and his wife died, the will stipulated an additional amount to have the material archived and published. The heirs put that part off. Till now. They insisted on handpicking the archivist."

"Did you know him well? Wilton Senior? I mean, Old Wilton?"

"We knew Lily, Mrs. Wilton. She was a real lady. Brought us lemon bars on her birthday, January 5. To brighten up the darkness, she always said. I met Old Wilton just once, although I knew who he was. Everyone did. He was the most important person in town."

I knew something about the death of a patriarch but said nothing.

"No doubt you've done your research," she said. "But the town websites are thin on details, and you should know the connections between the Wilton family and Wilton Springs. The Wiltons struck it rich in the late nineteenth century—they owned the Wilton Springs water company and a glass factory. They built a spa hotel based on the bathing hotels in Europe, which became a premier destination for the leading families of New York City. There'll be newspaper clippings that describe all that, and more."

"And that's how they made big money?"

She shook her head. "In the 1920s they ran a profitable business during Prohibition, shipping their glass bottles to Canada and sneaking them back down across the border filled up with Canadian whiskey."

"So the Wilton fortune is built on bootlegging?"

"Was it Balzac who said behind every great fortune lies a great crime? Actually, the glass factory burned down in 1929—you'll read about that, too. After the crash in '29, with their available capital they were able to switch to pharmaceuticals. Wilton Springs has long been a center for the health industry because of the mineral waters. Old Wilton sold the water company to a beverage conglomerate. He left a colossal enterprise for his grandchildren when he died."

"Grandchildren," I said. "Are there parents?"

"Yes," she said, with a sigh.

I looked up at the clock on the wall. It was 6:30. "Unless you want to cover anything else, I'll head home, and start bright and early tomorrow. Can you tell me where the restrooms are?"

Instead of answering me she sighed again. "You seem like a nice girl. You remind me of my little sister, who . . . isn't with us anymore." She paused. "Please, don't take this the wrong way, but I wish you hadn't accepted the position. You should never have come to Wilton Springs. Folks say the Wiltons are cursed."

"The Wiltons are cursed?"

"The curse . . ." She opened her mouth to continue, but just then we heard loud knocking on the door at the top of the stairs. Susan drew in a sharp breath, and her eyes darted toward the back of the room. She forced her lips up into a smile. "The restroom is upstairs and down the corridor on your left. I'll show you." The knocking continued as we walked up the steps.

When I opened the door no one was there.

CHAPTER TWO

Gentle sunlight leaked through bare patches in a ceiling of leafy trees as I walked back through the woods. I hadn't eaten since breakfast, and now all I could think of was food. A year ago, I might've celebrated my first night in a new place with a three-course meal at an upscale restaurant, perhaps at the recently reopened Wilton Arms Hotel, where guests were lounging on the terrace, clinking overpriced cocktails. I imagined sitting among them, washing coq au vin down with a glass of chilled Burgundy. I ignored these cravings, recognizing them for the distraction they were. I had to focus. It was up to me to liquidate my father's assets in order to pay the estate taxes, and I now needed to generate my own income, for the first time in my life. That meant being mindful of every single thing I spent money on, even if my salary was generous, which had been a key selling point of the position.

In town, I stopped at the supermarket and began filling a cart with basics. Pretty soon, the cart was nearly full. When I looked at the prices of the items inside, I put the imported Brie and aged Parmesan back on the shelves, and traded the Sicilian extra virgin olive oil for a California blend. The woman at the checkout counter scanned everything quickly, and then snapped open a plastic bag.

"Paper bags?" I asked with a smile.

She smiled back, and winked. *Trish*, her nametag read. She was petite, and very thin, a little younger than I was, with long, blonde hair and pale blue eyes.

When I turned to leave, she said, "Thanks, hon."

Back at home I reopened the windows, made scrambled eggs and toasted a slice of bread, then put in my earbuds and spent an hour cleaning. By the time I was finished the sharp smell of bleach was stinging my nostrils. Even after I closed the windows it was drafty, and I wore a sweatshirt in bed to keep from shivering.

I managed to sleep through the night, but woke up the way I did most mornings, with an aching jaw and throbbing gums. My heart was racing as I kicked the covers off. I must have had a nightmare, but there was no one to bring me out of it. Maybe the move to Wilton Springs and all the fresh air would cure me of the bad dreams. Maybe.

At 8:00, I received an email from Daniela, requesting all staff to attend a meeting at 9:30. I arrived a few minutes early, and we clustered inside her office, except for Luna, who wasn't working that day.

A woman with close-cropped platinum hair stepped forward. "I'm Detective Saunders," she said, "and this is my deputy, Officer Jackson." The younger man standing next to her glanced around at us and asked us our names.

After he'd written them all down, Saunders continued, "We are looking for information on a woman who disappeared in late May. She is a local Uber driver. Her name is Rowena, and she's twenty-five years old. She has a six-year-old son, Joshua, who lives with his father in Utica." Saunders passed around a 4 × 6 photograph. The young woman had a square face, framed by long ringlets, bleached at the tips. She wasn't smiling.

When Susan held the picture, she said, "I know her." We all turned to look at Susan. "Right, Daniela?" Susan said. "The northwest alcove?"

"Of course," Daniela said, "although I never knew her name . . . Rowena did you say?"

"Yes," Saunders said. "Rowena Kelly."

Mitch was nodding. Officer Jackson was writing notes on his pad. "Did she use the library?" he asked Susan.

She shook her head. "No. She rested here during the day. Well, she mostly slept. In an alcove a bit out of the way."

Daniela said, "She never disturbed anyone, so we let her be. She was clean and polite."

Saunders looked at Jackson, and then addressed Daniela. "When did she start . . . sleeping here?"

"I don't remember. Maybe two months ago?"

"It was more than that," Mitch said. "I remember seeing her back in February."

Jackson's gaze darted between Mitch and Daniela. "And when was the last time you saw her?"

"Not too long ago. Maybe last month?" Daniela said. "Right before finals week."

"Yes," Mitch said. "Exactly."

Andrea turned to Detective Saunders. "I helped her get a bag of pretzels that was stuck in the vending machine once. She was very grateful."

"Is she alright?" Susan asked Detective Saunders.

Saunders didn't respond to her question but turned to me. "You haven't said anything—did you recognize the person in the photograph?"

"She wouldn't have," Daniela spoke before I could say anything. "It was before Genevieve arrived."

Officer Jackson turned to me. "State your full name again, please?"

"Genevieve Tompkins," I said.

"Uh-huh," he said. "Are you a full-time employee at the library?"

"I work for a private trust, was hired to catalogue a family archive. So, I don't technically work for the college. But I'm here full time. And I just arrived in Wilton Springs."

"When?"

"Yesterday."

He nodded.

Saunders addressed all of us. "Is there anyone else who works in the library or your department who might have met her?"

Daniela said, "Yes. Luna."

"Luna?" Saunders asked.

"Luna Collins. She works here part-time."

Officer Jackson wrote down her name. "When does Luna come back to work?"

"Tomorrow at 9:00," Daniela said.

"Good," Saunders said. "We'll be back in the morning to talk to her."

"Thank you for your time," Officer Jackson said. Saunders said, "If you hear anything, please reach out to us." Saunders signaled to Jackson and he handed Daniela a card.

After the meeting I stayed in Daniela's office as everyone else left.

"Do you think there's need to be concerned? About that missing woman? Rowena?"

Daniela shook her head. "I know what you know, Genevieve. Let's place our faith in the strength of our institutions. Now," she cleared her throat. "I hope you're settled and ready to begin. I'll be interested to know what you uncover in those boxes. In fact, please check in with me after you finish each day. At least for the first week or two."

"I'd be happy to," I said, in a tone as cheery as I could muster, then turned and walked down to the basement. I was trying not to think about the cops passing around the picture of the Uber driver, mentally adding it to the Long List of Things I Don't Want to Think About, on which my father's death occupied the top spot. Work would be the best way to focus my mind.

I took the top off a box already on the table. Only a hint of mustiness rose up. Inside, there were many folders, papers tucked neatly inside them. I picked up the first folder and opened it. A Post-it note in faded yellow was stuck on the inside.

A single word, *Welcome*, was written in neat, cursive scrawl.

Someone communicating to the person who would be looking through these files? It must not have belonged in here. Unless the welcome was intended for me?

The first page was unlined computer paper. Penciled in different handwriting under the welcome note were the words *Wilton files 1990s Part I.* I turned the page over and shuffled through fifty or more business documents, lease agreements, and contracts. Straightforward stuff. The folders that followed contained similar papers. This box was already organized. I opened my laptop and typed in what I'd found. Then I labeled that box with an archival sticker and a number: *1.* I opened the next box. An index card with a title: *Wilton files 1980s.*

Inside were loose photographs, a Polaroid picture of a racehorse (Nelly, written along the bottom), standing next to a blond boy, and a picture of a huge log cabin. *Lake Charles House* scribbled beneath it. A 1990s real estate brochure featured a penthouse overlooking Central Park. Five million dollars. If all the files were as well ordered as the first two, the chronological sorting wouldn't take long.

I started making a family tree on the whiteboard on the wall, and entered names and information into the spreadsheet. The senior Wiltons—George and Lily Wilton, née Cooper—had two sons, Henry and George Jr. [middle name: James]. Henry had married Phyllis, and they had four children and lived in Florida. George Jr., George and Lily's younger son, who Russell Bailey said was referred to as James, lived in

Wilton Springs. He had married Barbara in 1987, and they had a son, Gabriel, and a daughter, Victoria. Victoria would now be twenty-seven. Gabriel would be thirty.

At the bottom of the 1980s/90s box was a family photo album. James and Barbara seemed carefree in the pictures, always smiling, on vacations in tropical locales or at various galas, he the height of preppiness in khakis and Ralph Lauren blazers. She looked tiny in one photo, wearing a sequined dress with shoulder pads, her red hair permed and fluffed up. Standing next to her, James appeared very tall. There were photos of Gabriel and another boy, identified on the back as Michael, maybe one of the four cousins. Gabriel looked like a miniature version of his father. There were pictures of pregnant Barbara, and Barbara holding her baby girl. Then Victoria as a toddler, gripping her mother's skirt. The last picture was a family get-together with three generations of Wiltons. The date on the back was 1998. I flipped through a second album, with older children. At the end of the day, I went to Daniela's office. "The two boxes I looked at were organized. Well organized," I said.

"I am not surprised," said Daniela. "Victoria Wilton interned here five summers ago, starting to organize the archive. Perhaps Mrs. Lily helped her. I'm glad you had a successful day." She turned to her computer. "See you tomorrow," she said, without looking back at me.

Emerging from the air-conditioning, I inhaled the fresh breeze as I walked through the woods, serenaded by birdsong. At home, I took a shower and then air-dried my hair next to the kitchen window while scrolling through my inbox, full of messages no one wants to receive, dealing with my father's old accounts and subscriptions, as well as a dozen condolence notes. I responded to each one, because if I didn't respond immediately, I never would. I fell asleep around midnight.

That first week, I woke up early every day, took a shower and had a long, cathartic wail, and walked to town just after eight, on my way to the library. I responded to a professor's ad for a secondhand bike and began riding to work. Here as elsewhere, I drank iced coffee, regardless of the weather. None of the coffee shops were crowded, probably because there were few students in town since the college summer programming hadn't yet started. I tried different places before settling on Wilton Grinds.

Wednesday morning, while waiting for an iced latte, I looked up to see Luna sliding my drink across the counter. "You work here?" I asked.

"Gotta pay the bills, pay off some loans," she answered. "Besides, I like keeping myself busy. I teach yoga, too." She grinned. "On Sundays."

Someone tapped me on the shoulder, so I stepped to the side. A white-haired woman reached for her cappuccino. A few minutes later Luna brought out another iced coffee and then walked over to me. "How about a drink tonight? Do you like live music?"

"Is water wet?"

She laughed. "Wanna meet at seven? There's a place on Main Street with decent bands."

The music venue Luna suggested was behind a tall brick building, directly across from the Wilton Arms Hotel. We followed a line of thin trees strung with twinkling bulbs to a huge back patio where a band of wiry guys on a stage were finishing a song with a clang of drums. After the clapping stopped the lead singer tapped the microphone. His black T-shirt was strategically ripped, and he had a goatee.

"I've been getting requests for a love song. So. This is dedicated to . . . all the ladies out there." The way he pronounced "lay-deees" made me purse my lips as if I'd eaten something sour.

Luna groaned. "Jeez. I've heard this group before. He used that line last time, too." A drawn-out instrumental intro was followed by the Guns

N' Roses song "Used to Love Her." Luna and I talked throughout the whole set.

"It took a while before I knew I wanted to get my degree in library and information science," she said, sipping a margarita with too much ice in a plastic cup.

"What influenced your decision?"

"Traveled a lot. On my own. I even drove down the whole East Coast."

"By yourself?"

"Just me, yeah. I went through a phase when I wanted to be a singer, wrote my own songs. Then I realized I didn't want to create. I used to dream of teaching abroad. Maybe someday. Above all I wanted to be active in a community. I've always loved books, information, the idea that you can go somewhere, and . . . learn. For free." She clasped her hands together. "I grew up in a small town, west of here, an hour to the closest library. I used to beg my mom to drive me. I became a huge reader. Good to have an escape hatch."

"Definitely. Any favorite books? Or authors?"

"My feminist hero is Anaïs Nin."

"*Little Birds*?"

"Damn, girl. You know your stuff! I've been reading her diaries. Did you know she published stories to pay her rent? The only way to survive in a man's world was to beat them at their own game. Same as today."

"Her writing is beautiful."

"Agreed. No doubt you know she was living a double life, with two husbands and two families, each in different parts of the country."

"Excellent role model."

"I like the way you think, Genevieve," she said. "Should we have another drink?"

"This is the most alcohol I've had in three months."

"I feel you. Were you doing a cleanse? Drying out?"

"No, I just haven't been craving it. I drink socially, and I haven't been social recently. My dad just passed away."

"Oh gosh, I'm so sorry." She reached across the table and rested her hand on mine, until I drew it away. "I know about grief, if you ever want to talk. I'm a good listener."

"Maybe some other time. I came here to leave the past in the past."

She touched my shoulder. "Let your emotions come and go. There's no wrong way to process trauma. And there's no time stamp on how long you get to grieve."

"That's a good way of thinking. The thing is, I wasn't close to my dad . . . toward the end. Makes me feel worse somehow. Like I didn't make an effort before it was too late."

"He was still your dad. The people we lose aren't always perfect, and neither are we. That doesn't mean you don't get to grieve."

"You're very philosophical, Luna."

"Someone I'm close to taught me how to think mindfully. I should introduce you sometime."

"Sure."

At the end of the set three drunk women went up to talk to the band members. The lead singer shook their hands eagerly and then walked in our direction until he was standing next to Luna.

"I'm Anthony," he said to her.

"Luna."

"Say, Luna, could you take our picture?"

"Okay," she said, and he passed her his iPhone. She motioned for me to join them as she followed them to the stage. Anthony posed with his band members while Luna took snapshots, and then handed his phone back to him.

"You're a good photographer," Anthony said, thumbing through the images. "What did you think of the set?"

"Musically you guys are fine but . . . the thing about the love song. The 1980s called and they want their jokes back. Misogyny has had its day, dude."

"Ouch," said Anthony. "I wasn't trying to offend anybody. Could I buy a round for you and your friend?"

"I don't accept drinks from strangers. And I'm still enjoying my watered-down margarita."

"Another song then. Just for you."

Anthony's rendition of "Like a Prayer" made both Luna and me chuckle, and after the second set ended, we let him buy us drinks. I went to the bar to buy another round and came back to find the two of them on one of the banquettes, heads silhouetted against the white brick wall.

I placed the drinks on the empty table adjoining theirs and retreated. Five minutes later I signaled to Luna that I was heading out. She pushed away from Anthony, stood up, wrote something down on a piece of paper, and handed it to him.

"Didn't mean to interrupt," I told her when we were back on the street.

"I'm a chicks-before-dicks kind of a person. If he wants to see me, he has my number," she said, flipping her hair to one side. "He's not the type I'd usually go for. So, how did your first few days go at work? What do you make of our lovable library team?"

The alcohol was now washing over me in waves, and my words came out slowly. "Everyone seems . . . nice, friendly."

"Working at the library is by far my favorite job. I'd go even if they didn't pay me. Probably."

"How many jobs do you have? There's the library, Wilton Grinds, and you teach yoga?"

"I have a fourth one but it's the least glamorous. As for the staff, they're weirdos, but that's what I like about them! Daniela's old-school and a bit stern, but she's got a heart of gold. She's wicked smart, speaks seven living languages, two dead ones. Susan is the sweetest—she has this animal rescue thing, even adopts homeless cats—she has like fifteen at home."

"Fifteen cats?"

"Something like that. She's razor-sharp, too, with encyclopedic knowledge of everything from sci-fi classics to T. S. Eliot. Best of all, she brings in fresh-baked brownies on Fridays. They're like . . . the platonic ideal of brownies."

"Yum," I said. "She said something strange to me on my first day, about how I shouldn't have taken the job? Any idea what that's about?"

She wrinkled her nose. "She might be superstitious. There's a lot of folklore floating around. I've heard stories of hauntings, dark things that happen in the woods at night. Susan was born and raised here, and has no doubt *seen things*. Or she could be talking about things she hasn't seen but are part of the accepted, local mythology."

"Also, the cops came to the library to ask about this woman, Rowena Kelly. You were off, but did you hear about it?"

"Yeah, they talked to me, too. I'd seen her in the library but we'd never spoken. Hope they find her soon. It's sad. Lots of people are struggling. Times are tough."

"For real. How about Mitch?"

"Mitch is like . . . a weirdo's weirdo. You know those English country gentleman outfits he wears? The three-piece suits?"

"Does he wear them every day? Don't they cost a fortune?"

"He buys them on eBay. That's how he can afford to. Oh, and he has a huge shoe collection that he wears with red socks only. But the shoes aren't leather. Because he's vegan."

"Eccentric."

She smiled. "But yeah. Everyone is super nice."

—∞—

At home I searched for Luna's social media accounts. Her Instagram handle was @lunamoonpriestess396. Her page was aspirational, and she had eight hundred followers. Recently she had started a business making T-shirts with life-affirming quotes on them.

> "The greatest glory in living lies not in never falling, but in rising every time we fall."
>
> —Nelson Mandela

> "Spread love everywhere you go. Let no one ever come to you without leaving happier."
>
> —Mother Teresa

The last one was my favorite.

> "The future belongs to those who believe in the beauty of their dreams."
>
> —Eleanor Roosevelt

CHAPTER THREE

When I arrived the next morning, Luna was in the staff lounge, holding a cup of coffee that I could smell from across the room.

"Last night was really fun. Drinks again soon?" she said.

"Whenever you're free!"

"I finished my big spring cataloguing project, so Susan just assigned me to work with you, be part of your team." She smiled brightly. "You can command me to get your coffee and dry cleaning, and pay me a pittance, as if I'm the average, college-educated intern in late capitalist America."

"It seems a bit below your pay grade and skill level, no? But hey, how great!"

"You're cool, Genevieve. And I hear you've got your doctorate, which is something I could never do, so I'm low-key in awe of you."

"I didn't actually finish my degree."

"Whatever. It's nice to have another person my age here. I'm off to meet with Daniela, but I'll be back shortly."

I finished up Box 2, and explained my procedures to Luna. She helped me lift a dusty box onto the table I'd been using as my desk. As I went through the contents, Luna entered important dates into the spreadsheet I'd been updating, and she fleshed out the family tree. The big box, which had been organized, contained mostly hundred-year-old contracts. I leafed through pages concerning Wilton marriages, and a late nineteenth-century contested divorce.

A few hours later, in the same box, I found papers from the early 1850s pertaining to Henry Wilton, George's great-grandfather, who'd been called a visionary and whose statue I passed on my way to work every day. The expansion of Wilton Springs had been Henry's own personal vision, and he'd become the first mayor of the incorporated Town of Wilton Springs, previously a village. He'd initiated the construction of an aqueduct, intended to distribute water throughout New York State, and even possibly all the way to New York City, which had been plagued by fires and diseases such as cholera, lacking a steady supply of clean water. But the work on the aqueduct had proceeded so slowly that the funds dried up before the system was completed. By then some reservoirs were up and running, and soon they provided water throughout the state.

Other documents described how after surviving the Civil War, Henry Wilton had returned to Wilton Springs and started the construction of the aqueduct. On a Sunday morning a few months into the project, his body had been found floating face down in the aqueduct, a "nasty gash" on his forehead. Henry's eldest son, Henry Wilton II, had been elected mayor of Wilton Springs, but he had died "an unnatural death" halfway into his first term, leaving behind one son, Albert Wilton. I looked into the cause of Henry Wilton II's sudden death. According to an article in *The Wiltonian*, he'd fallen through an ice-covered lake, and drowned. Henry II's son, Albert Wilton, had been elected mayor, in 1910. Albert's own son, George, was the one referred to by people who were alive now as "Old Wilton."

The next day, when Luna wasn't there, I researched the glassmaking industry. George Wilton's eldest brother, Henry Wilton III, had been in charge of the Wilton Glass Factory. I found newspaper articles about Frederick Wilton, the middle brother, an "alchemist" who was certain he'd found the fountain of youth in the town's mineral springs. Apparently his experiments, combining spring water with dangerous chemicals, had led to his accidental death, likely by mercury poisoning.

Luna worked again the following Monday, and after a few hours we opened the fourth box. Inside one of the folders were newspaper articles pertaining to the glass factory. In 1929, the Wilton Glass Factory, on the outskirts of town, had burned down, and twenty-eight workers had lost their lives. Firefighters had struggled to keep the fire contained within the factory walls so it wouldn't spread to the town. According to an article from *The Wilton Springs Herald* from June 18, 1929, the fire had been caused by a burst pipe carrying natural gas to the factory. Glass manufacturing was dangerous, with report after report of accidents with matches, overflowing molten glass, burst pipes, and, of course, arson.

Further inside the box, I found the obituary of Henry Wilton III, who'd been killed in the fire. A copy of a microfilmed article revealed that he and George had been involved in a lawsuit against each other, and after his brother's death, George had collected the insurance money. Another article suggested, in polite language, that the fire had been set intentionally. So far, I'd read about four different Wilton men—Henry, Civil War hero, had fallen into an aqueduct; Henry II had drowned in an ice-covered lake; Frederick, the alchemist, had died of mercury poisoning; and Henry III, who'd been killed in the fire. They had all four died untimely deaths. Maybe there was something to the curse Susan had mentioned. If one believed in curses, which I did not.

In the same box was a topographical map of Wilton Springs, dated 1736, with weird symbols on it. I didn't know what the symbols meant so I made a note, snapped a photo of it, and moved on.

Luna worked with me a few times a week, although her schedule changed frequently. Sometimes I had her organize the papers in one box in chronological order and input the initial data entry while I reviewed documents. Luna was diligent, and she didn't let me cut corners, which she said she'd learned from Susan. She was a hard worker, and often arrived before I did. It was nice to have a work buddy. We had inside jokes, and we talked about books a lot, too. Luna had read more than anyone I'd ever met. Free use of the college gym was one of the perks of our job, and she told me she read while on the treadmill. "As long as I'm not going too fast!"

One morning Luna ran downstairs to the basement and held up a book. "Have you read this?" she asked. The title was *Embracing Your Divine Feminine*: *With Affirmations to Preserve Health and Inner Calm, and Attract Happiness and Wealth*.

I took it from her, leafed through, then handed it back. "I don't read much . . . nonfiction."

"And I rarely make recommendations, but this book is next level! It'll change your life."

"What's it about?"

"Using the power women have within us to get whatever we want."

"I can see the appeal, Luna. Who wouldn't want to attract happiness and wealth?"

"I'll leave it on your desk after I finish memorizing it! You're welcome in advance."

I started bringing two sandwiches as well as cookies on the days I knew Luna would be there for lunch, which she happily ate, promising me free coffees at Wilton Grinds.

One afternoon I showed Luna an article I'd found about Albert Wilton.

"He was mayor until 1919," she said. "I already added him to the family tree, here," she pointed.

"But we haven't seen anything else about him until now," I said. "Albert started a company bottling the carbon dioxide present in the springs near the geysers in the state park. His company had been drilling for natural gas to make soda water to be bottled in Wilton glass bottles and sold all over the country. However, this depleted the water table of the springs. Wilton's gas company got caught up in statewide efforts to save mineral springs by banning carbon dioxide extraction. By an act of the New York State legislature the same year, Albert was forced to sell his company's holdings. Ousted from Wilton Springs in 1920, he took the money he'd been paid for the company, along with $200,000 he'd stolen from municipal coffers, and fled. A note of apology written by Albert was found in the company safe. Here it is!"

"Incredible," she said.

I handed her a yellowed piece of lined paper clipped to the article.

> *Darling Frances, I regret I must confess to having been inappropriately intimate with a woman named Myrna Swan. I can no longer live, not only in Wilton Springs, but on this earth, knowing the shame this will bring the Wilton name. Please do not look for me. I have decided to take my own life, and plan to jump off an ocean-going vessel. Raise the boys according to your fine principles always, and please tell them nothing of this.*
>
> *Your own adoring,*
>
> *Albert.*

I took the article and yellow paper back from Luna. "According to the article, Albert was never seen again," I said. "He was known as Mayor Houdini. But these days no one has any idea who he is, or was."

"Does it say what happened to all that money? Or to Myrna Swan?"

"Nope. Myrna was probably his cover. The money disappeared with the Houdini Mayor. Do you know anything about the geysers?" I asked.

"They're part of the state park," Luna said.

"Really? I'd love to see them."

"Want to go hiking out there? I know some trails."

"How about this weekend?"

Early on Sunday Luna drove us to the state park, on the edge of town, a couple miles from Main Street. We followed the signs to 3-Mile Springs Trail, which Luna told me ran parallel to several open springs. "Indigenous people knew about this area for thousands of years, and the healing properties of the spring water. This land was considered sacred," she said.

"One of the mineral springs was called the Medicine Spring of the Great Spirit," I said. "Today only twenty out of hundreds of springs are left. After the Mohawk were kicked out of the area around 1720, European settlers started developing the land, depleting the water table until the area was turned into a state park."

She sighed. "You already know more about the history of Wilton Springs than I do even though you arrived five minutes ago—I'll just let you guide the tour."

We passed a couple of families as we walked. Soon, we reached what looked like a natural water fountain. There was a steady stream of water jetting up five or six feet toward the sky and thumping down on the wet ground.

"They call it a spouter," she chuckled.

"Is that the same as a geyser?"

"A spouter is caused by natural carbonation, whereas in geysers it's heated magma." She stepped closer to the spring, her shirt getting increasingly wet. "It's perfectly safe to drink," she said.

"How does it taste?" I asked.

"Interesting. I wouldn't call it good. Wanna try?"

"I'm not thirsty," I said. "Maybe later."

We sat down on a bench and didn't talk for a while, both taking in the calm beauty of the park, the sounds of birds singing and the sputtering spring.

After a few minutes I turned to her. "Thanks for bringing me here, Luna. Being out here, far away from the city, feels like pushing a reset button."

She stretched her arms up. "You're really from Manhattan. Can you believe I've never been?"

"To New York City? Seriously?"

She shook her head. "I grew up in the sticks. I'm not . . . worldly and sophisticated, like you. What was growing up like? Did you go to prep school? I'll bet you've been places I've only read about. Provence. Seville. Let me live vicariously through the adventures you mentioned that you had with your mom."

I scooted away a bit and crossed my arms before responding. "In a lot of ways my childhood was great. But we moved constantly, which meant always making adjustments for just about everything. As for my mom, you've heard about those men who leave their wives for another woman? The other woman is my mom."

Luna opened her mouth and raised her eyebrows.

"She made sure to empty my dad's bank accounts before leaving him, and went on to the next Rich Husband. Her current husband turned out to be worth less than he'd advertised so she's now on the hunt for number four. She's always been super overbearing, and super charming, too. The life of the party. Early on she made me her best friend, took me everywhere with her. I mean, everywhere. It was a lot. Too much."

Luna laughed. "Even that sounds kind of idyllic. My mom had a substance abuse disorder and was locked in an abusive relationship with my deadbeat dad. He ran off with someone else and we moved around a lot. Until she OD'd. Painkillers."

"I'm so sorry. How old were you when she died?"

"I was sixteen. Raised myself. Got into college with a partial scholarship."

"You're . . ." I couldn't finish the sentence.

"I'm a survivor. Nothing can break me. I mean, I have my good days and my bad days like anyone else. Shitty memories. Whenever I'm unhappy as an adult I remember it was a million times worse as a kid. And I was helpless to do anything about it, back then. Powerless."

"Relatable," I said. "Are you an only child?"

"Yes. Thank goddess. And you?"

"Sort of. I have a half-brother from my dad's previous marriage who lives in LA. I don't really talk about him."

Luna shrugged. "I'm good at keeping secrets. I've got plenty of 'em. Or don't tell me," she said. "That's fine, too."

"We met only one time, actually. My dad left his mom for my mom so I'm sure that complicated his feelings about me. He wasn't at Dad's funeral."

"That's sad," said Luna. "Are you and your mom very tight?"

"She's not speaking to me at the moment."

"How come?"

"My dad died penniless, cleaned out by his last wife just the way my mom worked him. Anyway, my mom let me know in no uncertain terms that she wants me to snag my own rich husband while I'm still young. She's pissed I took the job here. I'm glad to be away from her."

Luna tilted her head back. "Be kind. Everyone you meet is fighting a great battle."

"I like that, Luna."

"Hey, I gotta get back soon. But let's come again sometime."

"Next weekend?"

"I can't. Working both days."

"How about drinks one night?"

She shook her head. "I'm volunteering every night this week. Which reminds me, do you have any old clothes you want to give away to a good cause?"

"I didn't bring much with me, but I might have a few things."

"We're collecting stuff for a women's center just outside Wilton Springs."

"It's great you find time to volunteer, I mean, with all your jobs. I'll look through my closet and see what I can find."

"Thanks, Genevieve." She narrowed one eye. "I'm curious. Do you have a boyfriend? Girlfriend?"

"Not at the moment," I said. "You?"

"Nah. Single and ready to mingle." She stood up. "I date men, mostly, but also women."

We started going down the path, Luna leading the way. Maybe because we weren't looking at each other, I began to talk about something I hadn't discussed with many people, what had happened with my ex-fiancé, Owen. "We were together in the same PhD program, and then he started sleeping with someone else." This was the first time I'd brought up Owen or our breakup since I'd found out he'd died in a freak accident.

"What a dick," she said, as we approached the parking lot. "I've been with guys like that," she sighed. "I mean, how awful that he died. Not that you could have saved him."

I didn't respond, and we kept walking, neither of us speaking, until we reached her car.

As we were driving out of the park, I pointed up at a derelict brick building that was nestled in the trees near the top of one of the larger hills.

"What's that building, Luna? Looks right out of a horror film. Don't tell me it's an abandoned psychiatric hospital that's now haunted."

"Close. Old TB hospital," she said. "Tuberculosis. People were sent here for the fresh air, on top of the hill. The salubrious breezes. Conveniently away from everyone, so they could just fade away peacefully."

"Fade away? You mean . . ."

"Die, yeah. Nothing could treat the disease. Thousands died, and not peacefully either, but coughing up blood in agony. People of all ages, including young kids. Back then, there was no effective treatment. The hospital was built in 1912, and closed in the early '60s with the advancement of antibiotics."

"Can we visit?"

"If you have a death wish, sure. It's closed to the public. And haunted as fuck. Visitors have fallen down shafts to their deaths, as if pushed by invisible forces. No one wants to touch that thing with a ten-foot pole. Actually, it was briefly open in the late '60s through early '70s."

"Reopened as what?"

"A real hospital, specializing in medical research. But then it closed again. I guess it was too far out of the way."

I looked up again, with a broader view. "There's a cool formation that looks like someone's face, in profile." I pointed up and to the left at some protruding large stones on a hill near the hospital building.

"They're known as the Lowell Rocks. Presumably after the Wilton Springs witch, but no one knows why they would be named after her. Maybe because they look like her face!"

Luna dropped me off at home, late in the afternoon, and that night I slept a full eight hours, waking up the next morning feeling refreshed, happy. My jaw didn't hurt, and I hadn't had any nightmares. At least, none that I remembered.

CHAPTER FOUR

The next day, after I'd just taken the lid off a new box, I heard shoes clicking down the stairs. A male voice cut through the silent air. "Hey there, I'm Gabe. Wilton. Are you by any chance . . . my mom said something about a historian? Cataloguing our family records?"

"I am. Genevieve." I recognized him—an older version of the boy in the photos, made flesh and blood. The same thick hair, now light brown, darkened with time. He was wearing a deep-blue polo shirt that set off brutally turquoise eyes. He was handsome in a conventional way, and he knew it.

"Genevieve . . . what?"

"Tompkins," I said.

He tapped his fingers on the table. "So nice to meet you, Genevieve Tompkins. Do you want to grab some food with me tonight?"

"How could I refuse such a gracious invitation?"

"Excellent. I'll show you one of my favorite local haunts. I can pick you up at seven. Where are you living?" His eyes widened when I told him about the Bailey cottage. "That old dump? I'll tell my folks they need to up your stipend."

A few minutes before Gabe was due to pick me up, I changed into a sleeveless blue-and-white cotton dress I'd bought on clearance at J.Crew and tied an ancient blue cashmere sweater around my waist. At 7:03 a beat-up black Honda pulled up next to Russell's house, where I was waiting. Gabe stepped out of the car and went around to open the door for me. He was wearing a crisp, white button-down shirt and designer Italian jeans.

"You look nice," he said.

"I clean up okay," I said. I hadn't put on makeup in six months but that was on a need-to-know basis.

"Do you like New Orleans cuisine?" he asked, when we were both inside the car.

"Do they have beignets?"

"The best you'll ever try, Genevieve."

The restaurant was at the base of a hill that led up to Main Street. The attendant managed to find a spot for Gabe's car in the parking lot marked FULL, and when the host said, "Our estimated wait time for a table is two hours," a man in a suit appeared and escorted us inside. We followed him past a full bar area and were seated near a fireplace. Gabe plunked down next to me on the banquette, and the man in the suit moved the silverware into place.

"You must be a regular," I said, after the man walked away.

"Dinner here is the perfect way to thank you for doing this nice stuff for my family."

"It's my place to thank you and your family for hiring me."

"Not that you need the money. Peter Tompkins was your father, right? The Peter Tompkins?"

I cleared my throat. "The very one." I stopped talking and he caught the hint.

"Sorry for bringing that up. My condolences, by the way." His cheeks flushed red. "So, you actually enjoy spending hours with old pieces of paper, without anyone around. In the middle of nowhere."

"It's my favorite thing to do."

"To each his own," he said, turning toward me and lightly brushing his hand over my forearm. I flinched. A pretty, young server came over to take our order, and Gabe glanced at her. A flash of something went through her eyes as she looked at us. Where had I seen her before?

"You're . . . Trish, right?" I asked, remembering her name tag.

"Yes! Wait, hon, did I check you out at the Giant the other day? You asked for paper bags."

"That's right," I said.

She smiled. "I work here part-time. The Giant cuts my hours in the summer."

"Nice to see you," I said.

Gabe barely acknowledged her although she flirted with him and called him by his first name when she delivered our drinks. I had ordered a glass of white wine but waited to take the first sip as it had arrived ice-cold. "Tell me about you," I said to Gabe.

Gabe downed his old-fashioned in three gulps as he told me his story. "After college I moved to Uganda. Helped build housing."

"How long were you there?"

"Two years. Fell in love with a girl. A doctor. But getting her a visa to come to the US proved difficult, and she kicked me to the curb anyway."

"You went back to New Orleans?"

"Lived in New York City for a couple years, thought I'd move out to Brooklyn and be a writer with a capital *W*. Just a phase."

"David Foster Wallace in hipster clothing?"

"Pretty much. Obviously, you can picture it."

"There were quite a few of those types with me in grad school. Then what happened?"

"Didn't work out. Why are you giving me that look? A bit of a cliché, right?"

"No, no. I'm not judging you."

"Then, I broke up with my girlfriend just before moving back home." He studied my face for a reaction.

"Oh. I'm sorry."

"It's alright. More than alright, actually."

The food came and we talked about the gumbo as we ate.

"Have you ever been to New Orleans?" he asked.

"Nope."

"It's fun. Party town. Just don't go during Carnival. It gets pretty crazy, even for me." When Trish appeared, Gabe asked me if I had room for dessert.

"Come on, I know you're pining for the beignets," he said. "Do you want to eat them with hot chocolate? I do."

The beignets arrived—four of them, covered in a thick layer of powdered sugar. Gabe ordered a "sipping bourbon" and didn't touch his hot chocolate.

Pushing my plate with half of my second beignet away from me, I sat back. "I'm in a food coma," I said. "Is it possible to order an espresso? A double."

"Of course," he said, looking around. When the tiny cup arrived, he cleared his throat. "Now is the time in the evening when you tell me you're seeing someone," he said.

"I'm not." I paused. "But it is . . . complicated."

"Is that complicated in an, 'I don't want to do this again, Gabe,' way, or an 'Ask me out again, please, Gabe?' I'm struggling to read you."

"I've had a nice time. Really."

When I offered to pay for half the dinner, he said, "They won't even bring me a check. It goes on the family account."

"Okay, but my treat next time," I said, as we stood up.

"I like that idea," he said.

Trish waved at us as we walked by. Gabe kept his eyes straight ahead, but I stopped and said, "Goodnight, Trish! Thanks. See you around."

In the car Gabe switched the radio on and then off, and slowly drove up the hill away from the restaurant. It was so dark. The lights were off in most of the big houses we passed. I rolled down my window and some cool air drifted inside. There were few other cars on the road.

At the next corner he stopped the car and leaned in. "Can I kiss you?" Without waiting for my answer, he gently steered my face toward him with his left hand. As his lips brushed mine, I did not turn away.

"Wait," he said. "I know where we can go."

"You can just drop me off at my house," I said, but was thinking about the soft kiss.

He drove in the direction of my house, and then he pulled into the parking lot of the funeral home, and turned off the engine.

"Is this your usual . . ."

"Hookup spot? No. But no one will disturb us here. Does it freak you out?"

"I should go home."

"You are almost home," he said, and kissed me, tentatively, letting the tip of his tongue run over my lips. I hadn't been touched by anyone in over a year. He smelled good.

He inched toward me and his hand found my waist, then slowly moved down and pinched my hip.

"Ow," I said, curling my fingers around his wrist, and placing his hand back in his lap. "Fooling around isn't a good idea. Not that we work together, exactly, but, kind of. Thanks for dinner, though," I said, unbuckling my seat belt and reaching for the door handle. "I'm serious about getting the next one."

He straightened up in his seat. "Okay. I totally get it." His face had turned bright red and splotchy, as if I'd just slapped him. He turned the key in the ignition. "I don't think you can get through that hedge. I'll drive you."

As we exited the driveway of the funeral home I noticed a large, dark-colored car with tinted windows on the opposite side of the street. It wasn't a hearse. The lights were off, but someone was in the driver's seat, although I couldn't see their face. I glanced at the clock.

"Wow, didn't realize it was after midnight," I said.

He stopped the car in front of Russell Bailey's house, jumped out, and ran around to open my door even though I was halfway out by the time he reached me. He leaned toward me, his head parallel to mine, and squeezed my shoulder gently. Pulling back, he said, "Guess I'll see you . . ."

"Soon," I said.

"Reach out anytime."

CHAPTER FIVE

The following morning, I texted Gabe to thank him for dinner, but didn't answer his reply. Two days later, waiting for coffee at Wilton Grinds, I saw someone tall, wearing a red baseball cap, then noticed Gabe's wavy hair peeping out underneath. I took a step forward, but a brunette bounced toward him and put her hand on his cheek. I turned around and walked in the other direction. Running into people, friends or mistakes, was something to expect in a small town.

Luna had told me about another, longer trail opposite the geysers, and Saturday night I set my alarm for 6:00 A.M. so I could ride out there, hike, and ride back before the sun became too intense. That evening brought the first big thunderstorm of the season, lights dancing and illuminating my room on and off, rain thumping the roof, and thunder blasting the hills surrounding us, all night long.

It took me twenty minutes to ride out to the trailhead, where I stashed my bike behind some trees. The ground was still wet, with puddles forming on the side of the road and in the dirt. I walked out past the nineteenth-century swimming pool housed in a big stone building that looked like a palazzo, and kept going up past the spouters and geysers we'd seen until the signs indicated I'd reached the other path Luna had described. The ruined TB hospital loomed high on a hill in front of me.

There were some beautiful rocks here, striped in unusual patterns that made them look like petrified wood, something I'd seen only in geology textbooks. No one else was around, just me, the colorful rocks, the birds, the springs, and my thoughts, which I was trying to switch off. I kept walking.

After a while I stopped to catch my breath, closing my eyes and inhaling deeply. The quiet was interrupted by the sound of a dog barking, once, twice, then frantically, and very close to me. I heard a woman's reprimanding voice. As I continued on the uphill path, the barking and the voice got louder, and I could hear a sort of thumping.

"Digger! Stop! Digger! Come!"

I could see them now, a small woman with long stringy hair trying to rein in a large German shepherd, who was like a machine producing a lot of dirt flying in the air. Then the woman let out an audible gasp that escalated into a stifled shriek. She dropped the leash and put her hands over her mouth. She saw me, and cried out, "Help!"

I didn't know how to discipline dogs, so I just stood there.

"My dog!" she screamed. "I need help!" She picked up the leash again and yelled, "Digger!" as she yanked, and was yanked back by the dog in a violent tug of war. She looked back at me. "HELP ME!" she demanded.

Running toward her, I could see tears streaming down her face. I reached for the dog's leash just below her hands, and pulled. I was a lot taller and maybe stronger than she was, but Digger was determined, and I stumbled.

"Damn it!" she shouted.

I dropped the leash and the woman yelled out, "There's another one!"

I looked down. Digger was uncovering . . . a body. Or body parts. I could see two legs, not connected. A sickening sweet smell hit me and my knees almost collapsed. There was what looked like . . . was . . . an arm. With a hand. And a few feet away another arm. A leg, puffy and milky-colored, with a foot, the toenails purply-black. The skin on every body part was covered with dirt.

"Holy shit," I said, trying not to gag.

"I can't stop him once he's on a scent," the woman cried, stepping back. "That's why he's named Digger."

I also stepped back, and stumbled over something, nearly falling.

"Phone! Do you have a phone?" she was screaming at me.

I leaned to one side and pulled my phone out of my pocket and handed it to her. She shoved it back at me. "Your password!" Her voice was strained and raspy. She was whimpering, looking at me and then at Digger, who kept barking and scratching the ground.

I took the phone from her, stood up, and hit the emergency button as I walked away from her and the sound of her whining, barking dog. When someone answered, I said, "This is Genevieve Tompkins. In Wilton State Park. A hiker's dog found . . . a body. Covered in dirt and . . . There are two legs. Two arms. More. We need the police. We're up past the geysers, on the five-mile path. No, no fire," I said. "No one is hurt, or bleeding. It's not me. It's a body. A dead body. In the dirt. No, we are not in danger. We don't need an ambulance. I don't know where. Where it levels out a bit. Okay. Oh, we might need a vet for the dog, too. Yes, I'll share my location with you."

Digger had stopped barking and started panting, as if out of breath. I had to create a contact on my phone with the emergency services number in order to share my location, and then I walked back over to the woman, who was down on her hands and knees. I could see part of a torso, at least that's what I thought it was. Half covered in dirt and dead leaves. I was buzzing in some sort of emergency mode and looked at it analytically, wondering how long it had been out there in the elements. The smell was so strong it burned my eyes.

"Digger," the woman begged, her voice hoarse. The dog turned around and walked over to her, and licked her face, which caused her to reel back and retch. Then she was hugging him, her head buried in his fur as she sobbed, saying his name over and over. I crouched down next to her, and stroked her hair, then her shoulder. "You're okay," I said. "Digger's okay. Help is on the way."

A siren wailed in the distance, growing louder before it stopped. It seemed to take a long time before three first responders arrived wearing backpacks and carrying gear. As I greeted them I pointed at the dog owner, who was calmer now, and sitting on the ground.

"Her dog dug up a dead body," I explained. The shepherd began growling but she shushed him.

"I'm a veterinarian," said one of the two men, and they both walked toward the woman and Digger.

The third responder, a young woman with a low ponytail, pulled out a notepad and started asking me questions.

"I'm Lizzie. Your name, please, and address and phone number?"

I gave her the information.

"Your dog?"

"No, he belongs to that woman," I said, gesturing toward her.

"What is your relationship to her?"

"None. I don't know her. I was walking and she screamed for help and we tried to pull her dog off the body, although at first we didn't know what it was. The dog's name is Digger."

She arched her eyebrows. "What were you doing out here so early?"

"Exercising before it gets too sunny. And crowded."

"Point to the direction you came from, and where you stopped."

She asked a lot of questions, all the while glancing in the direction of her colleagues. The vet was talking to the woman. The other guy was taking notes now. Someone else came up to the trail and waved. "The photographer," said Lizzie.

She looked at her phone and wrote down the time. "Please stay right here," she said. She walked over to the guy taking notes and conferred with him, then returned. "Thanks for your cooperation. But I'll have to ask you to leave now. We need to secure the area for the photographer and other authorized personnel."

Starting to walk away, I saw two more people climbing up the trail. I recognized them as the detectives who had come to the library to circulate the missing Uber driver's picture, Saunders and Jackson. "What are you . . . doing here?" asked Saunders, who was wheezing, as was Jackson. They were both wearing backpacks, and Saunders pulled hers off while Jackson walked toward Lizzie.

I explained what had happened. My emergency mode had faded and I felt lightheaded, as if I might faint.

She scrunched her eyebrows. "Miss Tompkins, is it?"

"Yes, Genevieve."

We stood there for a minute while she caught her breath. Jackson came back and said to me, "Sorry, miss, but we need to clear this area." He squinted. "You're from the library."

Saunders turned to him. "She was out on a walk."

"Could the body belong to . . . the Uber driver whose photo you showed us?" I asked.

"Impossible to know just yet," said Saunders.

We heard someone running toward us and turned to look down the path. A man in his mid-to-late thirties was jogging up the trail effortlessly, his cowboy boots making loud clumping noises. He tilted his head toward me when he reached the detectives. Saunders said, "Miss Tompkins is just leaving. She's an uninvolved bystander."

"My phone was involved," I said, but no one responded.

Jackson turned to me after a few beats. "Thank you for your help."

The smell lingered in the air. The heat and humidity were rising and there was no breeze. The wooziness stayed with me as I took one staggered step, and then another. I wanted to get away, to go home, but my body was holding me back.

The guy in cowboy boots stepped closer to me. "Are you okay?" he asked. When I didn't answer, he turned to Saunders. "Do you have any water in your pack?" She rifled through it.

"You'd better sit down," he said, gently steadying me as I started to lose my balance.

"I'm fine," I managed, letting him help me down to the ground. Saunders passed him a water bottle, and he opened it and handed it to me.

"Drink up," he said. "Not too quickly."

Saunders knelt down and gave me a thumbs-up.

"Is that smell what I think it is?" asked the new guy, turning to Jackson.

The three of them spoke in low voices and started walking away from me.

After a few minutes I felt much better, and stood up, then slowly hiked down the trail toward my bike. I was still feeling a little wobbly, so I walked the bike all the way back home, peering behind my shoulder every so often. I was covered in sweat by the time I reached the cottage, my hair wet. I took a shower that lasted too long, then got dressed, all the while trying, and failing, not to picture that scrappy dog unearthing pieces torn from someone's not-long-dead body. When the memory of the sweet, rotting smell inevitably came back, clawing deep inside my nostrils, I ran to the bathroom and threw up. I stayed on the cool bathroom floor for a while, grateful it was Sunday, and I didn't need to go to work.

For the rest of the day, I couldn't keep anything down except for plain crackers and seltzer. I thought of calling Luna and telling her what had happened, or my mom, but I didn't really feel like talking, so watched

TV instead. I made it through a few episodes of one of the later seasons of *Gossip Girl* and then went to bed. I woke up hungry and cold in the dark and looked over at the glowing alarm clock. One A.M. Forcing myself out of bed, I decided to go down to the kitchen to make myself a peanut butter and jelly sandwich and boil water for tea. But when I began climbing down the steps, I heard a slow, methodic rapping sound.

Panic seized in my chest and I froze. Had I remembered to close all the windows on the ground floor and lock the front door? Once the sound stopped I waited until my heart began to slow and then took light, deliberate steps to avoid making any noise. When I reached the foot of the staircase I saw that the door was locked, and exhaled. I thought about what Russell said, that Wilton Springs was so safe people didn't even have alarms here. I wished for one now. I slid into the kitchen and grabbed a big knife. Gripping the handle, I walked around, opening closets, looking for movement. But everything was sealed shut, no signs of forced entry. My New York City habits had saved me.

A breeze blew across my shoulders, even though all the windows were closed. The wind had picked up again outside, probably another storm system building up. I heard the same sound again. This time not so loud. The wind. That's all it was. Air.

I plunked down on the couch, turned on the TV, and half watched another episode of *Gossip Girl* until around 2:00 A.M., knowing I'd be exhausted the next morning. Finally starting to doze off, I imagined a woman's voice whispering, "You should never have come here. Now it's too late."

The words repeated themselves, over and over again. "Now it's too late. Now it's too late. Too late, too late," they pulsated, in tandem with my heart.

CHAPTER SIX

Having never lived in a small town before, I didn't know how quickly everything traveled—news, rumors, colds. Soon enough, they spread to everyone. The next day, Daniela stayed home with an upper respiratory infection that was going around.

"I didn't think Daniela knew the concept of time off," Susan said, shaking her head. "And it had to be right now, didn't it?"

"What do you mean, 'right now'?" I asked.

"I heard you saved the day," she said. "Severed limbs, a stray dog. Right?"

"I just called 911. And the dog wasn't a stray. Have they identified the body?"

"Yes. Belonged to a local girl. Lived locally, that is."

"Rowena, the Uber driver whose picture they showed us?"

"No. She worked in the grocery store."

"Why would anyone have wanted to kill her?"

She pushed her glasses up her nose. "I heard she had an abusive ex and a restraining order. Someone in my yoga class said she was having an affair with an older guy, a family man."

"How awful for her own family," I said. "Did she have children?"

"No family at all. She was an orphan, putting herself through night school on minimum wage. Imagine." Susan shook her head again, and blinked back tears. "Where did you find . . . her body? Where in the state park, I mean?"

"Close to the old TB hospital."

"Oh," she said. "I can't believe you went out there. By yourself. That place is . . . well, you shouldn't go anywhere near it."

"What is it about that hospital, Susan?"

"Ask Mitch. His mom was a nurse there."

The next day, Luna slapped a copy of the local newspaper, *The Wiltonian*, on my desk. "Well this is fucking freaky," she said. "You're like the hero."

"Hardly," I said.

"Tell me . . . " she said, her eyes widening. "Wait. Don't. Tell me later. I'm working at the coffee shop today but couldn't not stop by after I heard." She took off, bouncing back up the stairs.

I glanced down at the newspaper. The front-page headline read, in big bold letters, "Murder victim remains found in Wilton State Park."

I skimmed the article. "Body parts were identified by the Wilton County Medical Examiner as the remains of 25-year-old Troy (NY) woman Patricia Baranski, police announced Monday. The dismembered human limbs—two legs and two arms, along with parts of a torso—were found in Wilton Springs State Park, dug up by a dog out on a walk with its owner. Another hiker called the police. The victim's head has not been found. The police will confirm no details except that the crime status is a 'suspected homicide.' An unidentified male has been taken into custody."

Next to a blurred-out picture, which must have been of a limb, was a small photograph of Patricia Baranski's face. She looked familiar. It was Trish! The same woman who'd served me and Gabe at the restaurant.

I walked up the stairs and went in the bathroom. I stood at the sink and stared at myself in the mirror, gripping the cool porcelain edge until I stopped trembling. I had seen Trish, talked to her, only a few days ago . . .

Smiled at her. And now she was dead. Murdered. There had been so much death around me in the last year. Maybe I was the one who was cursed, not the Wiltons. I had the opposite of the Midas touch.

I ran back downstairs and dove deep into a box I'd already opened with files from the 1940s, the period I had started to focus on in the PhD program I'd abandoned. I found a packet of love letters between George and Lily during their World War II courtship.

"Darling Lily," one of the letters began, "We said we wouldn't get married until my safe return, since too many of your friends are already widows, but my longing for you is great, and thinking of you is the only thing that encourages me to go on. These are terrible days."

I imagined what it must have been like to have a wartime courtship. Reading these love letters allowed me to shove all the images and smells of the weekend incident out of my head. I read a stack of George's letters, and one of Lily's, in a pile of what must have been one hundred, noting details in the spreadsheet. I'd ask Luna to catalogue the rest the next time she was in.

After finishing the box from the 1940s by mid-morning, I pulled the cover off a new box. I pulled out a few folders and found another note written in the same handwriting as the "Welcome" note, and the same handwriting as . . . Lily's love letter? This one read, *Dearest V., I've tried to organize these as best I could, to make your job easier. I hope one day to discuss everything with you. Miss you. Love always.*

V. must have been Victoria Wilton. The notes were from Lily to her granddaughter.

Mitch, Daniela's assistant, had a thing for puns, and often brought me lunch on the days when Luna wasn't working. On that day, a little later than usual, he came downstairs with a boxed lunch and put it on my desk, beaming. He was wearing a tailored suit, this one grey pinstripe, but the pant legs were too wide and too long, lending an unintended clown effect.

"Quinoa with root vegetables and herbs," he announced proudly. "Never *turnip* your nose at a healthy meal!"

"Good one," I said. "This looks delicious. I keep forgetting to ask you. Susan said your mom worked at the old TB hospital. Ugh. Scary place. Do you remember her talking about it?"

"It is a scary place. And *was* a scary place, back in the day. A few times I overheard my mother talking to my aunt about the horrors she saw. I was young and didn't understand, but I remember the two of them whispering, and the terrified look on Aunt Shirley's face. Mom used to tell me if I wasn't a good boy the hospital ghosts would come get me. Things changed a lot when the Wiltons took it over in the late '60s. Toward the end, it was scary in a different way. They couldn't get all the spirits out."

"Wait, the Wiltons owned it? Get the spirits out? What do you mean?"

He put his hands on his hips. "Do you know why ghosts go out to bars?"

"Ghosts? Bars?"

"For the *boos*!" He chuckled, and I chuckled, too.

"Genevieve," he said. "I've been thinking. I know how much you enjoy your research."

"Well," I said, "some days are more interesting than others, as we all know."

"As we all know, those who don't like libraries find themselves in a *bind*! No, but seriously, I've gotten into it myself. Privately. Lately, I've seen some things that I can't unsee."

"Like what sorts of things?" I asked.

"If only Daniela weren't so diligent, I'd have more free time. But when the cat's away the mice will play." He took in a deep breath and began to recite, his arms rising up and outstretched, palms facing the ceiling. "You paths worn in the irregular hollows by the roadsides! I believe you are latent with unseen existences! You gray stones of interminable pavements. From the living and the dead you have peopled your impassive surfaces, and the spirits thereof would be evident and amicable with me."

"Is that . . . from something? Sounds familiar."

He dropped his arms and ignored my question by asking a question. "Do you know how many tunnels there are, under the United States alone?" I shrugged, and he continued. "Ten thousand! Ten thousand tunnels. The U.S. military keeps them a secret of course, they don't want us to know." He interlaced his fingers and lifted them over his head, then cradled the back of his neck.

"Is that the thing you 'can't unsee'?" I asked, making quote marks with my fingers.

"They use the tunnels as a more efficient means of transport. Especially for the aliens. It's the fastest way to transport the aliens without anybody noticing."

"Mitch," I said. "I need to get back to work."

"Okay, I'll go back up now. It's time to give you your *space* . . . Get it, space?"

He tossed one hand in the air. "You don't believe me, do you? You're like everyone else." His expression turned hard, cold. "You don't have to believe me. What I'm saying is the truth. Not the Disney fairy tales you read or hear about in the mainstream media."

"Thanks again for lunch, I'm sure it's *out of this world*," I said, hoping he would laugh, but his expression remained impassive. After he left, I stood up and stretched.

In the afternoon before I went home I saw Susan alone in the staff lounge, wearing red-rimmed glasses that matched her bright red top.

"What's up with Mitch?" I asked. "I tried to talk to him about the abandoned tuberculosis hospital but we quickly left the land of the rational. I didn't realize he was into conspiracies."

She rolled her eyes. "Don't pay any attention to him," she said. "About a year ago he started with these"—she tapped her head with four fingers—"cuckoo theories. His wife finally had enough and left him. No kids.

Now he has too much time on his hands. I suggested he pick up a normal hobby like gardening, but no, he wants to investigate whether the moon landing was a hoax. Poison."

"I can't believe someone so well educated could fall for that," I said.

"Anyone could believe anything, in the right state of mind," she said, her head bobbing in place as if she were agreeing with herself.

I sent Daniela an email, describing the love letters between George and Lily, the note to "Dearest V.," and other things. *Good. Thanks, Genevieve,* she wrote back.

The next day during my lunch break, I Googled James and Barbara Wilton and found recent photos of them at numerous charity dinners, their names on lists of donations to high-profile causes, although they were never big-ticket donors. After our date, I'd Googled Gabe Wilton, but hadn't found anything except his name mentioned in pages dealing with the family foundation.

Scrolling down, I saw a headline from a local newspaper. "Bainsville Senior Drowns at Lake Charles." I clicked on it. "Officials confirmed Victoria Wilton, under the influence of alcohol, became fatigued while swimming at a late-night party at her parents' house on Upper Lake Charles." The date: August 24, 2014. I read the article three times.

Why hadn't Gabe told me his sister had drowned? Why hadn't Daniela, or anyone who worked with me here at the library?

"Hope you're making some friends," I heard Susan say late in the afternoon, startling me. I'd been standing alone next to the water cooler, possibly talking to myself.

"Trying to," I said. "Susan, is there a reason you didn't tell me that Victoria Wilton died? Daniela said she interned here five summers ago. I found Lily's notes to her in a few boxes."

"Pardon me, dear, but it seemed a particularly grim subject for your first day."

I nodded. "Still, you could've told me after my first day, that she not only worked here, but she was working here when she died."

"I was thinking it's a shame Luna isn't around more often. But I'm glad she's here some of the time, since it must be difficult to meet people your age. You're not a student or on the faculty so you fall between two chairs."

"It seems as though you're trying to change the subject, so I'll say that I've never lived in a small town before and assumed it would be easier to meet people here than in the city."

"If you want to meet other people close to your age, you might want to seek out Cecile's group."

"Who's Cecile? What group?"

She had started to move away, and then turned back. "Genevieve," she said in a quiet voice. "Listen, I'm not one to gossip. But there have been rumors . . . that Gabe Wilton was seen with a new woman in town."

"And?"

"And that he had . . . sex with her . . . in his car. He doesn't have a good reputation. I want to warn you, since no one else will."

"Warn me? You think it was me? It wasn't!" I said. "He did hit on me, although please consider that private information. But you don't need to warn me along those lines."

"Not just because he's a womanizer," she continued. "Although he was involved in an ugly story a while back."

"Ugly how?"

Her gaze shifted from left to right. "It was maybe ten years ago. One of the young ladies he'd been seeing was found dead. In his bed. They said she had a heart condition, but—"

"Are you serious? I Googled him—"

"The family covered it up. Gabe moved away for a while. Africa, I believe."

"Wasn't there any sort of investigation?"

"Apparently not," she said, her shoulders rising slightly.

"Is that what you wanted to tell me? When you warned me about the Wilton curse?"

She put one finger to her lips, and then lowered her hand. "I just wanted to alert you. About the son, I mean. And the rest of it, too." Susan's voice had dropped an octave, and she continued, "Stay out of the state park, Genevieve. It's not safe there. Don't wander by yourself in isolated areas. Be careful."

"Okay," I said.

"Promise you'll stay on well-lit roads if you're out by yourself late at night."

"Why should I avoid the state park?"

"Besides the fact that you found a dismembered body there? Well, having lived here for as long as I have, I know that ghosts haunt those woods."

I interrupted her. "Susan. Listen. I did not have sex with Gabe Wilton in his car. How ridiculous! And I still can't believe that Trish was the person whose . . . remains . . . I discovered in the park. As you said, I'd avoid it for that reason alone. And I don't believe in ghosts. Or curses."

She tapped her glasses on the table. "You believe in history, right? In the past? Right?"

"Obviously."

"Well. Ghosts are just history demanding to be remembered."

CHAPTER SEVEN

When I received an invitation to "Sunday Brunch at the Wilton Residence," I assumed the Wiltons wanted to eyeball me and learn about my process in person. I wondered what, if anything, Gabe had told his parents. I was curious about them, too. I dressed in a lightweight knee-length pleated green skirt and matching green sleeveless silk blouse, which I thought looked appropriate for brunch but also professional. It was a sunny, cloudless day. When I arrived at the address on Main Street, I realized I'd walked by the property several times before. The house wasn't visible from the street, as it was set back into the landscape, surrounded by high trees, and, I now noticed, an eight-foot-high black metal fence. At the entrance gate, I typed the code I'd been given into a keypad, and the latch clicked open, allowing me in. I wandered up a long, curved Belgian-brick driveway, past a multidoor garage. From my work in the library I recognized the white brick house, colloquially known as Wilton Castle, and knew that it had been constructed in the early twentieth century by George Wilton's father, Albert, before he disappeared with the Wilton money and the stolen city funds. The home appeared larger up close than I had imagined while looking at the photographs. The windows on the ground floor had bars on them, which I didn't remember from the images.

Gabe opened the door when I arrived, a few minutes early. He looked me up and down and smiled. "You chose the right color to wear in this house, Genevieve." Then he leaned in to hug me and I stepped back, extending my hand for him to shake. "Okay, then," he said, then looked around. In a quiet voice he went on, "I'm actually meeting up with some friends at the lake pretty soon, but I'll stick around until you greet the folks."

"Did you . . . ?" I started to ask him if he'd been spreading false rumors about us, but someone walked in the foyer and started fussing with a plastic floral arrangement.

The air inside was warm and stale as we walked down the hallway. Despite their wealth, the Wiltons didn't believe in air-conditioning apparently. Gabe showed me into a formal living room so large it could have once been a ballroom. It smelled like a museum, which I liked, and was filled with designer-upholstered couches dotted with too many needlepoint pillows featuring horses and dogs. There were maybe eight overstuffed chairs, all covered in the same fading chintz. Four or five brown tables with lamps and more plastic flower arrangements on them. Everything needed dusting. The drapes—faded and floral—were the same green hue as the carpets. Everything looked at least forty years old, but not as a vintage-cool aesthetic. All the windows were clamped shut.

"What can I get you?" Gabe asked.

"A glass of white wine," I said.

"Wine it is. Do you prefer Chard from Sonoma? Or New Zealand sauvignon blanc?"

"The varietal doesn't matter, as long as it's ice-cold." He slipped through a concealed door off to the side of the room, and I crossed over to one of the bay windows that looked out over a lawn, or meadow—the tall grass needed mowing. Next to the window was another dusty brown table, this one covered with family photographs. George and Lily's wedding picture was behind James and Barbara's, both in tarnished silver frames. There were other framed photos, babies being christened in long gowns, Gabe and Victoria at different ages, wearing school uniforms.

"Listen," I heard Gabe say as he reentered the room with an opened bottle of Chardonnay. "About the other night after dinner . . ."

Just then another door swung open and James and Barbara, trailed by a bichon frise, collar jangling, walked in.

"Genevieve, I'd like you to meet my parents, Jim and Barbara," Gabe said, as he poured me a glass of wine.

"Good afternoon," they said, in unison, and shook my hand, Barbara first, then Jim.

Gabe gave me the wine, pecked his mother on the cheek, and then looked back at me as he headed toward the door. "Back soon," he said, waving as he left.

I pushed some hair matted with sweat off my face, and sat down on the couch across from Gabe's parents, my employers, feeling as though this were another interview even though I already had the job. Jim took a drink from a frosted martini glass that was too full and spewing cloudy liquid over the top. Barbara sipped a peach-colored drink before setting the crystal glass down on a wooden coaster on the pietra dura table between us. They were older than they'd been in the photographs I'd seen, but both of them remained attractive. Vibrant. Less glamorous, however. Less happy, understandably. Barbara's once bright-red hair was brassier, white roots growing in. She was wearing a long, opaque white linen maxi dress and Chiclet-sized diamond studs. No makeup except for a coat of nude lip gloss. Jim's wavy, silver hair was brushed back and in place, but didn't have that gel-sculpted look. His skin was tan and smooth, taut around his blue eyes, which were wide open. He was wearing a light-blue Oxford shirt and dark jeans with a Ferragamo belt, a navy-faced Rolex around his wrist. It was obvious where Gabe's good looks and style came from.

After making small talk, Barbara said, "Tell us a bit about you. About your background. Your educational background."

I crossed my hands in my lap. "I was a history major in college, earned a master's with distinction in American history, and started a PhD program, but then I had to attend to some personal family issues and decided to leave the program."

As if he hadn't been listening, Jim said, "We're so grateful you're working on the family archive. It's what Pops always wanted."

"Tell me you aren't bored to death," Barbara said. "What have you unearthed?"

"So far, a lot of reports and newspaper clippings, and business documents. And some fun love letters."

She beamed. "Aha. From which time period?"

"The boxes I've opened are from the '40s and '50s, and the '80s and '90s. And some from the nineteenth century. Early 1850s. I haven't made a dent in them."

She stirred her drink. "You're probably aware that my husband's family arrived in the seventeenth century from England," she said.

Before I could respond, Jim smiled at me with teeth freshly whitened and shiny. "My wife is an armchair historian."

Barbara lifted her head. "I was a history major in college." Then she stood up, offered to refill all three of our glasses, and left the room.

"We're here to help," Jim said. "But we don't want to be in your way." Glancing at the door Barbara had walked through, Jim cleared his throat. "We know your last name, and one of the reasons we hired you, in addition to your scholarly qualifications, is that we appreciated the fact that you would . . ." He paused, smiling at me. "We knew . . . we assumed, you would be circumspect. Discreet. About our family."

"Of course," I said.

A few minutes later, Barbara returned with our drinks, trailed by a young woman who set up three black lacquer tray tables, one in front of each of the three of us. It was the woman I'd seen arranging the plastic flowers after Gabe answered the door. She was pretty in a pixie-girl way, her dark hair short and swingy. Her white shirt, though, was stained, and her jeans were ripped around the knees. She left the room and then returned with a full tray, which she put on a sideboard. With robotic motions she put a platter of sandwiches on the coffee table, then plates and tableware wrapped in linen napkins in front of each of us before leaving again without speaking or making eye contact.

We began to eat, making small talk about the weather and movies. Then I heard a banging noise. Barbara went over to the window, opened it, and a goat snout popped up, knocking over a potted plant on the inside sill. The bichon stood up on its hind legs and started yapping.

"Quiet, Pippi!" Barbara said to the dog, followed by a loud, "Stacy!" Right away the young woman rushed back into the room. She saw what had happened and turned around, then returned carrying a brush and dustpan. As Stacy bent down to clean up the mess, Barbara brought a sandwich to the window and fed the goat from her hand.

"Is that a pet goat?" I asked. I'd never seen a goat outside of a farm on a school trip.

"Barbara adopts them," Jim interjected.

Barbara put her hand up. "They're used by . . . Wilton pharma . . . you see."

"For R and D," Jim said loudly. "Animal testing."

"Honestly, it's barbaric, the testing," Barbara said. "It's important we treat them well—after all that they do for us. They lead a good life now. I see to it."

"Barbara bounces from one charity to the next," Jim said. "She still sits on the board, on the ethics committee . . ."

"Daisy was Victoria's favorite," Barbara said. "She loved those goats."

"The librarians mentioned . . . didn't your daughter, Victoria, start to organize the archive?"

A long pause in which no one spoke made me regret asking about Victoria. "Our daughter was an intern there one summer," Jim said, standing up, and stretched his arms. Then he leaned down and scooped up our plates and walked out of the room with them, the little dog nipping at his heels. Barbara looked over at the platter of sandwiches, as if she might feed another one to the goat, but instead returned to the couch and asked me what I was reading. She hosted a monthly book club, and was caught up on all the current bestsellers.

Jim returned with a fresh martini. This was number three, at least. He wiped the side of the glass with one of his long fingers, took a delicate sip, then said, "Please follow me. There's a painting in the house I'm certain will interest you."

I glanced at Barbara, who lifted her glass. "Excuse me for not joining you," she said.

I followed Jim out of the living room through a butler's pantry and into the kitchen, where the woman who had served lunch was washing dishes.

"This is Stacy," Jim said. "She's been very kindly helping us out a few hours a week this summer."

"Hi, Stacy. I'm Genevieve. Nice to meet you," I smiled at her.

She didn't smile back, just nodded, still looking at the dishes in the sink in front of her. Her cheeks were slightly concave, the outlines of her skull visible underneath her skin. Then she did look up at me, with a direct gaze, her brown eyes lined with a thick layer of black kohl.

Jim and I walked out of the kitchen and into a long dining room. Thick, green velvet curtains framed ten-foot-high windows, and in the center of the room was an antique, almost-black wooden table that could have seated twenty. On the wall opposite the windows, gilt mirrors reflected our images back at us.

"Our dining room," he said, standing up straight, "has hosted foreign dignitaries, heads of state, Hollywood actors." A bronze bust of a man sat on a pedestal in an alcove. I recognized his eye patch.

"Henry Wilton, founder of Wilton Springs."

"You should lead this tour," Jim said, his eyes meeting mine. "Why are you smiling?"

"I was remembering a conversation I had with a friend in grad school. She said growing up there were the rich kids who lived in co-ops with elevators that opened onto their apartments and then there were the kids with busts of their family members in the living room."

"And which one are you? Were you?"

"Neither," I said, with a shrug.

At the far end of the room hung a life-sized portrait of a seated woman, dressed in an early twentieth-century gown, black with puffed sleeves. Her expression was austere.

"My grandmother," he said. "Painted by Sargent. Or maybe one of his disciples. Too good to check, as the journalists say."

"Frances Wilton," I said.

"That's right! She died before I was born. What have you learned about her?"

"She was married to Albert Wilton, alias Mayor Houdini. He had a mistress named Myrna Swan and fled Wilton Springs with $200,000 after a scandal with the water company."

"Yes, I remember hearing about the scandal with Albert. Great portrait of her, don't you agree? I wonder what happened to Albert's portrait. *Damnatio memoriae* I suppose. These paintings give this house a lot of character in my opinion, although my wife thinks they're creepy. I understand your dad has quite the art collection."

"Had," I corrected. "All contemporary, though."

"There are more upstairs," he said, leading me through two ten-by-ten rooms, a door separating them.

"The first office is mine, and this one is Barbara's." Old-fashioned computers took up most of the space on the desks in each office. "This area used to be staff quarters," he explained.

I trailed Jim back into the front foyer and then up a grand staircase with a green carpet running up the middle, my wrist grazing a dark wooden banister, which smelled like polish but was dull and smudged. When we reached the top of the stairs I sneezed and looked back to see a cloud of dust particles we'd created as we ascended.

The library had floor-to-ceiling windows and French doors that led onto a balcony. The fraying green chintz drapes matched the chair upholstery. The shelves were stuffed with biographies, and a glass coffee table had an oversized art book, splayed open to a still life.

Some of the bookshelves had been removed, and in the open spaces were three paintings, two landscapes and a third one, larger than the other two, of a shiny brown horse.

"The landscapes are Thomas Cole. And that's Nelly," he said. "I rode her growing up."

I yawned behind his back as he led me out of the library and along a long corridor. "One more thing," he said. We stepped inside a room, which seemed even stuffier than the other parts of the house. A faintly floral perfume hung in the air. The walls were a blaring shade of Pepto-Bismol pink, and about thirty stuffed animals and too many pillows covered the bed. An immaculate little girl's room.

"Victoria's bedroom," he said. "She never moved back home after boarding school . . . I prefer remembering her this way . . ."

Jim went over to a dresser and touched a photo of himself next to a young Victoria seated on a white pony, a tiny equestrian outfitted in a velvet jacket and helmet, and miniature boots. "My Victoria was . . . perfect. Always smiling. Blessed with a beautiful face and figure. She was an outstanding student. A dutiful daughter. So forgiving. Especially when others . . ." He turned back to me and said, "I suppose you've heard. About what happened. Rich families don't have secrets, as you well know."

"I'm very sorry," I said, wishing myself out of the stuffy room, out of the whirl of smells and memories that weren't mine.

"Don't . . . Please don't mention to Barbara, that I brought you to Victoria's room. Or to Gabe. I'd prefer it if . . . Well . . . I'm sure you understand."

He bowed his head, and I followed him out of the room into the hall. A cold breeze washed over my neck and shoulders, and I shivered. Was there a vent somewhere nearby maybe pushing up air from the cellar? I closed the door and caught up with Jim, wondering if he, too, had felt the draft. We went down another staircase, to the back entrance to the house.

"Thank you for coming over," he said. "And for the work you're doing for our family."

"You are most welcome."

"Hope you'll find some good stuff." He lowered his eyes to the floor, then looked back up at me. "We've had our fair share of tragedy. My brother had a heart attack at the wheel, wiped out his entire family. At fifty-seven. And then, Victoria. I'm not saying these things are connected, but it's a lot for one family."

"Oh, I, I had no idea," I said, thinking back to the photo albums I'd seen in the library. "I'm so sorry for your losses. I know what it is to have a heavy heart, believe me."

"And then we have Gabe," he said. "I understand he invited you out to dinner the other night. What did you think of him?"

"He seems—" I reached for an adjective. "Outgoing."

"I'd put that one-word description in the category of damning-with-faint-praise," he said, with a half chuckle. "And you'd be right. I've had to yank him out of trouble on more occasions than I'd like to recall. If my mother were alive, she'd describe him as a rich man's son." He clasped his hands together behind his back. "Anyway. Do let me know if you have questions, or find anything interesting, anything you think you'd like to run by me. Here's my card." He reached into his pants pocket and pulled out a card with bent edges, his name and cell number on it. "I'm off to a tennis match. Do you play?"

"Not in my skill set, I'm afraid," I said.

"That's okay. Your skill set is already quite extensive," he said, a smidge of disappointment crossing his face. Women with my background were supposed to be good tennis players, equestrians. "Maybe we can meet for a drink one afternoon, and you can catch me up on your progress."

Alarm bells started ringing in my head. "Thanks so much for brunch. I'll just say goodbye to Barbara."

"No need. She's getting on a call. I'll give her your regards. Shall I take you home?"

"Just drop me in town anywhere, I've got some errands to do."

I sat in the front seat of Jim's red Porsche, and he put the top down. A few seconds of fresh breeze cooled me down. "Thanks for the lift," I said, stepping out. "I'll share more findings with you two when I'm further along."

"Yes," he said. "Please do." He smiled again, and ran his hand through his hair. "I'm interested."

CHAPTER EIGHT

Remembering Barbara's mention of the oldest Wiltons, I decided to look for evidence of them. The next day, Monday, I started out my week taking the tops off six more boxes until I found one with a piece of lined paper on top that said *Oldest Wilton Records*. I pulled out the first crinkled, yellowing page. The date read 1740. The material was parchment, shedding in the corners. A long list of names. I lifted out of the box the rest of the contents, which weren't in any particular order, put them on the table, and began sifting through the hundreds of pages. The handwriting on these documents was difficult to read, but I was able to identify wills, contracts dealing with land transfers, and receipts. I checked the dates where they were indicated. Luna was late that day, but when she came down I told her about brunch at the Wiltons'. I hadn't mentioned dinner with Gabe. I knew she would've told me if she'd heard the rumor.

Luna helped me sort what I'd found into preliminary piles. The oldest documents dated from the early 1700s. Either Luna or I entered pertinent information in the spreadsheet indicating not only the number of the box and the letter of the folder where each document was located, but also a short description of the document, the date, and any Wiltons mentioned. The family tree on the whiteboard was cross-referenced with specific files.

"This is just like a fake project I had to dream up in school," said Luna. "So I get what you're doing. When you compile enough data, patterns will emerge."

"Exactly. We're compiling robust data that'll form a foundation for future analysis. We want the information to be"—I took a breath and touched my fingers as I went down a list I'd memorized—"accurate, complete, consistent, reliable, relevant, timely, unique, and valid. And," I added, "if the analysis methods are designed correctly there will be minimal impact from outliers and only small deviations from the assumptions, although things sometimes get wonky when you're inputting material from literal centuries ago."

"I can't believe I'm doing real archival work!" said Luna, a smile spreading across her face.

In the documents there were references to John Wilton, who was "a prominent law man and landowner" in upstate New York. In the middle of one of the piles were a few loose pages more discolored than the rest. The handwriting was legible, but elaborate, and written in archaic language. It turned out to be a property deed, which included a lengthy description of the land. I read it out loud, and Luna transcribed:

> . . . beginning at a point marked by a cluster of large boulders up a steep hill, six miles northwesterly of the Plesser Valley, in a bog meadow. A brook of sweet water courses through this meadow, and the land on each side rises thirty or forty feet above. On the side next to the springs the ground is stony, but fit for cultivation; on the opposite side, barren. The bank adjoining some of the springs is steep and bound with a ragged ledge of lime rocks, incrusted with flint. From where it terminates, to the upper spring, there is an easy declivity from the land above, to the margin of the meadow. For some distance,

> the brook winds through the meadow in a serpentine course in some places completely bridged over with large tables of stone. The bank, covered with a considerable stratum of earth, appears to consist principally of a solid mass of rock. The remaining part is cracked into deep fissures, four or five feet wide, some shallow, and some discovering into long subterraneous vaults. These ruins extend perhaps one hundred rods or more, and were produced many ages since, by an extremely violent convulsion of nature. I have been induced to be thus particular in my description of the neighboring bank, not only from its singularity, but on account of a personal conjecture which I shall herenow make, that there may be some connexion between the causes of those deep fissures, and those that gave rise to the springs.
>
> I shall now describe the springs. The uppermost is several rods from the foot of the bank, and may be properly termed a well. It is of an oval figure, over four feet in its longest diameter. Its depth is undiscovered, though it has been founded with a pole many feet long. It perpetually emits air bubbles, the size of those in a bottle of cider . . .

At that point Luna stood up and said she had to leave, but I was so absorbed I continued reading.

After the description of the geography and geology, the document indicated that John Wilton had inherited the property from the Widow Lowell, in 1723. It said the Widow Lowell's death certificate was attached, although it was not part of these pages. Maybe I would find it later. Was the Widow Lowell the same person as Prudence Lowell? A different Lowell? I included "Widow Lowell" in the spreadsheet, and added "Prudence Lowell?" in a separate but linked entry.

On top of the next page, in a different hand than the rest of the text, a letter was written:

What follows is An Account of Medicinal Springs at Nebsonbick, in The State of New York, by Dr. Samuel Wilton, September 1, 1725

An additional sentence was written in the margins: *(Nebsonbick derived from a Mohawk name meaning "medicine spring")*

My dear Sirs,

In my previous letter, I mentioned some mineral springs, in the vicinity of this place, previously unknown to me. When informed of their existence and location by my brother, the Honorable John Wilton, I took the first opportunity to see them, and never had less reason to repent of a visit in my life.

These springs are such a production of nature as could be designed, not only to excite the admiration of laymen, but to engage the attention of physicians and chemists alike. They were unknown, except to the Mohawks (in whose country they are found) until 13 years ago, at which time they were discovered by surveyors. The land, for miles round, is a wilderness. The springs want merely to be introduced to the world, to render themselves of important service to the country. They are abundant in number, located sometimes a mile apart, situated along a long bog meadow, through which runs a brook. The land next to the springs is fit for cultivation. The taste of the waters is unpleasant at first, but habit renders them agreeable.

These waters appear, through chemical analysis, to be the similar to those long renowned in Europe, although superior to them in curative virtues, in part due to their impregnation with fixed air and calcareous substances. These waters will burst any earthen vessel in which they are enclosed, making it difficult to transport them unless the air be discharged first.

The patients I sent to sample the waters were forty in number, with rheumatic complaints, and all returned perfectly relieved of symptoms. Among these patients was a man of twenty years of age, who served in the regiment, troubled with pulmonic complaints. I sent him to the springs in May, and by drinking the acidulous water for a fortnight, his symptoms were removed.

A girl from Albany, resulting from a fall on ice, had ulcerous sores along her leg, with a swollen and angry appearance, resulting in pains and the inability to walk. After she had used the waters for a fortnight, I saw her again. The swelling and ulcers were but a dark and distant memory, her pain abated, her skin clear, and she was able to walk again.

The residents of the vicinity believe the waters a cure for intermitting fevers . . .

The letter stopped there, the next page missing. It echoed information about the history of Wilton Springs that I'd read on the bus trip and discussed with Luna when we went hiking. I went upstairs, intending to grab a textbook on the history of upstate New York that I'd seen on the front shelves, and go outside to read it in the shadiest spot I knew next to the library.

But there was no one in the library. I looked at my phone and realized it was 7:00 in the evening. It was still bright outside. I checked the book out myself, which Luna had showed me how to do. As I was leaving the building, I saw a copy of *The Wiltonian* on the floor that someone must have dropped on their way out. I picked it up. The headline on the front page was "New Leads Found in State Park Murder Victim Case." I put the newspaper in the paper recycling bin and biked home. Eating leftover tuna salad in the kitchen, I read a paragraph from the textbook, which had been published in the 1980s, and was fairly dated.

For generations, Indigenous peoples freely used, and carefully protected, the site of these springs, currently Wilton Springs state park property. By the early to mid-eighteenth century, however, several springs fell into the hands of physicians who, having tried the waters, were keen to profit from their use. These doctors, convinced of the medicinal properties of the springs, cleared the brush away from Old Spring and Washington Spring, and put in paths and drainage systems. Soon, they established private ownership of the property, and began bottling and selling the waters.

I wanted to tell Daniela about the doctors profiting from the springs and that John Wilton had inherited property from Widow Lowell, but she was leaving the next day for Boston to attend a conference. Original-source archival discoveries were what scholars dreamed of finding while slogging through reams of fusty, musty, dusty pages. And I had now made not one, but two major breakthroughs to report on.

CHAPTER NINE

Tuesday afternoon, as I was finishing sifting through another box, someone walked down the stairs and said, "Hello. Maybe you can help me?"

I lifted my head and saw a handsome young face with a full head of wavy, dark blond hair set over blue eyes. Bronze stubble around his jaw caught the light. Long, tan arms. He looked like an actor playing a 1950s all-American boy. I interlaced my fingers on the table.

"I'm looking for old documents from the medical collection," said the handsome face.

"The medical collection is not one I'm familiar with," I said. "Someone upstairs can probably help you, though."

"They said I needed to talk to Danielle."

"Daniela," I said. "She's the head of the department. She's away at a conference. I'm not sure when she'll return."

"No problem. I'll come back another day." He turned around.

"Sorry I couldn't help," I called to his back as he walked up the stairs.

The next day the handsome face showed up again.

"Daniela's still out," I said.

"I know," he said, crossing his arms across his chest. "They told me upstairs. But I came all this way, so I thought I'd stop by and say hi. What are you working on down here?"

"A legacy project for a private family. I'm archiving their papers," I said. Why was my heart beating faster?

"That sounds interesting," he said. "Someone who lives around here, I presume."

"I can't really say," I said, smiling at him.

"Oh, totally cool. Could I leave my contact info with you to pass along to the head of Special Collections?"

"Sure," I said. "Are you a grad student?"

"Med student."

He opened the messenger bag he was carrying and took out a notepad, then scratched something down on a piece of paper and handed it to me. "I'm Mason, by the way."

"Genevieve," I said, and the tight knot inside my stomach began to give way. "I'll give this to Daniela."

I waited until he was back upstairs before looking at the piece of paper in my hand. Mason Clarke. A Gmail address. And his number. Doctors' handwriting was always so messy, but I could read it. I went back to work. An hour later as I left the building, I thought I smelled his cologne, its deep, woodsy tones. The air outside was humid, sultry. I rode my bike home, adjusting the gears so I could pedal as fast as possible. After I took a shower, I stood wrapped in a towel and punched Mason's name and number into a contact on my phone, telling myself it was a precaution in case I lost the piece of paper he'd given me. I thought of texting him, so he would have my number, too. Had he been flirting with me a little?

Two days later I was standing in line at the coffee shop and there he was, four people in line ahead of me. Mason Clarke.

I waited until he ordered and then passed by me. "Hi, Mason Clarke," I said. "I gave your contact info to the head of Special Collections. I assume she's been in touch."

"Well, if it isn't Genevieve," he said. "What are you doing here?"

"Out in the wild? Did you think I lived in the basement of Special Collections?"

"Kinda," he said, his smile turning into a grin.

"I'm down there most of the time, but everyone needs a coffee break now and then. Are you getting yours to go, or staying here?"

"Staying, but class starts soon. Want to sit for a minute?"

Five minutes later I joined him at a tiny table near the open door.

"What year of med school are you in?" I asked.

"Third," he said. "Almost there, although it's hurting my wallet." His gaze met mine. There was something sad and, at the same time, almost feral about the expression in his eyes. That, too, was appealing.

"Ouch," I said. "I can imagine."

"What about you? Cataloguing a mysterious collection of a mysterious family."

"Not that mysterious. I checked and it's not actually privileged information. The name of the family that hired me is Wilton. Old family. Old money."

"As in Wilton Springs? Well, whaddya know. How old is the old money?"

"They have documents that date back to the eighteenth century."

"You're a historian?"

"I actually was going to be one, before . . ." I combed my mind for an appropriate euphemism. "Before life got in the way."

"As it does, Genevieve." He sighed softly. "What about your own family?"

"They live outside New York City, in the suburbs."

"Is that where you grew up?"

"In the city. My dad just died recently, so it's only my mom."

Little creases formed around his eyes. "I'm so sorry about your dad," he said. I could tell that he meant it.

"Thanks. He had pancreatic cancer."

"They're all cruel, but that one in particular. Fast, too."

"The end came quicker than I'd expected. I hadn't been as close to him for a while. It disappointed me that I was always the one to make the effort, but now I wish I'd made more of an effort before it was too late. Sorry for oversharing." Why was I telling him all this?

"It's okay. You can say whatever you want to me. And you're right, a relationship is a two-way street." He leaned forward. It did feel as though I could tell him anything.

I pivoted anyway. "What about you, Mason? Where are you from?"

I hoped he would put his hand on mine, and imagined what that would feel like.

"The Midwest," he answered.

"Anywhere in particular?"

"Indiana," he said, with an exaggerated groan. "Have you been?"

"Nope. That's far away. Do you go back often?"

"Not since before I started med school. No reason to. Not to see my family anyway. I have three older brothers, and each one tormented me in their own special way when I was growing up."

"Sounds challenging. Have you always wanted to be a doctor?"

"Since forever, yeah." He mussed his hair. "Wait, that's not true. As a kid I wanted to be a vet."

"That's sweet."

"Did you know it's more difficult to get into vet school than it is to get into medical school? Guess I wasn't smart enough. Always loved animals though. My family rescued an abused cat when I was growing up. At least I can say that for them. I only go back for weddings and funerals."

"Are there other doctors in your family?"

"I'm the first one in my family to go to college. They don't even believe in science."

My voice jumped an octave. "You broke the mold, Mason!" I paused. "That didn't come out the way I meant it to . . ."

He smiled. "No worries. You're super chill. I go to school with a lot of snotty people. Speaking of which, I should probably head out, but what are you up to later?"

"Later, as in . . . ?"

"Tonight. Want to come to a party?"

CHAPTER TEN

The address Mason had given me was on Main Street, on the opposite side of campus from where I lived, where in the late-nineteenth or early-twentieth century the slightly less well-heeled (or the newer up-and-coming families) constructed a second generation of ostentatious abodes. It took almost thirty minutes to walk there in my strappy sandals. I double-checked the address. Who lived here? A narrow turret with bloodred stained glass windows rose up from the dark-grey shingled facade of an enormous mansion that looked like the evil twin of its pristine neighbor on the other side of the looking glass.

The first person I recognized after walking through the front door, past the dimly lit foyer and into the adjacent living room, wasn't Mason, it was Luna. She was near a small fireplace standing apart from two women young enough to be undergraduates. She glanced up and waved, walked over, and threw her sweaty arms around me.

"Hey, babe! It's been what, a whole entire day since I've seen you? Woo—I have had a lot to drink. Was just about to head out," she said. "I didn't know you knew Emma!"

"Who's Emma?"

She narrowed one eye. "She's a junior at Bainsville. This is her house. Well, her parents' house. Usually, they rent it out to summer people, but she's living here until September, which is awesome. The Blackwells are as old as the Wiltons, and just as rich, but not on speaking terms with them, because, yeah, Wilton Springs is apparently not big enough for the two of them."

"Two dynasties."

"Tale as old as time. Shakespearean! So, you walked here? By yourself? It's a bit of a trek, no?"

"Tell me about it, my feet are killing me."

"You shouldn't walk by yourself after dark. Remember," she said, pointing her finger at me. "Dead Trish. Prob'ly dead woman who used to sleep at the library."

"The address was on Main Street, Luna. I had no idea it would be a half an hour walk. But anyway, I'm here, nothing to worry about."

"All you need to do is call me and I'll give you a ride! Better safe than sorry."

"Yeah, because you driving a car right now screams safety."

She crossed her arms over her chest.

"That was a joke, Luna. Feel free to laugh."

"Not all of us can afford to take Ubers everywhere," she said.

I walked her to the front door, trying to assess if she could in fact, drive home.

"Don't patronize me, Genevieve," she said, when I suggested she walk instead. "I'm fine. It's not far. I'm a big girl." Then she said the alphabet backward as she walked backward away from me. I waved goodbye to her when she reached the letter *H*.

Following the source of the music, I walked along a creaking parquet floor into an Olympic swimming pool–sized dining room, where a young, blonde woman wearing a short dress the color of fire was standing at an upright bar in the corner. Her manicured fingers were wrapped around a drink that matched the color of her dress. Her posture was relaxed, yet assertive, as if she owned the place. Just then someone called out, "Hey, Emma!" The woman in the short orange dress looked up and waved.

So, she did own the place.

On the bar were three different red-and-orange-toned drinks displayed on a tray, as if they were tropical plants or designer handbags. A skinny man with lines of blue text inked on his left arm was shaking and serving the bright cocktails.

I looked around and didn't see Mason. I had no interest in sticking around if he'd changed his mind about coming. I'd rather be home reading about eighteenth-century New York than hang with this crowd of already inebriated young strangers. But just as I turned to leave, Emma and her friends crossed over to a set of French doors and stepped outside. Maybe Mason was out there. I followed them onto a grey slate patio that gave way to a vast dark-green lawn.

Emma had walked over to a woman wearing an oversized, multicolored silk coat with long fringes that danced as she moved, skimming the floor and flaring out now and then. The back of the coat was machine-embroidered with bright-red hibiscus flowers in full bloom—reminding me of a Madame Butterfly-esque costume one might buy at a thrift store. Just at that moment she turned, and I could see that she was older than anyone else at the party, maybe in her mid-to-late forties. A professor?

I walked back inside, crossed through the dining room and then into the front hall. Why was I wasting my time at an undergraduate party? I opened the front door, ready to slip out, and Mason was standing in the doorframe. My heart thump-thumped.

He smiled. "Attempting an Irish goodbye, Genevieve?"

"I need to be at work early tomorrow . . ."

He looked me in the eye. "Can I entice you to stay?"

"I don't know. Can you?"

"Sorry I'm so late. Was finishing up some paperwork."

"Well, this isn't really my scene."

"What isn't?"

"Sorority girls," I said. "Filthy rich undergraduates."

He shook his head once, twice. "Don't be like that."

"Like what?"

"You know, negative. You gotta enjoy this life! It's not a dress rehearsal. No offense."

"You sound like my mother," I grumbled.

"Besides, there are some people I know you'd like to meet. Not sure if they're here."

He threaded his arm through mine, which I didn't mind at all, and led me into the house and then back out to the patio.

The woman in the flowery coat was surrounded by a new cloud of people.

"There's Cecile," he said. "She runs a spa in town. Have you been? I'm sure you know this has been a spa town for over a century."

"Are you into spas? Facials and massages? Pedicures, perhaps? You seem like a pedicure guy."

"Very funny. I've heard Cecile's spa is among the best in the Northeast."

"If you say so," I said.

"Cecile is kind of—a personality in Wilton Springs. Always surrounded by an entourage. And, on the weekends, they go into the woods and . . . I'm not entirely sure what they do. They're, uhh—this is going to sound weird, but they're witches. They practice witchcraft."

"They cast spells?" I asked.

"I guess. Isn't that what witches do?"

"So, you've seen them doing . . . witchy things?"

"Me? Nope. But I've heard."

"Intriguing," I said. Clearly, Mason wanted me to be intrigued. I was trying not to yawn.

"Shall I introduce you?"

"Maybe later," I said.

"How about one of those orange cocktails being passed around?" he said. "Would you like one? Or something else?"

"I'm good, but thanks."

Emma turned around just then and gasped. She walked over to Mason and threw her arms around his neck and knocked her right hip into his. "MASON!! I am so, so glad you could make it."

"I wouldn't miss this!" he said.

"Save a dance for me later, pleeease," she said, with a wink, before she sauntered away, dramatically swiveling with each step.

Somebody laughed and I looked over. Cecile had turned her hazel eyes my way. She walked up to me until she was so close I could see tiny bronze flecks in her dark irises. Her hair was wavy, and thick, past shoulder-length, greying a little at the roots. Her face was not exactly beautiful, but it was distinct. Original. She looked like a late nineteenth-century theater actress.

"Hello," she said. "I'm Cecile."

"Genevieve," I answered. I turned to Mason but he wasn't there.

"What a pretty name, Genevieve," she said, pronouncing it with a passable French accent. Her voice surprised me. It was gravelly, low. The kind of voice I could imagine singing jazz. When she leaned in to kiss my cheek, I stepped back.

She put her hands together and bowed. "I prefer the double kiss—as they do *en France*."

"Are you French?"

She blinked. "Probably somewhere in there."

"Cool coat."

"It's vintage," she said, pulling it around herself and tightening the sash. "What do you do in Wilton Springs? Are you a student? Bainsville?"

"No," I said. "I'm archiving the private collection of the Wilton family."

"An archivist!" she said. "How . . . scholarly!"

"Mason told me you run the spa," I said.

"Mason?"

"Yeah, Mason Clarke, he's a . . . med student . . ."

"Oh, yes. Mason! What a nice guy. You're his friend?"

I glanced across the lawn. Mason must have gone inside. "New friends—we just met."

"You are correct, I do run the spa," she said. "I haven't seen you there yet. Please come in soon and pamper yourself."

"I don't really do pampering," I said, standing up a little taller, "Mason also said . . . you do witchcraft?"

"We practice in the esoteric healing arts, yes. Some label us as witches. Usually men."

"Well," I said, "You might be interested to know that I recently found some documentation concerning a Widow Lowell, whom I'm pretty convinced is, was, Prudence Lowell. You've heard of her, I'm sure."

"Of course! She's the reason I started my group. We're inspired by Prudence's example. What others label witchcraft we consider empowerment. For young women especially. Words are spells, after all. But let's talk about this another time. Tonight, we are guests in Emma's beautiful home! Would you like to meet some more people? Or have another cocktail?"

"There I go, mixing business with pleasure. But, please give me a rain check. I'd love to meet more people, but I have an early morning tomorrow." I stuck out my right hand and she grasped it. Her skin was silky.

"You have good energy, Genevieve," she purred. "Come visit me at the spa one rainy day when you've got nothing better to do."

"Okay," I said. She turned away just as Mason appeared.

"Can I drop you off at your place?" he asked. "I know you're ready to leave."

I smiled. I could get used to having this guy read my mind.

CHAPTER ELEVEN

After my breakup with Owen, I'd wanted to move away. Somewhere isolated, somewhere different from anywhere I'd lived before. A place where no one knew my name. So many things were terrible, and heartbreaking, and sad. The worst part had been the realization that other people were fundamentally unknowable. For three years, I had believed Owen was my best friend, and I was his. I was wearing his mother's ring when I'd tapped on our shared desktop computer to look up the weather. Owen was away for the weekend. When the screen flickered into focus, I saw an unsent message hanging out in one corner of the wide screen. I had thought it was a draft Owen was writing to me.

I ran my eyes over the lines: "I'm fascinated by your face. Your eyes and lips. I've never felt like this about anyone before . . ." I smiled, and sat up straighter. It was the sort of thing he'd written to me when we'd been falling in love. I read it again. Then I saw. The email was addressed to someone named Holly. "I'm sorry I didn't tell you that I live with my fiancée, but I feel so lonely here . . ." I read the words over again and again. Each time they became stranger to me.

I'd printed it out and stared at the string of sentences on and off for several hours, sitting on the floor. But then I'd stood up, taken off the ring, showered, and dressed. Put on heels.

When I heard Owen turning the key in the lock, I was listening to James Taylor and crying just a little, the kind of tears you can hide, not the kind that might ruin mascara.

"How was your day? Were you with Holly?" I had asked, not wasting any time.

"Who?"

"I think you know."

"No. I *don't*. You're acting crazy."

"If I'm so crazy, then what's this?" I handed him the copy of the email I'd printed out. He read it frozen in silence, and hung his head. "Explain it. I'm listening."

Owen hadn't been able to explain it, though, or had chosen not to. I had gathered his things, and placed them, neatly arranged, in bags and boxes. I pointed to them and said, "Out. Now." Later, in the bottom drawer of his desk, I'd found three empty vodka bottles.

I had helped him find a new apartment. A studio close by. "Sometimes," my friend Silvia had told me, "things are so painful that you have to lock them away in a box on a shelf in a closet in your mind, and never open it." It sounded like a useful visualization exercise. I tried, but it didn't help.

Owen and I had coffee once a week. Then once a month, then sporadically. Then not at all.

Ten months after the night of the email a friend had posted a large photo of Owen online. His hair looked longer and wilder now, but I'd immediately recognized his big, white teeth in the smile that once stopped me. I read the words under the photograph. Owen had died in a skiing accident. I had almost forgotten him, and now I never would.

"I'm so sorry," my mom had said, when I'd called her. "But he was terrible to you. And you were so nice to him. But you'll forget, sweetheart. The good, the bad. Like I did with your dad. And Steve. And Cal. Even

Bertrand. You'll be okay. One day, it'll be as if that time with him never existed."

After her call I had gone into my office, which had been our bedroom, and opened a drawer I had kept closed for a long time. I pulled out a porcelain figurine, a broken elephant I'd given him on the first birthday of his that we'd spent together as a couple. He'd been surprised and touched that I had remembered elephants were his favorite animal.

As I ran my fingers over the cracks in the porcelain, I took care not to cut myself on the sharp edges of the hole where the second tusk used to be. It was neither comforting nor disappointing to know that someday I would no longer remember why the figurine had once been important to me.

Saturday turned out to be sunny and warm with no humidity and just a light breeze, the perfect early summer day. I laced up my running shoes, pulled on a Bainsville baseball cap, texted Luna where I was going, and went for a long walk along the Wilton Springs streets. An hour later, I was on the side of town closer to Emma's house and stopped to look at a grand Victorian standing alone on a street corner marking the outer edge of Main Street. The covered front porch was painted powder blue, and two vintage rocking chairs leaned against the wall between two unlit gas lamps. A sign on the door read *Earth Mother Holistic Spa*. Cecile's spa. By this time, my feet, which hadn't recovered from walking a few days earlier in my strappy sandals, were throbbing. Especially my right foot. Maybe there was some potion in there that would bring relief. I walked up the path and crossed the porch slowly, the buckled wood bending and creaking underneath my footsteps.

I pushed through beaded curtains into a warm space that smelled like incense and fresh herbs. Spread out on a large table was an array of crystals in a variety of shapes, colors, and sizes, each with a description of their unique properties. A rainbow of larger crystals was displayed in the windowsills.

The woman behind the desk had straight, ink black hair. A tiny silver hoop hung between her nostrils. When she didn't look up, I cleared my throat. "Hi there. I'm wondering if you have something that I could put on my feet. They're sort of aching. Blistered."

"Any blood?" asked the woman.

"I don't know," I said, looking around for a place to sit down and take off my shoes.

"You'd know if there was blood," she said. "Do you want a topical treatment, or some healing crystals, or stones? Or a cup of herbal tea with sea salt to balance your electrolytes?"

"Umm," I muttered.

"Mind you don't get dehydrated. In this heat." She passed me a menu and left the room.

I picked up a small, heart-shaped pink stone from the glass shelf closest to me. Rose quartz. According to the label, if I carried the stone around with me, and occasionally held it in my palm until it became warm, I could attract love. I pressed my fingers into its smooth curves. When it warmed up, I set it back down.

I flipped through the menu, which listed all the spa treatments—massages, facials, manicures and pedicures. Next listed were *Remedies*, including Sacred Chakra Healing, Crystal Healing, and Hecate's Herbal Wrap. On the next page, under *Private Sessions*:

"Let our skilled team guide you to the next level with our coaching sessions." These included options such as

Unlocking your esoteric healing powers
Manifestation session: success
Manifestation session: love

In the bottom right-hand corner, *Prices on request* was written in small letters.

"As you can see, we do things differently here." I heard Cecile's low voice echo through the room. She floated out from a door behind the desk and crossed over to me, bringing with her a halo of essential oil perfumes. "It's nice to see you, Genevieve. Let's go up to my office. There's something I'd like to give you." The woman with the ink black hair had followed Cecile back into the reception area and now reached to answer the phone.

At the top of a flight of narrow, groaning stairs, Cecile's office smelled like she did, all vanilla and burnt herbs, with a hint of musk. I sat down in a white wicker chair across the small room from her desk. The seat felt rickety and the cushion was very thin. My eyes ran along the floor-to-ceiling bookshelves on the wall.

A Compendium of Herbal Magick
Herbal Living
Wicca for Beginners
Advanced Wicca
Tarot: A Historical Introduction
The Crystal Bible

She watched me looking at the books and then said, "You remind me of someone."

"Why does everyone keep saying that? I . . . Did the woman downstairs tell you I was looking for something for the pain in my feet?"

"Yes," Cecile said. She took two steps and knelt in front of me. "May I?" Without waiting for an answer, she unlaced my sneakers and gently rolled off my socks. She tossed a fluffy white towel across her knees and opened a black-lacquer box that she'd set down next to my right foot.

Taking two hot, moist towels from the box, she wrapped one and then the other foot, and worked between the toes of each foot before removing the towels and putting them back into the box. From her pocket she pulled out a small vial and opened it. Her hands were warm, and so was the oil she poured over my toes. Soon I leaned back into what seemed to be the most comfortable chair I'd ever sat in, and watched as she massaged one foot, then the other, her touch confident but tender, and certainly healing. After a while my eyes fluttered shut.

I don't know how much time passed, but I opened my eyes again when she rang a low-toned bell, and the woman from the front desk appeared with another white towel, this one also warm when Cecile wrapped it around my feet.

"I guess this is pampering," I said, as Cecile stood up and walked around her desk to sit down, inviting me to sit in the chair across from her.

Once we were situated, she smiled. "Treat your feet with care. They carry you through life."

"How very true."

"There's something . . . unusual about you. I could tell when we met. You're an old soul."

I sat forward. "Does that mean I don't have long to live?" Susan's mention of the curse flitted through my mind.

"Not at all. It signifies this isn't your first lifetime. You've had many, actually. In this one, you have experienced a lot of loss. Early on, but also . . . recently. Am I right?"

I nodded.

"Have you ever considered harnessing your unique power, and using it as a healer?"

"Did you learn all this about me while massaging my feet?" I asked.

She continued as if she hadn't heard me. "I used the word *healer*, but could just as easily have used *witch*. The words *wit*, *witch*, and *wise* have the same etymology. They come from 'to know, to understand, to be someone of intelligence.'"

"From the Anglo-Saxon word *witan*, used to describe a wise woman."

"So, you do know something about witches after all. Not surprising."

"Research is how I make sense of the world. No doubt you know the word that's pronounced 'wit-cha' was spelled w-i-c-c-a, and means 'to turn, or bend,' as in turn of the seasons, or bending reality."

She was smiling and nodding her head almost imperceptibly. "Well, then, you'll understand that we will be bending reality on Sunday, Litha, and wiccaning a new witch. And you are invited to join us. Knowing of your interest in our famous resident wise woman, it would be meaningful for you to attend."

She leaned forward, and looked me in the eye. "The desire to become a healer often begins with trauma in childhood. We must experience darkness to understand life's fragility. I was abused by everyone I ever cared about. My mother didn't know how to handle a child who saw ghosts. After she died, I raised myself and my siblings. My younger brother, the one I loved the most, died when he was twelve. Congenital condition." Her voice was calm, even, and somehow it didn't seem odd that she would confide in me, a stranger.

"That's a lot of trauma for a young person. Any person. I'm very sorry, Cecile."

"You're an empath. It's a mixed blessing."

I said nothing.

She paused. "Modern people think in the past. They send texts, repeat behaviors, lose their free will to the comfort of habit. I'm not engaged with any social media. Are you?"

"Yes, but I agree it's a waste of time."

"You might consider a detox. It would help you reach beyond your conscious mind. Traumatic events produce emotional reactions, forming negative memories. Negativity holds you back. So it's imperative to learn to let go, even if that feels counterintuitive. Authentic self-confidence comes from feeling comfortable with uncertainty. You will find your true self when you are able to rest in the space of ambivalence."

"Wow. All that makes sense, even if I couldn't repeat what you just told me. I feel calm now. I'm not sure if it was the massage or your words of wisdom. Where did you learn all that?"

She smiled. "I've been studying for many years. Lived outside Portland, where even the local grocers know the therapeutic powers of oregano. I was taught by a shaman in Peru, and a machi in Chile. A woman in Mexico who knew Santeria. I combine the magic of different cultures with my intuition, trying, in my own small way, to correct the errors of our collective history and teach others." After offering me some water, which I declined, she twisted the cap off a glass bottle, took a sip, and then continued to speak.

"We forget that Western civilization was built on enslaving Indigenous peoples, that the planet is being poisoned and man-made fires consume forests while fish choke on plastic. We are encouraged to compete, to hoard resources as opposed to remembering that we are all one, together on Mother Earth. Magic, and witchcraft, instead, are about connecting with one another, loving each other."

"Earth Mother, that's the name of the spa."

"Exactly. All of our problems stem from the laws of men. Like the schoolteachers who called me evil because I was left-handed. The left side has always been associated with evil."

"*Sinistra* in Italian, similar to our *sinister*."

"Good knowledge!" she said, and took another sip from the bottle. "Litha is the dividing line between the light and dark halves of the year, a special time." She opened one of her desk drawers, reached inside, and passed a dark stone to me, and then another, and then two light-colored stones. "This is obsidian, the truth teller. And here's black tourmaline, a healer. And jasper, for the serenity of the mind. Finally, amethyst. For protection. It repels negative energy."

"Do I need that?" I laughed a little, but she had stopped smiling.

"Everyone does."

"Protection against what?"

"The selfish intentions of others."

I held the stones for a while, rubbing their hard and smooth edges.

"How much are they?"

"They're my gift to you. To a new friend."

"Thank you," I said, with not a lot of enthusiasm.

"Please join us on Sunday. The moon will be full. That's why we chose the date to wiccan someone—to inaugurate her into our group of witches."

"Your coven you mean?"

She laughed once. "We don't call our group that. The word *coven* comes from *convent*."

I leaned back, the chair pressing into my shoulders. "If you don't call them a coven, what do you call . . . your group?"

"We're just a loose gathering of like-minded individuals. We all enjoy nature, and each other's company. On Sunday we will thank the universe for our blessings and burn wishes for the next half of the year. We're meeting at Emma's house."

"I'm pretty scheduled on Sunday. But I appreciate the invitation."

"No pressure, but if your calendar opens up, the ceremony begins at twelve o'clock."

"Noon?"

She smiled. "Midnight."

CHAPTER TWELVE

I didn't plan to go to Cecile's witch-activity event, but on Sunday evening I thought that if I stopped by Emma's house for a few minutes, I could text Mason afterward and tell him I'd been there. And maybe I'd learn something that could be useful for my research on Prudence Lowell.

I rode my bike across town in the dark, arriving at Emma's house at 12:07. All the lights were off, but the front door was unlocked. I walked in and through the quiet rooms and stood by the French doors, which were open to the back patio. A number of women were standing in a semicircle, including Emma. They were young, probably undergrads at Bainsville. All were wearing long gowns—some frothy, some fitted—and looked like bridesmaids. What was I doing here? It struck me as being utterly contrived, even ridiculous.

I had decided to leave when I heard someone softly call out to me. "Hi, Genevieve! Cecile told us you'd be here as an observer." Then the others looked over and smiled at me, even Emma, before returning to their positions and recreating the semicircle. It was too late to slip away.

A small bell started to ring in the distance. Two at a time the girls clasped hands and began to walk, slowly, forming a line across the lawn and into the woods. I followed. After a few minutes, weaving through trees on a path lit by the bright moonlight, we came to a sloping hill and a clearing. The bell had stopped ringing. In the center of the clearing a large pile of branches, flowers, leaves, ribbons, and knickknacks had been assembled.

Cecile was standing in front of the pile, turned away from us, her arms stretched out and up. Her hair fell down her back in one thick braid. On top of her head was an oak-leaf crown. She was wearing a floor-length white silk gown. She lowered her arms and turned slowly to face us, and I could see that her face was painted white and covered with red and black markings.

When she began to speak, her voice was peaceful and deep. "Good evening. Let us acknowledge our appreciation of the divine mother. Breathe nature deeply into your bodies, and we will begin a guided meditation. Join hands, everyone, and hold on, for whoever breaks the circle lets evil inside."

I took one step back.

"Say, 'Hello, tree spirits. If you are here, befriend us.'"

They repeated the line in unison. "Hello, tree spirits. If you are here, befriend us."

"Each tree has fingerprints," Cecile said. "And everyone has a birth tree." She took in a deep breath and quickly blew it out. "And now, we say, 'Thank you,' to the trees, and give an offering." One by one, following Cecile, the girls picked out flower petals from inside clay pots and threw them into the pile. "Thank you," they each said, one after the other.

I took another step back.

"The Mohawk people lived here for thousands of years in harmony with nature, and in return the forests and springs of pure water blessed them with good health. The Mohawk did not fear death, which they saw as sacrificing themselves for others, or for nature, when necessary. They did not fear sacrifice for the greater good. When white men took over Indigenous land by violent conquest, the newcomers exploited the forest and springs, no longer respecting the primacy of nature. The only thing they worshipped was the almighty dollar. But once the best of the forest and the springs' bounty was stolen by them, it disappeared forever."

Everyone began to nod. Cecile raised her arms.

"Hear now the invitation to break the circle and then cast your worries of the past six months into the pile. Here is the green man." Cecile pulled something out of the folds of her gown, which appeared to be a lump of clay with leaves stuck to it, and placed it in the center of the pile. Then, one by one, each of the women put an object on the pile. Emma brought over a stack of papers, followed by a clothbound journal. Another woman tossed in a bundle of clothes.

"Here is the sun-water potion, infused with wild herbs. May I have a volunteer? Phyllis?"

Phyllis, a slight brunette with wide eyes, poured a flask of water over the hair of a thin woman with long black curls. So that was the new witch.

"If you have not done so already, place your spell items and protective charms used last season onto the heap." A few girls threw papers and other things on top. Cecile struck a match, touched several papers in different parts of the fire, and we watched as the tiny flames grew larger, until everything began to catch fire, the flames dancing, light reflecting off the faces of Cecile and of those gathered.

"Erce, erce, erce," Cecile chanted.

I took a step back each time she said the strange word.

The twelve young women repeated, "Erce, erce, erce."

Three more steps. I was now back in the trees at the edge of the clearing.

"We call upon Cerridwen, the great Welsh priestess . . . And you, Nomhoyi, Zulu protector of rivers." As Cecile paused, her arms lifted again toward the moonlit sky, the wind swirled around, blowing dresses and trees and hair, as well as leaves. Was this going to be a fire hazard?

Some of the ash from the smoldering pile blew my way, and I stifled a sneeze.

Cecile turned around, slowly, lowered her arms, picked up what looked like a staff, or a broom handle, and shouted, "We call upon ALL witches who came before us, and ask you for your guidance. Protect our new witch, Tessa!"

"Protect our new witch!" The young women raised their arms above their heads and swayed back and forth, twirling, looking skyward, reaching over to touch Tessa. The scene reminded me of a French surrealist film I'd seen a few years earlier, but I couldn't remember what had happened next.

Cecile was saying "Protect, protect, protect," lowering her voice until everyone was quiet. I noticed that she had unbraided her hair, which was blowing around her face. "In honor of tonight, I visited the marker today, the very place where Prudence Lowell was falsely tried for witchcraft. I held close to it, until I warmed the plaque itself, because that marker is all we have left of this once powerful witch. Then I sank to my knees, apologizing that no one had protected her." Cecile's voice was glutted by tears. "We must protect each other. We must give of ourselves, as generations of witches sacrificed themselves for us." She paused again. "Now I will run more solar water over the new witch." I was relieved to see the big barrel of water, which I hoped they would use to put out the smoldering pile.

Cecile dipped a copper bowl into the barrel and filled it up, then poured the rest of the water onto Tessa's hair until it was slick and dripping. "Let us now circle around Witch Tessa with our lit candles and call out her name, offering a blessing for each element. Everyone in your own time, whisper what you wish for Tessa. I'll go first. I wish for Tessa . . . the boundless resilience of water, the creativity of fire, the flexibility of air, and the grounded-ness of earth." The girls' voices were much quieter, and I heard only whispering. I turned my back to the group and started to walk into the trees, the path well lit by the moon.

"Repeat her name—Tessa," Cecile called out, and I heard voices calling her name and clapping. "Welcome, Tessa! Welcome, new witch!"

Even as I slowly walked away I could hear laughing, and encouragement. Then someone began to sing a melodic, traditional-type song in a language that sounded like Celtic.

I made my way home on my bicycle, walking it every now and then whenever a scrim of clouds covered the light of the moon. Susan and Luna's warnings—that I not walk alone in isolated areas—accompanied me, and I felt wide awake. But it was dead quiet, only some insects chirping. Two owls hooted to each other for a while. And just before I reached my rental I heard a dog yapping, somewhere in the distance.

Lying in bed that night, I thought about my college years, what I'd been like at Emma's age, and even earlier. By the time I was twelve, I had started missing school in order to accompany my mother on "adventures." Eventually, after my absences became longer and more frequent and one school after another refused to readmit me, my mother decided that I would be homeschooled. Some of the tutors she hired were better than others, but I always read widely and voraciously, which is really how I ended up with a decent education.

As a consequence, I hadn't made any friends my own age as a teenager. Even then I knew there was something unnatural about spending so much time with my mother and her companions, often men thirty years older than I was. Once, when I was fourteen or fifteen, I was standing in the kitchen mixing something in a bowl when one of her friends snuck up behind me. "Let me show you how to use a whisk," he'd said. Trapping me against the counter with one hand and arm, and grabbing the hand of mine that held the whisk, he rubbed up against me from behind. His erection grew against my lower back, and as it did he pushed harder against me and gripped my wrist tighter and tighter. The cleaning lady came into the kitchen just as I started to whimper in protest, and he'd released me. My mother didn't believe me when I told her about it. She said I was being melodramatic, that I was always begging for attention, making up stories. That was when I knew I could never trust her again. That I could never trust anyone.

Making long-lasting friendships had been difficult in college, too. My mother told me that she was my best friend, describing my classmates as jealous of me. When I reached my twenties, and she was between husbands, she insisted we go out together to restaurants and fancy hotel bars, places where we might meet society men. People often asked if we were sisters, which pleased her. For the most part, I didn't tell her about the men I went out with. She'd liked Owen though, perhaps because he'd known what to say to make her feel at ease. He flattered her in public as much as he flattered me in private. He also led us to believe that he came from a very wealthy family. In that and other ways, he'd fooled both of us.

I took in a deep breath and let the memories recede, as I played the witch ceremony over in my mind, chanting the chants and humming the music. There was nothing shocking about what I'd seen. Joyful frolicking around the bonfire. There was no nudity, nothing lurid. It seemed so innocent and fun.

Still, something about it bothered me, but I couldn't figure out what. I couldn't see or feel any negative intentions. Witchcraft and spells and evil spirits were all so obviously fake.Underneath it all, wasn't Cecile just guiding these young women along the path to become the best possible versions of themselves? Isn't that what we all wanted? What we deserved?

CHAPTER THIRTEEN

The following afternoon I was finishing up the box with the oldest Wilton records. Luna had been working with me all day, adding info to the spreadsheet as I perused the documents, and updating the family tree. It was easier to work when there were two of us. I picked up a document and almost right away noticed the name Lowell.

It was dated October 1735. The handwriting had flourishes and the spelling was strange, but with patience I was able to read most of it. I typed out everything I could read, leaving blank spaces where words were illegible. Quite a few had been crossed out.

Petition of Philip and Thomas Lowell for restitution of the property of the late Daniel Lowell

To his Excellency,

The humble Petition of Philip and Thomas Lowell, nephews of Mrs. Prudence Lowell, and Miss Felicity Lowell, daughter of Mrs. Prudence Lowell

That whereas our Aunt and Mother Prudence Lowell, was apprehended upon suspision of witchcraft, and being brought to a trial, was condemned: since her death the sheriff sent an officer to seize her property. The said officer required us in their majestyes name to give him an Account of our aunt's estate, pretending it was forfeited to the King; he seised upon it, to a considerable value; and ordered us to go down to the said property and make an agreement with the judge, otherwise the land would be forfeited. We, not knowing what advantage the Law might give him against us, and fearing we should sustain greater Damage by the loss of our inheritance, went to the judge accordingly, who told us he might take away all that was seised, if he pleased, but was willing to do us a kindness by giving us an opportunity to redeem it. He demanded ninety pounds of us, which he has obliged us by Bill to pay him within a month. We know not of any Law in force in this Province, by which her property should be forfeited upon her condemnation; much less can we understand that there is any Justice or reason, for the judge to seise upon our property. And tho it is true our own act has obliged us to pay him a Sum of money, yet we declare that we were drawn to it partly by the officer's great pretences of Law to prevent the loss of our inheritance.

Now we humbly pray this Hon'red Court to consider our case, and if it be judged that so much money ought not to have been demanded of us, upon the forementioned account: we pray that we may be discharged from that obligation, which the judge, taking advantage of our ignorance hath brough us under. And yo'r Petition'rs as in duty bound shall ever pray

10 October 1735.

Under the date Philip, Thomas, and Felicity Lowell had signed their names.

I pushed my seat away from the desk. After Prudence Lowell had been tried and executed for witchcraft in the eighteenth century, this letter had been written by her heirs, a daughter and two nephews, requesting the court to allow them to hold on to her estate, which had been seized upon her condemnation. Prudence Lowell had a daughter! But how had John Wilton entered the picture? I knew from another document that he'd inherited her property. Had he and Prudence been married, or connected in some way? Had he tried to save her? Other documents might answer those questions. I gently lifted the next document underneath the letter, which was written on one very long page.

The examination and confession of Mrs. Prudence Lowell

After hours of questiones which provoked negative answers, Mrs. Lowell, aged 30 yeares, at last confessed that she was a witch. And that earlier in the summer she left a red mark in the devil's book with the middle finger of her left hand that the devil would afflict Martha Wilton, wife of John Wilton, whom she named on the Sabath day for she wished so to seduce and have John Wilton for her husband, although he was married by law to Martha Wilton. She states to have borne a girl child that she claims to be the child of John Wilton. Says a witness wax poppits were found that she used to afflict Martha Wilton and the daughter of John Wilton, Anne, aged 2 years. Prudence Lowell confesses she attended the witch meeting and promised her body and soul to the devil and to worship him and that she hath lied when she said that she bore the child of John Wilton. She confesses that the child she carried and bore was not the child of

John Wilton but the child of the devil. Reverend Dr. Samuel Wilton examined the widow and found the witch's teat, to suckle the devil's children. She promises to confesse what she will further remember.

Prudence Lowell Signed and owned the X Mark
The above said confession of Prudence Lowell
Signed 31st August 1722
Signed before John Wilton, Jus{tice} of the Peace

So, John Wilton had been a judge, and it appeared he had seduced and then later condemned Prudence Lowell, the Widow Lowell, to death for witchcraft. And his brother, Dr. Samuel Wilton, had examined her and "found the witch's teat," thus assuring her conviction. Tucked inside in a partial envelope holding that document I found a second document, which crumbled a little as I unfolded it:

This day Complaint being made to me by ye Subscriber, by Martha Wilton, against Prudence Lowell that she is Highly suspected to be guilty of several acts of witchcraft lately committed on the body's of Martha Wilton and Mary Jessop. Justice of the peace therefore requires you upon sight hereof to apprehend and seize ye body of said Prudence Lowell, before ye Justice of the peace, there to be proceeded with according to law, for which this shall be your warrant.

Given under my hand and seal this fifth day of September 1722.

To provide proof of Prudence Lowell's guilt of witchcraft and sorcellerie she is hereby ordered to undergo a water test in the nearby Lake Hamilton. She will be stripped and bound by rope and throwne into the said lake. If she is innocent of charges her body will sink, but if she is in fact a witch she will rise onto the surface and float, for water rejects servants of the devil.

A small note was scrawled underneath the text: *The said widow Lowell floated, and was sentenced to be hung up by the neck until she is dead for her evil.*

I stood up, and put the documents in a separate folder, my hands trembling and my heart booming.

"Uhh, Genevieve, you're shaking," Luna said, looking over. "Are you okay?"

"I just discovered something remarkable."

"What did you find?"

"I'm not sure how familiar you are with witchcraft trials in the colonies," I said. "But it appears that one of the earliest Wiltons in this country was a judge, who may have had an affair with Prudence Lowell, the widow condemned to death for witchcraft. Another Wilton, Dr. Samuel Wilton, examined Prudence and found a so-called 'witch's teat' on her body, supposedly confirming that she was a witch. She was subjected to a trial by water, then failed the test."

"What do you mean by 'failed the test'?"

"If an accused witch sank and drowned, that meant the water had 'accepted' them, which meant they were not a witch. So they had passed the test, even though they were now dead. But if they floated, that meant they were a witch because water rejected servants of the devil. Prudence Lowell floated and was then convicted as a witch, and hung."

"Pure evil."

"Yes, and it gets worse. Listen to this. I forgot to mention that a few days ago I found another letter written ten years later by Dr. Samuel Wilton, who turns out was the brother of this John Wilton, about the unique medicinal properties of the springs here, encouraging financial investments. I read in a textbook from the '80s that some prominent doctors promoted the supposed medicinal benefits of the springs for financial gain at the time. Now I'm putting two and two together. By accusing

Prudence Lowell of witchcraft, these powerful men were able to seize her property, as well as the springs that were located on it. This document," I said, pointing, "explains that Prudence's daughter was attempting to regain possession of her mother's property."

"I'm not sure I understand."

"The Wiltons made up a charge of witchcraft in order to steal Prudence Lowell's land!"

"Oh. Wow. Have you told Daniela?"

"She was at the conference when I found the first document. I haven't seen her yet today."

"She should be back by now," Luna said, her voice rising. "Go and see."

I went to Daniela's office, and found her door ajar.

"Welcome back," I said, after knocking softly and walking in. "I know you have a lot of catching up to do, but do you have a minute to take a look at something downstairs?" I paused. "It's important."

"Sure," she said.

Downstairs, Daniela sat down at my desk and read through the documents. She examined each page carefully, flipping back and forth between the earlier and later ones. Luna and I watched her in silence for several minutes as she seemed to go over a checklist in her mind.

"What do you think?" I asked, after a while.

"Let us go back upstairs to my office," she said. When we were sitting down across from her at her desk, Daniela said, "You're right, Genevieve. Not only have you found evidence that unscrupulous men contrived to deprive Prudence Lowell and her heirs of their rightful property, you've unearthed primary source documentation about Prudence Lowell's trial for witchcraft."

"The famous witch of Wilton Springs!" Luna said. "And Genevieve found her."

Daniela frowned. "She was a *woman*, Luna. There was . . . is . . . no such thing as a witch. Witch trials were shams, intended to dispose of people who were disliked in a community, innocent victims of local jealousy, misogyny. They murdered women and men. *Not* witches."

Luna nodded.

Daniela continued. "During this time, widows were easy prey, with fewer relatives to defend them. People often had something to gain from accusing their neighbors of witchcraft. The silliest accusations, for instance, 'She caused dogs to bark in the neighborhood' or 'She caused the butter to churn on its own,' had deadly consequences. An accusation alone was enough to land someone in deep trouble. No 'proof' was required."

I said, "In this case, the Wilton brothers discovered Prudence Lowell was literally sitting on top of a gold mine, if only they could seize her property and gain access to the springs. What easier way to do that than accuse her of being a witch!"

"Of course, there was also prurience involved," Daniela said. "A fascination with, or rather pretending to need to find out, what sexual things the 'devil' did, which of course revealed more about the proclivities of the men doing the interrogations. The doctors examining these women played a role, too. So many were complicit in destroying innocent lives."

I said, "And the people who condemned Prudence Lowell—the men involved—turn out to have been Wilton ancestors."

"That comes as a surprise," said Daniela. "I wonder what else we can find out about them. I've stayed in touch with a visiting scholar researching early modern witch trials in the Northeast who spent time in our collections. I will let her know that you have found original documentation about Prudence Lowell. I will also inform the Wilton family."

"It's in one of the boxes that is well organized. I suppose it must have been . . . Victoria who did the work?"

"Hmm," she said. "With Lily's help, most likely. I must say it is incredible the material that implicates the Wilton forebears has been sitting around for centuries with no one the wiser."

Just then there was a knock on the door. Daniela took a moment before saying, "Come on in," her Spanish accent rising and falling. It was Mitch. He had a perplexed expression. "Daniela, you promised we would talk as soon as you returned," he said, not looking at me or Luna as he stood in the doorway.

"Okay, Mitch, I will be with you in just a moment."

She turned back to me. "As I said, I will reach out to the historian, and let you know." Mitch knocked on the open door and then stepped into the office. He wouldn't catch my eye as I walked by him.

CHAPTER FOURTEEN

Mitch saw me in the common room the next morning. "I heard you've made some interesting findings, Genevieve. I'm sure you don't know this, but the most famous resident of Wilton Springs is in fact a relation of mine. Many generations back. Eighteenth century. Prudence Lowell was related to my mom's family. I changed my name to Mom's maiden name. Lowell."

"How was Prudence related to your mother?"

"I did some genealogical studies. It's a link down a patrilineal line. I'll show you sometime if you're interested. You've probably seen the marker. The widow, Prudence Lowell, tried as a witch, on what used to be Lake Hamilton before it dried up. Poor Mrs. Lowell. Trial by water, then a public hanging. Hideous misogyny."

"Yes. I didn't know about the dried-up lake."

"Why would you? According to Daniela, now you've made a connection between long ago Wiltons and my ancestor. I'll repeat, please let me know what else you find in the archive along those lines."

"Will do."

"The future is no more uncertain than the present," he said, his eyes flying around the room. Then he tossed his head back and began to recite what sounded like a monologue.

How else dispose of an immortal force? . . .
. . . The brook was thrown
Deep in a sewer dungeon under stone
In fetid darkness still to live and run . . .
No one would know except for ancient maps
That such a brook ran water. But I wonder
If from its being kept forever under,
The thoughts may not have risen that so keep
This new-built city from both work and sleep.

He stopped, waiting for my reaction.

"Impressive," I said. "But I'm afraid you're keeping *me* from my work at the moment, Mitch."

"Yes, yes," he said, with a wave of his hand. "Going back up. *Witch* me luck."

After he left, I typed a few words I remembered from Mitch's performance into Google. They turned out to be from the Robert Frost poem "A Brook in the City." I read the poem through once. Twice. Then I noticed a missed call on my phone from Darwin Truesdale, the Wiltons' attorney, who had hired me. I called him back.

"Genevieve, I have spoken to Mr. Wilton today about your historical research. He discussed the matter with his wife, and they do not wish for you to pursue the inquiry into John Wilton's involvement in the witch trial. His family has been under much scrutiny recently, and he does not want to reopen painful wounds. These were his words."

"But . . . there's been a misunderstanding. These events occurred 300 years ago. Certainly, they don't cast negative light on the current family."

"Please allow me to remind you that you are employed by a private family, and you are a private person not connected with an institution.

If you find yourself at cross-purposes with the Wiltons, they might even decide to let you go."

"Let me go? You mean, fire me?"

"I would caution you not to proceed further if you don't wish to antagonize them."

"Wow. Okay," I said.

"I'm not asking you to stop the archival work. But do not pursue the inquiry into John Wilton's involvement in the witch trial. Continue cataloguing what else you find in the boxes. That is all."

I stood up, and squeezed my eyes shut, but could think of nothing to say.

"Besides Daniela," Truesdale said, "does anyone else know about your findings?"

Luna came to mind, but I said, "No." Then I remembered Mitch.

"Good," he said. "I encourage you to refrain from discussing your finds with others at this time."

I hung up and put my head in my hands. Why had the Wiltons given me the message through Darwin Truesdale, instead of Daniela? Was a call from their lawyer intended to intimidate me? I did a quick internet search. According to New York State laws related to the statute of limitations and something called adverse possession, the Lowell family could not make a plausible case to have the land returned to them, or be recompensed for it. I wanted to talk to Jim and Barbara themselves. My job was to archive the documents and make their contents available to other scholars and the general public.

I thought about Cecile's ceremony, and how she'd talked to me in her office about owning my emotions and the importance of embracing uncertainty. She'd said to let go, so I took a few deep breaths. Then I was surprised to feel a powerful resentment stir deep within my chest that moved straight into fury. I took some more deep breaths. If I'd met Cecile earlier in my life, I might not be so practiced in the art of ignoring my anger, an art I'd perfected over the years of dealing with my mom.

I decided to let a day go by, until I could put everything that had happened into some sort of perspective. That night I tossed and turned, and the next morning I woke up groggy and irritated. Hours passed and I was once again livid, and didn't know what to do with the anger. Coffee. I needed coffee. After dodging spitting rain on my way to Wilton Grinds, I was surprised to see Luna behind the counter. Normally she worked in the early morning.

When she looked up, I waved at her and she waved back, but she was focused on making drinks. She looked especially pale. I ordered an iced coffee, paid, and sat down at a table near the door.

A few seconds later, Gabe walked in and came over to my table. "Hey, stranger," he said, just as the cashier called out my name. I went up to the bar, picked up my iced coffee, and took a few gulps. Luna must have been in the back as I didn't see her. I went back to my table, set down my cup, and put both of my hands on the table to keep them from trembling.

Before too long, Gabe returned to my table and sat down across from me.

"Have you been avoiding me?" he asked, running his hand through his hair.

I took a sip of my cold drink and realized I'd found at least one source of the anger still swirling inside of me. I said nothing as he smiled at me.

He spoke again, "Everything okay? You seem upset."

I said in a low voice, "I do not appreciate you telling the entire town we had sex in your car."

"What? I didn't tell anybody about . . . anything. I mean, nothing happened in my car. As we both well remember."

"So, why did my colleagues ask me about what happened? What didn't happen."

"How should I know? That was like, two weeks ago? I didn't say anything, seriously." He tilted his head toward me. When I said nothing he leaned over the table until he was as close to me as he could be and said, "Genevieve, please believe me."

I wanted to believe him.

He sat back. "At least now I know why you've been avoiding me."

"I haven't been avoiding you."

"Okay. Sorry again. I'm glad you're still sitting across from me and aiming those pretty eyes my way."

"For now," I answered, suppressing a little smile.

"Is there anything I can do to get back in your good graces?"

"Actually . . ." I began.

"Name it."

I told Gabe about the documents I had found, and that I'd been instructed not to contact other scholars. "Would you please persuade your dad that the incident happened centuries ago, and the only people who will care are nerdy historians? State laws protect your family from any lawsuits."

Gabe smoothed his fingertips along the edge of the table. "I'll talk to him because you want me to but I know he won't change his mind. My parents have been touchy and inscrutable since . . ." his voice trailed off.

"Since your sister died? Gabe, why didn't you tell me about that?"

"Tell you about my dead sibling on a first date?"

"Gabe, will you please, please, try to convince your dad?"

"I'll talk to him, but I'm sorry, I won't pressure him, or my mom, about this. I know you left your PhD program, and I'm sure this seems exciting, but . . . And anyway, you are, well, you're working for us."

"Whaaaa . . ." I sputtered. Then I stood up and looked over at the counter. Luna still hadn't reemerged. I marched out the door, ignoring Gabe as he called my name. I stomped all the way back to the library, angrier than ever. As I began to climb the library steps I felt my phone buzz in my pocket. I fished it out and saw a text from Luna.

Hi, can you meet me?

Now at library, I wrote.

OMW.

There was a picnic table in the woods just behind the library where we often took breaks, and where Daniela smoked the occasional clandestine cigarette. I knew Luna would go there to look for me.

"Hey," she called, when she arrived. She was sweating and panting, as if she'd run the whole way. "I didn't know you were friends with Gabe Wilton."

"We aren't. I work for his family. We had dinner when I first got here. That's all."

Her eyes met mine. "I know you work for his family. And he is cute. Why didn't you tell me you had dinner?"

"It's not a state secret," I said, but she gave me a look. "How do you two know each other?"

"He used to come to my yoga class, then one day he asked me out. Couple months ago." She frowned and looked down.

"I hope he didn't mess with you, Luna." My concern for her dialed back some of my general fury at the world and my specific anger toward the Wiltons, all of them.

"No, no—nothing like that. Although it's true Gabe seems laid-back, but he's a player."

"I kinda figured."

She twisted her head in the opposite direction so I couldn't see her full face. Then she turned back toward me. "They have a lot of pretty girls who work at Wilton Castle."

"You?"

"Not me. Anyway, there are . . . stories . . . I'll leave it at that. What were you two arguing about?"

I wanted to ask about the stories of the pretty girls, but she didn't seem in the mood to elaborate. "Those historical documents about Prudence Lowell that I found. The family wants me to bury the information. Their lawyer intimated that I could lose my job if I shared the info."

"You could get fired for telling the truth? For sharing information about things that actually happened? I'm so fucking tired of rich people acting with impunity!"

"The thing is, regardless of what Jim and Barbara tell me I can and cannot do, the senior Wiltons wanted all of their files catalogued for posterity, made available to scholars. To everybody. That's why I was hired."

Luna stood up and arched her back, then bent down again. "This is so unfair. You're in the right here! Privileged, revisionist-history motherfuckers," she continued, clawing her hair back from her face. "If you're fired, I'll quit. Then I'll help you find your own lawyer to sue their greedy asses." She hugged me.

"Thanks, Luna. I'm going to have a word with Daniela." I smiled at her. "I appreciate your sticking up for me."

She smiled back at me. "I know that you're smart, and tough. I got your back."

CHAPTER FIFTEEN

I left early that day, half an hour after meeting with Luna. At home I took a shower, pulled on a fresh shirt and shorts, and made a salad with slightly wilting greens and feta cheese left over in the fridge. I drizzled on some good olive oil that I'd found on sale over the weekend but couldn't eat more than a few bites. I sat at the kitchen table, first scrolling through the latest news on my phone but then letting my mind twirl through the same thoughts about the archives and the Wiltons censoring my work over and over, until it turned dark.

I understood what grief could make people do. Could the Wiltons ever recover from the death of their daughter? Could any parent? But that had nothing to do with the information I had uncovered. It was eerie how Jim Wilton's "natural" reaction was to continue to cover up what was clearly a serious crime committed by one of his long-ago ancestors. And Gabe wouldn't bring up the issue and risk disturbing his father to lift a finger and do the right thing. Everything had been swept under the rug and was going to stay there. Why couldn't they see that the centuries-ago narrative was something of interest mostly to scholars, and some fringe people interested in the history of witch trials?

Maybe Cecile was right. Maybe the way society functioned today was some sort of conspiracy. Not the kind of conspiracy that Mitch talked about, but something bigger, if quieter. Complicity by complacency. The men bought into it, enforced it. They protected other men and therefore protected themselves. Privilege begets privilege. In the case of Prudence Lowell, the Wilton ancestors had enriched themselves. John Wilton used her for pleasure and then discarded her, murdered her, in fact, when she became inconvenient, which he knew from the start she would be. Then he and his relatives profited from her demise. She stood up for herself and her child, and he had labeled her a witch, which led to her being convicted, thrown in a lake, tortured. And then hung.

It was too much to think about. Too much.

I knew because of the petition to restore her mother's property to her and her male cousins that Prudence Lowell had a daughter. Could Mitch really trace his ancestry back that far? No doubt a lot of people in this part of the United States could.

I threw the salad in the compost bucket and went to bed, but it was too hot to sleep well. Around 3:00 A.M. thunder woke me up, followed by a long series of ghostly flashes brightening the dark room, as if they were strobe lights. There was something cathartic about the rain that pounded the roof for hours after the lightshow, the sky letting go of everything that had been building up. I spent the rest of the night alert, running over what I wanted to tell Daniela the next day.

I wet my hair and put on a freshly washed and ironed periwinkle linen dress, spritzing myself with a little perfume before I left. The rain had brought the heat down and the air felt lighter, cleaner. I left a message on Daniela's phone that I would be late that morning. Then I walked through town to the spa. The beaded curtains clicked as I slid through them and the receptionist I had seen last time looked up.

"How can I help you?" Her tone was softer.

"I'd like to see Cecile. I'm Genevieve by the way. We didn't officially meet last time."

"Jade," she said. "Cecile's not in her office at the moment. Can I give her a message?"

"Please tell her I stopped by." I took out a slip of paper from my bag and wrote down my name and number and handed it to her. The corners of Jade's mouth curled up. As I walked out the door, I heard Cecile call my name.

"Oh, hi," I said. "I'm glad you're here." She motioned to me to follow her and we walked up to her office. Lavender fog smoked out of the humidifier in the corner of the room. It smelled soothing.

"What did you think of the wiccaning ceremony?" Cecile asked. "The part of it you witnessed before you left."

So, she had noticed. I stammered, "I, I can honestly say I've never seen anything like it."

"That disappointing, eh?"

I shrugged.

"The idea of witchcraft puts some people off. But the spells and sisterhood are important because they help create a community of support. That's the first step. Creating conditions that help them feel comfortable with each other. And themselves. When they learn to love one another, and themselves, that's when I can teach them how to cultivate their power, figure out what they want and who they want to be, and how to manifest it. Being a woman isn't easy. Never has been." She continued. "You're always welcome to join my group. I know a thing or two about being far away from family, friends."

"I'm starting to understand, I think, what you're doing," I said. "At first I thought you were trying to brainwash a bunch of undergraduates with incantations, but then I found something that has made me understand witchcraft, or whatever you call it, and women's role in society, in a completely different way."

"Is that what you wanted to talk about? How can I help?"

I leaned forward. "First of all, I wanted to ask you about the Wiltons. Do you know them well?"

"Barbara has been here for treatments. But she's a client, so I shouldn't even divulge that much. Why do you ask?"

"Well, it's nice to know about the people you're working for."

"The death of their daughter devastated them. After it happened, I offered Barbara a free session with the best medium in the country."

"Do you do readings? Tarot cards, or . . . ?"

"Rarely. It depletes my energy. But I wanted to offer Barbara the opportunity to communicate with the other side, so I called in a colleague. Here in Wilton, we're a small community, so we share our tragedies. I've cried for Barbara Wilton, more than once."

"And her husband, Jim?"

Cecile raised her eyebrows. "I have great sympathy for him, as well. He is weak, although many see him as strong."

"What about Gabe, the son? My friend, Luna, hinted I shouldn't trust him."

"Luna, you mean—the Luna who works here?"

"She didn't tell me she works here. Oh, yoga."

Cecile sat back against the chair and crossed her arms across her chest. "Luna's our best yoga teacher. What did she say about Gabe?"

"Just that he's a player. Trouble. And that a lot of pretty girls seem to work at Wilton Castle."

Her brow creased, and she leaned in. "Do you still have your crystals?"

"I left them at home today."

"You need them for protection!" she said.

"From what?"

"People are jealous of young, bright, talented people, especially women. Make sure you carry those crystals with you always, especially the amethyst."

"I'm almost sorry I moved here," I said. "I had no idea there would be so much drama."

"It'll be okay," she said. "You'll see."

At the library half an hour later, I told Daniela about the call from Darwin Truesdale. "Daniela, I'm sure you understand that if I'm not allowed to do the job I was hired to do then . . ."

"My dear," she said. "I hope you do not mind me calling you 'my dear.'" She smiled, and then continued, "You have misunderstood. And the fault is my own."

"It is?"

"The senior Wiltons requested that we organize and then publish all the materials in their archive. Jim and Barbara Wilton worked with their lawyer to be able to choose the archivist, you, because the mechanism for hiring was not spelled out in the will. They hired you, but they enjoy no jurisdiction over the actual position. Or the material. The only person the archivist must answer to is me, or the person in my position at the library. The senior Wiltons created a designated trust fund for the project, from which we pay you. You are under no obligation to do what Jim Wilton asks.

"As for Darwin Truesdale . . ." she stopped, looked out the window, and then turned back to me. "He has no standing in this matter. None."

"They don't have any control," I repeated. "That's . . . a relief."

"I also would like to tell you that I have been in contact with my friend, Dr. Hernandez, the expert on early modern witch trials. She is interested, although she is teaching a summer paleography seminar and won't be able to travel to Wilton Springs until next year. She emailed a list of books for you to read to acquaint yourself with the topic, and I have already emailed this to you."

"Thank you, Daniela! I will read them."

"I am not terribly surprised the archive offered up something of such import. The archive was waiting for this to be discovered. Victoria did not bring the documents to my attention, but she may not have realized their value." She stopped. "And! I almost forgot to tell you! I spent a delightful hour with the medical student Mason Clarke, showing him our collection of Vesalius illustrations. What a lovely and bright young man—unusual, in this day and age. He thinks the world of you, too."

I felt my face begin to warm. "I'm glad you were able to connect with him, Daniela."

She shot me a wry grin. "Very handsome, too."

After closing the door behind me, I noticed I wasn't taking such fast and shallow breaths anymore, and thought about what Cecile had said about anxiety controlling the mind. I checked out two of the books on Dr. Hernandez's list about witch trials in colonial America and spent the rest of the day reading. It was difficult to believe, but at that time one simple accusation could lead to a full-scale trial for witchcraft, and a trial was often tantamount to a death sentence.

The most famous witch trial in history happened in Salem, Massachusetts, in 1692–1693. By the time it was over, 141 suspects, men and women, had been tried as witches. Twenty people were executed in less than four months, nineteen by hanging. One was pressed to death by heavy stones.

Between 1647 and 1697, nearly three dozen people were charged with witchcraft in Connecticut. Eleven were executed by hanging, and nine of the eleven were women. Two of the executed men were hanged with their wives. Those who weren't executed either fled their community or were banished.

Luna looked up from the box she was organizing and noticed me thinking aloud. "Find something else that's groundbreaking?" she said.

"I've been reading about the history of witch trials. This book I'm reading claims that the trials were confined to Connecticut and Massachusetts, but the Lowell manuscript described a trial in New York."

"The states' borders changed back and forth over the decades," said Luna.

"Oh, of course."

"Just a random piece of history lodged in my brain," she said, tapping her head.

"Obviously these trials were more widespread than originally believed."

"And now you have the source material to prove it," Luna said. "But what else? You have that look on your face."

She was right, I was thinking about something else. "Prudence Lowell was a widow with a young daughter," I said. "She didn't have any adult male family members to vouch for her. Back then, widows were expected to remarry immediately. Single women were seen as deviants from societal norms and as such were left devalued and vulnerable."

"Hmm—not just back then."

I shook my head. "When they became adults, Prudence's daughter and two nephews tried to reclaim her land and property, but clearly failed, as by then John Wilton possessed both."

"That was one of the documents you showed Daniela, right?"

"Yes."

"And remind me, you said John Wilton was a lawyer?"

"He was a judge, able to act with impunity, targeting Prudence specifically, because at thirty-one, she was considered an 'old' widow, with no one to stand up for her. He fathered her illegitimate child. He stole her property, her reputation, her life. The injustice makes my blood boil."

"Understandably. But ever since you told me about it I've been wondering, why isn't this public knowledge?"

"Well, it's not the sort of thing any Wilton would've been proud of. I don't know the statute of limitations on lying, defamation, murder, robbery, and manipulation of justice from a position of power . . ."

Luna twisted her hair into a bun. "That pretty much sums up the practices of patriarchy."

"I wonder what happened to the daughter," I said, mostly to myself, as I nodded.

I opened the next box that Luna had prepped for me. There was an envelope sitting on top of a cream-colored folder, in the same handwriting as the "Welcome" note.

There was one sentence. *Darling Victoria, I had hoped learning about your family might have brought us closer together, and it might still bring us together, but at the very least, it'll help you on your path, whatever path you choose. Don't forget me. I love you. Your Gran.*

"Luna," I said, holding up the note signed by Lily. "Did you read this?"

"Nah, I just put stuff in chronological order."

"It's another message from Lily, the Wilton matriarch, who left these notes for her granddaughter, Victoria, who was here for a summer internship archiving her family collection."

I handed the slip of paper to her and watched her read it. "This and other notes were left for Victoria to find."

Luna craned her neck. "So Lily used the archive to communicate with her granddaughter, without her parents' knowledge. If Jim and Barbara don't want you to share info about their family's role in a trial that happened three hundred years ago, they're not going to be happy about you digging into anything to do with their dead daughter."

"By the way," I said. "Daniela told me that I answer only to her. Apparently, the Wiltons' lawyer Darwin was just trying to intimidate me. They hired me, but they don't control the work I do here. And they don't pay me directly, either."

"That's great to hear," Luna said.

"As far as the notes from Lily go, I don't know. I guess I'll just ignore them for now. I mean, it's sad since they're both gone." I shook my head. "By the way, you told me you taught yoga, but I didn't realize it was at Earth Mother Spa."

"That's right. Small world. Small town."

During my break, I called Cecile, and told her I'd uncovered some intriguing new information for her "modern witches," about Prudence Lowell. I knew the present-day Wiltons wouldn't want me to do this, which underscored the importance of sharing Prudence's story.

"That sounds fascinating!" Cecile said. "Perfect for us to discuss at greater length. You know what? How about tonight? We're already scheduled to meet at Emma's house."

CHAPTER SIXTEEN

I had worn sneakers, in case we were going to walk back into the woods, and in case I needed to run, but instead the group was standing near a circle of chairs on the patio when I arrived. They all seemed so young. Emma walked over to me. She was prettier, and more blonde, than I'd remembered. Her hair snaked down her neck and chest in two long braids, and she was wearing a short, tie-dyed sleeveless dress with a peace sign on the back.

"I'm Emma," she said. "I saw you at Tessa's ceremony. Nice to meet you, Genevieve."

I didn't want to tell her that I'd already been to her house, twice. "Thanks for having me."

She waved a couple of the other girls over, lithe and smiley, and introduced me. "This is Nicki, and Olivia," she said, just as Cecile walked out of the house and down the steps toward us. She was wearing a long, flesh-colored gown, with a tulle skirt.

After everyone was seated, Cecile said, "Instead of our regular meeting, Genevieve is going to share with you a tale of a persecuted witch of the past who lived in this very town." The girls continued to chat among themselves for a few more seconds and then went silent as they focused on me, their eyes wide with anticipation.

I introduced myself and explained what I was working on, and told them the basic story of the documents I'd found about Prudence Lowell, how she'd been accused of practicing witchcraft and then dispossessed of her property before being sentenced to death, it turns out, at the hands of the ancestors of the present-day Wilton family.

"Remember, everyone. It wasn't witches they murdered. It was women. *Innocent* women," I said, echoing Daniela's statement. Cecile was beaming as she turned to me. "It is my belief that you do not recognize your gifts as a storyteller, Genevieve. You are a weaver, an imparter of history." She folded her hands together as if in prayer, closed her eyes, and gave me a little bow. The girls clapped softly.

"Thank you," I said. "I'm honored."

"No," she said. "We are honored."

When I stopped talking Emma burst into tears, and as others comforted her, more of them started crying, some openly, some in little hiccups.

"I'm angry!" said Tessa, the new witch, standing up with her hands clenched at her sides.

"Good! Harness your energy," Cecile said to the group. "Whether it be anger or grief. It's all powerful. Don't waste it. We will learn how to direct our energy, but for right now just feel it, keep it alive. Remember, we're all agents of change in this world." She walked over to Tessa, who was now crying, and placed one hand on her shoulder, and began talking to her in a soothing voice.

A few of them came up to thank me. They were full of questions, and two asked if they could come look at primary sources in the library.

Was this how it felt to teach? To mentor? I felt a pang of regret for having dropped out of my PhD program. I could be working with young, inspired students. Instead, I spent my days hidden in a basement, working on documents that contained information that might never reach a wide audience. As I watched Cecile comfort Tessa and then some of the others,

I realized that her work as a healer and witch was more important than I had at first considered it to be. I wasn't cut out to be a witch, I knew that, but I, too, wanted to learn how to "harness my energy" and become an "agent of change" in this world. Was that possible? Too often in my life, I'd felt like loose Jell-O without a mold, searching for something to contain me. But now, something within me had been stirred, uprooted. I decided to keep that feeling alive, if nothing else.

As I walked home, the moon was bright and lit my path. The air was still and heavy. I wasn't afraid, felt as though nothing could harm me. I thought of Lily and Victoria and the notes in the archive. Were there more of them, and had Victoria read them, and if so, why were they still in the boxes? Had she reconciled with her grandmother before her life had been cut short?

The next morning, a Saturday, I flicked through my phone. No texts from Mason. I hadn't received a personal email in weeks. Just after my arrival, I'd read through a deluge of well-intentioned condolence notes, but even those had stopped. I hadn't reached out to anyone. I remembered what Mason had said, that relationships were a two-way street. I had a tendency to withdraw, especially during times of crisis, like after my breakup with Owen. My oldest, closest friends still kept in touch, but even they must have been exasperated sometimes by my lack of initiative.

Cecile had spoken to the group about reinvention. She'd said "Reality doesn't affect you, it reflects you." I thought about that as I went for a run, avoiding the state park, and that same day joined the gym at Bainsville, using a letter Daniela had given me on library letterhead. I emailed Daniela and asked her to put me in touch with her colleague as I'd read all the books she suggested and was ready to create a plan to publicize the new findings.

I had spent a lot of the day thinking about Mason, so when he texted a jolt of excitement ran through me.

Hey there. Wya? he wrote.

We arranged to meet for a drink in town, at a dive bar called Riotous Times.

I arrived ten minutes early and sat down at a table in the back after ordering sparkling water because I was thirsty and a vodka tonic to take the edge off. But what worked better than the alcohol was seeing Mason's glossy hair and the little crinkles around his soulful eyes.

"Can I get you . . . something to drink?" he asked, and we shared a laugh over the two glasses in front of me.

He went up to order and brought back a pint of something frothy, which he placed down next to my glasses.

"Cheers," I said, and clunked my vodka tonic against his beer glass, wondering how such a cute, charming, and smart guy could be single. It had been nearly two weeks since he'd dropped me off at home after Emma's party, our first and only date. Had it even been a date?

"Sorry I haven't reached out since Emma's party," he said, reading my mind. "It's just been so busy at school. And I haven't been in town."

"How far away is your school?"

"Forty-five minutes. If I speed," he smiled.

"And what's been going on?"

"Anatomy lab. It's kind of gruesome so best I don't get into details. Unless you want me to."

"Is that the one where you dissect corpses?"

"Cadavers, yeah."

"How do you do that? I'm not sure I could."

"You get used to it. I mean, there is the smell, which is very bad, and sort of stays in your nostrils."

"No need to describe, I think I smelled something like that when I found the remains of a murdered woman in the woods."

"Wait, what?"

"Her name was Trish Baranski, maybe you saw or heard about it on the news."

"Fuck, that's got to be tough. Are you okay?"

I drummed my fingers on the table. "It was a few weeks ago. Nightmarish. Definitely don't want to think about it."

"I'm happy to change the subject. How are you and how's work?" he said.

I told Mason about what I'd found out about Prudence Lowell and John Wilton, and then about talking to Cecile's group.

"You can read Ye Olde English?"

"In the early 1700s it was Early Modern English. Old English is Anglo-Saxon English, much older. You're right though, it's painstakingly slow to read some of the documents I'm finding. But I'm learning."

"Not that I know anything about the subject, but I'm impressed."

I let out a breath I hadn't realized I'd been holding and twisted my grandmother's ring around on my finger.

"Nice ring," Mason said.

"It was my grandma's. My dad's mom. Miss her."

His gaze met mine. "Grandmas make the world go around."

"Mine helped me through a few painful years. Then again, 'Life is pain, highness. Everyone who tells you differently is selling something.'" I leaned back in my chair, unsure if he'd recognize the quote.

"*Princess Bride* reference? Good one."

"Exactly," I said. "It was my comfort film as a kid. Even if it's scary in parts. I'm glad you got it."

"It's a favorite of mine."

"So you like watching films? When you're not saving lives?"

"I do. Nothing too scary though. Or arthouse high-brow. Mostly romantic comedies, come to think of it."

"What else do you like to do for fun?"

"Fun? What's that?" He arched his eyebrows. "Kidding. I just don't have much time for fun these days. Before I started med school I used to love to go to art museums. Someday, I'll save up enough to go to Italy and see the birthplace of Pinturicchio in Spello."

"I've been there! My mom rented a house in Umbria one summer. She was dating some Italian count."

He took a glug of his drink. "No way. That's the coolest thing I've ever heard. She rented like, a villa? Your mom must be awesome."

I laughed. "She's definitely unique. And that was a great summer, admittedly. So, are you an artist, too? Or you just have excellent taste in painters?"

"Me, nah. Well, I have dabbled. I wouldn't call myself an artist. But as a surgeon you develop an eye for fine details. Precision."

"Dabbled? You've painted some artworks?"

"A few canvases, yeah. Couple years ago. I should go back to it."

"Please show me sometime! If you want. I'd love to see them. Or one of them."

"Sure. As for what you generously refer to as my excellent taste, just because you're born in a stable doesn't mean you have to grow up to be a horse."

I laughed, and he leaned in close to me then. "It's nice to have someone to talk to, Genevieve," he said, holding my gaze. "It's nice to be your friend."

"Is that what we are?" I asked, the alcohol now circulating freely from my stomach to my head.

"Yes. And I'd like to get to know you better."

"I'd like that, too," I said.

I could feel my phone buzzing in my pocket. At first I ignored it, but the third time I said, "Just a sec. I need to turn off my phone," and pulled it out of my pocket. "It's Cecile," I said, standing up. "She's called three times."

She had hung up by the time I made it outside, so I called her back.

"Have you seen Luna this weekend?" she asked.

"No."

"She didn't show up for yoga yesterday morning. She's never missed work before. Or even been late. I've tried her but the calls go right to voicemail."

"She hasn't been at the library," I said, "but she's been off the schedule for a few days."

I looked toward the door, where Mason stood watching me, his hands in his pockets.

"When was the last time you saw her?"

"Last week. Maybe Thursday."

"Did everything seem okay to you?"

"Yes. She seemed distracted, but just a bit."

"Okay. I'll keep trying her. Let me know if she calls you."

"You let me know, too, please!"

She hung up.

"What is it?" asked Mason. "You look totally panicked."

"A friend of mine didn't show up at work. That was her boss. Well, one of her bosses. From the spa, Cecile. You know Cecile."

"That's weird, but I wouldn't freak out just yet. There's always an explanation for this sort of thing."

"I hope so. I need to see if I can reach her. I don't even know where she lives. Sorry to cut this short but I should go back home."

"Do you want me to put your bike in my car and drive you?"

"No, that's okay," I said. "I'm sure you've gotta get back and study."

"Yeah, going to head home and get some rest. Big operation on Monday."

"Thanks for . . . It was fun." I probably didn't sound convincing because I was thinking about Luna.

"I had a great time!" he said. "Listen, call if you need me, okay? I'll text you later." He hugged me for a few seconds and I took in the smell of his cedary cologne, wanting to stay tucked in his warm, strong arms.

After he drove away, I called Luna several times, but my calls went straight to voicemail.

I got on my bike and headed home, feeling a heavy charge growing in the air. Once back inside the rental, fumbling with the inner latch, I locked the doors and windows, then called Luna over and over for almost an hour. I had left all the lights off and undressed in the dark. Then I checked all the windows again, and the dead bolt on the front door, making sure everything was locked.

It took me a while, but I finally slipped into a deeper sleep that night. I dreamt about Owen, for the first time since he'd died. In the dream he'd called to tell me he was in rehab out in the Midwest. He wanted to see me. Could I come visit? But I was in California, surrounded by desert mountains and palm trees, so the answer was no.

PART II

CHAPTER SEVENTEEN

The next day, a Wilton Springs Police Department car was parked outside the library when I arrived a few minutes late to work.

Susan was sitting at her desk, arms folded in front of her. "The cops are grilling Daniela. They've finished with me. And Mitch. Guess you're next," she said, trying to lower her voice.

Saunders and Jackson walked out of Daniela's office, glanced around, then came toward me.

"Ms. Tompkins," Saunders said. "Do you have a few minutes to speak with us?"

"Of course," I said. "Please come down to my office." They followed me down to the basement, and I pinched my shirt collar away from my neck and walked toward the air-conditioning vent, breathing in the cloud of mixed sweat. Mine and theirs. The vent blew cold air up my shirt and I exhaled.

Detective Saunders was watching me.

"We're looking for information about Miss Luna Collins. Do you know her well?"

"Is she okay? What happened?"

"She's been reported as a missing person, and that is all we can share at this time. Please answer the question. Are you friends with Luna Collins?"

"I haven't been here very long, but she's definitely my best friend here. We work together a few days a week."

"Do you see each other outside work?"

"We've gone out for drinks. And pretty soon after I arrived, she took me hiking in the state park, to see the geysers. Near where . . ." I paused. "Trish Baranski was . . . found."

She nodded, and I glanced over at Officer Jackson, who was writing everything down that we said.

"Could . . . their cases be connected?"

"As I said, we have no further information to share at this time. When was the last time you saw or spoke with Ms. Collins?"

"Last week. Thursday. After her shift at Wilton Grinds. It was around 1:30 P.M."

"Where did you speak with her?"

"We met outside the library, out back at one of the picnic tables."

"And how did she seem to you? Did she express concern about money or a personal situation?"

"She seemed fine, and didn't mention anything specific about her finances to me. She told me once she was saving up to get a degree in library science. Can you tell me what's going on? Detective Saunders, please." My eyes searched hers. "Do you think she's okay?"

Her expression was flat, her tone methodical. "Right now, we're interviewing those who knew her or know where she might be."

"Gotcha," I said, even more unsettled.

"What about her other friends, or partners? Did she ever talk to you about past relationships?"

"She's not in a serious relationship at the moment, but she dates people. Both men and women. She went out with Gabe Wilton. A while ago. I'm not sure when." Jackson's eyes seemed to flicker when I mentioned Gabe's name.

“Thank you for your time,” Saunders said. “If you hear anything further, please reach out to us.” Saunders signaled to Jackson, and he handed me another card with her name and number.

“I have one already,” I said. “But thanks.”

I began breathing shallowly and quickly, feeling as though I couldn’t get enough oxygen into my lungs. After they left, I took in a deep breath and rushed up the stairs, not exhaling until I pushed through the glass doors and was outside in fresh air. I watched Saunders and Jackson getting in their car, then looked at my phone. There was a message from Cecile, asking me if I could meet in her office, after the spa closed at 7:00 P.M. I texted back a thumbs-up.

I tried to focus on the documents in the box on my desk, but just kept seeing Luna’s face. I flipped through files and took notes until I started to feel queasy. Information didn’t seem to register. I’d have to look over my notes later. I didn’t feel like eating lunch. The hours passed slowly, but eventually it was fifteen minutes before 7:00 P.M. I still wasn’t hungry. The sky was still light as I rode my bike, weaving through the woods, pedaling faster and faster, my heart rate surging with any small noise or rustling.

One of the gas lamps on the facade of the spa was lit up when I arrived, but otherwise the building was dark. “Hello?” I called, as I walked in the unlocked door. I heard creaking above me, so climbed the carpeted stairs to Cecile’s office. She was sitting at her desk, typing at the computer. It was the first time I’d seen her without makeup and casually dressed. Her hair was loose, frizzed out, and dripping off her shoulders. She was wearing a black tank top and jeans.

“Hi, Cecile. Are you okay?” I asked.

She flattened her lips together. “I’m pretty worried about Luna.”

“Me too. The police interviewed me and the rest of the staff at the library.”

"They were here, too. Let's hope they find some leads soon. Luna is one of the good ones."

"Has she ever missed work before?"

"She's never even been late," Cecile said, her brow creasing. "I overheard one of the officers say that Luna's phone and wallet were found in her house. When I drove over there I saw her car in her driveway."

"The cops asked me about her friends and partners. I mentioned Gabe Wilton to them, even though I think they just went out on a couple of dates. But I'm not sure who else she might've been involved with."

Cecile shrugged. "You'd probably know more than me."

My mind flashed to the night we'd spent at the bar, listening to live music, her banter with the band leader. "I forgot to tell the police," I said. "We heard live music and she exchanged numbers with the lead singer. Shit. Maybe I should call them."

"Yes, you should." Cecile sighed. "She did have a lot of energy, not that she ever complained. I don't know how she found the time to date, juggling all those jobs."

"Yeah. She always seemed so positive about everything. Except the last time I saw her . . ." I stopped then stood up. "What about Gabe Wilton?"

"What about him? I can't imagine that she ran off with him, if that's what you mean."

"No, I just thought . . . Well, I hope she did run off with some rich young guy, and that she'll call us tomorrow from London," I said.

Cecile smiled. "I hope that's what happened, too. But if not, Luna is a strong person. She's got street smarts. She'll be okay," she said, but her voice cracked at the end.

"I wish you could cast some spell and bring her back."

"If only." She sighed again. "We can manifest it, though."

"I'm still not sure I know what that means, but I'll try anything."

As I walked downstairs I read a text from Mason.

All ok? Did you locate your friend?

No, I wrote back. *This sucks.*

Do you have time to meet up? he wrote.

When/where?

Tres Amigos @ 9?

Not hungry.

Riotous?

See you there.

On my way to the bar I called and left a message with Officer Jackson about Anthony.

CHAPTER EIGHTEEN

At Riotous Times we ordered at the bar, and then found a free table. I downed half an inch of vodka in three seconds.

"What happened with your friend?" Mason asked, as soon as we sat down. "Is she okay?"

"Luna. The police received a missing person report. Maybe from Cecile? I forgot to ask her."

"Have you seen Cecile? Is she worried?"

"Yeah. The police interviewed the library staff, including me, and also Cecile and the spa. And I'm sure the people at Wilton Grinds."

"Do you have any idea where she could be?"

"I know she was working four jobs, one as a barista, one in the library, teaching yoga at the spa, and a fourth one. She was saving up for library school, and paying off loans."

"She sounds like a serious person. I understand why you're worried."

The distress in his eyes mirrored mine. "Thanks for being so supportive, Mason. But we don't have to talk about this. I'm probably not the best company at the moment."

"Understandably. You're good company, though, no matter what. And, you know, I'd like to be there for you. To spend more time together. Listen, umm . . ." He ran a hand through his hair. "Jeez. I'm rambling . . . I get so nervous around you."

"Don't be. It's just me."

"Hi, you."

"Walk me home?" I said.

"Should I throw your bike in my car and drive you?"

"I feel like walking," I said, looking up. "If that's okay."

"Whatever you want. I can come back here for my car later."

We walked with Mason standing on the other side of my bike, its frame creating distance between us, a barrier that felt comforting. Why was I like this? I walked quickly, then slowed down, then sped up again, and each time, Mason adjusted his pace. When my house was in sight, I turned to him.

"I'd invite you in for a nightcap," I said, "but . . ."

"You don't have to explain," he said. "I'm not going anywhere. Let's take all the time you need." He cupped my shoulder with his hand, like a friend, and our eyes locked for a few seconds. I wanted him to kiss me, and imagined for a couple of seconds the feeling of his lips pressed against mine.

He spoke. "If you ever need anything, just call me. Anytime. Day or night. I'm used to being on call, so you won't bother me." He brushed the back of my hand. "With everything that's been going on, I'm worried."

"Thanks, Mason," I said.

After watching him walk away, I continued down the path and around the corner to the front door. A Barbie torso, naked, headless, its arms and legs removed, was sitting on the doormat. A white envelope was next to it. I picked up the doll and envelope and went inside, double locking the door behind me.

I switched on the light in the foyer, and set the torso down on the table in the hall. With shaking fingers, I opened the envelope. A typed note: "Silence is golden."

I started to call Mason but another call was coming in at the same time. It was Cecile.

We started talking over each other. She had received a "message," as well.

"We shouldn't discuss this over the phone," she said. "Can you bike over to the spa?"

I biked over as quickly as I could, cicadas singing in the heat, which hadn't yet broken. Bruised clouds hovered low in the darkened sky above. I walked inside and closed the door behind me. All the lights were off, and Cecile was standing in the reception area. Using a small flashlight, she led me into a massage room without windows. We sat on the floor and she passed me something the size of an index card. It was a photograph. Of Luna. Tied up, against a white wall.

In big, black letters, someone had written in Sharpie: *Don't look for her. If you go to the police, she dies and then you're NEXT.*

"Cecile," I gasped. "Why is this happening? Why does someone not want us to look for Luna?"

"I have no idea."

"We've got to tell the police."

She pushed her hair away from her face and her gaze shifted from one side of the room to the other. "I don't know, I don't know. I'm terrified of putting Luna's life in danger. At the same time, how can I not? And how would whoever is threatening us even know if I went to the police? I have to tell them." She pushed away from me, and looked like she wanted to punch something, or someone.

"Who is they? Who would be threatening us?"

"Where's the Barbie you said they left for you?"

I pulled out the doll torso from my bag and handed it to Cecile. Her mouth formed an O.

"Disturbing, right?" I said. "Headless and limbs torn off. The same way Trish's body was found in the park. Found by me."

"I'll give this to the police, too," she said. "Did you say they were the same ones you met within the library? I have the detective's number already in my phone." She pulled her phone out of her pocket and tapped it a few times, then positioned it next to her ear. A minute later she gave me a thumbs-up and started to talk. She left her name and phone number and said it was urgent.

"I'm not sure I feel safe going back to my house by myself tonight," I said, after she hung up.

"You shouldn't. Let's both sleep here tonight, although obviously whoever is threatening us knows where I work. We can just keep all the lights off. Bring your bike inside. My car is at my house. If the detective calls back, I'll tell her to meet us here in the morning. But let's try to get some sleep now."

"That's a good idea," I said. "I really don't want to go back home."

Cecile gave me a blanket and pillow, and I slept in the treatment room, on a slightly cushioned massage table that creaked every time I shifted positions.

I'm not sure what time it was, but in the middle of the night I felt a cool blast of air and then heard something that sounded like a loud screech, or a scream. I shot up from the table, having forgotten where I was. It was pitch black but touching the massage table, I remembered I was at the spa. Shuffling over until I felt the wall, I then found a light switch, and turned it on. The door was closed. I went out of the room and began to tiptoe around.

All the doors to the treatment rooms were closed, and no windows were open. Cecile was upstairs, but I didn't hear her. The cold air must have been part of one of my nightmares. I went back in the room and locked the door. I woke up when I heard the door unlocking and pulled the thin blanket up to my chin, my heart beginning to pump furiously. The door yawned open and someone approached the table, their tall silhouette blocking the light. The next scream belonged to me.

CHAPTER NINETEEN

"You scared the shit out of me," Jade said, slapping her chest and panting.

"Ditto," I said, my voice squeaking.

"It's bad enough with Cecile sleeping here, now her hangers-on are, too?"

"I'm not a hanger-on. It's rude to characterize me that way when you don't know what's going on."

"I'm not trying to be rude," she said. "It's more about Cecile. She's got a big heart, and people are always flocking to her. Like me."

I sat up, draping the thin blanket Cecile had given me around my shoulders.

Jade shook her head, and smiled a lopsided smile. "Everything alright with you? Trouble at home? I don't mean to pry."

"It's, umm, it's complicated," I said, because I didn't want to explain. "Just . . . dealing with some stuff."

"That's something we've got in common, girl," Jade said, and laughed a high-pitched and hearty laugh. "I just made some coffee. Would you like a cup?"

"Thanks, Jade, I'd love it."

Jade led me into the staff kitchen and poured me coffee from a French press.

I took a sip. "This is good coffee."

"Thanks. It's our own brew actually."

"I've had your tea. It's really delicious, too."

"We try. So, how do you know Cecile?" she asked, sipping her own cup.

"I met her at a party. Then went to a few of her witch events."

"You're one of her witches?"

"Definitely not. I mean, I started out more than skeptical . . . Not that I believe in anything remotely supernatural."

She shook her head. "I didn't used to either. Not before moving here."

"But you do now?"

"I've seen some crazy stuff. One time I was closing out and the chandelier in the foyer was . . . swaying. On its own. And then there's shadows. I've seen shadows moving on the wall. Weird drafts of air when all the windows are closed."

"I felt one, too! Last night, in this room. I've felt it in other houses, too. And . . . was I hearing things or did someone scream in the middle of the night? Maybe it was in my nightmare."

Her eyes dropped to the floor. "You did sleep in room *3*. There's always this weird draft in one corner of that room even when the window is closed and the air con is off. One girl who was working here quit because she couldn't handle it energetically."

"Do you know what the spa used to be? Before it was a spa?"

"It was a wreck before Cecile came along. She restored it in record time. It must've cost the earth. The contractor came down from Canada, so it might've been cheaper. But while he was doing the renovation he was involved in a freak accident."

"What happened?"

"He fell down a ladder, went into a coma, and never woke up."

"Falling off a ladder in a speeded-up renovation project doesn't sound like such a freak accident."

"Someone saw it happen. He was on the first step when he fell."

"Oh. That is weird."

"Totally," said Jade. "Someone at the library helped us research the history of this house. It was built in the 1800s, and belonged to a doctor. Relations of the Wilton family. You've heard of the Wilton curse, right? Well, the doctor and his six kids all died during an epidemic."

"Epidemic of what?"

"Typhoid or TB, one of those. Treatment room 3 used to be the nursery. I've walked in there in the morning and the lights were on, when I'd remembered having turned them off the night before. Other people have heard screams before, and crying. Guests have heard it. And therapists. Supposedly it's the mom crying for her dead kids."

"So you must've freaked out when you found the room locked this morning."

As if she hadn't heard me, she said, "I can't imagine losing a child." She looked down.

"Do you know someone who lost a child?" I asked her.

"Did Cecile ever tell you about her special-needs son?"

"She's never mentioned a son to me, no."

Jade looked in the direction of the door. "I think he was eleven when he died. I don't know the details, but his death and this spa is why she's in a ton of debt. Why she works so hard."

"That's . . . devastating. Poor Cecile."

Jade rested a hand on her hip. "I've never heard her complain or feel sorry for herself. Or brag about what she does in her spare time, volunteering at a suicide hotline, for one thing. She volunteers at a women's shelter, too." It must've been the same shelter Luna volunteered at, I thought, feeling a pang of despair.

"More coffee? You seem ready for it," she said.

"Do I look as bad as I feel?" I asked.

She poured me another coffee, then excused herself to start answering the phone at the reception desk. I got up and looked around for Cecile, but her office door was closed so I downed the rest of the coffee, said goodbye to Jade, and walked my bike outside.

Before I got on the bike, I dialed Mason, who agreed to meet me outside my house. He'd been in Wilton on an errand when I called him, so he was waiting for me when I got home.

"I'm glad to see you," I said, reaching out for a hug. He held me until I pulled back.

"You okay?" he asked.

I shook my head and quietly said "No," as tears began streaming down my cheeks.

"Hey, hey," he said, brushing my hair back from my face. "Let's go inside, and you can tell me everything."

My hands were shaky so I gave him the keys and he let us in. We sat on my couch and I told him about the note and the doll, and that now Cecile was being threatened, too.

"Holy shit, that's freaky," he said. "You need to tell the police. Or, I can go with you to the police if you want."

"It's okay," I said, "Cecile's already called them."

"Okay, then come stay at my place! I mean it. Or just show up. I'll keep you safe." I forgot where he lived, but I knew it was a few towns east of where we were, close to the medical school. "I hate the thought of you being in any kind of danger," he said.

"I'm okay here for now. Let's see how the day goes."

"The offer's on the table, it's not going anywhere. And neither am I. Unless you want me to."

"I don't."

He ran his fingers through my hair, and hugged me to him. When I leaned back, I looked him in the eye. He pulled me close again, cupped my face in his hands, and we kissed, softly at first, and then I was lost in the pleasure of it.

"I've been wanting to do that for a long time," he said, once we stopped.

"Me too," I said, smiling at him smiling at me.

He stood up. "This is weird, but, I gotta go. I'm late for rounds."

"Thanks so much for coming by this morning. I know you're so busy."

He blinked twice. "Not too busy for you."

After Mason left, I took a shower and dressed for work. The library was not open yet so I rode my bike back to the spa, where I'd left my sweater with my credit card in it. Jade wasn't at the front desk. I looked for her and saw her in the locker room and stepped in.

She was reaching up, both arms overhead. When I said hi, she turned, one arm still up to balance the box she'd started to pull out. I saw a long dark scar on her stomach before she quickly dropped her arms and smoothed her sweatshirt down, but not before I noticed another, smaller scar—or maybe a tattoo—near her hip bone, where her sweats sagged down, that looked like the letter *D*.

"I left my sweater," I said. "In treatment room 3, where I slept. I'll just go grab it. Thanks for the coffee this morning."

"Anytime," she said. She seemed like she was about to say something else, so I stood there. After a few seconds she looked up at me. "This might be TMI," she said, "but I used to be one of those women. In that shelter I was telling you about, where Cecile volunteers. She helped me out of a really low place. I'd do anything for her."

"I'm honored you shared that with me," I said.

She clapped her hands. "Okay, I'd better get back to work. We're short-staffed now that Luna's gone."

"I'm worried, Jade."

She stepped over and stood close to me. "Cecile showed me the Barbie you got. Pretty fucking creepy. And the photo of Luna all tied up. Jesus Christ."

I looked up toward the second floor. “Is Cecile still here?”

“Already left,” said Jade. “I’ll tell her you came by. And . . .” She put her hand on my shoulder and leaned in. In a quiet voice she said, “Watch out for yourself, Genevieve. Be careful.”

CHAPTER TWENTY

Over the next few days, I worked hard to stay focused on the Wilton archives. My mind kept wandering back to the Barbie torso and the note I'd received, "Silence is golden." Was someone watching me? Was whatever happened with Luna, or Trish, going to happen to me? For the first few hours each morning I concentrated on the work Luna had been prepping and finished sorting one box of documents and then another into chronological order. Then I'd go back to cataloguing. I ate apples and cheese for lunch at my desk—Mitch had stopped bringing me meals—and didn't look up again until the night guard kicked me out of the building. The third morning, I ran into Susan. I told her the story, ending with the note and the dismembered Barbie left on my doorstep, and watched shock distort her face. "Please don't tell anyone," I said. "I'm supposed to keep quiet about it, but I trust you."

Later in the day, she clattered down the steps to the basement. "I just thought of something," she said. "What if the doll was meant to remind you of a poppet, like the ones witches supposedly used to represent a specific person to cast spells on them? Whoever left it knew you'd understand the reference."

I gripped the table. "You might be right. In a document I read, a witness supposedly found Prudence Lowell's wax poppets, further evidence she was a witch. But who would know I read a document with that information, or even about its existence?"

"Good point," Susan said, and turned to walk back upstairs. Could the Barbie really have been a specific warning by someone who knew about my archival finds, or was Susan overthinking things? The latter was more likely, but I knew she was just trying to help.

Cecile called and said she wanted me to sleep at the spa again that night, but I told her I felt safer at home. For the rest of the week after work I'd bring my bike inside and keep the lights off, and heat up some soup for dinner in the dark. I only burned myself once. Mason and I texted back and forth for over an hour each evening, sometimes longer, even when he was on a night shift. Before I went to bed we'd talk and say goodnight, which calmed me down, and then I'd read in bed until I fell asleep. Each morning there'd be another text from Mason, always with silly emojis and a quote for the day, such as "Be yourself. Everyone else is taken"—Oscar Wilde.

During one of my meetings with Daniela, I let her know that I wouldn't be at the library every day as I planned to gather information about Prudence Lowell from other local history records in the area.

First I visited the Wilton Springs Archives, housed in a municipal, redbrick building, at the end of Main Street on a perpendicular side lane. I had an appointment with the archivist, but when I told him about my research, he explained that the archives only reached as far back as the 1970s. He steered me toward some lesser-known genealogical websites where I found out that Prudence Lowell's daughter, Felicity, had married into another family, the Blackwells.

By then it was noon so I stopped for a coffee and a salad before biking to the Wilton County Historical Society, which turned out to be a museum, housed in a former Georgian-style mansion, on the outskirts of town. "Hi, I'm conducting research on the Blackwells and would like access to your historical archives," I said to the man at the front desk, my voice bouncing off the high walls. He appeared to be the only employee there.

"I'm not cleared to grant you access to those files. We're understaffed right now. If you could write down your name and number, I'll have someone contact you."

Without thinking about it, I scribbled the name *Virginia Evans* in the margins.

He glanced at the signature. "Do you have ID, Miss . . . Evans?"

"Not on me at the moment."

"Are you a . . . student?"

"Researcher."

"What time period are you researching? You know the newer files are in the—"

"Wilton Springs Archives. I was there earlier. I'm working on eighteenth-century history. The Wilton family, mostly."

He flinched. "You're not a relative, are you?"

"No."

"That's good. Bit of a . . . mix-up some years ago." He scoffed. "Mix-up's putting it politely. They came in, in one fell swoop, and took a bunch of our files. They were all haughty-like, acting as if they were the bosses. But they had a warrant so we had to comply. I'm not sure what was in those files that they wanted so badly, but they must've paid somebody off to look the other way. It was their archive, they claimed. Their materials. I've never heard of such a thing, but what do I know? I'm just a lowly state servant."

"Who's they? The Wiltons? Which ones?"

He shook his head. "Let's leave it at that. I don't want any trouble. We were told to report on who comes in asking about those files, too."

"Of course," I said, glad to be wearing a baseball cap with my hair tucked up under it. "Please give them my name." I paused. "While I'm here I might as well visit the museum." After paying the admission fee, I wandered through the halls of the building, coughing on the thick, dusty air. I was the only visitor.

One room was filled with antiquated musical instruments and couches with red ribbons and signs that read Do Not Cross. The next room contained a series of black-and-white photographs, yellowing on the borders. I walked over to a picture in a frame, which appeared to be a family portrait. A father and mother with two small children. All dressed in black-tie. Their eyes were closed. They were lying on the floor. They were dead.

I let out a small gasp, and stepped back. "Yeah," I heard the man say, echoing my thoughts. I hadn't realized he'd followed me into the room. "That was common back then. Whole entire families photographed. Dead. Macabre, eh?"

"How did they die?" I asked.

"Cholera outbreak poisoned the water supply. Big scandal. Them Wiltons again, faulty infrastructure. No wonder they're cursed." He laughed. I hadn't remembered reading about the poisoned water supply.

I moved to the next room, where a floor-to-ceiling painting of a stern-looking man took up most of the wall. The label identified him as Eugene Blackwell, original owner of the house. On the opposite wall was a similarly sized portrait of Mrs. Blackwell, long tendrils of dark hair framing her round face. I wondered what Prudence Lowell had looked like. She deserved some sort of recognition, but instead she'd been murdered, and then forgotten, thanks to the Wilton family.

On my way out, I passed by the scowling man at the front desk. After one pedal on my bike, I realized there was something wrong with it. I stepped off and found a six-inch slash on the side of the front tire. I looked around but could see no one.

Telling myself not to panic, I started walking home, pushing my bike. So, someone in the Wilton family had been to the county historical society and taken some of the archive? Why hadn't Susan and Daniela told me? I would discuss it with them.

After a few more blocks, I heard someone behind me but turned around and didn't see anyone. I walked slowly and heard them again, at my same pace. I sped up and they sped up. I glanced back over my shoulder as I turned right at the next corner. A tall, slim man in glasses had stopped and was looking down at his phone a few feet behind me, wearing a hooded sweatshirt, with the word Bainsville written in crimson letters. He was too old to be a student. Was he a professor? I turned around and kept walking my bike toward home, faster now, my heart pounding, nearly choking me. I had reached busier streets by then, and semi-ran my bike all the way back to my place, double bolting the door once inside. I looked out the window. No one.

I texted Cecile. *Any word on the investigation?*

After work, three days later, over a week since Luna had gone missing, I rode my bike with a new tire to the spa. Jade waved me upstairs, where Cecile was packing what looked like ceremonial objects into a suitcase. I closed the door behind me.

"Have you heard from the police?" I asked.

She spoke in a low voice, almost a whisper. "I gave them the photograph. And the doll torso with the note. They've set up a special team, apparently. No one's contacted you yet?"

"No. Did they say anything about Luna?"

"No," she sighed. "I've been calling them twice a day. Nothing." She took a deep breath, then looked at me and forced a smile. "How are you holding up, my beautiful friend? You've lost some weight."

"I'm okay. Working hard. And I have a . . . friend . . . who's been . . . attentive. That helps."

"Hmm. I'm sure you haven't told this friend anything, have you? Is it someone from the library? Those threats seemed real to me, and the police think so, too."

"It's just my friend Mason. You said you knew him. He's a med student. But no, I haven't told him anything."

"I hope you can act normal around him."

"Kind of. He knows I'm upset that Luna's still missing." I felt tears building so I squinched my eyes shut and clenched my fists. Then I started crying.

Cecile stopped packing and came over to me and folded me in a long, soft hug. "Stay strong, Genevieve. That's the best thing we can do for Luna right now. That and keep quiet."

"Jade told me that you showed her the note and the photograph a few days ago."

"She saw the photo on my desk and was horrified. I only told her because I'd trust Jade with my life. She adores Luna."

"You're very close here, I know." I gestured toward the suitcase. "Going somewhere?"

"Tonight's a special night with my group," she said. "A ceremony called 'Drawing down the Moon.' Would you like to join? Might be good for you."

"Thanks, but, I don't think so. I'm just not up for anything remotely social."

"If you change your mind we'll be at Emma's house. At midnight. No pressure though."

"Okay," I said. "Let me know if you hear anything about Luna. Just text me the word *moon* in capital letters, and I'll know what you mean."

I helped her load her car and then biked back to my rental.

Mason and I texted later and longer than usual, and by the time we finished it was almost 1:00 A.M. I had been drinking coffee to stay awake in the mornings and was still totally wired, so I decided to bike over to Emma's to see if the ceremony was still going on. People in robes were walking out, some to their cars, but quite a few others were still there, standing around talking. Clearly the ceremony had ended. The first person I recognized was Emma, who gave me a delicate hug.

"So glad you made it," she said. "I didn't see you earlier or I would've made sure you looked like one of us." She went off and returned with a long, red velvet robe that matched the one she was wearing. When I slipped it on, the inside felt soft, and silky.

Someone came by with a tray of drinks in silver-colored goblets encrusted with red rhinestones. Emma took two goblets and offered one to me. "Want to try some of my witch's brew?" As she held out the goblet, she looked past me and her expression changed. "I wonder who that guy is, standing over there?"

I followed her gaze, but it was pretty dark out. "The one with glasses?" I asked, looking around. There was only one other man here, so they both stood out. "Are there men witches?"

"Men are welcome, but I've never seen that one before. He doesn't go to Bainsville and doesn't look like a professor, either. Would you offer him a goblet and see what you can find out? I'm going to look for Cecile."

I took the cup from her and approached the man in the glasses.

"Hi," I said, holding out the goblet to him. Just then, it occurred to me that he could be the person who had threatened me and Cecile. He could have Luna! I stepped back.

"Hi," he responded. "Neat glass. I saw someone carrying a tray of those."

"The owner of the house asked me to offer you a drink," I said. "Her own witch's brew."

"No, thanks," he said, "but please thank her for me."

He seemed as if he was about to turn around, so I blurted out, "Are you a witch?" I was still holding the goblet up, so I lowered my arm. "What's your name?"

"I'm Lucas," he said. "You could say I'm a witch in training."

"I haven't seen you at any of the other ceremonies," I said, although there was something about him that seemed familiar.

"I don't live in Wilton Springs. I drove up a couple days ago to hear Cecile speak. Maybe even meet her." He looked up. "There she is," he said. "Excuse me." Then he moved to the left of me, lowering his head as he walked toward Cecile.

I'd seen him before somewhere. But where? I took the goblet inside the house then went back outside.

Emma and Cecile came up to me a few minutes later. "Did you meet him?"

"No," said Cecile, "but Emma told me there was a man here she didn't recognize."

"He said his name was Lucas. And that he was a witch in training who wanted to meet you, Cecile," I said. "He said he drove here from out of town to hear you speak, and I thought he was walking over to you a few minutes ago."

She shrugged. "Lots of people come to Wilton Springs to meet me."

Emma said, "I think you should be careful. There's something off about that guy. Looks like a creep. I'm going to see if he's still here."

"What if he's the one who sent me the Barbie and you the photo?" I whispered to Cecile. "What if he has Luna?"

"Genevieve. Calm down. He hasn't threatened anybody. Emma will find him and bring him to me. Don't worry, I'll watch my back. Always do anyway. Force of habit."

I slipped off the robe and draped it over the back of a chair, then found my bike and made my way home as quickly as I could.

CHAPTER TWENTY-ONE

Whenever I rode my bike I started looking around to see if anyone was following me. Inside the library I felt safe, and soon I settled back into a routine doing the cataloguing. I told Susan what the man at the county historical society had said, and asked her whether Lily or Victoria had brought in additional materials at any point. "Maybe," she said, with a shrug. "I don't remember. But I wouldn't ask Daniela right now, she's deadlining on some big project."

I'd seen Mason twice since we'd kissed, but he'd treated me like a good friend. Both times we'd talked late into the night, but there had been nothing physical between us. We'd eaten dinner at two different restaurants—the first time he paid, the second time I'd insisted on splitting the bill.

"You're a breath of fresh air, Genevieve," he told me that night.

"What do you mean by that?"

"You're different." I smiled. He looked like he was trying not to laugh.

"What's so funny?" I asked him.

"Your teeth are black."

"What?" I asked, closing my mouth.

"It's natural. Red wine is high in tannins that bind to your teeth, and the acidity etches your enamel making it more porous."

I craned my head around to look in the mirror and ran my tongue over them. "Oh! They did turn black." Now I was laughing. "Why didn't you tell me before?"

He leaned back. "I find it endearing you don't care what people think. You're confident. Maybe that's because you grew up with money. Whereas I'm always second-guessing myself."

"I'm not as self-confident as you might think, Mason."

"Well, you seem to be. In an unassuming way. But at the same time, I feel like you need somebody to look after you. Especially with everything that's been going on lately. Could be me. The person to look after you, I mean."

I felt my face begin to heat up. "I, uhhh . . ."

He put his hand on mine. "You must worry people will want something from you when they find out about your family. But you can trust me. Those aren't empty words. I'll show you."

I smiled again, this time without opening my mouth.

After driving me home he walked me to the front door and gave me a hug. When he left I stood there. Why hadn't he tried to kiss me? Especially after what he'd said at dinner. A part of him remained inaccessible, as if he had a room he retreated to that was sealed off from the outside world. Maybe he felt emotionally safer that way. He had told me numerous times that he respected me. "You know I'm a gentleman, right?" he'd said that night before leaving.

Focusing on work was the only way I was keeping it together without giving in to my rumbling anxiety. In my attempts to put Prudence Lowell in context, I read about the witchcraft trials in Finnmark, in northern Norway, when a terrible storm in 1621 led to the drowning deaths of forty men off the harbor. The local authorities, looking for someone to blame to assume the immense weight of this loss, turned to several Norwegian women, accusing them of witchcraft. The innocent women were said to have invoked black magic to create bad weather to kill these men. They were further accused of having sex with demons and other acts of depravity. I wondered if it had been an effective way for the town to deal with mass grief. Probably not. Death followed by more death.

A few times a week I'd update Daniela, who knew a lot about witchcraft trials, and gave me more sources to follow. Late one Tuesday, after everyone else on the staff had left, I went to her office. "Daniela, have you heard anything about Luna?"

"The detectives promised to update me, but I've heard nothing so far. I know you are worried. As am I. But we are not experts. All we can do is do our jobs, and let them do theirs. I know it's frustrating, but we have no choice."

I blew out a breath. "What about her family? Have they been notified?"

"I wasn't aware she had family, Genevieve. There are no family contacts in her record."

The next day after work, I saw the owner of my rental cottage, Russell, lingering near my front door.

"Nice to see you! With all this . . . mayhem with the girls, err—ladies, the bloom is seemingly off the Wilton Springs rose. I hope we aren't in danger of losing you as a tenant?"

"Nope, no danger of that. And no complaints," I said. "I thought you'd be away until Labor Day."

"Nah. I like being here in the summer. Even when it's hot. My wife's the one who can't stand being landlocked." He paused. "I know you're interested in history," he said. "Along those lines, I have something to show you." He turned back toward me. "At my house."

"It's getting late," I said.

"Won't take but a minute. It's a historical curiosity. Right up your alley."

Inside Russell's house, a slightly moldy, briny odor floated up. The furniture in the living room was covered with wide, white cloths. Russell stopped in front of a small door concealed in a wall under the staircase, and opened it.

"Go down," he said, pointing at a long narrow flight of stairs. I clutched at my arms.

"What's down there?" I asked, reaching into my bag for my phone, which I held up for him to see. "Maybe I'll take a photo?"

His eyes lit up. "The Underground Railroad operated out of this house. Enslaved fugitives hid in our very basement."

It was too easy to conjure up the fear of the people who must have hidden down there, having left behind horrific pasts, now risking their lives to escape through places like this, one at a time, lurching toward a completely uncertain future.

He nodded. "I told you there's lots of history in this sleepy little town. I'm lucky enough to live a part of it. Go ahead! Go and see for yourself. Don't take my word for it."

"I have a friend due for drinks any minute," I lied.

"Okay then. Another time. Or you could come back with your girlfriend."

"*He's* . . . claustrophobic," I said, lying some more.

"Oh, I see. Alright, then. Hey, I meant to ask you. I heard that a girl who worked at the library went missing. Have they found her yet?"

"Luna, her name is Luna," I said. "No, they have not found her."

"Well, I'm glad it wasn't you who went missing," he said, with a wink and a chuckle.

By then I'd edged my way back to the front door. "Thanks again for telling me about the basement, Russell," I said. But he had turned away and I wasn't sure he heard me.

CHAPTER TWENTY-TWO

Early the next morning, I received a text from one of the directors of the Wilton County Historical Society, granting "Virginia Evans" access to the archives. I didn't see the man I'd met the first day. His replacement was an elderly woman who didn't say much, but she did scrutinize me when I entered and left the building. I spent the following two days in a musty back room, looking through the documents in the Blackwell archive, which reached back to the mid eighteenth century. At the end of the second day, I found a letter in the file of one Mrs. Blackwell.

My dearest friend,

I know now that his true name, John Wilton, is not the same name as he haft given me. I do not understand how cruel this man must be to deny me what he promised. He told me that he wished me to be his bride. That he had lost his wife, as I had lost my husband. But his wife is very much alive. And together they have one young son and one daughter.

He is not the simple man he presented to me, but a powerful magistrate. I imagine his surprise when I will present myself there. He has not returned my letters. I suppose he throws them away, but I imagine his surprise there, too, for I am certain that he thought me ignorant. It was my husband who taught me how to read and write, how to balance a ledger. And when the fever took him, he asked me to one day marry again, to seek happiness with another. I believed that I had found him in this Mr. Wilton. But, my friend, I was wrong, and in this error I fear for my life. Alas, I cannot undo what has been done.

A few lines were obscured.

I intend for everyone to know that he is a liar and an adulterer.

On my way out I thanked the woman at the front desk. As I biked through town, which was surprisingly quiet that day, with few cars on the road, I made a mental note to figure out which Mrs. Blackwell might've been Prudence Lowell's friend. It was the hottest day yet of the summer, and even the breeze created riding my bicycle did not cool me down.

I couldn't wait to get home and take a cold shower. For a moment, in the stillness, excited by what I'd just uncovered, I felt a slight reprieve from the terror that had been ebbing and flowing since I'd heard that Luna had gone missing. The terror sometimes felt like grief, but no matter how it felt, normally it wouldn't let go. Just for a few moments, however, as I pushed my bike along the side of the house that led to the front door, I listened with some measure of contentment to the sound of cicadas. I began composing an email to Daniela in my head. Then I stopped. A woman was darting from the front of my house toward the Baileys' house.

"Hello?" I said, my voice raised, but she ignored me and picked up her pace. "Hey!" I called out. She turned toward me for a second and I recognized her as the young woman I'd seen at the Wilton house when

I'd gone there for brunch. She started running. Fast. From the Bailey property she ran into the street, and then she was gone.

I went inside with my bike, and saw an envelope on the floor, which she had presumably slipped under my door before running away. "Talk to no one about Luna," the typed note read. "She is beyond your reach."

Beyond my reach?

Had this woman also left the doll on my doorstep? Or worse, had she sent the photo of Luna to Cecile? I didn't know anything about her, other than that she worked for the Wiltons. Envelope in hand, I stomped out of the rental and started walking to Wilton Castle, breaking into a jog. When I reached the front door, I took a few slow, deep breaths before jabbing the doorbell. No answer. After ringing two more times I knocked. Nobody appeared to be home. I walked around the house and knocked on the back door. After ten minutes I was soaked in sweat. Maybe they didn't want me to know they were home. I'd return later.

I went back a few hours later, then the next day, and the next, early in the morning, and then again in the afternoon. On the third day, at 5:00 P.M., after the third time I had pushed the doorbell, Barbara opened the door. She was wearing a bathrobe, and her hair was twisted up in a towel, clear reddish droplets leaking down around her temples.

"Oh, it's you, Genevieve," she said, smiling easily. "Everything alright? Your work?"

She was acting as if nothing had happened. "It's going well, thanks," I said. "But I'd like to speak with the young woman who works for you. Stacy? I met her when I came over."

She paused.

"Young. Dark hair, slight," I said, shrugging my shoulders.

"I'm afraid you can't speak to Stacy," Barbara said. "She left us. With no notice, I might add."

"When?"

"It must've been a couple weeks ago."

"Well, she's still in town. She's been leaving . . . messages. At my house." I put my hands on my hips.

"Sounds . . . strange."

"May I have her phone number?"

"She doesn't have a phone. We gave her a work phone so we could reach her, but I found it on the kitchen table the day she didn't show up for work. That's how I knew she wasn't coming back."

I stood there, frozen, unsure of what to say next.

"I wish I could help you," she said.

"Sorry to bother you, Mrs. Wilton," I said, although I wasn't sorry at all.

That night I called Mason and told him what had happened. He drove right over.

"Have you contacted the police?" he asked. "I'll come with you if you want. Something's not adding up."

"Cecile's our conduit to the police. I called her right after I called you. So now they know about the doll and the note, the photograph, and this third message."

"Huh? What photograph? And what other messages?"

"Somebody left Cecile a photo of Luna tied up somewhere. The same night they left a threat-filled note for me, and a Barbie doll that had been . . ."

"That had been what?"

"Dismembered. I know, I know. The note to Cecile said Luna would be killed if she told anybody, and that Cecile would be next. We told the police anyway. Now you know everything."

"Why didn't you tell me?"

"To protect you, partly. And I didn't want you to worry even more than you were already."

He squeezed my hand. "You must've been terrified. Obviously, it stays between us."

"I'm trying to figure out how the Wiltons' household staff could be connected to whatever the fuck is happening."

"I don't know, Genevieve. Do you really think it has to do with the Wiltons?"

"Barbara was acting weird. Also, a man at the historical society told me the Wiltons had come in and seized a large part of their archive. Isn't that strange?"

"I doubt the danger has anything to do with the archives, Genevieve."

"Oh, and did I tell you about this creepy guy I saw at Cecile's last ceremony?"

"The ceremony where Emma's friend became a witch?"

"No, another one. It was called bringing down the moon, or something like that."

"I didn't realize you were attending these things regularly. What about a creepy guy?"

"He said he was a witch, that he was from out of town. But he seemed familiar. I think I've seen him somewhere else. He wears glasses and has a low, smooth voice. Maybe he's the one sending the notes to Cecile."

"Does Cecile know who he is?"

I shrugged and pulled my hands out of his and ran them through my hair. "Mason, I'm feeling on edge, and confused. I want to save Luna before she gets hurt and I feel like the police are slacking. For all we know there's still a killer out there who dismembered a woman!"

"Tell me what to do. What does the creepy guy look like? I'll find him."

"It's not the guy. It's just . . . Obviously somebody has Luna. And there's nothing I can do, except wait for the police to figure it out, right? And they haven't even contacted me! Why aren't they reassuring Cecile and me that we're not in any danger? Because obviously we are. When I moved here I was going through a rough time. But my life wasn't being threatened, nor the lives of two of my friends. I feel so helpless right now."

"But you know I'd do anything to help you, right?" He had that puppy dog look again, but it didn't seem as adorable as the other times I'd seen it. It was even a little annoying.

"If I close my eyes and think about what I would do if I could wave a magic wand, or drink one of Emma's potions, I'd return to my PhD program. I mean, with the material I found here about this widow who was murdered as a witch. I could start an original project about the persecution of women, with brand new sources. That idea is calling me right now."

"Well, who's to say you can't still do that? But, selfishly, I hope you don't leave anytime soon. I'd like to be part of your plans." He looked up at me and then back down at his hands.

"I'm sorry I haven't been around more, it's just that school is so busy right now. I feel awful you have to go through this by yourself. And one more thing."

"What?"

"I feel like I'm sort of out of my league with you. I mean, I'm a bit intimidated."

"I don't blame you for focusing on school. But intimidating? Me? I'm just me . . . and I can't be any different or less . . . anything."

"It's my own stuff. Things weren't easy for me growing up. I had to protect myself. It takes a while for me to let go, be myself with somebody." His body was angled away from me, but then he turned back. "I've never met anyone like you, Genevieve. You're talented, beautiful, dedicated. And you accept me for who I am. You recognize me somehow. You don't judge me. I trust you. All of that makes me feel like, well, like we'd be good together."

"As a couple?"

"Yeah. So I hope you're still around and when things let up at school. If you feel the same way I do. If so, can you maybe wait a little before you go?"

"I feel a real connection with you, Mason. I think about you. All the time. I—"

"Genevieve," he said, interrupting me, and I liked hearing him say my name. His face was beet red. He ran his fingers over his lips. "I'd better go. Thank you for talking to me, for listening. Is it weird I'm thanking you? I feel the need to. I want to see you again . . . soon. Please."

One step forward. One step back. Something about Mason's past traumas meant that anytime he got closer, emotionally, he needed to retreat afterward. Under normal circumstances this might have bothered me but right now I couldn't handle a new relationship that was too intimate. Not with my friend missing and her kidnappers at large, sending me threats.

CHAPTER TWENTY-THREE

The next morning I called Cecile and asked to meet her at the spa. She said she wasn't available until the end of the day, so I churned my way through an entire box in the library.

When I walked into the spa, Jade nodded at me serenely in the reception area. "Hey, lady," she said. "Go right on up. I've been waiting for you, but I'll lock up and head home. You holding up okay?" I shrugged. She put her hand on my shoulder and looked me in the eye. "The struggle we face today will develop the strength we need for tomorrow," she said, as she walked toward the door.

Cecile was on her computer and barely looked up to say hello. After a few minutes her hands flew in the air and she turned to me. "Forgive me for making you wait! Putting out fires."

I handed her the new note that Stacy had delivered and sat down. She looked at it and stood up, walked around the desk, knelt on the floor beside me, and wrapped me in her arms. "Stay strong, dear Genevieve. Light will conquer darkness. And I have protective spells surrounding you." She rocked back on her heels. "Best of all, I have some wonderful news! I heard from Luna!"

Blood rushed into my ears. "Really? How is she? Where is she?"

"She couldn't say where she was. I had a hard time reaching her, and couldn't understand everything she was saying, but she asked me specifically to tell you not to worry, that she was strong, and that she was positive she'd see you again."

"Can I call her? I've tried so many times and it always goes to voicemail."

"We could try calling her, but not right now. That energy is used up for a while."

"Energy?"

"We didn't talk on the phone. I spoke to her on a higher plane. It took so long to reach her that I've fallen behind in my other work. But it was important to connect."

"Higher plane? You mean, something to do with witchcraft?"

"Not exactly, but it would be difficult to explain, and I just don't have the strength right now. Someday you will learn all of this. I have so much to teach you! And Luna, too! You two have been sisters in another lifetime! And even closer than that! Twins!"

"Well, it sounds great!" I said. "I'm so glad she's okay. Did she tell you where she was? Or when she'd be back?"

Cecile stood up and walked back around her desk, beaming at me. "All in good time, Genevieve. It's important to have trust, and to assume the best."

I let out a sigh. I wanted some real-world information. "Now that you know Luna is okay, can you please tell me what happened when you talked to the police about her? When you showed them the photo?"

"They finally contacted me yesterday, late, to say they had some new leads. I meant to text you. That's all they would tell me, unfortunately. They promised that they had someone on patrol, who was keeping an eye on both of us. They assured me we were in no danger from the people who left the photo and the notes. Of course, one can only trust them so far. Who guards the guardians, as a wise woman once asked."

"Did they say anything else?"

She lowered her voice. "I was asked not to repeat it, but Genevieve, they asked me if I trusted you. When I said I trusted you completely they asked if I was aware you might leave Wilton Springs. I said yes, of course, although I had no idea. Is it true?"

"Why would they think that?" I said, sensing that whatever was going on was somehow larger than I'd thought.

"I know they talked to your property owner, do you think he told them? Mr. Baylor?"

"You're right. Mr. Bailey also asked if I was leaving. I wonder if he wants me out as a renter. Maybe he wants use of the cottage. He's kind of eccentric, so I'm always a bit guarded with him."

"I don't know if I could bear it if you left right now. And as long as you stay close, I can protect you."

"I appreciate that, Cecile, really, but for now I'd like to focus on Luna."

"Of course," she said. "Of course."

When I rode my bike back home it was late, and dark on my street. No lights were shining in any of the houses, and there were very few streetlamps. Susan had told me that most owners of the big houses left in the summer due to the heat. Even Russell had left me a note that morning that he was driving to Maine with his family to stay with his mother-in-law at the beach. I couldn't stop thinking about what Cecile had said. What to make of the "psychic chat"? I'd felt so happy when she'd first told me she'd spoken to Luna, but I had no idea what to think now. I should've pressed her to elaborate. At some point I must've fallen asleep because the next thing I knew light was seeping into the room from the honeycomb blinds.

CHAPTER TWENTY-FOUR

After breakfast, I rode my bike to the state park. I hadn't been to the area near the geysers since Trish's body had been found, so as I parked my bike under a tree and thought about the five-mile path, my heart started pumping faster. Stalling a bit, I sat down on a wooden bench, and retied my hiking sneakers tighter.

It was Wednesday morning, and there were only a couple of cars in the lot, including a Park Service pickup. It was a crisp day, not too hot at 7:30 A.M. I thought of Susan's warning me to avoid the park, but her reasoning appeared to have been mostly supernatural. Besides, it was early in the morning, not late at night. As I walked toward the trailhead, a car pulled into the lot.

Dark, boxy. I had seen that car somewhere. But where? Then I remembered: outside the funeral home, the night with Gabe Wilton. Was it . . . following me?

I rocked on my feet. I had to get to my bike. The car was pulling under the tree where I'd parked it. I walked in the other direction. I'd make a big loop and approach my bike from the other direction.

"Excuse me!" I heard the driver of the car say, already out of the car and looking my way.

"Ms. Tompkins," he called. "Do you have a minute?"

He knew my name. I started running, fast, but then stumbled, and couldn't catch myself. I went flying through the air and into the dirt, hitting first with my outstretched hands and left knee.

"Are you okay?" he called out, rushing over to me. "I'm so sorry."

By the time he reached me I had rolled over onto my back and was cradling my knee. He ran back to his car and returned with a blanket and a first aid kit, out of which he pulled a small bag that he mashed until it became an ice pack, which he placed in my hands. He gently lifted my head and arranged the blanket under it, and then ran back to his car again and reappeared with an enormous umbrella, which he held over me after he put the blanket under my head.

"I apologize for frightening you. But I need to speak with you. In private. It's urgent. And as soon as you sit up, you need to drink some water."

I remembered his voice. Why? Nothing made sense. I gasped slightly as the pain surged through me. "Who . . . are . . . you?" I managed.

"I'm a private investigator."

My brain kept churning.

"I know you've seen me in my car," he continued. "Probably a couple of times."

I stared at him. My whole leg hurt like shit.

"And we met, twice actually. The first time at the crime scene where the dog dug up the body."

It was the athletic guy in cowboy boots who'd known Saunders and Jackson. Who'd given me a water bottle on the trail the day Digger the dog had dug up Trish's body.

"And again at the witch ceremony. I told you I was a witch in training."

He slid off his sunglasses and replaced them with the glasses I'd seen him wearing that night at Emma's.

"Lucas."

"That's me."

"Do you have any aspirin or Tylenol?"

"Hold this," he said, handing me the umbrella. Then he fished around in the first aid kit and pulled out a bottle. "Take three," he said, handing me the pills. He took back the umbrella and with his other hand reached into his pack and took out a water bottle. "Do you want me to help you sit up?"

"I'm fine," I said, raising myself up and leaning on one elbow. I popped the pills in my mouth and reached for the water bottle.

"You really need to stay hydrated, too. In this heat."

I took a gulp of water. "What are you investigating," I asked. "And for whom?"

"A private case. For a private client."

Be more specific."

"The death of Victoria Wilton."

"An accidental drowning that happened five years ago?"

"Perhaps not so accidental."

I tried to stretch my leg out slowly in front of me and sat up all the way. "A private investigator."

"If you want to know anything about my credentials, I'm happy to supply more information."

"Who is your client?"

"That's confidential."

"But what you're investigating isn't?" I tried to hoist myself up to a standing position, but couldn't. I leaned back on both elbows. "I knew you weren't a witch."

"It was my cover."

I rolled my eyes. "And your voice is different."

"On purpose," he said.

"Why didn't you tell me who you were the last time we met at this park?"

"The local police don't like working with private investigators," he said.

"They seemed pretty deferential to you that day," I said.

"It's code around here that they agree to help, but it's mostly lip service. They really just talk and stall with the PIs."

"But why didn't you tell me who you were then?"

"Let's just say I didn't want them to see my cards."

"Meaning?"

"Meaning I had already decided then to ask for your help. And I didn't want them to know that I was going to ask you."

"Why did you wait until now to ask me?"

"I didn't want to freak you out. Also, I only today figured out how I could help you, so you might agree to help me. Given that you don't know me from Adam . . ." He trailed off.

I managed to stand, with his help, which made me wince, and cringe, and curse, in that order. When I was vertical I glanced over at my bike, baking in the sun. I didn't think I'd be able to ride it.

"And how do you propose to help me, Mr. Private Investigator, besides giving me and my bike a ride back into town?"

"I know that there's a dead woman and a missing woman, the latter being a friend of yours named Luna. Also, I know someone's threatening you. I think I can help you figure out who it is."

"And find Luna?" I said.

"And find Luna," he said.

I didn't ask him what he wanted to know about Victoria Wilton. Once we'd found Luna I'd give him all the help he needed. I memorized his license plate as he helped me hobble to his car. I hated getting in a car with a stranger but didn't feel like I had a choice.

He wrangled my bike into his car and drove me back to my rental, although I had him drop me in front of Russell's house and then limped to my front door, leaning on my bike. I called in sick and spent the day with my leg elevated and iced, taking two Tylenol every eight hours. I had suggested we meet at Riotous Times, at 9:00 P.M.

In the middle of a nap in the late afternoon, I was awakened by loud pounding on my front door. I looked out one of the windows and saw a police car. Had they found Luna?

"Sorry we banged on your door," said one of the two cops from the WSPD standing there when I flung the door open. They had removed their hats and taken a few steps back. "We tried the doorbell first," said the other.

The first one stepped forward and handed me a business card. "The guy you met in the state park is legit," he said. "We were in the same class at the academy."

"He's actually my cousin," said the other cop. "Well, second cousin. Kinda."

I looked down at the card. *Lucas Prendergast* it read. And underneath, *Private Investigator*. When I looked up the cops were already on their way back around the house.

At 8:30 I called for a taxi. It was a Wednesday night, so relatively quiet at the bar. I ordered a gin and tonic and Lucas ordered a Heineken. We found a table in the back.

"You don't look like a private investigator," I said, "but I guess that's the point?"

"I'm trying to fit in because I'm not from here."

"And you're not wearing your glasses."

"Yeah, well. Sometimes I wear contacts."

"So, you don't live here? How did your client find you?"

"I'm from a few towns away, but went to the police academy with some of the guys here."

"So they said. And one of them's your cousin."

"Not really, but our moms were real close."

I folded my arms. "Let's start by you explaining who you think's been threatening me?"

"I have direct knowledge that Gabe Wilton has driven by your house a number of times. Not lately. Anything you can tell me about Gabe? What do you know about him?"

I took a sip of my drink, which went into the wrong pipe, and I started coughing.

"A question for an answer. Okay. I'll humor you. I work for his family," I said, between coughs. "He invited me out for dinner soon after I arrived, and he hit on me. Then he lied about what had happened and told people we'd slept together. I confronted him and blew him off."

"Anything else?"

"Yes. Before Luna went missing, she warned me about Gabe. Said he was a player, that I couldn't trust him, or anyone in his family."

"So Gabe dated Luna, is a womanizer, plus he hit on you, and later on you had a disagreement."

"Pretty much."

"To demonstrate my willingness to share information with you, I'll tell you that my client insists that Gabe Wilton is innocent."

"Mrs. Wilton? She's your client, right?"

"I trust you'll appreciate that I'm not at liberty to divulge that information."

"Who else would want to investigate Victoria's death, five years on? And if Barbara is your client, then maybe you know why her employee left me two notes demanding I stop looking into Luna's disappearance? I thought you were going to tell me that's who was threatening me."

"You told the police about the notes?"

"Yes. I mean, Cecile did. She received some notes, too. Worse than the ones I got. And a photo of Luna tied up against a wall. Cecile told the police about all of it, and they're investigating. I hope." I paused. "Lucas. Let's push the restart button. The only reason I agreed to talk to you is you said you might know what happened to Luna."

"I never said I knew what happened to Luna, I said her disappearance was part of my investigation. Not just my investigation, the police investigation. As I said, they're supposedly assisting me. We actually do exchange important information. Sometimes the timing's a bit off, however."

I tapped my fingers on the counter. "Gotcha."

"One thing you have to promise me. Everything I discuss with you has to stay between us. Doing otherwise would jeopardize the entire operation. It's really important. Okay?"

"Unless my life or someone else's life is in danger," I said, "I'll agree to that for now."

He paused before continuing. "I think there's a connection between Luna's disappearance and Victoria's death . . ." He stopped and put his hand up. "Just a second."

He pulled his phone out of his pocket. "Yes," he said into the phone. "Really? What time? Are they sure? Get eyes on it tonight? Affirmative. Can I call you back? I'm in a meeting. A real one, yes. 10-4." He smiled and slid the phone back in his pocket before turning to me. "Listen, I'm sorry to cut this short, but I have to run."

"Now wait just one minute. That call was about Luna, wasn't it?"

His eyes floated up to the ceiling, but he didn't respond. "What happened to your willingness to share information with me?" I asked.

"Yes, the call was about Luna."

"And . . . ? Look, I might agree to help you, but you've got to tell me what you know."

"Can we talk tomorrow? I need to visit the cabin at the lake where Victoria drowned."

"Tonight? I didn't think anyone was living there. Not since she died."

"Someone on Lake Charles saw a woman matching Luna's description. Around the time she stopped showing up for work."

I rocked forward in my chair. "I knew it! Can I go out there with you? I won't get in your way. I promise."

He was shaking his head. "Absolutely not. No. It's not a good idea for a . . ."

I frowned. "What? A woman? Thank you for the sexism."

"That's not what I was going to say. I was going to say . . . a civilian. With a bad knee."

"Look. I'm going to insist on this," I said.

"I can't put you in any sort of danger. Although there are no known criminals out there."

"I could be an extra set of eyes."

"Can you please lower your voice?" he whispered loudly.

I huffed and crossed my arms, scowling at him. "This is hardly the equal exchange that you proposed, Mr. Investigator."

"Lucas," he said. And then added, "Actually, it would be safer if I went in your car if I can borrow it. Would you mind?"

"You've been following me but you haven't figured out I don't have a car?"

"Okay. I'll arrange for another car. But you're not coming."

"Wait. I really want to go."

"You need to rest your knee and put ice on it. It's late."

I sat up straight. "I can ice my knee on the way. And rest. I haven't slept well since . . . it's been a long time. Please."

"It's a two-hour drive."

I crossed my arms over my chest again. "One hour. Each way. Unless you drive like an old lady, and you probably do."

"On the contrary. I might need to speed. It'll be . . . bumpy. We won't even get there until midnight. Don't you have work in the morning? This is not a good idea."

"I can make my own hours. But do you think that a visit to this cabin could also lead us to Luna? And if so, why haven't the police been out there?"

"The police don't know about it yet, and I'd like to have a sniff around before they do."

"If you don't let me come tonight, I won't help you look for answers about Victoria," I said in a loud voice.

"Okay! Calm down. You can come to the cabin. But you'll stay in the car. And you've got to do whatever I tell you. No questions asked."

"Fine. Do you have a gun?"

He nodded once. "Yes, ma'am."

CHAPTER TWENTY-FIVE

By the time I thought about texting Mason we were already thirty minutes into the drive and there was no cell service. I was in the back seat sitting sideways with a cushion from the bar propping up my leg and another one behind my back. The bartender had given me two bags of crushed ice for my knee. I kept the chitchat to a minimum, except to insist that I wasn't going to stay in the car when we got to the lake house. To my surprise, Lucas didn't fight me on it.

Before reaching the lake we drove through a town with tiki bars and mini golf offerings for tourists, then several campgrounds. The streetlights dwindled until there were none. We continued along the same road, and veered right where the road climbed uphill. The houses became larger, more sparse. The road was pretty bumpy. Even in the dark, I could see that the lake was wider, grander, than I thought it would be—majestic, even. My mother hated mountains and lakes. She had always preferred seaside towns, places where she could arrange invitations to sprawling beachfront mansions.

There was a sadness about this place, and the lake, and as we wove through pine trees and small lanes, I decided I would not like to live here, even for all its beauty and tranquility. It was late, and dark, but even so the area felt isolated, still.

I knew what the house looked like from photos I'd seen in the library. Originally built in the 1930s, it had an old-time Adirondacks feel, thick, sturdy, and wooden. Lucas parked the car in some trees off the road and helped me out of the car after I threatened to scream if he walked off without me. It was completely dark, but after a while our eyes adjusted. The air was crisp and much cooler here, and I rubbed my bare arms, which were covered with goose bumps. Lucas walked a few feet into the trees and came back with a long and sturdy piece of wood that I used as a sort of cane. We made our way down the driveway and walked around the house, which was a lot bigger than it had looked in the photos. My knee hurt, but we went slowly, so it wasn't a problem. There was a dock out back on the lake.

Squeezing my eyes shut, I thought about Victoria, her last few moments. A young woman with so many possibilities. How had she died? Swimming? In a boat? Had she hit her head? What had her last thoughts been? A slice of moon glowed white and reflected off the shallow ripples stirred up by the breeze. A few lights twinkled in the distance on the other side of the lake. I heard a dog bark once. Twice. Then it was quiet again.

"Let's see if they left anything unlocked," said Lucas, trying the doors first and then the windows. Nothing budged. When he was back at the front door, looking in on the screened porch, I said, "I'm sure I don't need to tell you this, Mr. Private Eye, but how about looking for a spare key under the doormat." He kicked the mat, lifted it, and found a shiny key.

Earlier, my endorphins had been propelling me forward. My need, no, my desperation to find out something, anything, about what had happened to Luna had brought me out here. But now that we were here something didn't feel right. I sucked in a breath, anxious about walking into a house that belonged to someone else. To my employer no less.

We were not greeted by the musty smell I was expecting when Lucas pushed open the wooden door. We walked through the entrance hall and into a broad room with fireplaces at either end. The sliver of moon barely illuminated half the interior, but Lucas had a special flashlight that seemed to give off no light while at the same time allowing us to see in front of us. Everything was neat and tidy in this room, and sheets were piled in small heaps next to most of the dated furniture, although a few pieces were still covered.

"Someone's been staying here," I whispered to him. "They could be back any minute. Maybe we should go."

He stopped and passed me a pair of gloves, and I followed him into what turned out to be the kitchen. He opened the fridge, which contained a fresh carton of milk, several bottles of wine, and some beers. There was a bag of ground coffee sitting next to the coffee machine. Someone was definitely living here.

"We need to leave, Lucas," I said, but he had bent down and was looking at a small door with a lock on it, presumably leading to a basement. I tiptoed over to a window with a view onto the road. Nothing.

Lucas went upstairs, and I caught up with him, although I had to walk up one step at a time to accommodate my knee. There were three rooms off a narrow hallway, and the beds were made up. In the largest bedroom a king-sized bed that took up most of the room was covered by a knitted quilt that seemed to have the fresh imprint of a body on top.

Just then, car lights illuminated one of the walls, bouncing up to the ceiling and down, and along what seemed like the length of the house. He switched off his special flashlight and we both instinctively crouched, reaching for each other's hand. My knee complained and I squeezed Lucas's fingers. We heard the sound of a vehicle on the dirt road grow louder, closer, and then slow down. After a slight pause it drove on. Still, we waited, listening in the dark.

"It's okay," Lucas said, and he was right. We got our bearings and walked out. He locked the door again, and placed the key under the mat that he shifted back into its original position. I waited as he walked around the house one more time. When he bent down at the last window, I saw the handle of a gun peeking out of the waist of his pants at the small of his back. I wondered if he ever had to use it.

"Please give me your gloves," he said, and I peeled them off and handed them to him as we walked down the driveway. He walked slowly, sweeping the light in front of him and to the side. "Hold this, would you," he asked, handing the flashlight to me without looking. "Point it there." I could see nothing but he took about ten photos. When we reached the road at the end of the driveway I said, "I have no idea where the car is."

He reached again for my hand and led me to it without a word.

"Thanks," Lucas said, when he dropped me off at my house, right in front this time. "I appreciate your accompanying me. It's always best to go in pairs. That's why cops have partners. Although I would've preferred . . ."

"If I weren't a civilian, I know," I said. "And I would've preferred if we'd found out something about Luna. Do you think someone from the Wilton family could be living out there?"

"That's not an outlandish theory. The property does belong to them."

I rolled my eyes. "Do you think Luna was taken there?"

"No idea."

"But you think maybe she's been there?"

"Genevieve, I realize you are more than concerned about your friend, but I'm not a knight in shining armor who swoops in with all the answers. I'm collecting evidence in an attempt to connect the dots."

"Well, while you're collecting and connecting my friend is tied up somewhere, in trouble, maybe dead. And the only reason I wanted to go with you is because I thought it might help me find her." He started to say something but I turned and limped as quickly as I could to the front door.

CHAPTER TWENTY-SIX

It was difficult to find a comfortable sleeping position, but I finally fell asleep and didn't wake up until eleven. My knee felt much better, and was only slightly swollen, so I rode my bike to the library slowly, using only my good leg to push down on its pedal. Hot, forceful wind blew back my hair, seeming to scramble my thoughts. Lack of sleep didn't help. When I passed Daniela's office she called out to me, asking if I wanted to have lunch. Mitch and Susan were nowhere to be seen. I even wondered for a second about Luna, and then remembered. I forced a smile at Daniela and said I'd love to join her. Soon I was sitting across from her, slurping hot noodles I wished were cold.

"Are you . . . thinking about Luna?" Daniela asked.

I said nothing, but just nodded, squelching down anxious tears that were lying in wait beneath the surface, ready to spill over and fill up the room. But at the same time, I was glad she asked about Luna, as I'd started to worry I was the only one still thinking about her, wondering what had happened to her, thinking hoping wishing that she was alive and okay.

Late in the afternoon as I was slowly walking my bike home, my phone buzzed. It was Lucas.

"Can you talk?" he asked. "Not over the phone. Could we meet out at the trailhead?"

"Just left work. I'm exhausted and there's no way I can bike out to the state park. Feel free to come to my rental. I'm almost home."

Fifteen minutes later he was standing in my front hall.

"I drove back to the lake house early this morning. Took some photos." He passed his iPhone to me. "Do you know this woman?"

I spread my thumb and forefinger across the tiny image. "Yes! That's her! The Wiltons' helper. She's the one who's been dropping off those threatening notes outside my door."

"So, she works for the Wiltons."

"She used to. But Barbara told me she left, without notice."

"Her name?"

"Stacy."

"Last name?"

I shrugged.

"Did she know Luna? Were they friends?" he asked.

"Not that I'm aware of."

Mason called me in the evening and asked if he could come over.

"Sorry I've been kind of incommunicado the past couple days," he said, and gave me a hug once he was inside the cottage. "I know I've said that before."

"No worries," I said, not meaning it.

"How are you doing? Minus the knee. Ouch. You're icing it every twenty minutes, right? I can get you prescription ibuprofen, if you want."

I clasped my hands together. "Thanks. But I'm fine. Cecile talked to Luna."

"That's great, Genevieve! You see, you didn't have anything to worry about. Where is she?"

"Not on the earthly plane. Or the phone. It was a psychic chat."

He huffed. "So, no actual Luna. You must be going out of your mind. You need a distraction."

He stepped over to me, wrapped his arms around me, and pulled me to his chest. Everything about Mason soothed me—his height, his warm chest against me, his cedary smell. I took in a deep breath and then let it out.

He pulled back, still holding me at arm's length, a big smile on his face. "Let's do something together, for a whole day," he said. "Saturday?"

"Great!" I said. "But no hiking. That would be too hard on my knee."

"I'll figure it out," he said. "But clear your calendar for the entire day."

Saturday at 9:00 A.M. he was at my door, wearing dark blue jeans and a button-down T-shirt in a lighter-colored denim than his jeans. He had a big pack on his back. He looked like a young Paul Newman.

"Where are we going?" I asked. "Am I dressed appropriately?" I had on a light cotton green sundress that fell down to my calves and covered up the knee brace I was wearing.

"You look fabulous! We're just going to the farmer's market, it's not far. And solidly in my wheelhouse, having grown up on a farm. Give me just a sec, though. I need to put something in your freezer." I waved him inside and toward the kitchen. Then he helped me into his pickup truck and we drove over, parking in an open field.

The farmer's market was held twice a week, on the edge of town, in a large field under rows of tents.

I followed Mason around as he filled up his backpack with colorful local produce and cheese and a bottle of wine. By then, it was starting to get stiflingly hot. Mason found me a seat in the shade where I sat with my knee slightly elevated while waiting for him to return with the car. We drove around with the air-conditioning on full blast through several towns until he pulled into a restaurant parking lot. There was a large deck next to a river and we sat outside. The trees above us had tiny white flowers that floated down around us and into our food. "We don't charge extra for those," said the server, who addressed all her comments to Mason.

After lunch we drove to another little town and shared a cup of ice cream. We'd been listening to a special playlist that Mason had curated for me, a mix of contemporary country and romantic jazz. As we pulled into my driveway he brushed my hair away from my face and whispered in my ear, "I hope you're having a nice day, Genevieve."

Back at my rental, Mason wouldn't let me help him cook dinner, insisting that I sit up on my bed with my knee iced and elevated, so I did, the air conditioner moaning and struggling to cool down that room. I must have fallen asleep because he woke me by saying my name softly, and gently shaking me. He helped me down the stairs. "Your knee okay?" he checked—and then I closed my eyes at his request as he led me by the hand into the dining room.

"Okay to open your eyes," he said.

The table was set with linens he must have found in one of the closets, the mismatched dishes from the shelves, and some tableware I hadn't yet unearthed. There was a small vase of flowers that looked like the flowers growing in the Baileys' garden.

"Not bad for a farm boy," he said, pulling out a chair for me. "Now you sit down." He had a fresh pack of crushed ice for my knee.

He went into the kitchen and came back with two plates, each one with ravioli sitting on a bed of the market vegetables and herbs and cheese.

"You didn't see me buy this olive oil, did you," he asked, and my eyes widened as he poured it over the food. When he uncorked the bottle of wine he said, "My professor said this is the best wine produced in the state of New York. I put it in the freezer while you were resting. I hope it's cold enough."

"Did you make this ravioli? From scratch?" I asked, incredulous.

"Nah, it was frozen. I tucked it inside your freezer when I came by this morning."

"I'm impressed anyway," I said, after he had raised his glass and toasted "to us."

As we ate we talked about the day, just like a couple who'd been married for years. After he took the plates away he pulled a small container of ice cream from the freezer, scooped three balls into two bowls, and poured warmed-up chocolate over each serving, topped with fresh strawberries from the market.

"I could get addicted to this," I said, sitting back in my chair.

He leaned over and took both of my hands in his, his face flushed. "I'm addicted to *you*, Genevieve. Even when we aren't together, you're all I think about." Tiny hairs shot up along the back of my neck. "Leave the dishes," he said, as he pulled me up and led me to the couch, somehow bringing both of our wineglasses with him. He took out his phone and turned on some Brazilian jazz. "Turn your back to me," he said.

We rearranged ourselves, each taking a sip of wine along the way.

"Close your eyes," he whispered, and then began to massage my neck and shoulders, using only half of his strength.

"This is even better than dessert," I sighed.

"No talking," he said.

After a few minutes, I opened my eyes and turned to face him. We both leaned toward each other at the same time. His lips were gentle against mine, at first. After a few minutes we stood up, our hands moving and pulling, our bodies together and apart, stopping, holding, grabbing, knocking against each other as he helped me climb back up to the bedroom.

"I want you," he breathed, almost soundlessly. He lifted my shirt and undressed me slowly, caressing me as he did, as I undressed him. He closed his eyes, and I saw the veins in his neck pulsating. I straddled him, leaning to one side so as not to put too much pressure on my hurt knee, and began kissing his lips, his chin, his neck, quickly, hurried on by my desire. He ran his tongue over my breasts, as he gripped my waist. I reached over to my nightstand drawer, found a condom, and passed it to him. I expected him to be hesitant, new as we were to each other's bodies, but he kissed me deeper and deeper, and then he drew back, his expression half-wild as I straddled him again, gently. He let out a sigh as I pushed him inside me.

When it was over, I lay my head on his chest. I heard my phone buzzing, but I didn't know where I'd left it. I willed it to stop and fell asleep.

CHAPTER TWENTY-SEVEN

Early the next morning, Mason said he had rounds to attend at the hospital.

"Thanks for a wonderful night," I said.

"No," he said, taking both of my hands, and pulling me close to him. "Thank you."

He kissed me, then started to put on his clothes, then came back and kissed me again. He pulled back and said with a smile, "I have a condom, too." After about half an hour, he was fully dressed.

"I'll call you later," he said, as he walked downstairs.

"And thanks for the delicious meal." I followed him, wearing only a terry cloth robe. At the front door he pulled me in, slipping his hands under my robe and whispering, in a playful voice, "There'll be plenty of time . . . for seconds. Thirds."

I hobbled into the kitchen and saw that he'd done the dishes. How could I have slept through that? I started to make some coffee and then pulled my phone out of my pocket. It had been Lucas who'd called last night. I called him back.

"Do you have time to meet? It's important," he said, after answering on the first ring.

I barely had time to get dressed and ice my knee before he was knocking on the front door.

"I ran some intel on Stacy," he said, as we stood there with the door open. "She's twenty-five, has a record. Petty theft and drug possession. Moved here from Western New York, near Troy. Her ex-husband works in construction. She's filed two abuse reports against him. She's worked cleaning jobs mostly, but hasn't declared any income for the past two years. I was just about to drive out there to interview her when you called."

"Interview her? At the lake house? Is that a good idea? What if someone else is there? Like, the people who have Luna? Who knows you're going out there? Will you be safe?"

"Genevieve. I appreciate your concern. But this is not my first rodeo."

"Just out of curiosity, how many rodeos are we talking about?" I asked.

"Are you asking how long I've been in the business?"

"Yeah."

His eyes darted up and to the right, and then back at me. "Well over a decade. But I took a few years off to take care of my mom when she got sick."

"Oh. Is she okay now?"

"No," he said.

"I'm sorry."

"It's alright." He shuffled his weight from one foot back to the other. "Anyway, please let me know if you hear anything else."

"Do you have any news about Luna? I thought your partner or whoever saw her near the lake house. But it turned out to be Stacy. And how does that relate to Victoria? Or Luna?"

"It does, but I can't say how, not just yet." He had a canvas bag over his shoulder and he reached inside and pulled out something grey that looked like an old-fashioned Nokia my mom owned in the aughts. "That's why I asked to see you. This is a burner phone. We need to talk on this, not your iPhone. It can't be traced."

He handed the phone to me. It was heavy. "Thanks," I said. "I guess. Wish it weren't quite so . . . conspicuous."

"It's not a fashion statement. Hang on to it and be careful. Don't let it out of your sight. Or your bag. Don't let anyone else see it. Check it often. It's on silent and doesn't vibrate. And don't forget to charge it." He passed me an equally bulky charger.

"Got it," I said. "But what about Luna. What does Stacy at the lake house have to do with Luna? Is anyone making any attempt to find her?"

He cleared his throat. "I'm sorry, Genevieve, but my local contacts are saying there's no longer any active investigation. Only that Luna's a missing person."

"But . . . what about Trish Baranski's body? We both know she was murdered. And the threats to me and Cecile? And Ree—what's her name. The first missing girl. Rowena! That's too many missing or dead or threatened women to be a coincidence."

"They're saying the Baranski case, while gruesome, is most likely DV. Her former boyfriend is in custody."

"DV?"

"Domestic violence."

"How about the others? What are the police doing, exactly?"

"Look, right now, I'm your best shot at finding Luna."

"Why is that not reassuring?" I asked.

"You'll have to trust me here, Genevieve. And believe me when I say if you find out anything about Victoria, it'll help our common cause."

CHAPTER TWENTY-EIGHT

Two hours later I was sitting in my kitchen with my bad leg iced and propped up with pillows on a second chair, slightly hungover from the bottle of wine Mason and I had consumed. I drank two glasses of water and stared out the window. Lucas's burner phone was on the table, and I had my regular phone in my hand, willing messages to come through on both screens. I sat on the couch, and soon it started to rain. The gentle drumming on the roof lulled me to sleep for a few minutes, and then my normal phone buzzed. I picked it up and Mason's name lit up the screen. I smiled.

THANK YOU. I haven't had that much fun in . . . maybe ever? How are you?

I had a great time! More soon?

Absolutely. Don't stress. And don't work too hard.

Thoughts of Mason and remembering the feeling of his skin against mine sent pleasing shockwaves all over my body at random times throughout Sunday. Then early Monday he texted me again, explaining that he had to spend the next couple of nights at the hospital.

Lucas also texted me Monday morning. The first text on the clunky grey phone. *New info re: VW?*

Negative, I replied.

My knee was much better, so I didn't think about it when I rode to work. Instead, I thought about Victoria, and those notes I'd found that her grandmother had left for her inside various boxes. I had collected them, and Luna had ordered them chronologically.

I took them up to Daniela's office, and she nodded her head as she read through the notes.

I dragged my chair closer to Daniela. "They're from Lily to her granddaughter, Victoria, right? When she worked here?"

"Yes. That's correct."

"Why would Lily Wilton have left notes for Victoria in the archive, when they were both alive? Didn't they see each other often? At least in the summer when she was working here?"

"Her grandparents wanted a family historian." Daniela cleared her throat. "At some point, the generations became estranged. Maybe as a peace offering, Lily and George hired Victoria to work on the family archive. It was the summer she . . ."

"Died," I finished her sentence.

"Victoria was a strong person," said Daniela. "Caring. With convictions, integrity. But troubled. I shouldn't be saying all this. But I know . . ."

Someone knocked and Mitch walked in and tapped his watch. "Excuse me, Genevieve," Daniela said. "Let's talk another time."

I worked late and biked to the spa when the sun had gone down and it started to cool off. Cecile was leaving as I arrived but when she saw me she invited me back in. "I have some iced herbal tea, if you're interested."

"Witch's brew?" I asked, only half joking.

"Well, I'm a witch, and I made it," she said.

"Any news on Luna and the investigation?"

"One of the investigators came by in person to say they were following a new lead."

"Oh . . . that's interesting." But Lucas had said there was no investigation. Did that mean the police had discovered something and not shared it with him?

"What are you thinking about just now?" she asked. "You were literally lost in thought."

"I was thinking about Victoria Wilton. Did you know her? Her name has come up a number of times at the library, and in the Wilton papers. She died so young."

"Only the good die young," said Cecile, lifting her head. "And in Victoria's case . . ." Cecile glanced down and then back up at me. "Victoria . . . was a special soul. I loved her like a little sister. Like most privileged women, however, she didn't understand that there are always predators lying in wait, ready to take advantage, to hurt her. I tried to teach her the difference between trusting the universe and trusting her intuition. I tried to make her believe in herself. But in the end, I couldn't save her."

"I thought she drowned in a tragic accident?"

"Yes, it was tragic. 'Accident.'" She used her fingers to put quotes around the word. "I'm not so sure. Despite her privilege, Victoria was born into a life of difficulty. I met her when I taught yoga in town before I had the spa. After class one day, she confided in me, told me she hated her alcoholic parents who paraded her around as the favorite child. She was ashamed of what her dad and grandfather did. The big pharma thing. Kids at school had always bullied her. They were envious, of course, not only of her family's wealth but of her intelligence. Her dignity. She was a lot like you. That's one of the reasons I feel so protective of you."

"I wish I had met her."

"You would've been fast friends. I tried to teach her how to step into her own power."

"Like you teach undergrads in your coven. I mean"—I blinked my eyes shut, then opened them—"group," I said.

Cecile continued. "Victoria was an important part of my group. Her death was . . . a big loss. If only . . . if only I'd found her sooner."

We sat quietly for a few minutes, and then I tiptoed out.

CHAPTER TWENTY-NINE

At the end of the work day, Susan came downstairs, which was unusual for her. "I brought brownies a day early," she said. "Would you like one?" She passed the red tin to me.

"Always," I said, prying the cover off.

"I know you're upset about Luna," she said. "I am, too. We all are."

"Yes," I said. "I just wish I could do something."

She sighed. "I know how close you two were."

"You've lived in Wilton for a long time," I said. "You're a human cache of institutional memory here. Does it seem like a lot of bad things have happened to the Wiltons? Are happening right now, all at once?"

She pulled back. "What do you mean?"

"Daniela told me that Victoria Wilton was estranged from her grandparents. I know you knew Lily. What was going on there? And then she . . . Was it about the curse?"

"It's about the money. It's always about the money." She had lowered her voice and glanced at the stairs leading up out of the basement.

Susan switched off the overhead lights, so we were sitting in partial darkness. She arched her eyebrows. "The Wiltons are the law of the land in Wilton Springs," she said in a quiet voice. "Have been for a long time."

"How long?"

"In addition to their businesses, they were embedded in local government. They got away with all sorts of stuff. People turn a blind eye. Including law enforcement."

"What did they get away with doing?"

"Before that big corporation bought them out, the Wiltons paid people to be test subjects for experimental medications."

"As in, using the drugs on them after the drugs had been tested on animals?"

"There were official animal trials," she said, emphasizing the word *official*. "But most drugs were fast-tracked from the lab directly to the volunteers, who signed a statement waiving their rights in exchange for financial renumeration. A special program. Anyway, a private company can pretty much do what they want."

"I've never read or heard about anything like this."

"The people who agreed to be test subjects were promised a lifetime of financial security, but they had to be compliant and quiet. If they complained about side effects, or about the program itself, or even mentioned to anyone else that they were part of it, the cash dried up."

"Sounds like you know a lot about this program."

She cleared her throat. "My younger brother was a volunteer—he had gastritis. He'd been a wild child, racked up a lot of debt. The Wiltons offered to take care of him if he agreed to be a guinea pig. Six months after he started on the meds, he died of a heart attack. Thirty-five years old. I tried, and failed, to get anyone to investigate. They buried it."

"That's terrible, Susan. I'm so sorry. Did they do an autopsy?"

"My mother was still alive then. I didn't want her to know anything about it. And apparently, my brother had officially requested his body be donated to science, so even if . . ." She took a deep breath. "Anyway," she said, and stood up. She switched the lights back on. "Time to go home. Try to keep your hopes up about Luna. Without hope we have nothing."

I was still limping a bit, which made me feel somewhat vulnerable as I hurried to my bike, looking around to see if anyone might be following me. I fumbled while unlocking it and rode home as quickly as I could, pumping with my good knee. I knew the Wiltons were a powerful family. They had inhumanely used human volunteers for their drug trials. Was that the reason Victoria Wilton had been estranged from her grandparents? Had Barbara known about this program? What about the goats she fed and took care of?

I did some Googling, and found out that private companies still conducted clinical trials on volunteers in exchange for compensation. This was different from government-sanctioned drug testing, which had occurred at a shockingly high rate in the twentieth century, even after the Nuremberg trials had supposedly put an end to the governmental practice. There had been many examples of drug and disease testing on prisoners. The most famous case was the so-called Tuskegee experiment, when American public health workers had tested syphilis drugs on a large group of Black men in Alabama without their knowledge or consent starting in 1932. Although volunteering for drug testing with a private company was technically consensual, there were obviously a lot of ethical concerns.

Was this something the Wiltons were still doing? Was I crossing some ethical boundary by working for the family?

Lucas responded to my repeated texts on the burner phone with two words: *sorry busy.* The next day, Friday, I forgot to bring the big phone to the library. When I got home I saw that he'd called three times. I tried him back. No answer. Then later that evening he texted again. Just an address.

On my bike I followed Google Maps to a small street across from the old train tracks, on the outskirts of town. My knee always felt worse at the end of the day, so it took me a while to get there. I walked into a sports bar, empty except for Lucas sitting at the counter, watching a baseball game.

"I didn't know this place existed," I said, maneuvering onto the bar seat next to his.

"That's why I picked it."

"I'm glad you weren't worried about me riding my bike out here in the dark with my bad knee."

"You're very resourceful. I knew you'd make it unscathed."

I ordered a vodka tonic.

"How *is* the knee? All that biking back and forth to work must be great rehab."

"I'll live," I said. "But I may send you my physical therapy bill."

He tipped back the last inch of seltzer in his glass and asked for a refill, with lime, which the bartender was out of. Lucas peeled a loose strip of paper off his coaster and smoothed it down.

"What's the point of the spy phone if you never answer it?"

"Please don't call it that. And I always pick up."

"I called and texted you four or five times yesterday."

As soon as the bartender was out of earshot, Lucas said, "You were right, it was Stacy Fox I photographed at the lake house."

"And?"

"She's not working for the Wilton family anymore, you were also right about that."

I crossed my hands in my lap. "What's she doing at the Wilton lake house?"

"Seems like she's there socially."

"Socially?"

"She's a guest of Gabe Wilton."

I took a gulp of my vodka tonic. "She told you that?"

"She didn't want to talk to me. I only found out about Gabe when I mentioned that Mr. and Mrs. Wilton would be interested to know that she was staying there illegally."

"Did you ask her about Luna?"

"Yes, that's the first thing I asked her. She said she knew nothing, but I'm pretty sure she was lying."

I leaned closer. "Do you think she might lead you to Luna?"

"I'm a team of one, Genevieve. Well, two, counting you. Have *you* heard anything else?"

I stood up and put all my weight on my good knee. "I talked to Cecile, who knew Victoria, and had tried to protect her. From her parents. Said they were alcoholics, which I can attest to. Victoria was ashamed of her family's involvement in the big pharma thing. She was bullied at school."

Lucas had pulled out a notebook and was writing notes. When he was finished, he said, "Why did you try to call and text me yesterday?"

"In boxes of old documents I'm archiving, I keep finding these odd notes that turned out to be from Lily Wilton to Victoria, who worked for a summer in the family archive. But then Victoria died. And then Lily died."

"Do you think the notes would help me with the case?"

"That's what I was thinking yesterday, but now I'm not so sure."

"What about Gabe?" he asked. "I've been keeping my eyes open but haven't seen him around the last few days."

"Don't know," I said. "But the other reason I wanted to reach out is that one of the librarians told me about a hush-hush program the Wiltons were using—maybe still are using—involving human volunteers for their experimental drugs. Apparently, her brother died in one of the so-called trials."

"Hmm," he said. "Do you think Victoria was involved?"

"The program was run by the Wiltons," I said. "But I can't imagine she was involved in any way with drug testing. She was so young, and sheltered, but a bit of a rebel. If anything, they would've hidden it from her."

"Do you think she found out about it, and that's how, or why, she died? She might've been collecting information to expose them?"

"Do you really think they might have wanted to kill their own daughter?"

Instead of answering me, he looked at his phone. "I have to go," he said. "We shouldn't leave at the same time. You and your knee okay on your bike?"

"Was that a text about Luna? Is that why you have to leave? Cecile said yesterday that one of the investigators told her there was a new lead. Or is it about Victoria?"

"Both," he said. "The Luna case is very much alive again, contrary to what I told you the other day."

"That's good news. Any information on who sent us the threats? Are Cecile and I in danger?"

"I can tell you with certainty that you are 100 percent not in danger at the moment, but you should keep acting as if you are. Lay low. Go to work and act normal. Don't talk to anybody."

"Thanks for reassuring me," I said.

At home twenty-five minutes later, I texted Mason. Images of him, of us, in bed together, sometimes crowded out the image of Luna tied up that had been sent to Cecile.

Wanna come over?

He hearted it immediately, and I changed into a red lace camisole, and put a pack of ice on my knee. An hour later he rang the bell and stumbled through the front door. His clothes reeked of beer.

"I've been out with friends," he said, and leaned in to give me a smelly hug.

"Are you drunk?" I asked.

"One of my buddies ordered a round of tequila shots, and then each of us had to get the next round," he said. "We party extra hard on the weekends. Surgeons are the worst."

"We can just Netflix and chill." Forcing myself to smile, I brought him a can of ginger ale and a bowl of saltines. We made out on the couch, but I could tell he was too far gone for sex.

"I hate that you're seeing me like this," he said.

I shrugged. "We all have our moments."

"I should go home." He stood up to leave. My phone started buzzing. I ignored it, but it continued. Whoever was calling could leave a message.

"I need to pee," Mason said. When he was in the bathroom, I listened to my voicemail.

"Genevieve, it's Luna. I need your help. Please pick up."

I called back, but it went straight to voicemail. I called again and again. Four times. Five times.

"Luna!" I said to Mason when he walked back into the room. "That was a call from Luna! She left me a message!"

"What?" He fell onto the couch and closed his eyes.

"Now I can't reach her." I tried the number again, and again. After another six calls, a weak voice answered.

"Help me, Genevieve." Her tiny voice came out slowly, between breaths. "He hurt me. In his house. Near the lake."

"Who hurt you?"

"Gabe. Gabe Wilton," she whispered.

"I'm calling 911. I love you!" I said. "Stay strong!" The line went dead.

"Luna's in trouble!" I said to Mason. "I can't believe this, but Gabe Wilton kidnapped her."

"What?" said Mason, his eyes popping open. Then he sat up. "Call 911!" he said.

I'd already dialed, and someone was asking, "What's your emergency and location?"

"The Wilton house on Lake Charles," I said. "I'm not sure what the house number is. A woman named Luna Collins is there. She's been kidnapped . . . She just called me . . . She's in danger! She's on your missing persons list! My name is Genevieve Tompkins. Please send someone out there right away!" Then I gave them my address and phone number, and Luna's phone number. When I hung up, Mason was next to me, his hand on my shoulder.

I had to call Lucas, but wanted Mason to leave first. I turned to him. "You should go. I'm fine, really. I need to deal with this."

"Are you sure? It sounds intense."

"Yes, I'm sure. And you need to take it easy."

"I'm so sorry but I'm not sure I'd be super helpful to you at the moment anyway. You're right. I should go home, hydrate, and sleep it off."

"Fuck fuck fuck. I can't believe this is happening," I said, as if I hadn't heard him. Then my head snapped up. "You can't drive drunk. Go sleep in the bedroom. I'm going to keep calling Luna."

"No, I'm leaving," he said, staggering to the door and burping, as if he were trying to stop himself from throwing up. I pulled a sweatshirt over my lace camisole. I went into my bedroom, and called Lucas on the burner phone. He didn't answer, so I texted him. Then I called Luna again, three times in a row, but the calls went straight to voicemail.

Lucas texted back. *Driving to lake. Bad connection.*

I changed out of my camisole into a sweatshirt and waited two hours, then four, and then five. I must have fallen asleep on the couch because when I woke up to a sharp knock on my door it was after 3:00 A.M. I looked at the burner phone. Two minutes earlier Lucas had texted, *I'm outside your front door. Let me in please.* I opened the door to see Lucas standing there, his face smeared with big, black smudges. The smell of smoke pushed at me. I grabbed his hand and pulled him inside the house and could see his eyes were puffy and bloodshot. He had a dirty white handkerchief in his hand and kept wiping it across his brow. Soon, it turned black. He was shaking his head. "Sorry for showing up like this but I didn't want to tell you over the phone."

"What happened?"

"Let's sit down."

I went over to the couch and sat down but he just stood there. "Jeez, I don't want to get soot all over your couch."

"That's the least of my worries," I said, but when he just stood there I went into the kitchen, grabbed two dish towels, and spread them out on the couch. We sat down next to each other. He sat down and then I sat down next to him. "So, you were in a fire. What happened, Lucas?"

"The Wilton lake house . . . burned down."

I sucked in my breath. "Luna's dead?"

"No, no, she's okay. She got out."

"Oh, thank goodness."

"The police pulled three bodies out of the house. Dead bodies."

"What? Who?"

"My confidential sources say the first two were Rowena Kelly, an Uber driver who'd gone missing months before, and Stacy Fox."

"And the third?"

"The third is Gabriel Wilton."

PART III

CHAPTER THIRTY

I gave Lucas two glasses of water, which he downed eagerly.

"Want to take a shower?" I asked. "You can borrow like, a big T-shirt, and I don't know, a beach towel?"

"No, no," he said. "Appreciate the offer, but I need to go, and you need to sleep."

"I doubt I'll be able to sleep, Lucas."

"Try. I'll try, too. The next few days are going to be busy. For both of us."

After he left I lay on top of the bedspread without getting under the covers, holding my phone and staring up at the ceiling, an iced gel pack on my knee. I had received two texts from Mason.

Worried 'bout you.

YOU OKAY?

Presumably he was still sleeping the sleep of the inebriated so I texted back.

I'm fine. Talk later.

I called Luna again and again. And texted her over and over. In the middle of one text I dropped off to sleep, but woke up every few minutes, my heart racing, the smell of smoke still in my nose. Maybe she'd left her phone in the cabin?

The first call I received the next morning was from the police, asking me to come down to the station as soon as possible. They wouldn't tell me anything about Luna over the phone. I showered, dressed, wrapped my knee, and rode my bike there.

Officer Jackson showed me into a small office where he handed me a cup of light-colored coffee as I sat down. Detective Saunders walked in and shook my hand, then sat down facing me.

"Is Luna okay?" I asked, my voice rising and breaking off at the end.

"She will be, Ms. Tompkins," said Detective Saunders. "Thank you for calling 911. You saved her life." She turned to the other police officer. "Jackson?"

He cleared his throat. "Ms. Tompkins, we need to know, and this is just pro forma, where you were after you left work yesterday."

"I went home and I . . . Wait, are you questioning me as a possible suspect? May I remind you that I do not own a car? And I have a busted knee."

"He's in training," said Saunders. "Please just answer his questions. It won't take long."

I sat there, fuming. "After work, I went home. I rode my bike to a sports bar near the old train tracks east of town." Apparently, Lucas hadn't told them about meeting me there. Maybe they weren't supposed to know?

"And then?" Jackson asked.

"An hour later I was back home, and a friend came over. My boyfriend. While he was there Luna called me. I didn't answer at first, but then I listened to her message and called her back. I'm sure you can find the phone records between us. Anything else?" I asked, in as calm a tone as I could muster. They knew I'd been threatened, too. Probably just covering their own asses.

"No, thank you for your cooperation. That's it for today," Jackson said.

"Where is she? Can I please go see my friend?"

"They're keeping her in the hospital," Saunders said. "She's . . . They're taking some tests. No one is allowed to see her right now. I can't give you more details, although I will say she is doing remarkably well, considering what happened to her."

"Has her family been notified?"

"That's privileged information," said Jackson.

I rolled my eyes. Saunders took a sip from her coffee mug, stamped with the Wilton Springs Police Department logo, then said, "I just want to warn you, Ms. Tompkins, that when you do see Luna Collins, you might be a little shocked. Her appearance is somewhat . . . skeletal. I'm sure she'll be grateful for your support. And if you'd like, we offer free counseling services."

I leaned forward in my chair. "I'm okay. I'll be okay."

"Is there anything else you can tell us about Gabe Wilton, Luna Collins, Rowena Kelly, or Stacy Fox that may be able to help our investigation?" asked Saunders.

"I can't think of anything I haven't said already," I said. "But I'm . . ." A little tear slid down my cheek and we both stood up at once.

"If you remember anything," she said, "no matter however trivial it may seem to you, please reach out. You have our contact information."

At home I passed out on the couch for a few hours, then ate a yogurt, then went back to sleep. I woke up the next morning at 6:30 to my phone buzzing. I answered on the first ring. It was Luna!

"Hey, Gen. I've just. Been. Released. From the. Hospital." Her words came out slowly, one or two at a time, between huffs.

"So great to hear your voice! I can pick you up! I'll call a taxi right now. Be there within half an hour."

"Cecile. Took me. Home. In her car."

"Oh, that's great. How are you feeling?"

"You saved. My life. I don't. Know how. To. Thank you."

"Don't talk too much," I said. "Get some sleep. I'll come by with lunch. Or dinner. Or both."

"Resting. At home. Maybe tomorrow. I'll come to you. They said I need to walk a little. Move around."

The next day, which was a Sunday, I put together a "welcome home" afternoon for Luna, decorating my living room and kitchen with purple balloons (purple was her favorite color) and streamers, and filled a basket with gourmet food from one of the specialty grocers on Main Street, along with Luna's favorite lunch, a fresh baguette and brie.

As she walked through the door, she smiled, leaning on her cane. I thought she would still smell like smoke but she didn't. One of the benefits of an overnight at the hospital. But her bones seemed to jut out from under her skin. Her face and the whites of her eyes were yellowish, and her cheekbones were so prominent they looked sharp. She was very pale.

I went over to her with my arms out, ready to deliver a delicate hug. "I'm going to cry with happiness," she said, but stiffened in pain when my body met hers. I stepped back.

"I cannot believe Gabe kidnapped you. And kept you at the lake house! I was out there! You were in the basement! I could've saved you then. I feel horrible."

"What! When?"

"It's a long story," I said. "I'll tell you when you're feeling better."

I led her over to the couch and helped her sit down. She started crying, only a little at first, but then her whole body began convulsing in big sobs. I put my hand on her back.

After her sobs slowed, and then subsided, she said, "I feel so lucky. To be alive. I'd almost given up hope." She looked around her at all the balloons and streamers and the food basket and put her face in her hands.

I pulled out the bread and brie. "Ready for lunch?"

"I'm not hungry right now," she said, sitting up. "But I am thirsty."

I brought her a glass of water, and when she'd finished drinking it, I said, "I'll do whatever I can to help get you healthy and strong again. We've been so worried."

"We?"

"The staff at the library. And Cecile, of course."

She started coughing, so I brought her another glass of water, which she drank slowly. "I kept thinking about how pissed Cecile would be when I didn't show up to teach yoga. All I could think about was getting out so I could tell her it wasn't my fault." She lay one of her cold hands on top of one of mine. "And I thought about you, and our chats. That you're my friend and you cared about me." Tears were pouring down her face. I brought her a box of tissues.

"We don't have to talk about any of it," I said. "Not ever, if you don't want to. Why don't you have a bite to eat, drink some wine, and we can chat about nonsense?"

She sat up straight, and winced as she arched her back. "It might help to talk."

I turned my hand over and squeezed hers. "I'm here," I said.

Her voice broke as she began to speak. "Gabe was. A monster. That day, after I saw you, he called. Said he'd been thinking about me. That he missed me." She swallowed with some effort. "I didn't want to tell you. I was embarrassed. Because I'd warned you off him. He said he was preparing a surprise. For me, that weekend. 'Leave your stuff at home,' he said. 'Bring hiking shoes.' I canceled work shifts. I met him in our usual spot. Just outside town. He drove us to this gorgeous wooden lodge."

She stopped for a few seconds and looked out the window before continuing. "He prepped this incredible dinner. Opened a bottle of pricey wine. Said he'd fallen for me, that he realized he was. In love for the first time." She stopped again, and looked down at the floor. "He took me upstairs. To his bedroom. We had sex. It was like a beautiful dream. Until I woke up in some dark space with no windows."

"Holy shit," I said.

"I haven't even gotten to . . . the worst part yet."

"Is it too much? We can save the rest for next time—"

"No. I need to tell you. You're one of my closest friends."

"I'm here. I'm listening, Luna." I had to be strong for her, I told myself, and kept my face composed.

"I wasn't the only one there, Gen," she said. "There was another girl. A dead girl. In the basement. With me. 'Luna,' he said, when he came down the first time. 'Have you met your buddy? Rowena.' And then he started laughing. Said no one would hear my screams. Called me a slut."

I reached out and held her hand. "Oh, Luna."

"I can't believe I trusted him. He's a psychopath. A fucking psychopath."

"I'm so so sorry."

"He . . . kept me down there. Brought me food. Sometimes. Cans of beans with a pop top. I couldn't eat. Rowena's body smelled so bad. Even the thought of food made me retch. I had to force myself to drink water."

"Did he rape you?"

"We had sex just that one time," she said. "And it was consensual." She started crying again and I moved closer to her and she let me hold her in my arms for a while. Then she sat up and looked up as she said, "Sometimes I could hear stuff happening above me. One day I heard a lot of footsteps. Activity. Someone else had come to the house with him. But he didn't come down. Then a couple of days ago . . . he brought—" She started crying again, and gripped my shoulder fiercely.

I rocked her in my arms, saying, "It's okay, shhh . . . it's okay." Her teeth were chattering. "He brought in a garbage bag. Full of something. It looked heavy. He dropped it. Next to Rowena's body. A smell was coming from it, a smell I recognized."

"Stacy's body? No!"

"Blood . . . There was fresh blood seeping out of it. I could see it. Even across the room." She rocked herself for a minute and then said, "I didn't know it was Stacy. Until he told me."

"Jesus. How did you escape?"

"I unscrewed the only lightbulb. Hid underneath the stairs. Next time he came down, I whacked him on the head with a board. He passed out. Maybe he died. I don't know. Maybe I killed him." Her eyes were flashing but her face was white, even her lips were white.

"Let's finish this another time," I said. "You are paler than pale."

She was staring straight ahead, and as if she hadn't heard me, she said, "When I got to the top of the stairs there was a landline on the wall. I called your number, which I'd somehow remembered. As I ran out, I tripped on a rug or something. Knocked over a lit Coleman lantern. Saw this weird line of small flames moving away from me. Then crisscrossing the room. Gabe must have doused the lodge with gasoline. I don't know. I yanked the front door open by sheer force of will. Then heard a whoosh and was, like, lifted up. And out across the porch. Into some bushes. I looked back and the whole place was going up in flames. It happened so fast." She put her face in her hands.

"You're okay now, Luna," I said, shaking my head. "You're safe."

She hiccupped, and wiped her face with one of the tissues. She squeezed my hand.

We were both crying. "I missed you, Luna. I was so worried!"

She passed the tissue box to me. "I missed you, too, Gen."

"You need to rest and get strong again. I'll cook for you. I can come over every night. Or you can stay here. Whatever you need."

"I want to get back to work."

She hugged me again. It felt like embracing a little tree. I sat back in my chair, leaning into the plush pillow behind me. Luna clutched her stomach and closed her eyes. Almost immediately, she snapped them open.

She frowned. "Whenever I close my eyes, I picture those girls. I imagine the horrible ways they died."

"Don't think about them. Just don't."

Seconds later, she looked like she was starting to retch. She quickly stood up and rushed in the direction of my bathroom but then the retching stopped. She walked back to the couch and sat down. "How about some ginger ale?" I asked, softly stroking her back.

She pushed herself up again. "Sorry, but I'm feeling really sick . . . I'd better go home."

"Don't feel like you have to leave. You can just use my bathroom."

"S'okay," she said, thinly.

"Can I walk you back?"

"Cecile said she'd drive me. She's waiting outside."

I stayed home from work for three days, leaving the house only to deliver breakfast, lunch, and dinner to Luna. Sometimes she wanted me to stay, and other times she wanted to be alone. Whenever I wasn't shopping for, or cooking for, or talking to her, I was imagining the horror that she had gone through.

On the first day, two camera crews showed up at my house mid-morning. I didn't answer the door and hid out on the second floor. After an hour they left.

I hadn't reached out to Mason since the night Luna had called when he was there drunk. He had texted or called each day, leaving voicemails. Sometimes I'd text back, but I told him I couldn't talk and wasn't ready to see him.

After returning home from delivering dinner to Luna on the second day, a knock on the window startled me so much that I actually jumped. Mason was standing there, holding a huge bouquet of long-stemmed red roses.

"Sorry to scare you, gorgeous. I know you're going through a lot," he said, when I opened the door. "I'm not coming in. I just wanted you to have these. And I wanted to say . . . please don't shut me out."

"I'm not shutting you out, Mason, but I need to be there for Luna. And myself. That's all I can manage right now."

"Speaking as a soon-to-be doctor, I don't think you should be on your own right now. But I also think that you know what's best for you. Just remember, I want to take care of you." He kissed his fingers, reached out, and touched me on my forehead. Then he left.

A few minutes later I felt the phone in my pocket vibrating. I fished it out.

> *Hello, Genevieve. I was wondering if we could meet. I can't leave my house at the moment, due to media scrutiny, but please come over whenever you have a few minutes.*
> *Best, Barbara (Wilton)*

I let the message sit there for a few seconds without responding. I tried to imagine what was going on in Barbara's mind right now. I couldn't. Both of her children were dead. One had committed horrific crimes.

9 P.M. tonight? I wrote.

She replied within seconds. *Back patio.*

Outside, it had started raining steadily. I twisted my hair up under a baseball cap and pulled on my navy rain jacket. Ten or more people were standing outside the Wiltons' front gate, clustered together under a sky of black umbrellas and tented parkas, so I rode past them and pushed my bike into the trees, and snuck around to the back. I typed the code into the smaller gate there, the service entrance, and texted *through gate.*

She opened the door as I arrived. I pulled off my jacket, took off my shoes, and followed her to an enclosed porch that overlooked the backyard. We sat across from each other, five tea lights with flickering flames on the table between us. It was pretty dark in there, but I guessed that was the idea.

"You're limping slightly," she said. "Are you okay?"

"Hurt my knee. It's getting better. I'll be fine."

"You're sure?"

"Yes. Thanks." How had she summoned the empathy to ask about me and my silly knee injury?

"Lemonade?" she asked, pouring a glass for me without waiting for my answer.

"Barbara, I . . ."

She interrupted me. "I appreciate your concern. But I don't want to talk about my son."

"I understand." I let the conversation hang there.

"I want to talk about something else. You may have heard the Wilton family is cursed."

"Yes," I said. "I have heard that."

"Victoria certainly thought we were. Have you found anything she wrote in the archive? About that, or . . . anything else?"

I shook my head. "No."

"Victoria claimed she could clear our bad energy, reverse the curse. She said it would take a lot of effort because Wiltons had been involved in many evil deeds, over the centuries."

It started raining harder. It was very dark now, but flashes of lightning lit up the room every once in a while.

"Illegal alcohol," she said. "An aqueduct built with cheap labor that resulted in many deaths. The testing of innovative pharmaceuticals. None of this is a secret in Wilton Springs."

I wondered what she meant about the aqueduct. I hadn't read about those deaths. Her gaze shifted to the other side of the room. "She called it the 'Wilton blood money.' Or maybe that's how the bullies at school referred to it. But do you know how many lives have been saved because of patented drugs? Millions."

She reached under the tablecloth and fished out a little silver flask, opened it, and held it toward me. "Highly recommended on a rainy night," she said. "Or day."

"No thanks."

Barbara poured two glugs into her lemonade and then drank the glass down as the wind rattled the porch windows and the tea lights flickered in unison.

She sighed. "Jim's been . . . spending a lot of time in Manhattan. He's there now. It's . . . complicated." She waved her arm up and into the air. After a few minutes, she stood up and reached over to shake my hand. Hers was cold. "Thanks for coming over. I want you to know we appreciate what you're doing. And, Genevieve, we owe you an apology. Feel free to go through all the materials in the archives, nothing is off-limits. Invite other historians, too. Let it attract whatever attention it merits."

"Thank you," I said, not mentioning that I was already corresponding with others, and had spoken to Cecile's group.

As we walked to the back door she held on to my arm, as if for ballast, and said, "And if there's anything in there that Victoria may have written, or anything about what we, umm, discussed, let me know. Your work is important to us. It means a lot . . . meant a lot, to Victoria. Darwin will be contacting you soon. I want to double your salary. Jim won't agree, but it isn't his decision." She wagged her finger, a strange expression plastered on her face.

"That is more than generous of you," I said, unsure how to react.

"Keep me posted," she said, a bit loudly, her smile widening into a wide, slightly garish grin as I slipped on my wet jacket.

"I will," I said, slipping into my shoes by the back door.

I found my bike and started riding home, bundled up in my jacket, the cap not really shielding my face from the raindrops. Why had Barbara asked me to come over? To see if I had found any more info about Victoria in the archives, for starters. But Lucas would have told her that. Although maybe Lucas hadn't told her he was talking to me. It was too early to tell, but presumably Lucas hadn't connected Gabe's death or any of the other deaths with Victoria. He wasn't exactly figuring things out. And he obviously hadn't told the detectives he'd met me at the sports bar.

Barbara had given me permission to continue my research, permission that she and Jim must have known I didn't need, even though they tried to bluff me into covering it up. She chose to tell me this herself, without Jim, and she gave me a raise, without Jim's okay. Why? Because it was her last link to Victoria? Was she worried I'd leave, given what Gabe had done? I wasn't surprised she hadn't wanted to talk about Gabe. What could she say? Could anyone admit that their own child was a monster?

Maybe something else though. She'd said Jim hadn't been around a lot. I'd heard Mitch and Susan talking once about Jim's "women." And Russell Bailey had warned me when I first arrived—something about keeping daughters locked up when Junior was out on the town. And then Luna had said she wouldn't take a job up at Wilton Castle, no matter how good the pay was. And his inappropriate invitation to have a drink together and discuss my findings sometime. Did he go to New York City to cheat on his wife? Was that why Barbara drank so much? Was that why she was doubling my salary with the Wilton family money designated for the trust for the archive?

Her expression had been soft and sad when she talked about Victoria. But when she spoke about Jim she hadn't looked angry or vengeful, just . . . dismissive. As if he didn't matter.

I fell asleep thinking about the raise, and how that kind of money would change things for me. I had to admit it made me think differently about leaving Wilton Springs, although I wouldn't have considered moving away until Luna was totally back on her feet anyway.

The next morning, Daniela called to ask, in as gentle a tone as I'd ever heard from her, when I would come back to work, and I promised to come in soon.

On the third day, after breakfast with Luna, who looked a lot better and said Cecile was bringing her lunch and dinner, I biked home to change and grab my laptop. After tucking my hair under my baseball cap—my Virginia Evans disguise—I biked to the county historical society. I flashed my credentials at the front desk and went back to "my" room, where I started to review the material in the few remaining folders pertaining to the eighteenth-century Blackwells. There were more letters and receipts, contracts and records, which I added to the other data I was cataloging. I hadn't found anything about Prudence Lowell or John Wilton, so there was no reason to enter this material into the spreadsheet. Disappointing, but not unexpected.

The first few pages of the last folder were from the late eighteenth century. It didn't appear to be an organized group of documents. I noticed a document tucked in the back of the folder dated July 19, 1722. Right before Prudence Lowell's trial. I looked at the signature.

It was signed *Prudence*!

My dearest Felicity,

Your cousins will read this letter to you, or I shall come back to haunt them.

You, my only daughter will grow up an orphan, which causes me the greatest dissatisfaction. What displeases me even more is that your father is a cruel man, a man of many falsehoods, who made me believe he wished me to be his wife. He described himself as a widower as I am a widow, but I now know that he had a wife, and children. I know also he conspired with his brother to steal from me, and so from you and your cousins what is rightfully yours, my home and property given to me by my beloved husband may he rest in peace. To achieve this theft, John Wilton has accused me of devilry, of sorcery, of wicked things.

Goodbye, my daughter. I am confident your cousins will teach you many good lessons, so that you will be virtuous and kind, that you will grow into a fine woman, and one day meet a good man, who will be your husband, who will give to you all what I have been unable to provide. Marriage is a blessing, but a woman with independent means is able to provide more for her children. I hope your cousins will use their resources to return to you what is due. What is yours.

Know that I love you, and always will.

May you walk gracefully in the light of the Lord.

Signed lovingly from your mother,

Prudence.

I ran my fingertip over the faded ink. A letter from Prudence Lowell to her very young baby daughter, Felicity, who at age seventeen had married into the well-to-do Blackwell family. Had Felicity and her Lowell cousins ever recovered the property that rightfully belonged to their mother and aunt? Without a substantial dowry it was doubtful she would have married as well as she had, and led what must have been a prosperous life.

Mrs. Blackwell had been Prudence's friend . . . and perhaps her daughter's future mother-in-law.

The next letter in the file was a letter from Mrs. Anne Kuiper addressed to Mrs. Felicity Blackwell, dated May 8, 1745.

My dear sister,

The tender affection I hold for you, my dear sister, induces me to write you with regularity, as well my shame over the great neglect with which you were treated by our father in the home where we spent our juvenile years. Are your sons and daughters well? My dear Peter is of good health and cheer. Your goddaughters, Betsy and Mary, are five and eight, in good health and learning to sing and to sew adeptly.

Thank you for your last letter, the particulars of which you were kind to share with me, about your mother, and about the map, too, its sketched indications of entrances drawn and precise locations of certain springs. I will say no more about it, but know how I treasure this wisdom, and shall pass it along to my daughters when the time comes, as you bade me promise. I wish presently to visit the springs for their sakes and the danger small pox now presents.

A happy meeting between all of us is my sincere wish and prayer.

I shall never cease to be your affectionate sister and friend.

Anne

A security guard I'd not seen before let me know that it was closing time, and then left the room. I took a photograph of the letter.

After picking up dinner from the best deli in town, I took the back roads to Luna's place, slowed down by my knee, which was throbbing at the end of a humid day. Fortunately, the reporters had never figured out where Luna lived.

Her movements seemed easier, more fluid, and it was a relief to see her gain strength. Her face looked fuller, and red bloomed across her cheekbones again. She didn't want to talk any more about what she'd been through, and I didn't push her. "I want to keep it light from here on," she said. I had shared my Netflix and Hulu passwords with her, and often stayed with her late into the night watching reruns of *Friends* and Disney classics. She refused to watch anything with violence, murder, or crime.

Everyone was warm and quietly solicitous the next morning when I showed up at work. It was good to be back. Once I made it to my workspace in the basement, it took only a few minutes to find Anne Kuiper on the Wilton family tree. I confirmed that Anne was John and Martha Wilton's daughter, and that she and Felicity Lowell were half-sisters.

Within another ten minutes I'd found out what I had supposed, that Anne Wilton had married Peter Kuiper. I did learn that his family, Dutch farmers, had vast landholdings, hence the name of a town not far from Wilton Springs, Kuiperville. Peter Kuiper, who had fought in the American Revolution, had lived a long life. I found references to the Kuiperville Historical Society, which had an archive that apparently included a "cache of letters pertaining to the Kuiper family, 1710–1818." I contacted the historical society, and because nothing in the collection had been digitized, I arranged for photocopies of documents pertaining to Anne Kuiper from 1740 to 1770, and anything related to the Blackwell family, to be sent to me via interlibrary loan. I wasn't sure how long it would take, especially over the summer.

The following weekend, Cecile had offered to host a healing session for Luna. Luna was resistant at first, but I talked her into it. If anyone had the power to heal trauma, it was Cecile. I felt protective of Luna, as though she were my little sister. Sometimes, when we were together, she would zone out, as if she were in a space of her own. This wasn't something new after her ordeal—I'd noticed it before. I respected her distance. If I was over at her house when it happened, I would gently try to bring her out of it, but if that didn't work, I'd slip out.

One night after one of these episodes during dinner with Luna, I'd gone home and checked my burner phone, which I hadn't turned on in a few days. Now that Luna was back, I hadn't been so eager to act as Lucas's sidekick.

Meet me at Riotous at 10 pm, the text read, which he'd sent half an hour earlier. I debated whether or not to go, but I hadn't had anything to drink at Luna's, so I put my hair up under my baseball cap and rode to the bar. It was a Wednesday, and Riotous was empty except for one yawning bartender. Lucas was sitting at a table in the corner with his back to me. I hadn't seen him since the night of the fire. When I sat down across from him, I could see that he'd grown a scraggly beard. His hair was greasy against his forehead, and his glassy eyes kept blinking. He was nursing a glass of seltzer with lime. A vodka tonic was sweating on a coaster.

"How are things going?" I asked, sitting down.

He lifted his chin, aiming it at the vodka tonic. "Slowly," he replied. "Dealing with three, actually four, dead bodies, has been overwhelming for the police department of this sleepy town."

"I'm sure. Have they called in the FBI?"

"Everyone's determined Gabe is the perp."

"Do you agree?"

"Well, obviously Gabe can't testify. And Gabe's phone was lost in the fire. His email and cloud were wiped of all material. As in no trace of anything."

"Is that really a thing?"

"If you know what you're doing, and you have the connections, and the money, then yes."

"What about your own investigation?"

"Ongoing."

"Is Gabe Wilton now a suspect in his own sister's untimely death?"

"My client continues to maintain that Gabe was not involved in Victoria's death." He paused. "Nor with what went on at the lake house."

"Gabe is guilty of a double homicide. She's maintaining he's innocent? What bullshit." I picked up the vodka tonic and took two gulps.

"She?"

"C'mon Lucas. I know you're working with Barbara Wilton."

"I can neither confirm nor deny."

"Okay, let's reset. Thanks so much for your efforts to find Luna. Really."

"How is she doing?"

"Better. Better every day."

"I'm so happy for you, Genevieve. And I'm happy to have played a part."

"Anything I can do to help you? You asked me to meet, so you must want something."

"Please tell me what you know about Luna Collins."

I took another swig of the vodka tonic. "Why? Victoria died five years ago. Luna never even met her."

"I didn't say Luna's under suspicion. But she's a piece of the puzzle. It's possible she has some information that could help me figure out the truth about what happened the night Victoria drowned, even if she wasn't living here then."

"Sometimes I forget that at the end of the day, you're a cop." He returned my hard stare with something approaching weariness. "Can you please, please, leave Luna be until she gets her strength back?" I asked him.

"Just keep your eyes and ears open, Genevieve. I held up my end of the bargain. Luna is rescued and free. A deal is a deal."

"Fine."

Leaving the bar I muttered to myself. The idea that Luna could have been anything but a victim was just another example of what Cecile meant when she talked about the repression of women by the patriarchy. I would help Lucas if possible, but my first priority was to protect my friend and help her heal.

CHAPTER THIRTY-ONE

A few days later, Mason drove Luna and me to Emma's for Cecile's healing session. "I like the idea of being the center of attention!" Luna said, as we pulled up, and she clapped her hands together. "Cecile said we're going to Emma's indoor pool, and we'll have champagne. Yay, happy birthday to meeee!"

Emma and ten other girls, including me, were dressed in long, white dresses. I'd borrowed my dress from Cecile, who asked all of us to join hands and make a circle around Luna. After we each had a glass of champagne from Emma's parents' wine cellar, we switched to paper cups filled with Cecile's witch's brew, the detox tea they served in the spa. It tasted like licorice.

Then we all walked around the house to a long, covered pavilion over a shallow lap pool. Cecile asked me to pour some moon water through Luna's hair, and then together we lifted her up, walked into the lap pool, and laid her down in the water on a blue float. Two girls held the head and the foot of the raft, while Luna floated on the raft with her eyes closed. I looked at her body, studying her many tattoos, and saw one that I hadn't seen before, a Gothic-style capital letter *D* on her hip bone, big enough to see through the thin cotton of her wet shift. Where had I seen that tattoo before? Jade had one, too! I'd seen it that day in the spa. Emma sprinkled herbs and salt crystals into the water, and we gathered around Luna. Cecile began to sing in her low, beautiful voice. Luna quietly cried through some of it, although she smiled at times. Seeing Luna let down her guard and release her emotions made me tear up, too. Cecile spoke to each of us individually, explaining how Luna's trauma affected all of us, comparing the movement of negative energy to ripples in a pool.

After the session was over and Luna was wrapped up in one of the spa's plush bathrobes, Cecile began to speak. "Luna, who has come to us in a state of trauma, now emerges from the water healed. She has been kissed by fire, earth, and, air and is reborn strong and serene. We have unblocked her energy and given her back her power. She will not succumb to the ill-wishes of evil people. Let us chant together now." The girls began to chant in Latin, and I felt myself going into a semi-trance. I'm not sure how much time had passed when Cecile blessed us and then signaled for us to follow her out of the pavilion, which we did, in single file.

The night's cool wind made me shiver, and I rubbed my arms while running to retrieve my bike. I heard someone running behind me and stopped, then swirled around in a slight crouch. It was Emma, who rushed up to me and clasped my hand in hers. She smelled like jasmine. "You're such a good friend," she said. "I wish I had someone who loved me like you love Luna."

"I'm sure you have friends like that," I said, although I wasn't sure at all.

"If and when you decide you want to become a witch, I'll host the ceremony for you here."

"That's really kind of you to offer. I appreciate how all of you have included me this summer, even though I'm still pretty much a stranger."

"No such thing as strangers, only friends in waiting."

"I like that."

"Cecile sees something unique in you. She thinks you'd bring a special energy and light to our group. Would you consider it?"

Would I? My scalp was tingling, and the tingling spread down through my arms and legs and into my feet. “Sure.”

“You’ll make a great witch,” she said, and fluttered off.

The next day, I set up a meeting with Barbara to tell her about the letter I’d found from Prudence Lowell to her daughter. I was let into the house by a young woman I hadn’t seen before, who directed me through to the living room, where a man was sitting on the couch, drinking from a teacup. He was wearing a tailored jacket and tie, and I realized that the air-conditioning was on in the house this time. Remembering my brunch visit, I had dressed in a sleeveless blouse and short skirt. Now, I was cold.

“Darwin Truesdale,” said the man, scanning me with his eyes. “I represent the Wilton family. It’s nice to finally meet you, Ms. Tompkins. Mrs. Wilton asked me to relay the message that she’s under the weather.” There was a hardness about him, a man composed of sharp edges. Of course. My father had had a lawyer like Truesdale.

I wasn’t sure what to say. I just stood there.

“She apologizes for missing your appointment,” he said, “which she was looking forward to.”

“Why didn’t she text me to reschedule?” I asked.

He didn’t respond, but twirled the teacup in his fingers. “Would you care for a glass of . . . something?”

“No, thank you. If I can’t meet with Barbara, I’ll go back to work at the library. Please give her my regards,” I said, realizing that I couldn’t remember the last time I’d seen Jim Wilton, since he’d driven me to town after our brunch here. And now Barbara was “under the weather.” Well, they both deserved my sympathy, that was certain.

We exchanged polite goodbyes. He signaled to the young woman, who'd been standing nearby, and I was shown out.

—∞—

"You look fresh and cool," Daniela said, when I passed her in the library heading down to my workspace. I was still sweating, as I'd gone directly to the library. "Although you should probably have brought a sweater for downstairs. The administration keeps this building at sixty degrees."

"I dressed up for a meeting with Barbara Wilton, which got canceled, and the first time I was at Wilton Castle there was no air-conditioning. But, Barbara wasn't feeling well, or so I was told. By Darwin Truesdale ."

Her eyebrows dipped and then straightened. "He was here this morning."

"Busy guy."

"He is close to the Wiltons, legally and also financially. He represents the family trust, and now that their heirs are . . . gone—you understand. He's become a powerful man."

—∞—

Later that day Barbara called to apologize, and asked if we could meet the following morning, a Saturday. The reporters had abandoned Wilton Springs and were onto the next big scandal: A grisly school shooting had taken place in Colorado two days earlier, so Gabe Wilton wasn't generating national headlines anymore.

Barbara opened the front door herself, gave me a smile, and then led me to the covered porch area. Her gait seemed unsteady. She looked as though she had lost weight since the last time I'd seen her.

"Are you feeling better, I hope?" I asked.

"I'm fine. Must've been something I ate. I had to get it out of my system." She looked toward the lawn, then back to me. "Never mind. Tell me your news. And can I offer you anything? I didn't make lemonade, but it won't take me long if you'd like some."

"I'd rather tell you about the letters I found," I said.

Barbara listened intently, and when I was finished she said, "So, this woman accused of witchcraft—could she have put a curse on the family?"

"If that sort of thing is possible, Prudence Lowell certainly had a reason to do so."

"Interesting. I look forward to hearing what else you find on her. And one more thing. After everything that's gone on, no one would blame you if you wanted to leave. But I hope you'll stay. In addition to what we discussed, including your increased salary, I—Jim and I—would like to offer you a permanent position here. Now that, well, our estate will . . ." She didn't finish. I understood she meant that now that her children wouldn't be inheriting their estate.

I started to speak and she put up her hand, and closed her eyes for a second, gathering her thoughts, or perhaps suppressing a strong emotion. When she opened them again, she nodded. "We'll have even more funds to allocate to worthy causes. I'm hoping this might incentivize you, although I recognize many other places would benefit from your talents."

After that there wasn't much to say. In the early evening, I called Mason and invited him over. He was there within twenty minutes, as if he'd been waiting for my call, standing on my doorstep in a pair of worn-in jeans with a bottle of Malbec held behind his back.

He handed me the bottle, then picked me up in his arms and swung me around. "You said you have some news?"

"The Wiltons have raised my salary and offered me a permanent position in Wilton Springs if I'm interested in staying on."

He smiled. "Woo-hoo. That is excellent news indeed. I'm so happy to hear it."

He opened the bottle of wine and poured it in two glasses. We had a few sips and then stood there in the kitchen, our bodies pressed up against each other, and soon his mouth was on mine. We kissed for a while, and then I took off my dress and slowly undressed him. I grabbed his hands and put them on my breasts, my waist. I felt so desperate to feel him again, that I didn't even walk into the bedroom, but laid down on the couch, pulling him over me.

Afterward, I leaned on his chest with his arm around me, and he traced little circles on my shoulder. "I've been thinking about this, about you, for weeks, Genevieve. I've missed you so much. I want to do this every day."

We didn't leave the house, or my bed, all weekend, and I didn't check my phone once.

CHAPTER THIRTY-TWO

I woke up to a text from Lucas on the burner phone.

When u read this, meet me @ picnic table outside library u told me about. I'm here now, waiting 4 u.

I groaned.

"What is it?" Mason asked.

"I have to run out. To the library."

He sat up then let himself fall back down onto the mattress. "You're killing me, Gen. You're worse than I am. What could be happening at the library that can't wait until tomorrow?"

"I can't explain right now, but I'll call you, okay? Okay?"

"Sure, yes. Fine."

It was midday, the sun strong in the sky, and there was no breeze as I rode my bike to the library. Sweat was dribbling down my forehead by the time I arrived, and I could taste the saltiness in my mouth. I wished I could wash my face but the library was closed. Clouds had started to roll in, and the atmosphere felt heavy, the sky a pressure cooker about to explode with thunder and rain. But the heaviness didn't break.

"You okay?" he asked, when we were sitting down at the picnic table.

"I'm fine. I love really hot, really humid weather. Cut to the chase."

"I was intending to. Have you seen or heard from Luna in the past forty-eight hours?"

"I'm in touch with her constantly. Not yet today, or yesterday, actually. I had . . . company . . ."

"No need for details, thanks, suffice to say you've been busy. Luna's not at home. Hasn't been home since late Friday morning. After you brought her breakfast."

"What the hell? You're spying on me now?"

He shrugged and opened his eyes wide.

"Please don't do that again. I'm serious. Is that even legal? Anyway," I said, "Luna has started back up at work."

"I spoke with your colleague, Daniela. Luna returned to work at the library last Thursday afternoon. But didn't show up Friday."

"Daniela's not my colleague, she's more like my boss. Yesterday, you're right, I called and left Luna a message, but never heard back."

"Daniela said she went grocery shopping for Luna, but Luna wasn't home when Daniela stopped by with the food. It was too hot to leave the groceries outside on her doorstep, so she went back a few hours later. No Luna. Daniela called her multiple times, but no response."

"Why didn't you call me, Lucas?"

"I both called and texted you. Numerous times, but the burner phone seemed to be switched off. Even though I've specifically asked you not to turn it off, and not to forget to charge it."

I thought about my weekend with Mason and changed the subject. "When I mentioned it to her, Luna said she wasn't ready to talk to you yet. She said that talking with the police was really draining."

"Try her now, please?"

I called Luna, but the call went right to voicemail. I texted her.

Are you ok? Where are you? Please let me know when you get this.

"I'll let you know when I reach her," I said to Lucas, pretending to be calm. "First thing. Thanks for the heads-up."

I rode my bike to Luna's apartment and rang the bell several times, but she didn't answer. The door was locked. I stood on the tiptoes of my good leg in order to peer into the window that faced the street. Nothing looked out of place. Her desk, her couch, her kitchen, were tidy, just as when I'd seen them last time. For the rest of the day and evening I tried to reach her, and carried my phone in my hand, refreshing my messages over and over again. I looked at her Instagram. She hadn't posted anything new in a while.

At exactly 8:00 P.M. I received an email from a Gmail address with the name Luna Collins.

"What I experienced was too much for any one person to carry. It was a privilege to know you. You and Cecile were my closest friends. I love you. Please remember me. I'm sorry, Genevieve. Sorry I never said goodbye."

I closed the screen and held my face in my hands for several long seconds. My phone buzzed in my pocket. Lucas's number popped up on the screen. I answered. "The police just found Luna's body. In her apartment. Suicide."

I could hear the sound of traffic humming in the background. For some reason, the noise was comforting.

"I'm sorry, Genevieve," Lucas said, those three words echoing the email I'd just received. "Genevieve? Are you okay? Are you still there? Hello?"

When at last I started to cry, I was unable to stop.

CHAPTER THIRTY-THREE

When I woke up the next day I had a few happy minutes before I remembered what had happened. Luna. I'd found a true friend, then lost her, then found her, only to lose her again. This time she was gone for good.

I hugged myself, rocking back and forth, for hours. Lucas called six times. Eight times. I turned off both of my phones. When I turned them on again there were two voicemails and a text message from Mason.

Please call me. I heard the news.

I finally answered when Cecile called. "Genevieve, I kept calling but you didn't pick up," she said, then paused. I heard her take a deep breath before she continued, "I'm so very sorry. Can you come over to the spa? Whenever you can. I don't know if you're working today, or—"

"Yes" was all that I could manage as a reply.

A sign outside announced that the spa had closed early for the day, but Cecile had left the front door unlocked for me. Jade was not there.

After hugging each other without speaking, we went into the staff kitchen and I blurted out, "I can't believe I missed the signs. That I didn't stop her in time."

"Depression is like that, it takes over a person. I had a depressed uncle. One day he was—just like that. A zombie. Nothing anyone did managed to drag him out of it."

"Was Luna ever depressed? She never seemed sad, not even after what she'd been through. I know she had a troubled childhood. But she always seemed so happy."

She shook her head. "Don't beat yourself up. It's tragic, but not your fault."

I wasn't so sure. I started crying so hard I could barely breathe through the sobs.

"It's alright," Cecile kept repeating, holding me as she stroked circles on my back. "You're going to get through this. We're going to get through this. Together."

At the library, on Thursday, we held a memorial for Luna, outside by the picnic tables. Daniela said a few words. Some of Luna's colleagues from the coffee shop were there. A couple of cute guys around our age that I'd never seen before, probably admirers. Daniela announced that the following week, they were arranging one-on-one meetings with each of us. She said the college wanted the library to host a series of mental health awareness sessions.

Ten minutes after I was back at the cottage, Lucas texted and said he was on his way over.

"You're still having me watched?" I said when he arrived, a minute later, and I'd let him in.

"Why would you think that?"

"Because I got home literally ten minutes ago, and you're already here. You know what, I don't care if you are having me watched. I was going to call, and tell you that I wanted to talk."

"About what?"

"I know you respect the police here, but something doesn't make sense. Luna did not kill herself."

"Tell me what doesn't make sense," he said.

"I don't know, but—she was strong to the core. And think about the others. Rowena, Stacy, even Trish. What did they have in common?"

"They were all struggling to make ends meet."

"True, and they were small-town girls from around here. Underprivileged backgrounds. None had living parents or good relationships with them if they were alive."

"And your point is . . ."

"Luna didn't have money troubles. She lived modestly because she was saving up for library school," I said. "Okay, maybe she was a small-town girl who wasn't in touch with her family, but she had everything to live for. She was not suicidal. Ever."

"I actually agree with you on that," Lucas said. "But I still don't know where you're going with it."

"If Victoria's accident wasn't an accident, then maybe Luna's suicide wasn't a suicide. What about those threats Cecile and I received when she was missing? Is there a tie-in there? And something else. There's no way she sent that email to me. It didn't sound at all like her."

"Are you feeling okay, Genevieve? You seem a little . . . worked up."

I paced the length of the room twice, stopping when we were standing a couple feet away from each other. "Me? Worked up? Why would I be worked up? I can't think of a better way to spend my day than going to my beloved friend's memorial, and coming home to hang out with you, Lucas. Why did you invite yourself over here, anyway?"

He took a step back. "And before you answer, I have another question for you. Did Luna Collins have romantic interests? Any known boyfriends or girlfriends? Oh, wait, I know the answer: privileged information!"

"At this point I can tell you in all honesty that I don't know the answer to that question. But why do you ask?"

"Because you asked me when we first met, and I keep forgetting to tell you about Anthony."

CHAPTER THIRTY-FOUR

Lucas and I found a table in the back of the bar. The crowd was larger than it had been last time, with a different set of enthusiastic groupies sitting close to the stage. Once again, after Anthony opened with a Sheryl Crow hit from the '90s, he said that he was going to play a love song, the exact same as the last time I'd seen him perform.

After he started singing, Lucas leaned into me. "Do you actually like this . . . music?"

"Please . . ." I answered.

After a few minutes, he turned to me again. "Is it always this bad?"

"I've only seen him one other time, but it was the same."

After the set was finished, and a few women had taken selfies with Anthony, we waited until he came back from the restroom. As he passed our table I stood up. "Hi, Anthony!" I said, with a broad smile.

"Oh, hey," he said, nodding, "umm . . . ?"

"Genevieve."

"Great seeing you, Genevieve, and . . . your date." He nodded toward Lucas.

"Oh, that's my kid brother," I said, tilting my head toward Lucas, who had his hat down over his face and was on his phone. Anthony looked around, then back at me. "Can I buy you a drink?" I asked, batting my eyelashes, which were caked in mascara.

"Uh, sure. I'll have whatever's on tap."

We walked to the bar and I ordered two IPAs as we sat down on barstools. While we waited, I turned to him.

"Do you remember—when we met here last time, back in May, I was with my friend, Luna. Long dark hair, tall, and slim. Gorgeous." The bartender passed us our beers.

Anthony took a sip, and shifted to the right on the barstool. "I meet a lot of people at gigs."

I found a picture of Luna on my phone and showed him.

He took another sip. "Oh, right. The girl with the sister. Who has leukemia, just like my sister. We talked about that, and other stuff."

"Did you ever see her again?"

He ripped his paper napkin into two halves. "We hooked up, maybe twice, then she stopped answering my calls. She had like four jobs. Maybe five. She did not have time for me."

"You're sure this was Luna, right? Not some other . . . friend of yours?"

"Yes. I'm positive." He stood up with his drink in his hand. "Gotta go. Thanks for the beer."

As Lucas and I walked out to his car he turned to me. "Anything?"

"He said Luna had a sister."

"Do you think he was telling you the truth?"

"I have no clue. But if you think Luna is still a piece of the Victoria puzzle, maybe investigate Anthony? Find out if Luna did or didn't have a sister?"

He stood there, looking off into the distance.

"You will investigate, right? Isn't that what investigators do?"

"What else do you know about her family?"

"Her mom OD'd. Abusive dad. She put herself through college. We discussed this before."

"You said she was working four jobs because she was saving to go to library school. Maybe she was supporting her sister, too?"

"Possibly. And she said she was still paying off her school loans."

"Is there anyone else who might know about her sister? Cecile?"

"If Luna didn't mention her sister to me, I doubt she would've told her employer."

"I'll run some intel, see what I can come up with. Both on Anthony and the possible sister."

Later that night Lucas called me on the grey phone. "Anthony's clean. Was playing a gig that night so has a solid alibi. The story about Luna having a sister with leukemia checks out, too. Uninsured, obviously."

"Whoa," I said, pausing to let the information settle. "That's pretty crazy. But it proves my point, Lucas. Luna would not have taken her own life knowing that her ill-with-cancer sister relied on her."

"But couldn't the burden of that enormous responsibility, combined with the harrowing experience she'd just gone through, have pushed her to suicide?"

"Luna was loyal. And she was strong. Way stronger than I am. So no. Not buying it."

"Okay, so being kidnapped and almost being burned alive didn't affect her? Playing devil's advocate here, but . . ."

"Oh, it definitely affected her," I interrupted him. "But it didn't break her. There's a difference. And like I said, she seemed happier than I'd ever seen her." I threw my hand in the air. "It's as though the more we learn, the more confused I am. Is that how you feel in your job?"

When he responded, his tone was grave. "All the time, Genevieve. All the time."

CHAPTER THIRTY-FIVE

I called Mason later that night. "Sorry I haven't been in touch."

"You don't have to apologize. What can I do to make you feel better? Anything?"

"I wish you could. Unless . . . do you have a magic pill to make it all go away?"

"No, but how about a close friendship? With benefits?" He let a few seconds tick by before he said, "Just kidding. Listen, in my career, we see a lot of death. Also, I have. Personally. Starting with my dad when I was a kid."

"Oh . . . What happened? Do you want to talk about it?"

"Liver cancer. From his time in Vietnam, when he got exposed to a lot of stuff."

"Is that why you wanted to become a doctor?"

"One of the reasons."

"I'm so sorry, Mason."

"We all have our crosses to bear. I'm with you, though, Gen. Really, I am. I have a lot of respect for you, for what you do. You're amazing."

I blew out my breath quickly. "I don't feel amazing. Not tonight."

"What happened?"

"Long story, but I don't think Luna died by suicide."

"What do you mean? And what about that email she sent you? The suicide note."

"I think someone killed her, and then made it look like a suicide."

"But why?"

"Trying to figure that part out now. I'll let you know what I come up with."

"Are you sure that's a good idea? Sounds . . . dangerous? Maybe you leave the investigations to the pros. I know you've been threatened, and you have this theory that Luna's death needs to be . . . avenged? By you? Just remember, you can't be responsible for anyone else except yourself."

I let out a quick "Ha."

"What is it?"

"That's what my mother always used to tell me."

A few minutes after we hung up my mother called. I let it ring a few times before answering.

Her voice was loud and I held the phone several inches away from my face. "Genevieve, I've been following what's going on . . . in the news. Wilton Springs seems like a hotbed for . . . I don't know what exactly. Don't you think it's enough? You should get out of that town. Come home already."

"I'm okay, Mom. Things are going well with my job. Really well. I've met some great people, and was just offered a permanent position and a much larger salary. I'm learning a lot about American history, more than in the first two years of my PhD program, and—"

She cut me off. "You're not even attached to an institution with any heft. What's really keeping you there? It's so isolated. You're still young. You should be back in Manhattan. How are you going to meet any eligible men out there in the back of beyond? The clock is ticking, sweetheart."

"Aren't you busy enough with your stepkids that you don't need to be worrying about me and my ticking clock?"

"There's no need to be nasty. I was just calling to check up on you. Next time I won't bother. Besides. You're the child. You should be calling me."

"It's been busy."

"Well, I am very sorry to interrupt," she said, her tone coated in a thick layer of sarcasm. "I'll let you get back to your important life."

"It's not that, it's—" I started to say. But she'd hung up. I knew what would happen next. Her silent treatments sometimes lasted a month or two. That was okay. I didn't need her for comfort, or anything else. I was on my own, supporting myself financially for the first time, making my own decisions. It felt good.

My phone buzzed again. Thinking she'd had a change of heart, I answered. But it was Lucas.

"I've been trying you on the burner phone," he said. "The autopsy results just came back. No indication of foul play. Luna took a ton of sleeping pills, then got in the bathtub."

"Hmm."

"Also, she was missing a kidney. Had been removed 'recently,' they told me."

"Maybe she donated her kidney to her sister?"

"I don't . . . Hey, that is a good question. You've been asking lots of good questions. Ever considered a career in law enforcement? Long hours, little pay. High risks to personal safety, low rate of success commensurate with effort, elevated rates of depression and anxiety. High rate of attrition. Interrupt me as soon as I've convinced you."

"I may as well go back and finish my PhD because you literally just described my graduate program. Except for the high-risk part. Although if someone had told me a year ago about all the crazy shit that would happen while I was working in a library in upstate New York, I would've asked what kind of bad psychedelic trip they were on."

He chuckled. "Okay, I'll see if I can find out anything about the timing of Luna's operation. They also mentioned that she had the letter *D* cauterized into her hip."

"Luna had a bunch of tattoos."

"This was a brand."

"A brand? Oh, I remember! I did see a *D* tattoo on her hip. During the healing ceremony. When she was floating in the water. I think it was her hip. Left hip? Right hip? I can't remember. And something else about that letter . . . oh! I saw it on Jade, too. I wonder why."

Lucas texted me the following morning at eight that he was outside my house with a visitor. Still in my bathrobe, I hobbled downstairs, favoring my bad knee, and opened the door. There was Luna, standing next to Lucas, even more emaciated than she had been after escaping the burning house.

CHAPTER THIRTY-SIX

"I'm Sienna," said Luna's ghost in a feeble voice, thrusting her hand out toward me. "I guess you knew my sister."

"Your sister. Yes," I stammered, reaching out for her hand, my own shaking as I touched her cold, thin fingers. I wanted to hug her, to feel Luna close to me again in any way possible.

I showed them into my living room and then made a pot of coffee in the kitchen, which gave me a few minutes to recover. "It's so nice to meet you, Sienna," I said, walking out of the kitchen with a tray of mugs and the pot. Lucas and Sienna were sitting on opposite ends of the couch. His phone rang and he looked down at it. "I've got to take this."

"Some of Lucas's calls are a bit sensitive, so he'll wait outside. Won't you, Lucas?" I glanced at him.

"Of course," he said, with a wry smile, and headed to my front door.

I sat next to Sienna. She put on an N95 mask. "I'm so so sorry about Luna," I said. "Your sister was extraordinary. I mean it when I say I loved her."

She held up her hand. "When Mr. Lucas said Luna's death was being treated as suicide, I agreed to meet you. I want to help you. And him."

"Help us?"

"To find her killers."

I swallowed hard. "I want to help, too, however I can."

"Good. Mr. Lucas asked me if Luna was struggling with mental health. I said she was very stable."

"I also know that your mother—"

She interrupted. "Different moms, same dad. He wasn't the most . . . caring of parents."

"She didn't tell me much about her family. She was very private."

"Well, she told me all about you. She thought you were terrific. She called you the Duchess."

"The Duchess?"

"Because you're rich," she smiled.

"I'm not . . ." I started to say, but she kept talking.

"She admired you. I think she didn't want you to know about the trailer park where we grew up, or about me, her baby sister. Poor, sick Sienna. I was getting treatment the day of her memorial, or I would've met you there."

"Do you live near here? Did you two see each other often?"

"I'm an hour away. But it had been a good two months since I'd seen her, although we text a lot. Texted."

"Did she seem depressed to you? The last time you spoke?"

"Never. Luna doesn't do depressed. Didn't. She was always busy, working her ass off. That's how she was able to send me money for the treatments. She told me she was going through something big, something life-altering. Stressful. She didn't share any details. She always protected me, her baby sister. That's why I don't believe the suicide thing."

"Because killing herself would have been abandoning you?"

"Yes. And there's no way that email I got was written by her. First of all, we texted. Also the words were over the top. Luna was no bullshit. She told it to me straight."

"Who else would've wanted to harm her?"

"Dunno. She kept her dark side close to the vest. Hidden."

"Was she involved with anyone sketchy? Boyfriends? Girlfriends?"

"She didn't have time for any of that. Sometimes, but only short-lived stuff. Flings."

"Did she do any drugs?"

She patted her lap. "Mr. Lucas asked me all these questions already. No drugs. Luna was going to be a prim and proper librarian. Marry a sweet guy, have kids, put her past behind her. She started teaching yoga, said she was 'finding herself' through natural . . . something." She paused. "Natural medicine."

Tears were rolling down my face. Sienna started sniffling. We sat there quietly until I said, "I really miss her."

"I'm all alone now," she sobbed. "I'm all alone . . ." I put my arms around her, hugging her. After a while she pulled back, took in a few breaths, wiped off her face, and blew her nose.

"Sienna, what did you mean about Luna's dark side?"

She took a breath. "When Luna was in school, she used to . . . write papers. For rich kids. They paid her. Luna was crazy smart, but she didn't always use her brain on the right things. If anyone had found out about those things, Luna would've lost her library job, her dreams would've gone"—she blew on her fingers—"poof!"

I bent my head forward. "Things? What things?"

She bit her lip. "You gotta keep this a secret. She, uh, she killed somebody. Hit and run when she was drunk at the wheel in college."

My mouth popped open. "Oh . . ."

"The cops investigated, but somehow she skated. She said someone made it disappear." Sienna took a deep breath, struggling to sit up straight. "I thought you should know. But don't tell anyone else. I mean, it's not like she could go to prison. But . . . Even if she's dead, I want her memory to stay pure."

"I completely understand."

Sienna stood up. "I'm really tired."

We walked outside and Lucas was still talking in his car. But he waved at us and held up one finger.

I turned to her and asked, "One more question? Luna's kidney had been recently removed. They noticed when they were performing the autopsy."

"Mr. Lucas asked me about that already. Somebody made a mistake. She would've told me about that, for sure."

"What about the *D* branded on her hip bone?"

"Oh yeah, I asked her about that once. She said it was some dumbass sorority-girl shit. Not that she was ever in a sorority."

Later that day Lucas texted the grey phone. *No record of Luna Collins as a patient, or any kidney removals in the last three months, at any of the hospitals in a hundred-mile radius.*

I called him. "If Luna's kidney wasn't removed to save her sister's life, why was it removed? Do you think she sold it?"

"More good questions," Lucas said. "Wish I had the answers. All we know is the surgery was recent. The coroner described it as 'fresh-fresh.'"

Luna had kept so much hidden from me. The plagiarism scheme. The hit and run. A kidney surgery. Even her own sister. Had she been trying to protect me? Or protect herself . . .

The next week, I put my full attention on my work in the archive. I was being paid to devote my time and energy to that, not to solving what may or may not have been a crime case. When I thought of Luna, I would pivot to another task—fill in the family tree, read, double-check what I'd entered in the spreadsheet earlier in the week. Part of my job was to scan and upload anything that wouldn't be damaged by the scanner, which required my full attention, so I made it a priority. I found some boxes were better organized than others. I hoped to find a checklist that Victoria had organized, but it was probably on her laptop. Maybe Barbara Wilton would someday let me look at Victoria's computer, which was probably in the bedroom where everything had frozen in time.

On Friday afternoon, I stopped by Daniela's office at the end of the work day.

"The Wiltons offered me a permanent position, and raised my salary."

"That's wonderful!"

"I don't know. After everything that's happened, I'm not sure I want to stay in Wilton Springs. But of course I'll give you at least two weeks notice. Or a month."

She straightened up in her chair. "I do hope you will get through all the boxes. For the library, and other researchers. And, of course, for the Wiltons, but also for Luna, who was so dedicated to the project. She wanted to be a good 'team member,' as she told me. I saw her in here early in the morning before you started your shift."

"Did Luna ever mention that she had a sister?"

"Sister? No. She was an only child."

"Luna had a sister. Has a sister. I met her last week. She's staying in Luna's house right now. Daniela, did you know anything about Luna's past?"

She tapped her pen on her desk. "We should not be discussing personal matters. It is not appropriate." She switched off her lamp, and we walked out together.

Later that night, I called Mason and invited him to meet me at Riotous Times. His tone had a grumpy edge when he said, "I can't. I have to work late tonight."

"No problem," I said. "Talk soon."

When we hung up, I sighed. So much for being there for me when I needed him. I wanted a distraction, though, so I rode my bike to Riotous Times anyway. The air was dense. The heat had been oppressive all day and into the evening.

Inside, the bar was air-conditioned, but full of tourists, not surprising on a hot Friday night in August. I ordered a vodka tonic. Then a second one. I gulped them down quickly. I didn't like the taste of alcohol, but craved that feeling of numbness it generated. I sat there, waiting for my brain and body to unwind. I heard a little commotion, and looked over to see Emma at the entrance with a few of her friends. She kissed the bouncer on the cheek, and chatted with him as she twirled a strand of her hair. I didn't want to talk or for them to see me like this. I paid and left out the back.

Outside I checked my phones. No messages. A man I'd noticed across the street had crossed to my side and stopped in front of me.

"Hi there," he said. "You're pretty. Where's your boyfriend?" His breath smelled like whisky. I turned away from him and stared into my phone.

"My place is just up the road. Want to come over and get high?"

I put my hands on my bike, but he leaned closer and grabbed my wrist. "Hey. I said, 'You're pretty.' Say thank you!"

"Fuck off!" I yelled in his face. As he leaned back and loosened his grip on my wrist, I swung my arms out toward him, and hit him, missing his head but connecting with his shoulder, unloading as much force as I could. He staggered back. I pushed my bike away from him, and then I was on the seat, pedaling as fast as I could. Pumping, pushing. Raging. "Asshole!" I screamed to no one.

Inside, I locked and double bolted the door, turned around, leaned my back up against the wood, and slid down to the floor, buzzed from the drinks and the adrenaline. As I waited for my heartbeat to return to normal, I thought about what had just happened. Thanks, Mom, for those self-defense classes you made me take. I texted Lucas. *Call me.*

After answering on the first ring, I didn't tell him about the incident outside Riotous Times. He might've asked me why I'd gone out late drinking by myself, and I didn't have a good answer. Instead, I said, "Anything happening with the Luna investigation?"

"There is no Luna investigation. We have a body this time. Sorry to put it that way. Her death is considered a suicide."

"Have you talked to Cecile? Maybe I was wrong. She didn't know about the sister but maybe she knows other stuff."

"Is there other stuff?"

"You tell me."

"I can't talk to Cecile."

"Why not?"

"Cecile thinks I'm a male witch in training, remember?"

"But you said she never spoke to you. And you were wearing glasses. And a hooded robe."

"Well, I can't take any chances. But I'm thinking about someone who can, risk free."

"Your buddies at the station? Or those detectives?"

"Nah. I'm thinking about a woman. Someone she trusts."

"Emma?"

"Who's Emma?"

"Barbara?" I said. "Your client."

"Mrs. Wilton is not my client."

"Right."

"Actually, I was thinking about you."

"Me?"

"She trusts you, doesn't she?"

"I can absolutely talk to her. But you know what, if I'm going to do your job for you, I should probably be compensated."

I could hear the smile in his voice. "Let me see what I can do."

Cecile told me to come by at 7:00 P.M.

When I walked through the beaded curtains, Jade was behind the desk.

"I thought the spa was closed?" I said, my voice rising into a question.

She shrugged. "What can I say? The boss is a tyrant. I'll get her for ya."

Cecile came downstairs and wrapped me in a hug. Her warmth, her softness, and the smell of incense on her clothes was calming, much more than the vodka had been. She took my hand and we walked up to her office. "Poor Genevieve," she said, after closing the door. "I meant to call you earlier. It's just been so busy here. 'Tis the season."

"Cecile, have you ever met Luna's sister?"

"Luna has a sister?"

"She showed up at my house with a friend. Said Luna had told her about me. My nickname was the Duchess. Anyway—"

Just then we heard a series of thumps, like a pile of logs had collapsed.

Cecile ran down the stairs. I followed.

"Jade!" Cecile called. Jade was doubled over on the floor. She had knocked over several books and a lamp.

"I'll call 911," I said.

"No!" Jade rasped. "Don't . . . call." Her eyes were closing and she was writhing in pain.

I fished my phone out of my purse and was about to dial 911 when Jade pushed herself up off the floor, and swatted my phone out of my hands, and then leaned back and slid down the wall and onto the floor.

Cecile stared down at her. "Genevieve's right, Jade."

Jade's face was contorted. "No! This isn't . . . an emergency, I swear. Just—bad period pain. It happens to me."

"Okay," said Cecile. "Let's get you on the massage table and let you rest for a bit." She shot me a look. "Don't worry, Genevieve, I'll call 911 myself if she's not better in a few minutes."

Jade looked at me and forced another smile. "Thanks, Genevieve," she said, her voice still strained. "Don't worry. I'm fine."

Cecile glanced over at me. "I'll deal with this stubborn one. And I'll call you," she said, mimicking a phone with her fingers.

The beads clicked as I passed through the threshold. I texted Lucas and told him Cecile did not know Luna had a sister.

CHAPTER THIRTY-SEVEN

Early the next morning I walked to Wilton Grinds and ordered two double espressos in a row instead of my usual iced coffee because I was tired and hungover, but wanted to stay caffeinated in order to figure out my next move. I walked all the way back, figuring it was good therapy for my knee, which had become inflamed after my panicked ride home from Riotous the night before. Sienna was waiting for me on my doorstep. Once again, I thought it was Luna, and my heart began fluttering. I opened the front door, and Sienna followed me inside.

"You promised not to tell anyone!" Sienna hissed, when I closed the door behind us. "About what I told you about Luna. You told Mr. Lucas! I should never have trusted you. Either of you!"

"I did not tell him! I swear."

"You told someone!" she said, her voice hard. "I found a dead rat with no head outside Luna's front door. With this note." She handed it to me.

No one likes rats. If we catch you talking again, you'll wind up like this one.

"Oh, Sienna."

"No one knew except you. Just leave me out of your investigations. Mr. Lucas promised me I'd be safe." She was breathing quickly.

"Sienna, I didn't tell Lucas what you told me. I'm very sorry this happened."

"Sorry's not good enough. I don't even know why I came here. Luna's dead. This is the worst thing that's ever happened to me. It's my fault I made it even worse by telling her secrets to someone I can't trust."

"You can trust me! I would never put you in danger. I cared about Luna. I care about you."

"You don't care about me. You didn't even know about me until yesterday. You say you cared about Luna. Maybe! She can't tell me, she's dead!"

"Who else knew you were here?" I asked. "Has anyone contacted you besides Lucas? I want to help you."

"Stop asking me questions and stay outta my life, will you? That's how you can help me. You have everything in the world, and people like me and Luna, we work our asses off and for what? No one gives us any advantages!"

"I understand," I said, nodding.

"You don't understand, and you're not really sorry," she said, her voice shaking. "Stay the hell away from me," she said as she moved toward the door, somewhat unsteadily. She looked so weak. Her arms and legs were so thin. "I'm never coming back to this shithole, Wilton Springs." She slammed the door as hard as she could on her way out. I dialed Lucas to tell him what had happened, but he didn't pick up. I left him a voicemail, and then texted him. An hour later, I walked to the spa, limping a little for the last ten minutes.

Dark clouds swirled in the sky, and the wind had picked up, threatening a summer storm, fast and explosive. No one was at the front desk. I walked up to Cecile's office and told her what had happened with Sienna.

"Look, I don't know what the police have told you but I'm convinced Luna didn't die by suicide. Luna's killer is out there, if her sister got a credible threat like that. That means that you and I are in danger. I need to leave Wilton Springs. I wish you could come with me. Can you?"

She smiled. "No, alas, too many people need me here. But I understand your position completely. Just know that a lot of people would miss you. I would. Mason would, too."

"You've talked with Mason?"

"I ran into him recently. He's very concerned for your safety, and mine."

I reached out and took her hand. "I'm just so worried about both of us. Are you sure you don't want to leave with me? It would only be temporary, until everything gets sorted out."

"Don't worry about me. I have—"

"Crystals, I know."

"I was going to say I have people close to me who protect me. And angels, too, who are always around. They won't let anything bad happen to me."

"I'm not sure I have any angels."

"You do. I can see them. A matriarch. A grandmother. Your father's mother. The ring you wear, it belonged to her, right?"

I stammered. "Yes, how did you know—"

"I've been seeing spirits since I was a little girl. Would you like to speak with your angel guides? I should show you some ways you'll be able to protect yourself, no matter what."

"Do you believe the Wilton pharmaceutical company has been conducting unauthorized medical experiments, and that that could have something to do with what's going on?"

She froze, and paused before she said, "I, I don't know."

"Cecile. Tell me what you do know, please."

"I've heard the rumors, too. But I can't tell you whether or not there's any truth to them."

"The other day, with Jade. Could she have been one of the volunteers who took their drugs and had an operation? She didn't want me to see it, but a few weeks ago I noticed she has a big scar."

"Jade's medical history is something I know about, but it would break confidentiality for us to discuss that. She has been through a lot. I'll say one thing—she's lucky to be alive."

"That's not exactly comforting."

"The things we do here have power, Genevieve. The mind is strong in ways that no one understands. There's nothing that you want that you can't have, if you work hard enough for it." I wanted to believe what she was telling me.

"Emma said you two had talked about . . ."

"About my conversion. At her house—"

She interrupted me. "It's not a conversion. It's a new way of looking at life. According to the belief systems of ancient cultures I've studied, there are different kinds of births and rebirths, leaving your mother's womb is only the first. We'll be ready for your wiccaning whenever you are. But I never want you to do anything that makes you uncomfortable. I just want what you want for yourself. What is it that you want most in the world, Genevieve?"

"Peace of mind would be nice."

"Okay, I can do that. What *else*? Dream big."

"Independence, a permanent career, to be free of the yoke of my family."

"That is something I've helped people overcome. Families are constructs."

"Did you help Victoria overcome that?"

She frowned. "Victoria, why do you ask?"

"I've been thinking about her, recently."

"Victoria was my biggest failure. She wouldn't let me help her. Believe me, I tried. I'm like you, Genevieve. I take responsibility for other people. Victoria was like a child to me."

"Jade told me you had . . . a child."

She looked down and didn't speak for a few seconds. "I had a son," she said. "Kyle. He died when he was eleven. He had a disability. He needed a transplant and"—she struggled to take in a breath—"and they were unable to find a donor. In time."

"I'm sorry. I'm so sorry, Cecile."

"That's life. We play with the hand we are dealt. I built my world around Kyle, gave him the best care that I could, until it was . . . too late." She swallowed.

"What about Kyle's dad? Did he help you out at all?"

"My ex?" She made a noise that sounded like a laugh. "He did nothing for Kyle. He remarried. Moved on. It takes a special kind of man to be a father to a special-needs child."

"Do you have anyone in your life now?"

"Nobody serious. Lots of bad men out there, with ill intentions. I stay away from negativity. Most are takers. I won't settle again. I'm waiting for a good one. Someone real." She pushed up her sleeve, revealing a gold bangle with pavé diamonds, glinting in the light. "Everyone needs a secret admirer," she said, with a cryptic smile, twisting it around on her wrist.

We hugged and I left and walked home quickly. It had started drizzling, and the streets were dark. I locked all the doors and windows and checked them three times, and went to bed with the big kitchen knife on my nightstand.

The next morning I arranged to meet Barbara after lunch. When she opened the door, her hair was disheveled and she was wearing a wrinkled shirt that was buttoned incorrectly. We sat together in the enclosed porch, and she poured me a glass of lemonade. I took a sip, but it was too sour to drink.

"Are you doing okay?" I asked.

"I had another bout of nausea again last night. It might be Jim's concoction."

"Concoction?"

"A weight-loss and wellness drink the company's been developing. It worked marvelously the first week and I was already feeling improved mood and energy. It's in the lemonade," she said, pointing at my glass. "I figure every woman wants to lose a few pounds and gain some energy, no? Drink up!"

"Thanks," I said, as I reached forward and put my glass on the table.

"How's work going? Any new discoveries?"

"I've been analyzing the data, and wondered if you could answer a few questions."

"Of course, Genevieve," she said. "I want to help."

"Do you believe in the so-called Wilton curse? But before you answer, do you agree that a statistically high number of Wiltons, almost all men, died mysteriously over the generations?"

I waited, as if these were the sorts of questions all archivists asked.

She folded her hands in her lap. "What I know with certainty is that my husband and his brother were rivals. His brother was the favorite and the heir apparent. Even before my brother-in-law and his family were killed in the car accident, my father-in-law had cut Jim out of the family business entirely. It wasn't until after Old Wilton died that we found out he'd left everything to the grandkids. Jim was given nominal control over the family foundation, though Darwin Truesdale—you met him—actually runs the foundation, which provides some income. Just enough to get by on. Everyone here thinks Old Wilton set us up for life, but he actually pulled the rug out from underneath us. Although now there is a . . . recalculation. Darwin is helping me. He's figuring it all out."

"It was sort of similar with my family. People assume I'm loaded, but I actually didn't inherit anything from my dad."

"You need a lawyer. Like Darwin."

I leaned forward and pushed the glass of spiked lemonade away. "I know about the private detective you hired, Barbara."

"What private detective?"

"The one . . . investigating Victoria's death."

"Peretti? I don't think he could help with your father's will. Although he is the best of the best for death investigations. Or at least he was, before he retired. He's back on the West Coast now, with his grandchildren."

She refilled her glass and drank half of it before setting it on the table again.

I sank back into the crunchy cushion, and spent the rest of the half hour listening to her prattle on about the book she was reading for her book club.

As I rode my bike home, my phone buzzed. It was Lucas. I didn't pick up. Could I continue to trust him? He hadn't been hired by Barbara, so who was he working for? Maybe he was trying to find out something about Victoria in order to get leverage over the family. Maybe Lucas wasn't a private investigator at all. Maybe he was a journalist. It wouldn't necessarily explain his gun, and those special gloves and flashlight he had, but he'd never shown me a badge. Did private investigators have badges? He certainly hadn't seemed very professional when I first met him, dressed up as a male witch. Well, first I met him in the state park. And the detectives knew him. And those policemen who came by my house. Were some people in on whatever he was in on? It had also occurred to me that when Lucas had told me about the police finding Luna's body, I'd received her goodbye text only minutes earlier. Something wasn't adding up.

I let his next two calls go to voicemail.

Everyone in Wilton Springs had been so nice to me. But could I really trust anyone?

CHAPTER THIRTY-EIGHT

The following morning, Monday, the library was closed for an annual training day, and I didn't work for them so I decided to take the day off. The sound of lawn mowers droning woke me up, and when I left the house an hour later to pick up breakfast, Russell Bailey was standing there, surveying his newly trimmed lawn. He waved me over.

"Ah, Genevieve, how are you doing? I'm back in town for the day."

"Hi, Russell. Seems like the ice maker's broken in the cottage."

"Want me to send someone over to fix it?"

"That'd be great."

"It may not be so easy, everyone's on vacation, but I'll try. For you. How about a glass of ice water in the meantime? I could fill a bag of ice for you to take back to your freezer. C'mon in."

Something about his big old house felt dank and creepy, not only because it shared a boundary with the funeral home. The rooms were small, and there were a lot of them. It was like walking through some sort of maze to get to the kitchen. I wasn't sure I could find my way back out if I had to. Russell poured me a glass of water over two ice cubes and carried it as he walked out of the kitchen into the next room, and then the next one, where he pulled the white sheet off one of the sofas, gesturing for me to sit down. I turned to an uncovered chair and sat there instead.

"How's your work going?" he asked. "Is everything here as historically fascinating as I promised?"

"I've been learning a lot. About the Wilton family." I inched to the far end of my seat. "What do you know about them? Any juicy tidbits that would be helpful to connect the dots in my analysis?"

"I know you talked to that lawyer of Barbara's the other day, Truesdale. Maybe he gave you some information about the Wiltons."

"Are you and Truesdale friends?"

"Friends? With Truesdale? Ha. No. A categorical no. As an attorney myself I can tell you that Truesdale is too clever for his own good. And self-righteous. I steer clear."

"Then how did you know I spoke with him?"

"Genevieve, this is a small town. Word gets around."

I put the glass down on the floor next to me. "And you know the nature of our confidential conversation? That Barbara wasn't feeling well and couldn't meet with me."

"No, of course not! I was just pulling your leg. I saw Truesdale's car in town, and I saw you on your bicycle at the entrance gate to Wilton Castle about an hour later."

"You know what Truesdale's car looks like?"

"He's there all the time. Like I said, he's Barbara's lawyer."

"You mean Barbara and Jim's lawyer."

"No, Barbara's lawyer. Barbara's parents left her a healthy sum when they died twenty years ago. Old Wilton cut Jim off ages ago." He nodded. "Without Barbara's inheritance they would've had to sell the castle a while back. Jim pretends to dabble in new business ventures."

"What kinds of businesses?"

"He invests in the spa for instance. He's over there all the time. He doesn't want anyone to know his wife supports him. He's too proud."

"I've never seen him at the spa, and I'm there all the time."

"They're discreet."

"They? Does he have a girlfriend he meets there?"

He skipped over my question and said, "Jim's parents, the senior Wiltons, they always knew what was going on. That's why the money went to the kids."

"And now the money Jim's parents funneled to the trust for Victoria and Gabe is reverting back to Jim and Barbara?"

"Did Truesdale tell you that?

"No, but it had to go somewhere in the family, right?"

"It'll go to the family foundation, which is what I'm assuming Truesdale was discussing with Barbara. Mrs. Bailey said that now that the kids are gone, Barbara is fed up with Jim's hanky-panky stuff and wants a divorce. But she wants part of the Wilton inheritance to make up for all those years she's supported the family. I hear there's no prenup, so I don't imagine she'll have any luck, even with Truesdale's maneuvering."

"Hanky-panky? Like, what I think hanky-panky means? Is that why you warned me about him when I first met you?"

"Yup, he's a serial hanky-pankier."

I raised my eyebrows.

"Everyone in town knows. We just don't put it in the newspapers, like you city folk do. I've read about your mom on page 8."

My eyes narrowed. "Have you," I said.

"Well, Mrs. Bailey has."

"Did you say everyone in town knows about the Wiltons' marriage? Or Jim's wanderings?"

"Yes, but there's been enough donations to make sure everyone here minds their own business. Police department. Fire department. Hired drivers. Shops. Those two pretty girls who got killed—Rowena and Stacy? They worked for the Wiltons as housekeepers. Something about that whole story seems fishy. Mostly the Wiltons wanted to exonerate their son. They'd like it to seem as though someone else murdered those girls. But everyone knows Gabe had something to do with it. And that girl who died in his bed. Not to speak ill of the dead, but he was a slippery one, that boy. If he'd grown up, he would've turned out even worse than his father."

"You are a font of information, Mr. Bailey."

He shrugged.

"Speaking of which, I'd better get back to work."

"It must be easier to look into someone else's family history, rather than looking inward toward your own."

I was struck by how goofy and at the same time unpleasant he was revealing himself to be. One more person in Wilton Springs I couldn't trust. I looked at my phone. "I could use that ice you mentioned. Then I need to go home to do some work."

"Yes, you just said that. All work and no play makes Jill a dull girl, too, you know. Why don't you join us for a casual family barbecue one of these days? You're at that library all the damn time. Even on the dog days of summer! But we'll have to wait another week or so. I'm leaving tonight."

"Meeting up with Mrs. Bailey?"

"Tomorrow's her birthday. She asked me to take her to someplace that doesn't have cell service. I found a B&B up by the Canadian border. Anyway, let's catch up before Labor Day, sounds good?" He walked me into the kitchen and filled a Ziploc bag with ice.

"Sounds good." I gave him a thumbs-up, and he escorted me to the front door.

CHAPTER THIRTY-NINE

A few hours later, Mason texted me.

I should bring you something sweet. What are you in the mood for?

Can't think of anything.

Fresh ice cream for lunch?

Never a bad idea.

An hour later he was standing outside my door, each hand holding a pint. "I hope it's not too melted," he said, as I let him inside.

We sat on the couch and ate our ice cream in silence until there was nothing left. Then he took my hands in his. "Growing up, we used to say that ice cream cures all."

"Meaning?"

"About the other night. I'm sorry I couldn't come over when you called. You caught me at a bad time—one of my hospital patients—died—it was awful. But I wanted you to know." He lowered his head, and when he lifted it his face was flushed. "I realize we come from two different worlds, but I've never felt the way I feel when I'm with you."

I moved closer to him on the couch and kissed him. "It's the same for me, Mason. But I have something else to tell you. I'm thinking about leaving Wilton Springs."

He drew back away from me, his hands sliding down my shoulders. "What? You can't leave."

"Part of me wants to stay. But the Wiltons are involved in something dangerous. Whoever exposes them risks getting . . . silenced. It's no coincidence both Wilton kids are dead. I haven't sorted it all out, but I talked to my landlord, and others, and I no longer feel safe here."

"That all sounds . . . scary. Let me know how I can help. Whatever you decide, I'm with you. Makes no difference if I don't see you every day."

"I just need some time. Of course, I don't want to leave ..." I paused. "You."

"I understand," he said. But I registered the disappointment flooding his face. He looked as though he might start crying. Instead, he kissed me once, twice, and then was on his way.

I went to the library the next morning. I had to prepare my departure carefully, and slowly. Mitch followed me down to the basement wearing a plaid suit and cradling a cardboard box, a crooked smile plastered on his face.

"Hey, Genevieve," he said. "Did you see the goldfish upstairs, reading the new thriller?"

"Goldfish? What are you talking about?"

"It was hooked!"

"Ha, very funny."

"Package arrived for you." He laid the cardboard box on my desk and then jogged back upstairs, humming a tune. I looked at the label. It was the interlibrary loan material from the Kuiperville Historical Society I'd requested. I sat down at my desk, opened my laptop, spent about ten minutes online, then opened the package. Inside were six green folders with the photocopies I'd requested of documents pertaining to Anne Kuiper, née Wilton, during the years she'd spent there, from 1740 to 1779, as well as any other extant material related to the Blackwell family during that period. I leafed through the pages of the first folder, then started entering identifying information into my spreadsheet. Just before my lunch break, in the third folder, I found a letter from Felicity Blackwell addressed to Anne Kuiper, whom I knew was Felicity's sister, Anne Wilton, before she married into the Kuiper family.

To Mrs. Anne Kuiper
July 10, 1753
My dear sister,

I fear the fever that now afflicts me will soon end my life, so am I compelled to formalize your knowledge of certain things we have discussed, for I have nary another friend in this world save yourself.

By my own crude hand I have drawn a map indicating the location of secret caverns that lie beneath the springs in the hill where my mother's cabin once stood, beneath the Ancient Rocks, where last summer and two summers past and three summers past we spilled blood by the full moon in honor of the goddess.

It is recognized by law of this land that our blood father and his brother are the owners of the springs and its lands. But through me and now you, only the daughters have knowledge of the caverns. I pass along this map to you, Anne, and trust you will pass it to your daughters, along with the information I have imparted. My daughters and yours will then pass the knowledge to their own, much like the Mohawk who choose their Queens from among the brightest of their girl children, passing wisdom from one generation to the next.

Anne, the time has come. In addition to showing your daughters the map and teaching them how to find the entrances, also be sure to tell them that my father, our common father, denounced my mother as a witch and had her killed. Tell them what my daughters know, that on account of his treachery I sought out and discovered secret knowledge, and taught myself the ways of the witches of the woods. I summoned demons and learned occult spells. And with that terrible knowledge I have cursed not only the springs, but the water that flows beneath our land. Tell them that with dark words I have cursed the men who would prosper from what is rightfully not theirs to own. That nothing good may usher forth from those depths. My anger over my mother's unrighteous death fuels the evil still swelling within my heart, which grows weaker day by day. Thus have I placed curses on all men who bear the name Wilton. Tell your daughters, dear Anne, that each night before sleep I whisper these words as if they were an incantation, a prayer:" May not one Wilton son know peace as long as he breathes."

Your sister in life as in death,

F. Blackwell

The curse! I gripped the desk in front of me as I read the last words over again and again. I'd just found historical proof that the Wilton curse was real. But Prudence Lowell hadn't cursed John Wilton for condemning her to death. Instead, John Wilton's daughter, Felicity, had taken her revenge against her father by learning "the ways of the witches of the woods." Both of John Wilton's daughters—one by Prudence and the other by Martha—had "spilled blood by the full moon." Blood sacrifice, in other words.

Two of the daughters referred to in the letters were ancestors of Mitch's, if what he'd told me was true. He said he had the genealogy to prove it. I would ask him about it.

There was more to reflect on. "By my own crude hand I have drawn a map," the letter read. I remembered finding a map with strange symbols on it, something I'd seen soon after starting work down here in the basement. I searched my spreadsheet. There was no digital copy, but the notes said the original was in Box 7, folder 47. Box 7 was easy to find, but when I pulled off the lid I could see right away that the documents were in piles, rather than organized in folders. How had the papers ended up this way? Had someone else gone through the box? It took me forty-five minutes to reorder them, but I couldn't locate folder 47. No map. How had the papers ended up this way? Had someone else gone through the box? I looked again, and then went through Box 6 again, and then through Boxes 7 and 8. No map. Then I remembered.

A map with weird symbols had piqued my curiosity enough that I'd taken a picture of it, which I might have forgotten to print or download to the spreadsheet. Still, that didn't explain why the original map wasn't in Box 7.

Using the date on the spreadsheet, I easily found the photograph on my phone, printed it out, and started to examine it. Because I'd been out to the state park with Luna, and had gone running there myself, I could easily orient the items on the map. The springs were clearly marked. What Felicity had referred to as Ancient Rocks were now known as Lowell Rocks. I had seen them from afar and knew they were located near the old TB hospital.

A few weeks earlier, Mitch had brought in old blueprints of the hospital that he'd found among his mother's files. Written on them, in various spots, was the word *CHUTE*. Mitch had told me about "the chutes" although at first I'd thought he'd said "the shoots" and hadn't taken him seriously. I'd researched tuberculosis hospitals from the same era, which mentioned so-called death chutes, underground passageways in a few other hospitals in neighboring states through which hundreds if not thousands of dead tuberculosis patients were moved, undetected, out of buildings, without the knowledge of other patients at the hospital or residents in town. I'd thought the practice creepy and weird, and didn't include it in the database. But maybe Susan's brother been moved through one of the death chutes? Were medical experiments still going on out there? Luna had said the hospital was closed to the public.

Later that night I lay in bed and thought about the map, my thoughts always looping back to Luna. I thought about our first hike to the geysers, about her laughter. She had so much energy, working four jobs. But she played hard, too. I thought about her smile and how messed up it was that Gabe had kidnapped her and kept her in the basement with the other dead girls for so long. But not long enough to break her. Also . . .

I thought back to when she'd disappeared, and when she had reappeared. I sat up in bed and turned on the light. I'd seen her every day for weeks, right up to what I now knew was her kidnapping date, a Friday. Lucas said her kidney had been removed recently. Maybe illegal medical experiments were ongoing, and Gabe had been complicit. And Victoria had threatened to expose the whole thing, so he'd murdered her, or had her murdered? Was he capable of killing his sister?

Luna hadn't told me about having any kind of operation. But they could have drugged her, so she wouldn't have remembered what had happened.

But she would have told me if she'd found a scar on her body . . .

Jade's scar! Had Luna seen it? Did whoever was running the illegal experiments know she'd found out? Or they didn't know, but Luna had agreed to sell them her kidney for a lot of money, and then they'd killed her so she wouldn't talk about it, or because they didn't want to pay her? None of it made sense.

As these thoughts wove through my mind, I changed into hiking clothes. I wanted to go out to the old TB hospital and walk around. It was almost the full moon, which meant there would be plenty of light. If any sort of illicit operation was going on out there I'd take pictures and tell the police. Not the Wilton Springs police because the Wiltons owned them. I wished I could tell Lucas, but I probably couldn't trust him anymore, since I had no idea who he was, and who he was really working for. The evidence couldn't get into the wrong hands. I would send whatever evidence I found to my mom instead. She had a million connections and even though we weren't talking I knew she'd help me if I were truly in trouble.

I'd been taking care of my knee, and it was feeling strong, so I pedaled hard. Everyone except Sienna and I thought Luna had died by suicide. Going out to the old TB hospital might be a crazy idea, but the energy surging through me made think it was the right thing to do. It was something I COULD do. The only thing.

Then reality sank in. I stopped my bike and texted Mason. *If I don't check in with you tomorrow by 8 am, I'm out at the old TB hospital hunting around for some death chutes.* He would love waking up to that message.

As I approached the park I could see some of the old hospital through a clearing and followed a dirt road until more of it came into view. I leaned my bike up against the backside of a tree a little bit off the road and started walking. It looked like it would be a long climb. My knee would hurt tomorrow, but I didn't care.

Around the next bend I saw a bright light glowing in one part of the huge structure, which now looked as long as a full city block, although I couldn't see the details, as there were still other hills blocking my view, and lots of trees and tall underbrush. Then I heard something. Lights bounced around up ahead. I ran into the woods, tripping over a log and falling into some bushes. There was a low rumbling noise, some clacking, and creaking. A gate opening. The rumble got louder. The noises got louder. I put my arms over my head and curled up into a ball until the rumbling noise was right next to me, and then kept going. Looking up, I saw some red taillights and heard what sounded like a truck downshifting to a lower gear.

Just up the road I came to the gate I must've heard open and walked through it. If it was still open, did that mean the truck would come back soon? A high, metal fence encircled the building, and a large No Trespassing sign hung on the fence next to a big gate padlocked shut. Maybe the truck had driven out through a garage underground? I stepped through a hole in the fence where other people had obviously entered, avoiding the cut chain-link fencing, clutching my phone in my jacket pocket.

Graffiti covered the facade of the building—a jumble of multicolored names and nonsensical words. I stepped quietly and carefully as I approached the building, looking behind me every so often. Many of the bars on the windows on the ground floor had been sawed off and the glass smashed in, sockets empty of eyeballs, some boarded with plywood planks. In the bright moonlight I was able to find the front entrance. Just like the gate the truck had driven through, the door within the huge doorframe was unlocked and ajar. I pushed it open and stepped inside. It looked like a bomb had exploded. A grand stairwell running through the center of the big space had collapsed into an enormous pile of stone and brick. The air was thick with the scent of years of accumulated dust and death.

A hole in the ceiling let in the bright moonlight, but didn't light up some water puddles that I stepped into. I skirted some debris, as I looked for . . . what exactly? A chute? Bodies? Skeletons? Medical equipment? I heard something, so I crouched down low. It was a soft noise, but also scratching. Something moved overhead and I looked up to see a bird flying, maybe to or from a nearby nest. A cloud was covering the moon, so I turned my phone flashlight on and took a few more steps toward an opening in one of the walls, and then went down a long corridor into another cavernous room. The same rumbling noise started up and I crouched again, holding my phone against my chest. My heart was thumping wildly. What was I doing here? It was dangerous, and the truth was I didn't even know what I was looking for. I just wanted to find out if something was going on here, something that was related to whoever killed Luna. When I stood up and started walking again I felt a cold breeze swirl around me.

I smelled a sharp electrical smell, and walked in that direction until I saw a big metal door with light coming out from underneath it. I went up to it and turned the handle as slowly as possible, but it was locked. I heard a noise and turned around in time to see something moving that then froze in place. It sounded like someone was walking around. Was someone else here, following me? I took two slow steps back the way I'd come, thinking to hide behind a low wall I'd seen. A beam of light rounded the corner then stopped when it found me. All I could see was light.

"Hey," yelled a man's voice. My adrenaline kicked in as it had with whisky man.

"WHAT are you doing here?" said the voice. My heart boomed in terror. Then the light dropped away from me, and the man pointed it up under his chin so I could see his face. "Genevieve, it's me!"

It was Mason. We moved toward each other, and embraced.

"Shit, Mason. I thought Jim Wilton sent his hitman to kill me."

"I got your text and drove up immediately. You should not be here! Hobos hang out here and do all sorts of twisted stuff. It is totally unsafe. Let's go. I can't believe you'd do this. You almost scared me to death."

"Mason, I saw a map. In the archives. Underneath this building are natural, or maybe carved out, caverns. A whole warren of tunnels and passageways running miles under part of the park and Wilton Springs. There's an entrance beneath this building. The TB hospital transported dead bodies through underground tunnels. I think there's some secret subterranean space that's being used to conduct illegal experiments that were an offshoot of Wilton pharma. Luna didn't kill herself. Her death was part of something larger. Please stop and listen to me."

Mason stopped, but didn't let go of my arm. I'd never seen him angry before. "Genevieve," he said. "I want to protect you. Listen to me. You are not safe here. Neither of us is safe here. You've got to trust me. We've got to get out. NOW!"

"Okay," I said. I felt discouraged, but knew he was right. "I just wanted to do something. Find something and take photos. No one would believe me without proof, and apparently everyone is happy to forget what happened to her, case closed."

"Tell me all about your theories in the truck. But we have to go. Now. Before someone finds us."

We walked back through the opening in the fence just as it started pouring. We walked downhill through the woods, Mason pulling me up if I started to lose speed, encouraging me. "You got this! Heads up here. Go sideways here. Take my hand." I listened to his patter and held his hand, following him until we reached his truck. When he lifted me inside, I slumped down in the seat and started sobbing. "I'm okay, I'm okay," I forced the words out of my mouth. I wasn't okay. We were both drenched from the downpour, and it was still pouring, lightning flashing over and over. "I just hope we don't meet anyone coming up the hill on that road."

"Did you see anyone drive out earlier?"

"Yes," he said.

"Me too. Not a good sign."

He shifted the car back into a low gear and drove, using his parking lights except when it came to the turns.

"My bike," I said, as we drove out of the entrance to the park.

"Not something you need to worry about right now," he said, driving a little faster. We skidded a bit on the next turn and he slowed back down. The rain had started to let up.

"Mason," I said. "Can you take me somewhere? Your house? Out of Wilton Springs? Until I can sort out in my head what's going on?"

"I've already thought about that." He was silent for a minute, then began driving away from town, not toward it. My eyes were closing.

I opened my eyes what seemed like a few seconds later but I wasn't sure how much time had passed. "Where are we going? Your place?" I asked.

"A buddy of mine has a cabin up on Lake Charles. I have the keys. I was planning to surprise you with a romantic weekend, but we'll push it up a few days. Hope the sheets are clean."

"That's a good friend to have." He squeezed my hand and then downshifted.

CHAPTER FORTY

We were leaving Wilton Springs. Everything was going to be okay. We continued driving, and the road seemed empty of cars. Labor Day weekend was ten days away. Soon, the students would flood back to campus, and the residents would return from their summer getaways.

The rain started coming down again. Blobs of water and what seemed like hail began falling like daggers on the roof of the car, blurring the windshield, making it difficult to see.

"I'm going to pull over," Mason said. "Visibility's terrible."

I could barely hear him the storm was so loud.

"What?" I screeched.

"I'm going to pull over!" he shouted.

As we waited on the side of the road, I opened the window, just half an inch, but the rain started coming in horizontally, so I closed it again. Mason lay his hand on my shoulder. "Hey," he said, softly. "I got so scared tonight. I'm not sure this is the best time to tell you this, but I love you."

I started crying.

"Wow, that's never happened before, ouch," he laughed and I did, too. "I hate to see you so upset. How can I fix this?"

"I don't think you can, Mason."

"You can't hide out forever. I mean, you can, but. Did you call the police?"

"No."

"Why not? Do you want me to call?"

"No!" I said. "We can't call them."

"Why not?"

"Because Jim Wilton controls the police. I was trying to tell you. The Wiltons are . . . above the law in Wilton Springs. Jim controls everything. He's dangerous. We need to leave and never come back. The Wiltons' evil spans generations."

"What do you mean?"

"It's all a jumble. Jim's brother and his wife and kids all died in a suspicious accident. Jim's father disinherited him, left everything to the grandkids, Victoria and Gabe, who are now dead. And Jim was conducting his own unethical operation."

"Which was?"

"Using humans like guinea pigs to test new drugs."

"Is that even legal?"

"Yes, if the subject consents. I saw this woman who works in the spa—Jade—collapse in pain but she wouldn't let me call 911."

"Why would she have refused?"

"Maybe because she doesn't want anyone to know that she had been a subject of the Wilton tests. They could ruin her financially, or even kill her. The people in the studies were on the fringes of society, without families. Taken advantage of by a rich and powerful man. First there was the supermarket checkout woman, Trish Baranski. Her body was found in the state park. The other two women who died, Rowena and Stacy, both worked for the Wiltons. It's possible all three volunteered for the experiments. And after they died, their bodies were burned. Susan, at the library, said her brother was involved in a drug trial, and he had a heart attack and died. Of course, no one investigated it."

"I can't believe this."

"They need to reopen Victoria's case and Gabe's. Find out how they really died."

"The Wilton family has given money to the medical school and the hospital where I'm a resident!"

"It's the foundation that gives the money. None of it comes directly from the family. Jim wants people to think he's the big donor, but my neighbor says everybody in town knows all the money is Barbara's."

"Barbara?"

"Jim's wife."

"Isn't the wife complicit?"

"No. It's still fuzzy, but I think Jim hired this fake private detective to pretend to look into the deaths of his children, maybe to hide the fact that Jim's the one who arranged to have them killed, in order to access their inheritances, in any way he could. At the very least, he'd collect life insurance money that he took out on them."

"Listen to what you're saying. A father murdered his own kids? And you really don't think the wife's in on it, too?"

"No. And I have to warn her."

"About what?"

"I think he's been poisoning her with a weight-loss drink. He's been cheating on her for years. They don't have a prenup. If anything happens to her, he gets her money. And the kids' money."

"Shit. Did you reach out to her yet?"

"I texted her but want to tell her in person. Jim's obviously having me followed."

"Tomorrow we can reach out to law enforcement outside of Wilton Springs," said Mason. The rain had lightened up again, so he shifted the car back into drive. The sky was clearing. "I'm amazed that you put all of this together. Clever woman."

I looked down at my phone. Two texts from Lucas. He was sending them to my regular phone now. *All good? Worried I haven't heard from you. If you don't write back, I'll have no choice but to send out a search mission :P*

"Who are you texting?" Mason asked. "If I were you, I wouldn't tell anyone where I was, or who I'm with. Especially now."

"Just Daniela to say I won't be at work tomorrow. You're right. No more texting. I'm going to turn off my phone."

"Good."

I switched it off. I was losing signal anyway.

We kept driving. When we reached the area of the lake where the Wiltons' house used to be, I thought I could smell smoke. I felt my heart fluttering. A few tears slipped down one cheek and the other.

Mason squeezed my hand. His fingers felt so warm. "You're going to be okay. I'll never let anything bad happen to you."

Tears were streaming down my face. "It's hard to be back here, by the lake. Can't help thinking of Luna and what happened to her."

It was almost 1:00 A.M. and very dark when Mason stopped the car. We were on a desolate part of the lake, with barely any other houses around. I started to relax. No one could find me here. Even if I turned my phone back on, I doubted there was any cell service.

Mason opened my door and took my hand. We walked along a long, dirt path through tall weeds that scratched my legs until we reached a small log cabin. "When you nodded off I reached out to a friend of yours. She can help."

"She?"

We opened the door, and I stepped inside, greeted by a warm smell of incense and herbals that I recognized immediately. Sitting in a faded-white Adirondack chair, wearing a long, black gown, was Cecile.

CHAPTER FORTY-ONE

I threw my arms around her. "This is the best surprise! Did Mason tell you what happened?"

She gave me a tight squeeze. "He gave me the address and said to meet him here. It's great to see you, too, love."

"Mason said this house belongs to one of his friends. Are you the friend?"

She smiled. "Nope. It's not mine. He's been keeping this place from me, the little shit."

Cecile and I walked around the house, her heels clicking on the uneven wood floors, and we peeped in at both of the bedrooms, which were so dusty inside I started to sneeze. Back in the kitchen, Mason was preparing a snack. He had opened a bottle of white wine, and was squishing it into a bucket of ice. He turned to Cecile.

"Genevieve's figured it all out. Soon, we'll expose the Wiltons' evil, together."

I put my hand on his shoulder. "We'll have to put together a compelling case, especially since we can't trust the cops in Wilton Springs."

"You've probably got it all written down on your laptop, knowing you. But right now, go sit down in the living room, take a load off," Mason said. "I'll bring this out in a minute."

Cecile drew in a deep breath. "Mason said you've uncovered incriminating evidence?"

"Yes, about Jim Wilton. He's a crook and a philanderer. In addition to those two women who worked for his family, I think he arranged the murder of his own children. I need to warn Barbara. I wanted to meet her in person but it's too dangerous. Is there Wi-Fi here?"

"How do you know she's not involved?" asked Cecile, as we sat down next to each other on the couch in the living room.

"Because she's the one with money. Jim is trying to poison Barbara, and run off with one of his girlfriends. Barbara looks worse and worse every time I see her. Actually, in the archive I discovered the Wiltons really were cursed, but . . ."

"Hold up, slow down," Cecile said to me as Mason came into the room. She had pushed up her sleeve and was twisting the beautiful bangle that she'd shown me. "Let's have some wine. We all could use a drink."

Mason poured white wine into two bell-shaped glasses and handed them to us.

"Not cold enough, but it'll do for now," he said, as he poured a glass for himself.

"I didn't know you drank anything stronger than moon water, Cecile," I said.

She smiled. "On occasion I'll have an adult beverage. Everything in moderation."

Cecile clinked her glass against mine and leaned her head in, nearly knocking mine. Then she sat back and stared up at the ceiling, then back toward me. "Very few people are able to succeed at it. Moderation. Everyone tends to want it all, don't you find?"

"I guess. I've never considered it."

"You wouldn't have, growing up like you did. Probably seemed natural to you." She paused, putting her wineglass down.

"I suppose."

"Think about a girl like Luna Collins. Grew up with nothing. Lost her mom. Gets a partial scholarship and puts herself through college. Cuts corners where she can—writing papers for privileged, lazy kids, who go on to get top paying jobs, and inherit money from trust funds, all the while Luna sinks deeper into debt, no matter how gifted and hardworking she is. Add to that a sister with a life-threatening illness, who she has to support. What's a talented young woman to do?"

The room reflected back to me, and I felt a surge of vertigo. "So, you know about Sienna, the sister. I thought . . . She told you how Luna made money in college?" I asked.

"You, Genevieve Tompkins, were a little shocked to hear that she hustled her way through school weren't you. Even though you thought of Luna as a close friend, right? You'd never stoop to doing such a thing, I'm certain," she said, emphasizing the word *stoop*.

"I sympathized with Luna, and her circumstances. I told her all the time how impressed I was by her accomplishments."

"And what if you were a young woman with nothing, and some rich boy came along promising everything, but really just wanted to get in your pants, and move on to the next. How would that make you feel?"

"Not good."

"And might you be motivated to seek revenge on such a person, once you realized they were just playing you?"

"I'd be pretty pissed. I remember how it felt when I found out my fiancé was cheating on me." I turned to Mason. "Could I have a glass of water?"

"Water's turned off here," he said. "Have some more wine."

"Okay," I said, turning back to Cecile. "Where is this going, Cecile?"

"It's not going anywhere, it's an exercise in empathy, which I think all of us need to practice." She shook her head. "Must be difficult. For someone who's never had any real challenges in life."

I lifted my glass and took another few sips of wine.

"And what of such a man's mother?" said Cecile, her voice acidic. "Who taught him to unconsciously label women either those to wed or those to bed, those to bed being the ones who didn't come from the right family? A wealthy woman in her own right, complicit in the crimes of her husband, might do such a thing. Like she might control every aspect of her daughter's life in order to mold her into a docile, well brought up girl and repeat the cycle. Even when she could've done so much more."

My heart had speeded up. I thought the wine would make it slow down. "You're talking about Barbara Wilton. And Victoria."

"Is that woman's life worth saving, considering that she's been the cause of so much misery?"

"I'm not following you, Cecile. Barbara hasn't done anything wrong."

"Does she deserve your goodwill? She and her husband's family are responsible for so much oppression, and suffering. Centuries of it." I could see the little purple veins in her forehead throbbing as she spoke. "I've devoted my life to helping unfortunate people, to giving others a chance. If it were up to the Wiltons and their ilk, the unfortunate people would be dead. Like my sweet, little boy. Do you know how much his medication cost me every month? American society is broken, Genevieve."

"There's a lot that's wrong with it."

"Everything. Everything is wrong with it. I know you know that."

"I dooooo." I didn't mean to sound emphatic. The word just came out, and kept coming.

Cecile stared at me. "The ancient cultures I've spent my adult life studying emphasize the importance of sacrifice for the greater good. The idea of *do ut des*. Have you ever heard that phrase? It means, literally, 'I give that you may give.' Stretches back to Roman law. Or, consider this, the Norse eddas tell the story of the mighty Tyr, who sacrificed his own hand—allowed it to be bitten off by the wolf Fenrir—in exchange for the world to live in peace until Ragnarok. Druids sacrificed criminals in order to win battles. Human sacrifice played a prominent role in pre-Columbian societies. In ancient Sweden, kings would sacrifice one of their sons to Odin every tenth year, and eventually their own lives, permitting themselves only ten years of rulership. Why is it that in our modern society, sacrificing oneself is seen as idiotic, and wealth is hoarded by the few? All matter is finite, yet the societies that redistributed resources to create equality have been all but destroyed. Greed governs all."

I leaned my head back against the top of the couch, taking a break from her words and her hard glare.

Mason was standing in the doorway, watching us. He came over to refill my glass of wine, and rubbed my neck. "How you feeling, babe? Any calmer now?"

"Yes. Calmer. Definitely. I think." Even though I'd only had one glass of wine, it was having a powerful effect on me. Unless I closed my eyes, everything started to spin, as if I were on a merry-go-round. Then the room seemed to be slanted over to one side, and it looked as if I were seeing it from upside down. I thought of the Hanged Man from the tarot deck. And then the room disappeared altogether, and I only saw darkness.

CHAPTER FORTY-TWO

I woke up in a blank, dimly lit space wearing sweatpants and a sweatshirt that didn't belong to me. The place felt cold, too cold for a summer afternoon. Where was I? What was happening? I heard voices outside the room, and a few minutes later Cecile walked in followed by Emma, who was wearing a lab coat and carrying a tray with food on it, which she put on the bed over my stomach. She pulled a plastic bottle of Wilton Springs water out of her coat pocket, twisted the top off, and handed it to me. Then, without saying anything, Emma walked out of the room.

"You were out for a while," Cecile said, soothingly.

"Where am I?" I asked. "Did I pass out?"

"Take a deep breath. And you need to eat, please."

"I'm not hungry. I feel sick to my stomach. And I have a massive headache. I'm not sure I can even stand up. Is there any coffee? Or a Diet Coke? I'm on the verge of a migraine."

"You're feeling the passing of your old life," said Cecile.

"What?" I sat up, and threw the covers back, but couldn't move because something was stopping me. I looked down, then up at her. "Cecile! There are straps around my ankles! What's going on?"

"The transition is more difficult on some than others," she said, standing up straighter, her hands clasped behind her back.

Panic pushed away my confusion. I bent over and tried to take the straps off. They had locks on them. "What the fuck?"

Cecile shook her head. "With the negativity in your voice, you won't be able to hear what I am about to tell you."

"I'm not being negative!" I said. I reached down to the straps on my ankles but couldn't see how to loosen them. "Help me!" I insisted.

Cecile ignored me and began talking. "You smart girls need things explained in the simplest of terms. In plain language, I'm starting a new society and way of life, open to those who believe in what I'm trying to accomplish."

"Which is . . ."

"Equality for everyone. A new order, inspired by what historical revolutions have failed to create in the past. The movement is growing, one person at a time." She looked at me, and then continued. "The system is based on female empowerment. On a redistribution of resources. I told you that I specialize in getting people what they want, and what they need."

"Why am I strapped in here, Cecile? Simple question."

"Mason and I believe in you, Genevieve. We'll be stronger with you. If you were in charge of the world, it would be a better place. I know you care about other people, about social issues, about justice."

"Mason . . . ?"

"My right-hand man, even if we're both lefties," she said, and tapped the tray on my lap. "Eat your food. You need to get your strength back."

"You drugged me? Or Mason did! With the wine?"

"Join us."

"Us?"

"We're together, a team. A special team. But it's not just the two of us. There are many who believe in my path. As I said, we'd be stronger with you. You've got the discipline. You remind me of Victoria. She was strong, like you. Rebellious. She didn't believe the lies that American society fed her about what women could and could not do."

"What do you want from me?"

"Your compliance, which won't be automatic, I know. You did too much investigating on your own, without having it all properly explained, and now you can't see things in the right light. But I'm hoping you'll come around. Like Emma. It took her a while to understand, but now she loves what we do. She supports the cause. And not just financially."

"Is that why you chose me, for my money? I don't have any!"

Cecile waved her hand in the air as if to dismiss me.

"My mom is heavily in debt," I said. "I had to sell my dad's houses, his cars, artwork, everything—in order to pay the estate tax. Now I need a job to pay my bills."

"No need to prevaricate, Genevieve. I've read in the papers—"

"The papers don't know shit. I'm telling you the truth."

"If that's the case, I can make you rich again, Genevieve. Do you want to join us, or don't you? You'd be well compensated if you find other women to join. Like Luna did with you."

"Luna . . . recruited me?"

"Perhaps it's more accurate to say that she helped guide the hand of destiny." She looked down and then raised her face to mine. "Then Luna got greedy, and we had to part ways."

"It was . . . you! You killed Luna! Because you couldn't control her?"

Cecile winced. "It's not about control. It's about strength, teamwork, helping each other. As women." Her eyes ran over my face. "You never hold on to something quite so tightly as the moment before you let it go."

"So it was never the Wiltons. It was you all along. You and Mason. And Emma. And . . . whoever else."

"More people in Wilton Springs are with me than against me. I've spent a while cultivating friends. All kinds of friends."

"Why do you need me if you have Emma and her money?"

"You're smarter. More capable. I already told you. It's not about money."

"She's younger. Easier to control."

Cecile pursed her lips. "As women we alone understand our own unique challenges and can support each other."

"You support other women, yes, but not Barbara Wilton. Not Victoria."

"Don't put yourself in the same category with them. They're spoiled, entitled. They lack empathy. Victoria never had the star quality that you have. And you have a good heart, too."

"Oh. That's why you wanted me. You think I'm naive."

"Good and naive aren't the same."

"So, what's your proposal? Now that you know I can't bankroll you?"

Cecile crossed the floor to the opposite side of the room and walked back and forth, as if she were a professor about to start a lecture. "Do you know how many people around the world are desperate for organs? Beyond desperate. Without a certain organ they would die." She didn't pause for a response. "Millions. And in the United States it is illegal to sell one's organs. That's a good example of the nanny state. Do you know how much organs are worth?"

This time she waited, but I just stared at her.

"All the organs and tissues in one person's body are worth millions of dollars," she said. "And in most modern societies the powers that be watch human beings die in the name of legalese and individual freedoms, rather than let generous, compassionate individuals sell what belongs to them in order to help someone else. That's not only ableist, it's applied eugenics. Politicians, and those who elect and enable them, decide who lives or dies. I would've paid anyone any amount to save my son. But that was not an option available to me. At the same time that he died on a wait list, people are living in wells of poverty and debt, people who will never make it off the hamster wheel. Can't you see a way those two groups might mutually benefit each other?"

"Organ harvesting."

"I would describe it differently. Let's say there's a young woman, in the prime of her life. She's had fewer opportunities than others, and although she's trying to succeed, things have not turned out well. Maybe she has a criminal record for a petty crime. She's in a jam and can't pay her way out. Such a person cannot get a regular job, no one will hire her. So, what does she do? And how can I help? That's what I ask myself, if she comes to me.

"First, I help her get clean. But that's not enough. Oftentimes she owes money, or she's got an abusive partner, or she's trying to get custody back of her child. Then it's time to become creative. In the new order, we're all equals who help each other. Because helping her in turn helps someone else, someone who needs something this young woman has but doesn't need. Let's say her second kidney. Removing it won't change her life expectancy. But it's a matter of life and death to the other person. To her it's a matter of money. Doesn't that seem like a fair exchange?"

"If I don't agree to join you, will you kill me, too?"

Her mouth twisted up. "My dear, you are jumping to unnecessary and inaccurate conclusions. I think you'll see it our way and join us. I empower women to regain control of their lives. I do the work that society is supposed to do. Doesn't that speak to you? You're a caring person. Not so our politicians, who only pretend to care. I save lives."

"And you profit from them."

"I take a very small fee, for arranging the transactions."

I said nothing.

"Can you see what I'm trying to do?" said Cecile. "How beautiful it is? I've never asked you for anything, which should show you that you're worth more to me than your bank account. I care about the real Genevieve. And I honestly believe you could help us. What do you say?"

"I think, yes. Alright," I said, trying to sound enthusiastic.

"Alright? Alright what?"

"I'll help. I will. What you're saying actually does make sense. I've never thought of it that way before. I want to be part of it. I believe in you, Cecile."

She clapped her hands together once. "I am so, so glad to hear you say that. Now, there's someone who would like to check on you." She put her finger to her lips as she walked out.

A few minutes later, Mason walked in. "Hello, gorgeous," he said.

"Mason! Can you unlock these straps," I said, pointing at my ankles. He shrugged, so I said, "Okay, can we talk about what Cecile is doing? Please, can you explain it to me?"

"Shh . . . relax. Cecile said you're on board. Aren't you glad I introduced you to her? She's extraordinary, isn't she?" His tone seemed different. It was dreamy, reverent.

Panic and confusion pushed away some of the fog still clouding my mind. I almost reached out for his hand, but stopped myself. "Cecile said the two of you were . . . together?"

"Together? In a way . . . Cecile is my sister."

I stammered. "Cecile's your . . . your sister? You're her brother?"

"Cecile was adopted by my family. But she was the one who raised me."

"Are you adopted, too?"

"My mom adopted Cecile and her younger brother when she thought she couldn't have children, then years later my brother and I were born. Cecile took care of all of us boys. Even while she was in nursing school."

"Cecile's a nurse?"

"She had to drop out. Doesn't mean she's not brilliant, though. She's smarter than I am. She's the one who came up with this idea for an alternative society of the future."

"Is that why you went to med school? Because of Cecile?"

"She encouraged me for sure. When I was in college she got me a job in a hospital shadowing a surgeon, working as his assistant. We used to practice suturing grapefruits."

"So you're part of all this, part of . . . the organ harvesting?"

"We don't call it that, Gen. We're helping people stay afloat. Cecile saved Jade, for example, saved her life, helped find a way to finance her education. Jade's a certified spa therapist now. She's working at the front desk, but soon she'll have clients of her own."

"Did she give up one of her organs? Is that why she has that huge scar?"

"Just one kidney."

"And you performed the operation. Also on Luna?"

"I've never done anything that these women didn't want themselves. That they didn't volunteer for. Rowena, Stacy, Trish, Luna, Daphne, Kathy, the others."

It took a tremendous amount of effort to stay calm. "You performed the operations on all of them. More than just the four I know about. How many more?"

He bent over toward me and kissed me on the cheek, and moved around to my lips, which he pecked. Then he left the room before I could ask where he was going or when he was coming back. Over the next twenty minutes, I drank all the water in the bottle that Emma had given me.

He walked back in half an hour later, wearing a white lab coat. I'd never seen him dressed as a doctor before. He shook his head when he approached me.

"Mason, can I leave now? Or can you take these straps off my ankles?"

"I just had a talk with Cecile. She wants proof you're serious. About your decision to join us."

"What does that mean?"

"The way you came around wasn't organic, she said. Wasn't . . . seamless, the way it was supposed to be. You went out on your own, asking questions, digging deeper, even after you were warned. Cecile's worried you may not be serious about your commitment. To the cause."

"How do I show I'm serious? I can't make a donation."

"Not a monetary one. But a donation like some of the other girls have made."

"You mean . . ."

"I'll do the operation. I'm very good at it—it's very safe."

"I believe you're a great surgeon. And I believe in what you're doing. What you're both doing. I want to help. But at least two of the girls who were operated on died."

"They didn't die because of my operations," he said, punching out the words. "They were in poor health to begin with—drug addicts who'd abused their bodies. Long suicides, basically."

"I know you're skilled, it's not that . . ."

He took a step back. "But, my love," he said, his voice back to its gentle tone, "how would we know you're not just pretending, not going to run to the police?" He picked up my right hand and kissed it. "Unless, and please forgive the expression, unless you have some skin in the game?"

"I understand." I did understand. If I refused to go along, they would kill me. "And I'm ready to make the sacrifice. I only need one kidney, right?"

"Oh darling, that's wonderful. You won't regret it, I promise. It's very simple, and after it's over, everything will go back to the way it was, and we'll be so happy."

"I really need coffee. And lunch. Or breakfast? What time is it?"

He shook his head. "I'll have them bring you something else to eat and drink. You have to rest before the procedure. I need to leave now for the hospital and assist in another surgery."

"Everything's moving so quickly. I still feel really groggy from whatever was in my wine. Don't you think I need time to get that out of my system before you put me under again?"

He shook his head. “We must proceed ASAP.”

“How about tomorrow morning, when you’re fresh?”

He laughed once. “You’re not trying to stall, are you? Let’s just get it over with.”

He put his hand on my forehead and ran his fingers, tenderly, through my hair. “I really think you should rest now, my love. I’ll give you something to calm you down,” he said, as he pushed me down gently, but with force. He pulled a syringe out of his pocket, and said, “Lie back, and try to relax.”

He rolled up the sleeve of my sweatshirt and then pulled a little packet out of his pocket. I squeezed my eyes shut and winced as he stabbed my forearm with the needle, which he dropped into a metal tray. He tore open the packet—an alcohol wipe—and pressed it where he’d punctured my skin. “Count backward from ten,” he instructed.

I made it to seven.

CHAPTER FORTY-THREE

When I woke up, bright, fluorescent light was shining in my eyes. Through a dull headache, I could see that the room wasn't fully in focus. And it wasn't the same room I'd been in before. My mouth felt very dry. I now had on a hospital gown, tied in front. No ankle straps. I heaved myself out of bed, tested my balance, and stood up on bare feet. There was an unopened bottle of water on the counter so I carefully stepped across the room and drank it. Maybe it was the adrenaline, but I felt pretty alert. How many hours had it been since Mason had knocked me out? When would he return? I waited a bit longer until most of the wooziness had faded, and then walked to the door. It was unlocked. I opened it and looked out. Silence. Darkness. I could see that it was a hallway. I stepped out of the room, shutting the door behind me. I didn't know whether to turn left or right but knew I had to get away. I chose left.

Walking slowly and quietly in total darkness, I trailed the fingers of my right hand along the wall in order to feel my way. I came to a door, twisted the knob gently, and it opened. The only light came from two small green dots next to what I hoped was a light switch. I pushed it, and lights came on. I found myself in what looked like a modern, fully equipped operating room, with a long, padded table, mobile headlights, a stainless-steel sink, plastic containers filled with liquids in a rainbow of colors, and a row of steel cabinets with glass doors filled with scalpels and other instruments. In front of the cabinets was a cart with more instruments individually shrink-wrapped in plastic pouches, on shelves. And a monitor.

I heard something and flipped off the light. I waited. When it was quiet again, I silently turned the doorknob and tiptoed out of the room. I continued down the hall, my hands crawling along the walls, trying to determine something, anything. After another five minutes of walking, the hallway stopped.

I turned and continued along the back wall of the hallway. A few steps in, I felt a change in the material I was walking on. I dropped to my hands and knees and felt around. My hands ran over a latch of some sort. Just then, I heard a door opening and closing. A light came on at the far end of the hallway where I'd come from. Muffled voices. Other lights started to click on. I wrapped my fingers around the latch and pulled what turned out to be some sort of thick plastic cover, about three feet in diameter. I was able to move it easily, and then look into a porthole. Off to one side, a metal ladder was bolted to a wall. At the other end of the hallway I heard some shouting. Barefoot, I started to climb down the metal rungs slowly, taking care not to slip, not bothering to replace the cover above me.

When I reached the bottom, I looked all around me. I was in some sort of corridor, or tunnel, which was dimly lit. Wall lights flickered and hummed. The ground felt freezing on my bare feet as I began to walk. The air was damp, and very cold, in the high forties I guessed. The path under my feet was clean without much debris, although there were loose pebbles. I could make out a brick, snakelike construction running through the center of the ceiling on kinds of stilts. I was walking along a narrow path next to what looked like some sort of trough. I thought of what I'd found in the archive and realized I was probably inside part of the old aqueduct.

I reached another metal ladder bolted to the wall but kept going down the path, picking up my pace and starting to run, as fast as I could, which was not fast also because my knee was not fully healed. Soon, I was winded and shivering, and my face was wet with tears, but I had to get farther away.

I didn't hear anything behind me in the tunnel, and slowed down. By the time I caught my breath, I saw a third metal ladder attached to the wall, which I climbed up. At the top was another three-foot porthole closed with a cover. I pushed on it but it was difficult to open more than an inch or so. Something was covering it. I had to hold onto the ladder with one hand and push the cover and whatever was on top of it to the side. My arms were trembling and I thought I was going to have to climb back down when I saw a beam of a flashlight sweeping down the tunnel where I'd come from.

With a surge of energy I pushed up, and through the hole, and crawled out. There was a familiar smell of incense, lavender, and other herbs. It was warm and humid.

When my eyes began to adjust, I could just make out that I was in the basement of the spa. I was back in Wilton Springs? I stood up and looked around. I was in the locker room. A nightlight was on in the bathroom and shower area, which oriented me. Red numbers glowed on the clock that dipped down from the ceiling. 7:03 P.M. The spa was closed.

How soon would they discover I wasn't still in the room where they'd left me? When they found me, would they kill me?

I put the cover back in place, and as I smoothed out the carpet, floorboards started creaking above me. I could hear a muffled conversation upstairs. My temples throbbed, and my throat felt as if it were stuffed with sandpaper. I needed water, but couldn't turn on the faucets in the bathroom because I knew that they moaned when in use. Now the voices above me were distinct, closer. Were they coming down to the basement? Bending my head, and folding my arms into my chest, I managed to squeeze into one of the tall lockers, closing it gently behind me, letting the lock click shut. I waited inside the locker until my breathing and heartbeat slowed to normal and I heard the front door of the spa thud closed.

I opened the locker door, walked to the bathroom, turned on the noisy faucet, and dipped my head in the sink, drinking water sideways, gulping it down with a lot of air. Had Mason said how long his operation at the hospital would last? My neck hurt. Everything hurt. I had cut something on my right foot and it was stinging. And I was trailing blood. I reached for a paper towel and looked in the mirror. Someone was standing behind me. I spun around.

"Jade," I gasped.

Her eyes widened. I remembered what Cecile had said about Jade's unwavering loyalty. I'd need to choose my words carefully. "Hi, Jade!" I said. "I don't know how I wound up here. I woke up in a bed wearing this gown, and walked until I found a ladder. I think I was in a sort of trance. I was waiting for Mason, and—"

"You need to get out of here, Genevieve. You're in a hospital gown, so I know what's going to happen to you. Do you have any idea?"

I nodded. "Yes."

"So, you've agreed to it? Are you with them?"

"No!" I said. "I'm not with them. Mason gave me a shot, but I woke up and found a tunnel and . . . I'm very, very scared."

"You should be scared," she said. "But I can try to get you out of here. Let's go."

I hesitated.

"NOW, Genevieve! You promise me you're not with them, right?"

"I promise."

"Are you sure? Wait, did they send you? They suspected I was wavering. How did you escape?"

"Down a hallway, I pulled off a cover and saw a ladder. People were coming my way so I went down the ladder. I ran through a tunnel and climbed up another ladder into the spa. Look at me! I'm all bloody and scraped! I'm not with them. But how do I know I can trust you?"

"We've got to trust each other. But we don't have much time."

"Jade. I need something more."

"Okay, okay. Remember those body parts that you found in the park? The day with the dog? Mason gave Trish's body parts to Luna to dispose of, and she was supposed to take them upstate but ran out of time and panicked, so she asked me to help her and we buried the arms and legs in the park. Is that enough proof?"

"So you were with them then, how do I know you're not with them now?"

"Genevieve! I woke up when I had to deal with a chopped-up body without a head! If you think I'd make that up, then I'm out." Without waiting for me to respond, Jade reached up into one of the cabinets above the lockers, and passed me an Earth Mother sweatshirt and a pair of leggings, which I quickly slipped on, throwing off the hospital gown. "What size shoe do you wear?" she asked.

"Ten," I said.

"I'm a seven and a half. Cecile's an eight. But I'll check the lost and found."

She opened one of the lockers and pushed some things around until she pulled out a pair of sneakers and handed them to me. I slipped my bare feet inside. They were too big. I tightened the laces, hoping I could run without tripping.

Jade ripped open a packet of water bottles and gave one of them to me. I slurped it eagerly as we made our way back to the porthole.

"I don't think we should go down there," I said, as she started to pull the rug away. "Someone with a flashlight was behind me on the path."

"It's the only way," Jade said. "Whoever was down there is long gone now. And if they thought you'd climbed up into the spa they would've called me. Okay, you go first, and I'll put the cover back in place."

When we reached the bottom she gave me a pocket flashlight. "Don't use it until you really need it." She turned hers on and we started walking through the tunnel.

I got winded trying to keep pace with Jade. After only a few minutes she turned around. "Whatever he gave you is really slowing you down. You're going to have to move faster," she said. "And keep drinking water to flush out the drug. Here's another bottle."

"What is this place?" I asked.

"The tunnels, you mean?"

"Why are they so well-maintained?" I said, but Jade had started trotting ahead.

She turned her head sideways as she spoke, then swiveled back straight ahead. "Before the tunnels there were just a bunch of caverns," she said. "Natural geological ones, formed millions of years ago. Lots in this area. They were dug out, shored up, formed into tunnels to transport things. Contraband. Canadian whisky smuggled south at the time of Prohibition. During the Cold War the military started using the tunnels, made more. Connected them. Built fallout shelters and bunkers. But after the Wall fell, it was all abandoned. The tunnels were forgotten. But Cecile . . ." She stopped at a corner and looked left and right.

I took a breath. "Why are you helping me? Mason said Cecile saved your life, and—"

She turned to me and said in a crisp whisper, "My life? Please. The only person Cecile is interested in saving is herself." She put her finger to her lips. "We've got to talk quietly now," she said and we took the left path. After a few minutes the tunnel widened and she stopped until I caught up with her.

She whispered, "In the beginning, yes. I fell for it. I was in bad shape. Cecile helped me get clean. Off the streets. When I was better, she brought up some nasty stuff about my past. Used it as collateral and said I had to work for her. At that point I didn't have a choice. But now I know the real reason she wanted me to get healthy is because she wanted my kidney."

"Oh, I'm so sorry, Jade!"

"She promised I'd get out of debt, said the kidney would bring in a big sum, I could start my life over. But no money ever hit my account. When I told her I was leaving, Cecile went batshit crazy, said if I left, or even told anyone, she'd kill me. Later she apologized, said she needed me, that I was her only true friend. She promised they'd take care of me. She and Mason. But now I'm stronger. I didn't know how to leave, I was scared, but when I saw you in that gown it was like a switch flipped. It's a lot easier saving you than saving me. Or trying to, at least."

We heard a loud clunking noise. In front, or behind us? We flattened ourselves against the wall and looked in both directions. After a few seconds we started walking again. "And how did you find out?" Jade whispered in my ear.

"I . . . uncovered some stuff, and thought the Wiltons were doing illegal experiments, and murdering people. I thought you were involved. When I saw your scar that day, I started asking more questions. Yesterday I went to check out the old TB hospital, and Mason met me there, like he was rescuing me, took me to his friend's cabin on Lake Charles."

"And Cecile was there, right?"

"Yes! I told her about the Wiltons. She talked a lot but I don't remember what she said because Mason spiked my drink. I woke up underground somewhere, and even after I agreed to be part of their plans, let them take my kidney, they drugged me again. I managed to get to the spa. You found me."

"We may still be screwed," she said. "If they find us they'll kill us both. When they killed Luna, I knew I was next."

"Do you know where we're going?" I asked.

"Cecile had an old map in her office that she hid behind some books. She told me to study the routes of the tunnels. I have a vague idea where we are. Can you go any faster?"

"I'm going as fast as I can."

"'Kay."

"I can't believe we're what, running for our lives? Cecile is so . . ."

"She pretends to be a hippie who teaches self-empowerment and healing, but that's just a ploy to lure rich girls like, sorry, like you. And Mason. He seduces the girls, and then they're hooked. So it's a double whammy: Cecile the earth mother figure and the hot guy, seemingly crazy about them. Everyone knows Mason went after you, even though he's married to Emma."

I felt a churning deep in my stomach and grabbed her arm. "What?" I said, but then we heard another loud clunking sound and stopped again.

"Let's go," Jade said, after what seemed like five minutes.

"What else don't I know about?" I said almost under my breath as we started moving.

"Gabe Wilton. He wasn't the most upstanding guy about town, so people barely even questioned his death, even his parents."

"Cecile and Mason killed Gabe Wilton?" I asked.

"And made Luna say he'd kidnapped her, when it was actually Luna who lured him out there, pretending she wanted to seduce him. With Gabe gone the Wilton inheritance would revert to Jim. You know Cecile was sleeping with him, working that angle, right?"

"Holy shit" was all I managed to say. We kept walking. "I had no clue."

"They kept it under wraps," said Jade.

"Why did Luna agree to seduce Gabe? Did she know they were going to kill him?"

"They'd blackmailed Luna with stuff from her past, and then threatened to kill her sister when she threatened to blow their cover if she didn't get paid."

"I knew she didn't kill herself," I said.

"Once each of us realized the money we were promised after our operations wasn't coming, we started questioning things. That's when we became inconvenient liabilities. After Mason operated on Rowena, she got an infection that gave her jaundice. Mason snuck her out of the hospital, but we never saw her again."

After we walked for a few more feet I said, "I just realized something, Jade."

"What?"

"They burned down the lake house not only so Gabe's inheritance would revert to Jim, but to hide the fact that the dead girls were missing kidneys."

"It's worse, actually," Jade said, shaking her head. "Mason didn't kill them right away. He took other live organs, not just kidneys. Corneas, livers, I don't even know what. Mason did something with Trish's head. For a while it was on ice in one of the coolers at the spa. I heard Cecile tell Emma the organs were sent in the coolers through the tunnel system, sometimes all the way up to Canada, the same route they used to run moonshine way back when. But the bodies weren't always moved upstate. They didn't have a solid plan for the bodies."

The path became sandy, and Jade grabbed my hand. "Hope your strength is back. We need to start running. Let's exchange numbers in case we get separated."

I patted down my pocket. "Shit! My phone!"

"Wait. Cecile put a phone in her safe at the office!"

"Do you have the combination?"

"Yes, but we can't go back there now. I could, but not you."

"I know someone who could retrieve it from the safe."

"Someone who could break into the office? Call her on my phone and I'll give her the combo. Wait, no cell service down here. Shit. We can't call her."

"It's a he. Lucas. He's a detective I trusted, then didn't trust, but . . ."

"How do you know he's not with Cecile?" Jade asked.

"I'm pretty sure he isn't. Do you have a better idea? Can we just call 911 when we're out of the tunnel?"

"No. Cecile has a lot of friends in first responders."

"How much longer till we get out? And where?"

"I'm not sure where we'll get out, but I'm trying to get us away from Wilton Springs. Ten minutes or less? Once we're out we can call your detective. Here, put in his number," she said, holding out her phone.

"I don't know his number!" I said.

"Well, we can't go back to the spa just for that. Once we're aboveground we can crash at my girlfriend's place and figure it out from there."

"Okay," I said. "Wait! Did you hear that?" We stood there and waited, holding hands. I had heard something. Maybe there were rats down here?

"Ready to run?" Jade said. "It can't be too much further." I took a deep breath and crouched down, ready to lunge forward, but then heard footsteps, crunching.

"Hello, ladies." A voice I recognized bounced off the walls.

CHAPTER FORTY-FOUR

Emma moved into the middle of our path, blocking the way. Jade stepped back and grabbed my arm.

Emma pushed up goggles on her head and aimed the gun she was holding at my chest. "Oh, Genevieve, there you are. Trying to run away, weren't you? Jade, why are you with her?"

Jade tightened her grip on my arm. "I was on my way to bring some supplies Cecile asked for and found her wandering around. I was taking her to surgery prep. She's out of it. Kept saying she wanted to call Mason."

Emma clicked her tongue. "Did you tell Cecile?"

"Of course. She didn't pick up, so I left her a message," Jade said.

I inched closer to Emma, blinking my eyes. "I was in a daze and got lost, and ran into Jade. She said she'd help me. Get back. I'm really thirsty. I need to talk to Mason."

Emma's eyes narrowed. "I wonder how Genevieve could find her way into the tunnels from the surgery area. Hmm. It's not that I don't believe you two, per se, but what is it Lenin said? 'Trust is good, control is better'?"

Jade stepped toward Emma. "You know I'm loyal to Cecile. I'm the one who found Genevieve. Now you're trying to take credit."

"Emma," I said. "I'll go with you." I smiled at her and held my hands up. "We're friends, right?" Jade had turned around and was walking back in the direction of the spa.

With the hand that wasn't holding the gun Emma pushed me around and shoved me forward. I started walking, slowly. "Mason said he injected you with enough benzos to knock out a pony," she snarled. "He said he wasn't sure if you'd wake up again!"

After a few more minutes of walking she started up again, "We were never friends, Genevieve. You were someone I tolerated. I hate everything about you, from the way you dress to how entitled you are, even though you pretend otherwise. How many events at my house did you crash? I told Cecile we couldn't trust you. Keep walking. I know a shortcut back to the surgery center."

"Did you know you descend from a famous witch, Emma? I found the history of—"

She cut me off. "I don't care about any of that."

I was deliberately limping even though she kept pushing me and knocking my back with the butt of the gun. After a few minutes in silence, she grabbed my arm and forced me around until I was facing her. She was grinning as she shook the gun in my face, grinning as she said in a singsong voice, "Did Mason tell you I'm his assistant? You know I'm premed, right?"

I continued acting groggy, slowing my words, hoping Jade was on her way to get my phone and call Lucas. Or figuring out something else. But I wasn't sure. "Mason said you believe in Cecile. Me too, Emma! I believe in Cecile. But, well, I'm kind of confused about this whole thing. Why do you believe in Cecile?"

"'Why?' she asks. Because I have a sense of right and wrong. Convictions, which I would be wasting my time trying to explain to you. *Walk!*" She turned me around and pushed me again and I felt the gun in the small of my back. "Faster!"

"You really are devoted to Cecile's cause, Emma, right? As dedicated, I mean, devoted, as I am?" I stopped but she shoved me forward.

"If you really believed in her, Gen-e-vieve, you would know that Cecile is pure love. I'm ecstatic about the utopia she's already started to create, a world based on everyone getting what they need. Most people go through life without gratefulness. I used to be like that. Then Cecile showed me how she was helping other women. I'm talking about real charity. Not the bullshit philanthropy my mom and her friends do to make themselves feel better. The only reason modern society looks down on the organ trade is because of outdated religious laws. In Wiccan culture—" She paused, and then continued. "To sacrifice, and to give life, is the highest form of altruism one can aspire to."

"Wow. You know so much. Mason said you were smart. By the way, did the operation hurt when you had it?" I spun around and looked at her, then squeezed my eyes shut and opened them wide. I had remembered a move from my self-defense class and was about to try to grab her gun, but Emma tucked it into a deep pocket of her jacket.

"I haven't had to make the particular sacrifice they're asking you to make," she said, her voice quieter than it had been. "They know I'm willing but they need me for other things. I recruit good candidates. I would never have tried to recruit you, though." Her scowl flipped into a smile. "And Mason said he wouldn't want to disfigure my perfect body. He can't imagine me with a scar." She spat out her next words at me. "It kills me to think of him in bed with you, even though I know he's faking it. Another sacrifice I made for the greater good."

I opened my mouth but no words came out.

"Fuck," she said. "My night goggles ran out of juice." She pulled a huge flashlight out of her bag, turned me around, and clicked on a bright light that lit up the tunnel before us. She pushed me forward and we continued walking. I stumbled every ten or twelve steps.

After walking in silence for another few minutes we reached a metal ladder bolted to the wall and she told me to stop.

"After you," she said, and clicked the flashlight off. I climbed up the metal rungs and crawled out through an open porthole, which led to a long, tiled hallway, this one with plenty of light. There was a row of closed doors on one side of the hallway.

At the third door Emma took me by the arm and pushed me in front of her and into a large room. An operating room. Mason was there, standing next to Cecile. They were both wearing white lab coats.

"Why, Genevieve, hello. We've been missing our guest of honor," Cecile said, wagging her forefinger. "The party can't get started without you. Take off your shoes and clothes and put that on." She pointed the gun that Emma had passed her at a hospital gown.

"What you're doing is shameful. Disgusting," I said, as Emma crouched down and started unlacing my sneakers. I heard Cecile click something on the gun. Emma wrenched the shoes off my feet. The only thing I could do was try to stay upright. "You're psychopaths," I said, looking around the room. With surprising strength Emma grabbed the waist of the sweatpants and yanked them down along with my underwear. I raised my voice. "Murderers!"

As Emma pulled my sweatshirt up and off, Cecile faced me. "I'm a respected member of society, dear Genevieve. People love me, look up to me. If you'd gone to the police you'd have been laughed out of town. Or they'd have sent you to a psych ward."

"Not everyone believes your lies, Cecile. You can only keep this going for so long. You're going to get caught."

Emma pushed me into the wheelchair, plucked up the gown, and tossed it at me. She stepped over to Mason, pulled him toward her, and wrapped her arms around him. She gave him a full-body hug and a passionate kiss, which he returned, his hands running up and down her body.

"Okay, kids," Cecile said. "Let's get going."

Where was Jade? What was taking her so long? Had she made it to my phone and reached Lucas? Or had she gotten cold feet? As Mason snapped on blue gloves, Emma wrapped the gown around me. As soon as she turned away, I leaned over and then shot up out of the wheelchair and, using my fear and rage as fuel, I swung my arm back and then forward, pummeled my elbow as hard and fast as I could into Cecile's face, hearing and feeling her nose bones crunch. "Oww!" she screamed as blood shot out all over both of us. The gun discharged as it hit the floor. "You little bitch!" Cecile bellowed, her hands cupped over her nose.

Mason jumped toward her. "Are you okay, Cecile?"

"Get—get, get her! Don't let her go!" Cecile was shouting, holding her hands over her face as the blood streamed down her lips and chin. I'd run across the room and was twisting the door handle, but my hands were slippery with blood. I twisted and pulled but couldn't open it. We were locked inside the operating room.

"Emma!" Mason shouted. "Take the handcuffs out of that drawer and cuff her! To the wheelchair!" Emma had picked up the gun and now whacked the side of my head. I fell down, thudding onto the floor.

"Don't just stand there. Put her on the damn table already!" Cecile screamed, breathing heavily, her voice stifled. I felt hands grabbing at me and wrestling me onto the table. Emma, her hands shaking, passed him a large syringe. My eyelids were fluttering open and closed but I could see him bend down, lift my gown, and jab the needle into my thigh—fast, practiced. My mind was racing but immediately it began to slow down. My limbs turned limp, useless. My eyelids felt heavy and began to droop. The chill of the metal through the thin pad soaked through my gown, and kept me from giving up, giving in.

"All ready," I heard Emma say, in an excited tone. "Bring her over."

Forcing my eyes open, I could see Mason's handsome face and strong, tan arms. He clamped a clear, vinyl mask over my mouth. I wanted to scream but when I breathed in, I swallowed the gas from a machine that had hissed into life. I stretched my eyes open again. Cecile was moving into my line of sight. Clumps of gauze were taped over her nose, but glistening blood was still dripping down over the edge of her lips and off her chin.

My mind shifted to a memory of the last time I'd had surgery, when my tonsils had been removed. I was eight years old. I remembered being terrified. My mother and father were still together then, but in the last year of their marriage. They were in the process of separating, arguing every night. That day they'd brought me to the hospital together, each hugging me before I went in.

I remembered the loving, concerned look that had played across my mother's face, one that I had never seen before, or since. My father had looked so helpless, as if he might cry. The doctors had tried to cheer me up, promising me that my parents would have to feed me all the ice cream I wanted when I woke up. I remembered going to sleep and seemingly within seconds waking up, feeling great.

It was alright to let go, I told myself. The lights went dim, then dimmer still. I heard them talking, their voices muddled, as if I were hearing them from underwater.

"I thought you said you gave her a bigger dose this time," Emma said.

"Why is this taking so long?" Cecile said. "Maybe you should give her some more."

"Don't tell me how to do my job. I'm perfectly capable—"

A whooshing sound blew through my ears.

Then I heard shouting. "Stop! Everyone freeze!" The sound of things dropping, clanging.

"Shit!" Cecile was saying. "Mason!"

The other voice, heavy on top of Cecile's. "FBI! Put your hands where we can see them. Hands up! Up up up!"

And then I went back under, letting go, as if someone had nudged me through a wide, black screen, and I sank down, floating away from the shouting. Away from the sharp noise and the pain. Away from the fear.

EPILOGUE

I woke up once again in a hospital bed, but in a real hospital this time, and my mom was standing across the room. Vases filled with bright flowers sat on every horizontal surface. The biggest bouquet was closest to me, and I could see one card with a picture of the library on it, so I guessed that was from the staff. For a few minutes I couldn't remember why I was there.

"Mom," I rasped, my voice so weak I wasn't sure it was audible. I tried to smile as I watched her cross the room until she was standing over me. She reached down and patted my hand, gently. "Shh—" she said, her voice warm and comforting. "The doctors said for you to rest. No need to speak until you're ready."

"Okay," I said, although I felt ready now, even if I wasn't sure what I was ready for.

When I was able to walk up and down a flight of stairs, they discharged me, and I moved back into the Bailey cottage for a few more weeks. I had agreed to train a new archivist at the library and to assist with the investigation. Two days after leaving the hospital I was escorted by a driver in a shiny black Suburban to Lucas's FBI office, which was in Albany.

I couldn't help smiling when I saw his real name and credentials on a sign on his open door as I walked in.

Caleb Matthews
FBI Special Agent

"I knew you weren't a witch," I said.

He stood up to shake my hand. "That was maybe not my most effective disguise."

"I can't think of a less effective one," I said as I sat down across from him at his desk.

"I'm glad you haven't lost your sense of humor," he replied.

"And your little Columbo act?"

He smiled sheepishly and shrugged. "I didn't really plan that part. Also, I didn't want you to hold anything back from me, so I downplayed my creds and law enforcement status. I wasn't pretending, however, when I said we made a good team."

"We did. Make a good team. The only thing I wasn't convinced about was your witchiness. You didn't exactly fit in with Cecile's crowd."

"I take that as a compliment."

"So, they sent you to investigate Cecile's group because it was a recognized cult?"

He took a deep breath, and let it out. "It started when I read the report about Victoria Wilton's death, and suspicions of cult activities in Wilton Springs, New York, so close to my hometown."

"So that's true. You grew up in the area."

"A lot of things I told you were true."

"What else did you tell me that wasn't?" I asked. "I have a very low tolerance for lies these days."

"I'm about to explain everything," he said, "and I apologize for . . . bending the truth."

"Apology accepted. Back to your illegal cult investigation."

"Actually, cults in and of themselves aren't illegal. But if the big personality at the helm, Cecile in this case, defrauds or manipulates the cult's members to gain financial benefit, that's illegal. We'll also prosecute her for enacting physical and psychological abuse. One instance, the dead women—and living ones—all have the capital letter *D* branded on their hip bones."

"What does that stand for?"

"Daughter. Cecile was the 'Mother.'"

"Earth Mother Spa." I looked down and then at the wall. "She was so charismatic. Those vulnerable young women did whatever she asked them to do. They agreed to the tattoos, right?"

"By agreeing to be branded they signaled their desire to belong to Cecile's 'family,'" he said. "In return, she promised them love, safety, and financial well-being. Or they agreed to it because they felt they had no choice. In the same way, eventually, they agreed to have their kidneys harvested. They believed her when she said it was all going to turn out great. But it didn't turn out great, did it? That's called defrauding. None of this applies to the chosen ones, obviously."

"The chosen ones? Like Emma?"

"Cecile relied on the well-off ones to provide her with a steady income. The worst part of her plan was reserved for young women on the margins of society, those without resources or a reliable network of family or friends. Initially you were targeted as a chosen one."

I sat up straight. "How horrific. Just like, who to wed and who to bed."

"Huh?"

"Oh, just another thing Cecile talked about. Too depressing to think about right now. Go on."

He took a sip of coffee. "Once again I apologize, Genevieve, for misleading you. But I couldn't reveal anything until we had evidence of wide-scale criminality."

"Just how much did you know, and when?" I asked.

"Victoria had been hanging out with Cecile, who as an outsider in town was under suspicion, although she'd made a ton of local friends by the time I started the investigation. When that dog dug up Trish, we had a second body, but there was no direct link to Cecile. I didn't know until later that Trish had been part of Cecile's coven."

"Group," I said. Then my hand flew to my mouth. "I can't believe I said that!"

"Anyway, after Victoria's accident and the lake house fire, when we identified Rowena and Stacy, we had three bodies loosely connected to Cecile. But Gabe's death confused us. We couldn't figure out Cecile's motivation. Luna's apparent suicide also threw me off."

He took a gulp of coffee and continued. "I called you a bunch of times late that Sunday to tell you I had to run a weeklong training session because the scheduled instructor got the flu, but you never answered. When you still hadn't called back by Wednesday, I canceled the 250-student lecture ten minutes in, and raced to Wilton Springs with lights and sirens."

"Really? I was totally in the dark meanwhile. Literally and figuratively."

"And when we finally got down inside the surgery room, I freaked out when I saw all the blood everywhere, thinking it was yours. But it was from Cecile's broken nose! Your handiwork! Impressive."

"Yeah, that elbow slam felt good. And my turn to say sorry. I totally trusted you until I found out from Barbara that she hadn't hired you. I figured you must've lied about everything."

"Wait, I never actually told you that Barbara was my client."

"I know, I know, but it all got tangled up. Apologies."

"None necessary."

"So how did you find me, Lucas? I mean, Caleb."

"Your colleague, Mitch, at the library. When they interviewed him after Stacy's body turned up, he went on and on about secret tunnels under Wilton Springs, and brought out a copy of an old map with a red

X over the TB hospital. I was driving to your house when Jade called me from your phone and said you were in the tunnels. She told me later your phone had died, so she couldn't explain what she meant. But I flashed on that interview with Mitch and took the dirt road toward the hospital, which I've known about since I was a kid. I got there and the little sister of somebody I know was outside 'guarding' the place. When she saw me, followed by four backup police cars, she ran down to the surgery room with us right behind her. And there you were!"

"So the local connections . . ."

He leaned back in his chair. "I gotta say, tunnels! Amazing. I need to know more. They were literally under my feet when I was growing up, and I never knew about them."

I shook my head. "I still can't believe Mitch was the one who saved me. Reminds me of my late father's favorite expression, 'Even a broken clock is right twice a day.'"

"Good one."

"I'm probably going to write about the tunnels one day. I'll send you a copy."

"A ton of grist in tiny Wilton Springs for your historian-career mill, eh? So you're going back to grad school? That's what your mom said you'd probably do."

"When did you talk to my mom?"

"At the hospital, while you were still pretty out of it."

"She didn't tell me you visited!"

"Only every day until you were out of the woods."

"Well. Thanks, Lucas. Caleb. Matthews, is it? Caleb Matthews?"

"Yup, that's my name. And you are most welcome, Miss Tompkins. It was an honor. And a pleasure." He frowned and then we looked at each other and both broke out into smiles.

"If you say so . . ." I said.

"So what are your plans?" he asked me. "After the yacht trip on the Aegean for Labor Day weekend with Mom's new family. Yes, she told me about that, too. When do you fly out?"

I tapped my nails against his desk. "I don't. She must've forgotten to tell you that boats make me seasick. I'll be too busy filling out applications for PhD programs. My true love. I'm certainly not cut out for the true-crime life."

"Genevieve, please know that I am, we are, grateful to you. For everything you did to help the investigation. And are doing."

"I didn't *do* anything. It just . . . happened."

"You did manage to stop a world-class criminal network."

"Not alone. You had something to do with it."

"Right, but I was just doing my job. You went outside of your comfort zone . . . by a wide margin." I shrugged, and he continued, leaning forward. "Listen, Genevieve, don't sell yourself short. Promise me? Even if we don't ever see each other again, here's the takeaway: You're special."

"And you, too, Lucas. I mean, Caleb."

"You can still call me Lucas if you want to. It's my middle name."

We both smiled again.

"Anyway," he said, "I gotta go, but I hope our paths will cross again. Under better circumstances. And not in Wilton Springs."

"I'd like that. You have my number. Reach out anytime."

"Okay if I hug you?" he asked, standing up.

"Of course!" I replied. It wasn't a bear hug, but it felt good to be so close to someone I could trust.

I couldn't sleep that night. As much as I didn't want to, I kept thinking about Mason. Despite everything I knew about him, everything he had told me, and everything I'd learned later, I still loved him. Not the actual, evil Mason, but the sweet, sensitive, vulnerable man I'd thought him to be. I kept wishing there were an on-off switch for my feelings. I hated him, I didn't forgive him, would never forgive him, but in a far-off corner deep in my heart I still cared.

But I was clear with myself that loving an evil person didn't make me evil.

Healing my heart, like healing my body, would take time.

The next morning a text came in from Barbara.

Can I treat you to a glass of lemonade? Or a five-star dinner and a bottle of Cristal Champagne? Whatever you want! Name it.

Lemonade sounds nice, I wrote back.

When I went to see her a few days later, she'd straightened her hair and had it cut in a stylish bob. She was wearing a fitted red dress.

"I love the new look, Barbara," I said.

"I just put Wilton Castle on the market, and I already have an offer," she said. "I'm moving to the city." We sat down and she poured the lemonade. "And I'm divorcing Jim. I shouldn't have waited to file papers until after I found out that his mistress was trying to poison me. He didn't even know!"

"His mistress?"

"Cecile. The wellness drink I thought was helping me lose weight was killing me. Jade said Cecile had her drinking it but she poured it down the drain. Stacy died from it."

I sat back against the chair. "I'm so sorry, Barbara."

"Don't worry about me," she replied. "Uncoupling from Jim is the best thing I've done in a long time. As for the rest of the nightmare . . . all of those dead girls. I'm . . ."

We both sat there without speaking until she put her glass down, and said, "I've been thinking. About the Wilton Curse. It skipped my husband but hit both my children. I guess there's still time for it to catch up to Jim. He's the last Wilton. Does that mean it would end for good?"

I didn't have an answer, so we were quiet again, until she cleared her throat, and said, "I asked you here, Genevieve, to thank you. In person. For warning me. For helping me."

She bowed her head and started to cry. Just a few tears at first, and then I started to cry, too. After a while she came over to me and I stood up and we faced each other, all the pain and anger and confusion and sorrow swirling around us, through us. She lifted her arms and leaned into me, and we hugged, not speaking. For those few moments I felt that thing Cecile had often talked about but never given to me. I felt love.

We heard a knock on the door and Jade walked in. She strode over to me and wrapped me in a long hug.

"Jade's going to be working with me for a while," Barbara said, "as a personal assistant. After she finishes her collaboration with the FBI, that is."

"How great!" I said.

"I was worried about being prosecuted," Jade said as she sat down, "until the FBI reassured me they understood that I was a victim, too. Working in that spa, I knew stuff. But Cecile made sure I didn't know how it all connected. Most of the girls are still devoted to her. Turns out there are experts in the department who know how to deprogram people who've been in cults. It's going to take a while to sort out the matrix of names of those involved, not just in Wilton Springs. I'll help with that."

"Emma knew everything," I said. "Didn't she?"

"The investigation's still ongoing, so keep this quiet, but Emma will be considered an accessory to major crimes. She gave Cecile and Mason close to two million dollars!"

Barbara was shaking her head. "Victoria used to babysit Emma when she was little. I wonder what her parents think. They were never around. And Emma was always in trouble."

Jade said, "One of the experts I spoke to said that Cecile and Mason gave Emma a sense of self, belonging."

"Excuse me, ladies," Barbara said, standing up. "I have a quick call with my lawyer. It'll only take a few minutes."

As Barbara closed the French doors behind her, I turned to Jade and said quietly, "How long had Jim and Cecile been seeing each other? You told me about them in the tunnels, but I don't know the details."

"Cecile cozied up to Jim—the richest man in town—by offering grief work to him and Barbara after Victoria died."

"I thought everyone in town knew that Barbara had all the money? And that the inherited Wilton money was going straight to Gabe and Victoria, not Jim?"

"At first, Cecile didn't know, and as a way to get to Jim she targeted Victoria, who'd transferred to Bainsville after more than one suicide attempt at her previous college. She was fragile when she met Cecile, who introduced her to yoga. And spells. And her brother."

I sucked in my breath. "Mason? Victoria Wilton?"

Jade rolled her eyes. "Yes, Genevieve. Mason and Victoria. While she was working with those family papers, Victoria found some old maps and showed them to Cecile. The maps indicated the location of secret tunnels underneath Wilton Springs. From the springs and into and out of town. Cecile, who'd been giving yoga and spiritual enlightenment classes out of a storefront on Main Street, bought the derelict house that's now the spa because it had a tunnel entrance in the basement, revealed on the map. Cecile did a full reno, but apparently—before I arrived—as soon as the job was completed the contractor conveniently fell down a ladder. They blamed ghosts.

"Which reminds me, Jade continued, "you remember the weird currents of air you felt that night you spent in the treatment room? They come from the tunnel entrance, not poltergeists. Anyway, the discovery of the tunnels became a key element in Cecile's business plans, which grew in scope." She counted off on her fingers as she said, "Ample refrigerated storage, easy transfer of organs with no one the wiser, hidden access to the hospital."

"Was Victoria on board with Cecile . . . and her vision?'

"She didn't know about the big picture, none of us did. But then Victoria started blabbing about the tunnels to Mason. Remember, Victoria didn't know that Mason was Cecile's brother. Cecile had demanded that Victoria not tell a soul about the tunnels. I think the two of them argued about other stuff. Then Cecile staged Victoria's accident up at the Wilton lake house."

"Cecile killed Victoria?"

"Yes. Right after Victoria retrieved all the papers with info about the tunnels from the archives, turned them over to Cecile, and we burned them during a 'sacred purification ritual.'"

"I found a weird old map in the Wilton files, but it went missing. I photographed it, though."

"Cecile was aware that the originals, and maybe copies, of maps were still in the files, which hadn't been disturbed since Victoria died. It's no coincidence that Luna was helping you catalogue the Wilton papers. Cecile told Jim to forbid you to investigate Prudence, as she thought it would lead you to the tunnels. He played it like he and Barbara wanted their privacy, and Truesdale was the legal guy delivering the message. I love it that you blew them off."

Just then, we heard the French doors opening, and Barbara walked in. "That took longer than I thought it would," she said. "Now I have another phone meeting in five minutes. Ahh, life in the fast lane. But before you leave, I want to hear about your witch stuff, Genevieve. Jade said you had a new project."

I took a sip of lemonade and said, "Yes! Last week, I got an email from *Historical Witches of America* about newly passed legislation clearing the names of accused witches in the United States beyond Salem. My boss, Daniela, had given my contact information to the person spearheading the effort, whose foundation wants to hire me to research Prudence Lowell."

"Isn't that so cool?" said Jade, turning to Barbara.

"Does that mean you'll stay in Wilton Springs a bit longer?" asked Barbara. "Maybe train Jade to carry on with the archives?"

Jade was shaking her head.

"Anything's possible," I said.

"And the witch foundation?" Barbara asked me.

"I outlined Prudence's story and the story of Felicity Blackwell and her half-sister, Anne Kuiper, John Wilton's daughters. The foundation asked about the daughters' tombstones. Although Prudence wasn't given a burial, Felicity must've been buried in the Revolutionary War-era cemetery in Wilton Springs, and Anne in Kuiperville. I'm not sure if I want to go further with the whole inquiry, but I do like the idea of Prudence Lowell being exonerated. Justice is still justice, even three hundred years later. Right?"

"For us historians, three hundred years isn't that long," Barbara said.

"Agreed. In my mind, there's some parallel universe in which Prudence escaped, not using witchcraft but via the tunnels, maybe with her friend Mrs. Blackwell's help."

Barbara looked at me with a sad smile. "Speaking of Prudence, have either of you heard about the petition going around to rename Wilton

Springs Lowell Springs? I was the third person to sign, after someone named . . . Mitch Lowell—" Her phone started ringing. "Here's my call! Thank you, my lovelies, for sharing this moment with me. I'll walk you out and call them back."

Jade and I stood up and followed Barbara out of the house. I glanced at Jade and a flash memory of her running beside me in the tunnel came barreling back toward me. My legs were starting to shake, and I took in a deep breath of Wilton Springs air to steady myself. Autumn would be arriving soon, although that afternoon the sky was leaden and the humidity was oppressive. I thought about the cloudless spring day when I'd stepped off the bus from Midtown Manhattan, full of hope, mixed with grief, ready for a fresh start.

As we were preparing to say goodbye, Barbara held me at arm's length and said, "I can't believe we hired you only three months ago." She pulled me in and whispered, "Thank you." The bell tower rang three times. Time to go home and start packing. Even after a lifetime of moving from place to place, it never got any easier.

Barbara turned and leaned in to hug Jade. I stepped back and watched the older woman's thin arms enveloping Jade's sinewy figure. Barbara held Jade tightly, tightly, as if she were holding on to a little girl who might fade away, who might disappear.

And then Jade and I were off, skipping down the steps, lightly bumping shoulders, laughing, feeling older, feeling younger. Feeling free. Ready.

ACKNOWLEDGEMENTS

A second novel is a challenge. I learned so much from the first that I wanted to channel into the second. I would like to send heartfelt thanks to everyone who contributed to this journey!

First and foremost, I would like to thank my brilliant editor, Luisa Cruz Smith, whose spot-on editorial eye made this book the very best it could be. Many thanks for your patience as the novel underwent several transformations.

Thank you to Otto Penzler and Charles Perry, it is an ongoing dream to be published by you both!

Heaps of gratitude to the whole Mysterious Press team, especially Julia O'Connell. Many thanks to Michael Pintauro, Nora Nussbaum, and Lisa Liu, for helping craft this book into its polished version.

My wonderful agent, Jody Kahn, read early drafts and is the best first reader anyone could ask for. Thank you for the excellent suggestions on both micro and macro levels. I am immensely grateful for your tireless precision, care, and belief in me.

Thank you to the incredibly talented authors Lauren Nossett, AJ Finn, and Clémence Michallon for their generous words and time.

Thank you to the extraordinary Lauren Cerand for your guidance and great insight, especially in the world of publicity and marketing, and expert event/tour planning.

Thank you to Ryan Gilbert, the manager of The Mysterious Bookshop. Your knowledge, enthusiasm, and fellow Sagittarian luminosity are deeply appreciated.

To my husband, Bjørn, I am grateful for your endless patience and support during my (many) long writing and editing days. Thank you for cooking delicious meals and always listening to me go on and on about a bunch of people and stories I made up in my mind.

To my family, especially Abby, Rick, and Sara, thank you for all the love and support and fun.

Thank you to the inimitable Patrick Monahan, not just a brilliant writer, but also my dearest and oldest friend, for reading an early draft and for steadfast encouragement. We always say this to each other, but I couldn't do any of it without my pal.

And most of all, to the readers, who make it all worthwhile, thank you for staying with me.